Ruth Nichols is ... novel, *The B...* ... Headline. She has also written a number of works of fantasy. An academic, she lives and works in Toronto, Canada.

Also by Ruth Nichols

The Burning of the Rose

What Dangers Deep

A Story of Philip Sidney

Ruth Nichols

HEADLINE

Copyright © 1992 Ruth Nichols

The right of Ruth Nichols to be identified as the author of the Work has been asserted by her in accordance with the Copyright, Designs and Patents Act 1988.

First published in 1992
by HEADLINE BOOK PUBLISHING PLC

First published in paperback in 1993
by HEADLINE BOOK PUBLISHING PLC

10 9 8 7 6 5 4 3 2

All rights reserved. No part of this publication may be reproduced, stored in a retrieval system, or transmitted, in any form or by any means without the prior written permission of the publisher, nor be otherwise circulated in any form of binding or cover other than that in which it is published and without a similar condition being imposed on the subsequent purchaser.

All characters in this publication are fictitious and any resemblance to real persons, living or dead, is purely coincidental.

ISBN 0 7472 4007 8

Printed and bound in Great Britain by
HarperCollins Manufacturing, Glasgow

HEADLINE BOOK PUBLISHING PLC
Headline House
79 Great Titchfield Street
London W1P 7FN

To
Peter Craigie,
unforgotten teacher and friend.

Then shall two be in the field: the one shall be taken, and the other left.

Two women shall be grinding at the mill; the one shall be taken, and the other left.

Watch therefore: for ye know not what hour your Lord doth come.

Matthew 24: 40–42

What dangers deep I passed, it folly were to tell:
And since I sigh to think thereon, why, *Fancy now farewell*!
George Gascoigne, *The Green Knight's Farewell to Fancy*

One

A camp of the English army in the Netherlands, 1586

A mist had risen from the ground, bringing with it a perfume of burnt wood, of horse-dung and of plants fresh with night and darkness. Occasionally a horse stamped, its hoofbeat dulled by the moist earth, or a fire cracked, releasing poplar-smoke from a fissure of coral ash. Washing, strung from lines, hung motionless, mildewing and pickling in smoke from the still air. Above the tents – peaked squares where shadows moved across the lights – the stars shone humid and gentle. There was no moon.

Someone put back a tent-flap and stood for a moment against the light of his own door, looking at the stars. A man tall enough to pass for six feet, and English by the set of throat and jaw that betrayed the dental consonants of his native tongue and not, for instance, the labial muscularity of French: though he did speak French, and excellently. In Italian his proficiency had been good; German he had refused to learn.

English also by his air of physical competence, which was that of a man who worked hard and who gave orders to other men. Handsome enough, though his skin had begun to crease at the forehead and around the eyes; dark blond without being fair. His eyes were a concentrated and brilliant green-grey, almost a lichen-grey, with black lashes. He wore a leather jacket over shirt and hose, and was alone, having sent his servant away.

He frowned at the stars and turned back into the makeshift chamber, which smelt of oiled canvas and of the beeswax candles he allowed himself for his reading's sake. A camp-bed stood already made, its sheets clean; a chest lay strewn with books; and on another chest a cuirass damascened with gold showed the dent of the armourer's proof-bullet. *But was it a Spanish bullet?* wondered the man, as he moved back to the desk set with ivory and inlaid woods. On it lay a letter, which he picked up and read again.

Outside stretched the night-silence, charged yet leisurely, of a war already decades old. For this officer could die, and others like him, before Spain would let go of its Protestant, heretical and rebel Netherlands.

The servant had sharpened quills for him – Ambrose Hyde, the same man who had gone with him to Poland twelve years ago, towards the end of three years' education and travel on the Continent. Hyde's master frowned again – *they were the three best years: I know that now* – mixed ink-powder with water, and wrote:

Philip Sidney to his beloved friend, greeting.
My dear, I rejoice that you married. Yes, of course I remember you, and your sister also. No, Frances my wife has no children yet: she was fifteen when I married her, and I have not wished to hurry her. As for your own pregnancy, do not fear it: surely with two deliveries already safe behind you . . .

Perhaps some perfume came from the paper covered with her fine, squared, sloping script. If so it was a delicate scent, accidentally communicated or even imaginary – a suggestion of lemon-balm and roses; and suddenly he remembered her voice entire. An alto voice speaking the Court French that had been their idiom, for through all the events of that winter in Kraków *actual* contribution in Caesar's day was, I believe, the export of tin.

Nevertheless our King Arthur was, I suspect, a late-Roman general; and from the time when the Legions, called homeward, deserted our island, we began to create a civilization of our own, cobbled out of little Saxon and Danish kingdoms. In the past four hundred years several royal dynasties have succeeded each other. Henry Tudor, whom we call Henry the Seventh, became our King by conquest at the Battle of Bosworth Field.

In fact, however, the Tudors have had difficulty in establishing a dynasty, for their stock does not run to living males. Their sons have been by-blows, sickly short-lived princes, or children dead in infancy; and their daughters have thriven and caused war. Henry the Eighth, the only other Tudor male after his father who lived a full lifespan, divorced or destroyed six wives, not in lechery but in his desperation to beget a king, and to save the country from the civil wars bred by female contenders and by the men who use them.

My maternal grandfather, John Dudley, Duke of Northumberland, was beheaded after plotting to marry his son to one such young princess. She was to have been Queen, and her husband – my uncle Guildford, who was executed at the age of eighteen years – was to have been King-Consort. But all three – grandfather, uncle and little princess – had their heads chopped off instead, and King Henry's true heirs succeeded him: the late Queen Mary Tudor (who was my godmother), and the present Queen Elizabeth.

This treasonous grandfather of mine was, it seems, an excellent father. He married my grandmother Jane, and despite the disgrace he brought on us, he remains fiercely loved by sons (including my uncle Robert, Earl of Leicester) and daughters (including my mother, the Lady Mary Sidney) who have taught me also to love his memory. Indeed I count it my chief honour that through my mother I carry the disgraced name of Dudley.

A word about Uncle Robert. After my grandfather's fall, his children sought safety in hardworking loyalty to Queen Mary. Their chief hope of regaining power depended on the exploitation of a personal affection; for Her Grace Queen Elizabeth deeply loved my uncle Robert, whom she had known from her childhood. The first scandal of her reign was the expectation, widely accepted in Europe, that she would marry him (she had just appointed him her Master of the Horse).

At the worst conceivable moment his wife, Amy Robsart, was found with a broken neck at the foot of a staircase. Her Grace imprisoned my uncle while two coroner's juries acquitted him of murder – a legal verdict no one has any just reason to doubt, though at the Court of France a wit was heard to remark, 'The Queen of England has married her groom, who has killed his wife to make room for her.'

This scandal was only one of several reasons why Her Grace chose, to my uncle's profound disappointment, not to marry him. She must have remembered his brother the little King-Consort; and in any case the bestowal of her marriage (and therefore of her progeny, troops and money) upon some prince of France or Spain was too important a weapon to be wasted in marriage to one of her own subjects.

My parents have known Her Grace all her life, and despite rumour they do not doubt that she has remained virgin. I believe she fears the consummation of love. When her mother, Queen Anne Boleyn, gave him only this daughter and no son, King Henry had Anne murdered upon a charge of incest with her own brother, and of adulteries so promiscuous they cast contempt only on her accusers. Never in her life has Her Grace been heard to speak her mother's name; but my father believes she knew how Anne Boleyn died by the time she was five years old.

She and my uncle have remained loyal and intimate. Whatever rumour may say about his ambition (and rumour said truly), he loved her and wanted children by her. Until his late and secret marriage to Laetitia Knollys – another scandal – Her

Grace's refusal had denied him a legitimate son. Accordingly, for much of my boyhood, *I* was his heir. He has been a kind patron to me.

My mother, the Lady Mary, was a daughter of the treasonous Duke of Northumberland. She sought refuge in marriage with a good man whom she loved. She was once extremely pretty, but the smallpox disfigured her early in the present reign, and she now seldom leaves home, and never without wearing a black velvet mask.

My father Sir Henry Sidney, whom I respect and love, has fought Her Grace's battles in Ireland, and lost them as (I believe) every English general will always lose them; and he pays his troops out of his own purse because Her Grace, she says, is poor and forgetful. I had two sisters who died in infancy, and have also a brother Robert and two other sisters, Ambrosia and Mary.

I feel, as you can see, affection for them all. I have been loved, and have loved most earnestly in return. From my boyhood I felt an ardent desire to *work* for my family, to deserve their affection and to restore their fortunes. From the tutors they gave me and from my schools (my parents sent me at ten years old to a school away from home) I learned to be a scholar and a soldier; to ride, to dance, to fight, and to master music, mathematics, philosophy and languages.

As for my faults, I am quick-tempered. Impulsive anger and rash speech are my chief faults, I think. From the time I was twelve or thirteen – a little too young – I desired women; and lust tormented me with those ecstasies and obsessions that make the young so ridiculous and so unhappy. I was always in love, and always writing verses; and so pestered one charming creature that she took to uttering 'No' in doubles and in quadruples – 'No, no, no, no!'

Well, I extracted a verse-chorus from it: I often cobbled the poor thing's refusals into metrical form. Once she conceded me a kiss. In my eagerness I nipped her, and had to apologize in verse; then assured her that only more kisses would stop my babbling. And so I harried her into surrender. The sonnets stopped immediately.

When I was seventeen my parents trusted me sufficiently to send me abroad for my education. With me I took a gentleman-servant, Ludovic Briskett, and my body-servant Ambrose Hyde. I was in Paris on the famous Feast-day of Saint Bartholomew, when the French King, urged by his mother Queen Catherine de' Medici, set his Catholic subjects to massacring his Protestant subjects through the streets of the city. I have seen, from my hiding-place in the English embassy, a soldier swing a little girl by the hair until he broke her spine against a wall; a naked man dangled by his tormentors from a window five storeys up, until they let him drop; a raped woman impaled on a pike.

The leader of the French Protestants, Admiral Gaspard de Coligny, had been convalescing from a wound. He was dragged from his sickbed, stabbed to death and thrown from a window into the courtyard, where the King's soldiers cut off his head. It is said that children could be seen playing with human corpses in the streets of Paris after this massacre. It was on Saint Bartholomew's Day that I learned to hate the cruelty of Catholicism.

I had made new friends in Paris. Several of them died that day.

Thereafter I studied in Italy, and met many scholars. But my parents had allowed me only three years abroad; and two had now gone by. I had only one more year in which to learn all I must. And so things stood with me in the autumn I turned twenty – the October when I rode from Vienna to Kraków to attend my godfather's wedding.

Restore to me, then, the body I had when I was twenty years old: a body whose grace and endurance, whose elastic strength I took for granted – and that body's other, unrecognized gift: an avid quickness of mind. Just a few weeks turned twenty, I was, though I did not know it, an excellent young machine. No hidden reserve of strength or intellect had yet betrayed my demands upon my own capacities; and those demands were as merciless as the intelligent young can make them, when something drives them and they know their own goodwill. With the innocent arrogance of twenty I did not dream that muscles could stiffen and mind move more slowly; that Time might someday prove, to me too, that although youth is not happy, its strength and health contain many of the other elements that make life good.

Did I feel young? In a sense, yes: I was aware, as if by comparison with something not consciously recognized, of my lack of experience. The brevity of my own history troubled me. As if to make up for my own inadequate story, I loved to cherish and remember the years we had lived together, my family and I. Already too in this final year abroad I felt the pull towards home; and that fretted me with a sense of work unfinished.

It was October – too late at night for travellers to be safely on the road, but events had delayed us, and the wedding was tomorrow morning. A group of horses stood on a hill, their riders looking down at a city in the dark. Behind us our hired guard shifted and trampled, their horses' feet cracking, in the ruts of the road, the first crisp panes of ice. Brown leaves lay furred with rime. Our breath hung before us in moonlit plumes.

'We must not stand too long, sir,' said Ludovic Briskett. 'They will already have locked the city-gates, and they warned us in Paris that these forests are full of outlaws.'

'Then the outlaws will be as cold as we are.'

He was a trim, olive-skinned man who came only to my shoulder. His born name was Ludovico Bruschetti, though we had Englished it into those sounds whose drawling 'a's' and blunt initial accent so insult (he said) any foreign language we attempt. 'We are *marks* sitting here, sir. Or have you forgotten someone slashed your packs at the inn two nights ago? What was he looking for, do you think? Money? Surely not: the packs were too light to hold anything but clothing.'

'Jewels, then,' I said. 'I should have pinned a note to my bags telling him how my tutor once had to turn me out in trunk-hose made from my old velvet cloak because we were too poor to afford better.'

'Whereupon your uncle of Leicester, on your tutor's appeal, sent you sixteen excellent suits made up by his tailor – proving, sir, that you were never as poor as your father's wages keep *me*. A letter?' He did not mean to let it go.

I met his eyes in the cold light, and after a moment saw his eyes drop. 'But there was no letter.'

'There lies Kraków, sir.' It was the soft voice of Ambrose Hyde, muffled further by the sore throat that had made him miserable these last days.

I glanced at him. 'I've hated to keep you riding, Ambrose, but I dared not leave you alone to follow us.' (Not with the slasher of packs riding somewhere behind us, alert to learn what I knew: for if there was no letter, there was a message I had memorized before I fed the letter into the fire.) 'We'll get you a warm bed when we reach Sir Antony's house. It must lie somewhere down below.'

In later weeks I came to know well the landscape that lay before us. In a few hours, daylight would restore to walls their tints of grey and biscuit-pink; to the river its shadows of trees; to the landscape its tattered yellows, broken by the lacquer-red of rowan-fruits and the orange of a tree I had heard called *jawor*. But now a landscape of small hills lay under swarms of cold white stars. Moonlight shone on a river where barges lay at rest. A clean stroke of moon-silvered wall broke at an angle and was lost in trees. I saw clusters of pale spires; the swell of Castle Hill, crowned by a fortress as great as Windsor, which I had already learnt to call the Wawel; and the roofs of huge churches to which experience was to give their proper names – Saints György, Anna, Stanislaw, and the uneven spires of Sancta Maria.

What Dangers Deep

A light winked out in some remote window.

'What if they have locked the gates?' said Ludovic.

I shrugged. 'If we can't rouse or bribe them, we'll seek shelter at some house outside the walls. I should hate it, though. We'll have to find an inn at dawn, and wash and unpack in haste, for I *will* not quarter us on Antony Marshall on his wedding-morning . . . Wait, someone is riding up from the town.'

So they were: a small party of horses.

'Then let's go down to meet them,' replied Ludovic Briskett. Both of us laid our hands on our sword-hilts, and I gestured our people forward.

The two parties approached each other and halted. A voice called in the Latin that enables any traveller – Italian, French, German or English – to understand any other traveller: 'Have I found Master Philip Sidney?'

'I am he.'

'Then welcome, sir, from Sir Antony Marshall and all his household. We were beginning to scrape together enough money to ransom you from bandits.' The man rode forward: I saw in him the ascetic blond handsomeness that marks the Polish men before age coarsens them. 'I am Adam Kózmian, the Ambassador's steward. Welcome to Kraków.'

I smiled and shook his hand; we turned to ride together. 'How is Sir Antony, Master Kózmian?'

'Rehearsing his wedding, sir, at this moment, with the priest, three exhausted ladies, and servants laying a cold buffet.'

'*Three* ladies?'

'Mistress Dorotea' (this was the bride) 'and her two sisters, sir. They are her maids for tomorrow.'

'I see. Have they closed the city for the night?'

'Yes, but they'll let us in at the Barbican: I've bribed the guards there. So we must cross the river, then ride rightwards along the verge.'

The bridge proved to be timber which echoed beneath our horses' hooves. The huge squared logs came, I guessed, from the Polish forests that provide the best timber in the world. Below us slipped water with its sucking labial sounds.

I felt tired, but curiosity moved me to say: 'Master Kózmian, why a timber bridge?' In spite of its magnificent carpentry it seemed to me rustic and makeshift.

He replied: 'We do not bridge the Vistula with stone. We can cut this bridge into the river in ten minutes if the Turks come; and they lie eight days' march away in Hungary.'

I felt a chill raise the hairs on my forearms. The sound of horse-hooves changed to a thud on frosty ground.

We were now cantering along a line of trees, their colours – green, orange, butter-yellow – latent in the dark. A wind wakened; leaves pattered, their shadows hazing a wall that had seemed a crisp line when viewed from the hill. Now it rose above us – squared blocks of stone in which the moonlight picked out flecks of quartz-silver.

'Has this city a king tonight, Master Kózmian?' I said.

I wish, even now, I had put it more kindly. We had ridden for days through a rich, forested kingdom that tempted the Turks whose front line of advance lay so near; and I knew that, dangerously, this kingdom lay undefended. It could not afford to remain so for long. King Zygmunt August, a learned and capable man, had died two summers ago, leaving no son. Even had he done so, the Polish Parliament (which they call the Diet) would not automatically have chosen that son to rule them – for the Poles, like the English in ancient times, elect their kings.

And the Diet's choice had fallen on Prince Henri, one of the fragile, vicious sons of Catherine de' Medici, Queen Dowager of France. Henri was an aesthete who enjoyed perverse bedfellows and a modest reputation as a soldier, which, fostered by distance and by French efforts, alone accounted for his election.

What Dangers Deep

However, when they saw him the Poles did not like him, nor he them. So he had pined at Court in Kraków, cultivating the arts and setting Catholics against Protestants, until his brother's death had suddenly made him King of France. And then, to universal mirth, he had run away one night, abandoning his indignant Polish subjects.

This history amused me; and I fear that a rather cruel laughter coloured my question to Adam Kózmian.

'Has this city a king tonight, Master Kózmian?' I therefore said, for not every rumour might have reached us on the road.

'Not since June, sir,' he replied.

It had been the month of Henri's escape. Behind me I heard Ludovic Briskett laugh.

Kózmian reined in. Even in the dark I knew Briskett's face was scarlet. 'I do not think I know this man: your servant, Master Sidney? Let me tell you why we need a new king, gentlemen, and why my country's misfortune is not a joke for your servant to laugh at. We are your bulwark against Islam, and your defence against Russia too. If the Turk moves past us or over us, then France may become as Muslim as conquered Hungary. Our Grand Chancellor, *Pan* Jan Zamoyski, has no equal in Europe except for Lord Burghley or Prince Willem the Silent; and the French, who made my nation a laughing-stock this summer, have no man as good. We need a commander, and we need taxes to make war, because war is occurring on our frontiers at this instant and is not going to stop.' I could hear Kózmian's breathing, the paced breathing of controlled rage. 'And now introduce me to your servant, if you please.'

Briskett swept off his cap. 'My name is Ludovic Briskett, Master Kózmian, and I entreat your pardon. I meant no mockery, I beg you to believe me.'

'*I* beg you: the fault was mine,' I said.

'Very well.' Kózmian nodded; we moved forward again. 'No, gentlemen, tonight we have no king: the Diet has as yet elected none.'

'Did King Zygmunt leave no blood-kinsman you could choose?' I demanded.

'Only his sister, the Princess Anna. We cannot risk a Queen-Regnant: if we elect Anna she must marry a warrior, though she is forty years old. There is the Grand Chancellor, *Pan* Jan Zamoyski, but I hear he has refused the Crown.' (I knew Antony Marshall's bride was a niece of this lord Zamoyski.)

Ahead of us rose a round fortress, its gilt spires shining coldly in the dark. 'Refused it? Then who,' I said, 'enforces civil order?'

'The nobles, each in his own fief. And there is little order. You will find Kraków a dangerous place.' Kózmian pointed. 'That is the Barbican; beyond it lies Saint Florian's Gate. *Pan* Zamoyski is still called Grand Chancellor by habit, but since King Zygmunt's death he has no more standing than any other lord; and all have too much power, I think. *They* want no king at all.'

'Lest the Crown curtail their own power?' I said. 'It was so in England too, during our civil wars. Our best poet, the Earl of Surrey, was the eldest son of such a clan – the family of Howard.'

'A poet who was also a prince? What became of him?'

'King Henry cut off his head.'

'Excuse me, sir, but I have heard he also did that to your grandfather.'

'Then rumour belittles us, Master Kózmian – for he cut off my *great*-grandfather's head as well.'

Kózmian gave a shout of laughter.

'And while he sat in prison waiting,' I added, 'he wrote a book called *The Tree of Commonwealth*, in which he warned of the dangers to the State arising from greed and corruption.'

Kózmian grinned. 'Fearing his experience might die with him?'

The great belly-shape of the Barbican rose direct before us. From its watchtowers I could feel the attention of the sentries.

What Dangers Deep

We rode through in darkness, and down a short avenue. Now the city-wall stretched in front of us again, pierced by one of those humble ancient gates that are little larger than a door – and defensible accordingly.

Kózmian turned to me. 'This is Saint Florian's Gate. Florianska Street runs straight up from it to Market Square and the Mariacki Close. The Ambassador's house is the corner building, where the street meets the square.'

The gate opened, again in silence and without visible sentries. We passed the low arch, which smelt of ancient stone and urine and the delicate bitter scent of marigolds. Set into the wall I saw an icon that gleamed gilt in the dark; someone had set a pot of pine-boughs before it. As we passed it, Adam Kózmian made the sign of the Cross. Later, remembering, I was glad for him.

Saint Florian's Gate closed behind us. In front of us stretched Florianska Street, a lane of varying darks: flat house-fronts, each narrow panel of windows rising to the scrollwork of the roof. Iron, wrought into crosses above the doors, closed shopfronts with cages of thick round bars. Here and there high up, candlelight showed a gentle, secretive glimmering, or shutters enclosed it further to suggest a magic privacy.

'How still it is,' I said.

Adam Kózmian pointed. 'A straight run up the street, sir, as I said: the corner house. Then one goes through a tunnel into the courtyard. The porter will let us in.'

We did not know then that the porter was lying dead, and the front gate battered in. I stood up in my stirrups, listening to a silence that seemed choked with potential sound. 'What—?'

And then they came, clattering quietly out of their sufficient distance on either side of Saint Florian's Gate: armed men moving with the leisure of skilled purpose, closing to fill the road behind us.

'Christ,' murmured Adam Kózmian. '*Ride!*'

After that I remember a surging of motion, sound and darkness. Beneath windows that preserved their discretion we pounded down the street towards the great open square, where for all I knew a second ambush might await us; yet we were being herded precisely in that direction, by whom and why we did not know. Above us a few windows winked into darkness; at none did any face appear. The citizens of Kraków knew better than to help strangers shouting in the street after dark.

An arrow whickered over my head; wall-stone splintered from its impact, and one horse swerved, blinded, and went down with its rider. I twisted around to glance back. Our pursuers seemed to be men of a single household, to judge by their red turbans and the gleam, in the dark, of very rich armour. Some lord's house? A joke? Young men on small horses, beautiful in motion. Two or three shouted to me, laughing. Somewhere behind them, strangely, I heard singing.

And so we surged down the street, and swerved in a body of chaos on the edge of a paved square that seemed limitless and empty. 'The archway!' shouted Kózmian. Stars streamed. The bulk of a church with uneven towers cut past me on the left diagonal, as something, whipping down on me from above, nearly jerked me from the saddle. It was a thrown rope. I cut through it: the dully smouldering amber and emerald of lit church windows righted themselves again.

I could see the archway of the corner house, but there was no gate, and men seemed to be fighting there. 'Through it! Through it!' cried Ludovic. We dived for the tunnel, fighting our way.

'Who are they?' I shouted to Kózmian.

'I don't know,' he called back. 'But get to the front door if you can.'

'They're following us through into the inner court!'

We had been used, I now guessed, as the head of a ram: the front gate battered down, the household barely roused to its own danger, and the guests driven down the street – guests who must be received, through a confused defence, into the safety of the house. It had taken much care and more luck; and they were indeed following us through.

What Dangers Deep

In a courtyard seething with motion I felt Kózmian's hand on my shoulder, and the atrocious ache told me how the lasso had hurt me. He pushed; I slid from my horse, and my splayed palms felt the wood of a door that slid open to receive me. An arrow killed Adam Kózmian, and Ambrose crowded me into the light of a hallway. Behind me my servants were struggling to shut the door; and a man whose voice I had known since he held me at the font came forward to embrace me. 'Philip! God be praised we have not lost you too.'

Panting I stared at my godfather – at servants, a priest, frightened women. 'Who are they, Antony?'

'I have not,' replied my godfather with stoic cheerfulness, 'the least idea. But we have a rescuer coming if we can hold out for half an hour: I sent a runner over the roofs five minutes ago.'

He held me away from him. My breathing steadied. I focused my eyes on the familiar face: a high-cheeked oval with sparse ginger hair and small kind eyes that frowned with a perpetual anxiety. 'And now make your duty to the ladies. Are you hurt?'

'No, but your steward is dead. I'm sorry: an arrow took him from behind while he was covering me.'

'Then,' said the high mellow baritone that seldom changed for emotion, 'let us avenge him as we have means. This is the lady Dorotea Zamoyska, tomorrow my wife; and Yolanta, her sister; and Maria.'

White-faced they curtseyed to me: Dorotea, whom I guessed to be about thirty, a beauty with a withered arm; the slender tall Yolanta, with eyebrows thick as a boy's and serious dark eyes; and a pretty little blonde with exquisite features and eyes slyer and cooler than her sisters'.

Someone handed me a crossbow. I said: 'If you have men on the roof, let me go up.'

'I will, but Robin of Leicester will have my head on a plate if you get killed. Remember, Philip, this is my wedding-eve. This may be a prank, or may pass for one.'

'A *prank?*' I was about to follow his servants up the stairs. In a corner a woman was tending Ambrose's hurts. I heard in my voice the shrill false rage of exhaustion. 'I counted five men dead.'

'I know. Up to the roof, then, and lie close: with the mêlée down here, they may not pick you out against the sky.'

I climbed two staircases and a ladder, and emerged on to the slates of the roof, which was flat. 'Lie beside me, sir,' whispered a servant in English. 'How many bolts have you?'

'Six in the quiver they gave me. Damn, it's half empty.'

'Then,' said the man, 'pick your mark and kill with each bolt. They had the gate down before we knew. We have stores of ammunition, but you may not get another six arrows, not where you are lying. Kill for me the man who killed Adam, if you recognize him.'

'Under those red turbans? Whose uniform are they?'

'Daniel Balinski's, a great lord in the city. And no, I know no reason.'

And so I was looking straight down at him when a man rode into the courtyard. He was clean-shaven and wore no headgear; his saddle-cloth was a grey wolf-pelt, and his robe was silver cloth-of-gold, his belt studded with white opals.

He raised his hand: the fighting stilled. Drawing his horse's head tightly round, he circled and gazed up at the archers lying ready to shoot him. A big blond man, very strong, with a straight nose, blue eyes, and a mouth perfect as a woman's. He noted us, smiled, and called: 'My lord Ambassador Marshall: Forgive us. We will pay the blood-price of your men. We ask only a sight of the bride.'

In the silence someone kicked a tin lantern that had fallen from its wall-hook: it rolled with the uneven clatter of a dented bucket, and was still. Under the arch a man was weeping. I saw Adam Kózmian: he lay with one arm pillowing his face, and the blood beneath his head shone black in the torchlight.

And then the door opened.

What Dangers Deep

Hazed in the candlelight from the hall stood Dorotea Zamoyska, her green dress torn. Antony hovered behind her, and I knew how he hated to let her go in front of him as his shield; and knew, as if I had heard them quarrel over it, that she had somehow insisted.

I noticed with pity how deftly she concealed the left arm, withered by some fever to child-size. Her sleeve swept down to hide it, and with her strong right hand she lifted her coif from her head and shook down over her shoulders the hair that testified publicly to her virginity – for only maidens wear their hair loose in public. In a shining dark brown fall it veiled her to the hips. *She is very intelligent: it is a dangerous risk*, I thought. For the softness of it – the womanly gentleness in that atmosphere of masculine uncontrol – invited rape. For a moment the silence hung ambiguous.

And then, clothed thus almost visibly in the sacred virginity of a bride, Dorotea curtseyed to Daniel Balinski. In a clear alto voice she said: 'My lord, you have come to wish us well at our wedding?'

He bowed, and controlled, with skill, his sidling horse. 'And to bring you a gift, my lady. Here it comes.'

Antony had joined Dorotea, drawing her unobtrusively back into the doorway. There they stood as file upon file of small boys dressed in red and silver entered through the archway and formed into ranks. The man beside me was grinning, but not with amusement. He glanced at me and said with pantomimic gentility: 'His chapel *choir*. Famous as far as Paris. You won't hear a better.'

'His *choir*?' I whispered.

A man with a baton mustered the boys; other men, also in red and silver, entered, huge flat baskets slung from straps about their shoulders. From these they flung bags of gold net that jingled with small objects. Balinski glanced up at us again: I swear his eyes met my own. He gestured, and a golden bag, deftly flung, hit my companion on the shoulder. We tore it

21

open. Out tumbled almond-cream pastries, sticky green glacé cherries, walnuts fried in honey, marchpane apples no bigger than the ball of my thumb, each with a leaf of crimped green velvet.

'Wedding-favours,' murmured my friend.

'Do you think they're poisoned?' I said.

He shrugged. 'Do you care?' And, lying side by side on the slates, we devoured them.

The choir began to sing – a pure, single tone, sweet as a pang on the palate. And they were singing, adequately enunciated, words scoured from God-knows-what obscure volume in the university library. They must have enlisted some wandering English scholar to teach them pronunciation, for they were singing inteliigibly in English: a compliment, I suppose, to the bridegroom. I knew the words: a lover's appeal, triumphant in its dignity, decency and grace.

> Now certës, Lady, since all this is true –
> That from above thy gifts are thus elect –
> Do not deface them, then, with fancies new,
> Nor change-of-minds let not thy mind infect:
>
> But mercy him thy friend that doth thee serve,
> Who seeks alway thine honour to preserve.

'Why are you laughing?' demanded my friend.

'The Earl of Surrey,' I murmured, and shook my head in apology.

Another man had come quietly, on foot, into the courtyard, noticed only by a few. Because of my vantage-point I saw the first stir of motion around him. A big, powerful man, excellently dressed in the short boots and belted gown of a Polish nobleman. A short-sleeved coat of black velvet fell to his ankles and served him, with fashionable negligence, for a cloak. He carried his hat in his hand, and beneath his mantle I saw the line of a curved sword.

What Dangers Deep

He seemed alone; yet around him all sound, all motion died. At last he came to stand beside the mounted man. His head bare, his hands clasped on the felt brim of his hat, he gazed up at the rider, ignoring the bulk and the hooves that could have killed him. His plain face, with its small eyes and lumpish nose, was smiling. In a voice that startled me by its power and beauty he said: 'My lord, I have come to take the ladies home.'

'Not before my choir has finished its wedding-song.' Balinski's lighter voice yielded him nothing.

'By no means,' replied the man I now guessed to be Jan Zamoyski, Grand Chancellor of Poland. 'I will stand with them and listen; and then, as the ladies are tired, we must wish you good night. I have detained your brother at my house, to ensure that your men depart without quarrelling with my own, who have filled the whole square.'

After a long pause Balinski bowed. The Chancellor also bowed from the shoulders in return, and mounted the steps to join the bridegroom and the bride. As I scrambled back down the ladder into the attic I heard the choir's collective voice resume:

> There is a rock in the salt flood,
>   A rock of such nature
> That draweth the iron from the wood
>   And leaveth the ship unsure.
>
> She is the rock, the ship am I,
>   That rock my deadly foe
> That draweth me there where I must die
>   And robbeth my heart me fro.

When I came quietly down the stairs I found them there in the tiled hallway: the servants fallen silent; Yolanta and Maria collapsed into each other's arms in an embrace of exhaustion; Antony, and beside him Dorotea, her hand held high by the uncle whose power shielded her.

Yet softly as I moved, Zamoyski heard me. His head turned. I saw the round, unremarkable face – the nose too large, the skin slightly flawed with smallpox, the pursed pink mouth; and brown eyes of a hard and bright intelligence. For an instant he weighed me, his assessment – and he knew it – pinning me to the wall. Then with a smile he released me.

Through the October night, pitch-perfumed with smoke from the torches, the children's song rose:

> A bird there fleeth, and that but one;
>   Of her this thing ensueth –
> That when her days be spent and done,
>   With fire she reneweth.
>
> And I with her may well compare
>   My love that is alone,
> The flame whereof doth ay repair
>   My life when it is gone.

* * *

The door had shut behind us and, under the watch of Zamoyski's pikemen, the courtyard was emptying. The dead had been lifted gently from the cobbles; I had sent my servants to bed.

'Jan,' said Antony, 'this is my godson, Philip Sidney.'

He shook my hand. 'Master Sidney, your uncle of Leicester has written entreating me to be a father to you. I will not threaten you with that, but only with an invitation to my house as soon as I can contrive. And I hear well of you from my friend Hubert Languet. You are fortunate to have studied with him.'

'I shall count myself so all my life, sir.'

Zamoyski turned to Dorotea. He can have been barely ten years older (how had so young an uncle inherited the guardianship of these girls?) but his bulk and grace might have belonged to a man of fifty. He laid his hands on her shoulders. 'Dorotea, I am bitterly sorry.'

What Dangers Deep

'It was foolish of *me*, sir, to choose a rehearsal at night.' She had begun to shake: Antony clasped her shoulders with quick alarm. She passed gently from the arms of one man to those of the other. With her head against his shoulder, Antony said, 'Tell us, Jan, what happened here this evening? I know a bridegroom is fair game on his last night.'

'Balinski might indeed prefer that the city think precisely that.' Zamoyski glanced around at his women: the slender, vixenish Yolanta, who was gathering her hair into the hood of her cloak, her large white hands trembling slightly; and at Maria, whose prettiness I now focused.

Which of the two was the elder, I wondered? Aged nineteen or twenty and no more than a year between them. *Taller seems elder*, I thought. I had already chosen Yolanta for my favourite; Maria I liked less. She was the shortest of the three, with a sturdy, muscular grace; and her face was pretty almost to excess, despite the strength of its bones. Her pale yellow hair, now limp with sweat, fell in crimped waves; nose and mouth were perfect, and her eyes were blonde-lashed and grey-blue. I did not like mixtures of prettiness and spite, I thought with the cruelty of fatigue. Her beauty lacked sweetness, and I felt a young, unkind pride at preferring the plainer sister.

'What happened here? A wedding-jape,' said Jan Zamoyski. 'In fact an attempt on the women, or so I guess: not Dorotea, but Maria or Yolanta. Either would suffice him, if she could be captured.'

'A forced bride.' Yolanta's voice – of the three she had the truest soprano – was calm.

He nodded. 'Or simply a hostage.' Since I alone looked puzzled, he turned to me. 'Master Sidney, my house is impregnable, as you will see. This one is relatively unguarded. The fault was mine in leaving them vulnerable even for this one evening. Balinski was prepared to turn the attack into a wedding-prank if the timing – your arrival, the battering of the gate, my own inexcusable inattention – did not favour him.

When he entered the courtyard he already knew my troops were approaching through the streets.'

'My runner reached you, then,' said Antony.

'Of course.'

'But why capture your nieces, sir?' I demanded. 'Could he not ask, if he desired to marry one?' *And if he meant rape* – I thought but did not say – *why did he not care which girl he took?*

'He could ask, yes. But he wanted a prisoner, and one for whom I would be afraid. He wants no king, Master Sidney, or else the weakest of the candidates. With a hostage he believes he might frighten me into compliance.' Zamoyski shrugged. 'But I will vote as I please, and the Diet will listen to me. And now we must leave. Dorotea, let go, you will see him in the morning.'

'But tomorrow night,' said Antony softly, 'your sisters will go home alone.' He leaned down and kissed her on the mouth, a soft, skilled kiss, while we pretended to look at other things.

'Master Sidney, I hope you have not been hurt?' It was Yolanta's voice suddenly addressing me.

I started, and felt the blush I hated scald my skin. 'No, mistress, I am whole, only weary.'

'Then good night, sir.' She smiled – a thin-lipped smile made wry by fatigue – and turned away.

So did Maria; but for an instant I saw her eyes linger on me with a steady dislike.

By one o'clock in the morning six wooden chests, each large enough to coffin a man, had been piled in the archway to form a makeshift obstacle. The gate-wright would come tomorrow. The house had at last fallen to darkness and silence when Antony and I, carrying a lantern, walked across the courtyard to the bath-house. We still wore our swords.

The bath-house rose before us: a little square solid building. It had no windows; from its chimney drifted a plume of smoke underlit with colour from the furnace. In the main house the last panes went dark.

What Dangers Deep

Now all four wings of the embassy enclosed us in a square of solid black. Stars glittered in the frost – beads of sparkling, brilliant white. Behind them receded the lesser jewels, until they faded into a glow thronged more and more faintly with sparks beyond the reach of sight.

Antony paused, staring upwards. 'They comfort one, don't they.'

'I find they steady me,' I said softly. 'Perhaps because they exceed us, and do not change.'

He produced a key and opened the door. We found a small, candlelit annexe ventilated by window-slits near the ceiling, and lined with scrubbed wooden benches. On the walls hung pegs for clothes. As we began to undress I said, 'I do not like Kraków, Antony. As to that, I did not like Venice either.'

'Why?'

'It smelt.'

'God save us, an Englishman abroad. But you've come to hear a course of lectures, haven't you, as well as to see me married?'

'Yes, at the Collegium Maius.'

'Then do not defend yourself, like an Englishman, with contempt for what really frightens you. Every state in Europe, Philip, is torn or threatened by civil war, and every one in answer has increased the power of the king. Only in England and in Poland will you find a parliament.'

'A parliament of nobles.'

'Yes,' said my godfather serenely.

I had unbuttoned my doublet, and was pulling off my shirt. 'Then to whom are you Ambassador, Antony? To the Diet?'

He shook his head. 'I *was* Ambassador to King Zygmunt, and then to King Henri, of fleeting memory. Did you go to Court in Paris?'

'No, because I hate the French Queen Dowager.'

'Then I can confirm one rumour about King Henri that you may find useful someday.' Standing stark naked he picked up a towel and tossed it to me. 'He enjoys being flogged on the buttocks while wearing women's clothes.'

'Under what circumstances precisely,' I demanded, and followed him into the sweating-room, 'do you think I might find this useful?'

More clean-scrubbed benches, and the metal tray of stones I had grown accustomed to from the public bath-houses at our inns. Antony picked up a ladle and poured water on the stones, which the fire had heated from below. I had learnt not to handle these smooth, cool-seeming lumps of granite. A second ladle, a third, and steam filled the room. We sat down to sweat out the dirt and exhaustion of the day.

'I shall build a Turkish bath-house when I get home,' murmured Antony, 'and invite Her Grace to compare it to her own bath at Greenwich, where every wall is lined with mirrors.' He leant his head back against the wall, his eyes closed, his face puckered with weariness.

'You'll get no sleep tonight,' I said. 'I'm sorry. Do you mean to go away afterwards, you and Dorotea?'

His eyes opened. 'Yes, to Vienna in a day or two. Oh, I'll sleep for two hours, and she, poor lass, may get three or four. Did you think her beautiful?'

'Yes.'

He nodded. 'The fever destroyed her arm when she was eight. She has that astonishing sweetness of nature I have found in some crippled people, both men and women. Since Anne died I had not dreamed I could be so in love.'

'I'm glad, Antony.'

'*Antony*.' His blue eyes, as deceptive in their anxious mildness as his face and voice, opened suddenly. 'When did we drift into *that* equality, my child?'

'When I grew to be a man.' Affection for him, and disinclination for this kind of play, made my voice gentle.

Antony grinned. 'You were eighteen inches long, and squalled when I gave you into the arms of King Philip of Spain, your other godfather. He had married your godmother, poor Queen Mary, which made him – God save us – *our* King for a few years, until his neglect killed his wife and he went home.' He pointed to a seam across my naked shoulder. 'How did you get that scar?'

I glanced down at it. 'Ned Dyer: a friendly fight.'

'And how are the family – your mother and father, and Ambrosia and my little Mary?'

'Oh, they're writing sonnets to Mary.'

'But she's ten years old!'

'So was Surrey's Geraldine. Ambrosia had the scarlet fever, but seems to have recovered.'

'I'm sorry.' He frowned with concern.

'And Father is Lord Deputy of Ireland again.'

'I hope he has better luck this time . . . No, I am not Ambassador to the Diet. I am the *former* Ambassador, detained in Kraków by my personal affairs. I do not want to take Dorotea from her kindred – not yet: a first marriage for her, and so late . . .' I nodded. 'She is learning English. Meanwhile Queen Elizabeth finds my delay acceptable.'

'You could replace Rafe Sadler in Paris,' I said.

Antony shrugged again. 'When there is a king in Poland, Philip . . . I am told Prince Willem of Orange has offered you his daughter.'

'I did not like his daughter, Antony,' I said, 'and I do not mean to marry till I'm thirty.'

Naked, oiled with sweat, we stared at each other. Willem of Orange, called the Silent, led the rebellion in the Netherlands: for my other godfather King Philip also ruled Holland, and half the Dutch had turned Protestant and hated him.

'You want work,' said Antony. 'Here *is* work. Accept what Willem offers you and you would have, by inheritance of marriage, leadership of the Protestant war in Europe, whose moral head Willem became when the mob cut off the head of Admiral Coligny in Paris.'

'I am devout, Antony,' I said, 'but not devout enough yet to kill men for my religion, nor brave enough to die as Coligny died.' I leaned forward, aware of strength, solidity and grace, remembering the humble envy I had seen in my elders' eyes. *Will I envy the young when I am old? If so, I vow I will have the dignity never to show it. How does life betray and disappoint them, that my elders look at me with such envious hope – with a humility that shames and frightens me for them?* 'Antony, I will do all I can. Let me alone.'

'I am sorry, Philip.' With care he settled back against the warm wall. 'There is an illusion that will tempt you when you are forty. I have heard women speak of the desire for a last child – how, at forty, the longing tricks them, torments them – even makes the belly ache. And at forty, for a few years until you conquer it, something in you will cry out in suffering and say the lie you swore you would never believe: *These young people will be more than I ever became.*'

'Someone slit my packs the night before last,' I said. 'And someone used the cover of Balinski's attack to pick me accurately from the rout, and nearly dragged me from my saddle.'

The small eyes with their ginger lashes considered me. Then without a word Antony got up and went into the next room, the *frigidarium*. I followed him. Here clean white towels lay closed from the damp in cupboards, two velvet robes hung on pegs, and on the benches stood the buckets of cold water I had learnt laughingly to dread. My godfather lifted a bucket and emptied it over me: I whooped with shock, and did the same to him. We shivered and shook ourselves. Antony said, 'It's worse in Sweden: there they expect you to go and roll in a snowbank. So you carry a letter?'

'So I think the thief believed.' The second bucket descended; the icy delight and cleanliness of it made me shiver. When I had doused him again, I reached for the towel and said, 'No, spare me a third. There is no letter to steal. I bear a verbal message from the Privy Council to Father Caspar Laurence of the Society of Jesus.'

What Dangers Deep

'The surgeon whose lectures you've come to hear? He's the most famous doctor in Europe.'

'Yes. And he is the friend of Cardinal William Allen, and close friend to Father Robert Parsons, who lead our own Catholic rebels in exile on the Continent.'

Antony towelled his neck. 'What does the Privy Council wish to say to Father-Doctor Laurence?'

'Last spring,' I replied, 'he sent word in secret that he wishes to die at home, not in traitor's exile; and that if Her Grace would pardon him he will recant, and tell all he knows of Catholic plots to kill the Queen.'

He reached for his robe. 'So she has decided to make trial of you.'

I thought of Her Grace's face as I last saw it, a face whose youth was a memory that belonged to my parents, not to me; the oval face the portraits will make seem so inexpressive. Her eyes are light brown and brilliant, the pupils distended with short sight, and the high cheeks, fine narrow features and skin of a translucent delicacy may once have given her the kind of prettiness that vanishes – an attraction that must always have been elusive to describe. Now her face has thinned to a nervous and intelligent austerity, and my elders say her resemblance to her paternal grandfather, King Henry the Seventh, cancels the ancient slander on her birth. Still, it suits half Europe to believe that slander.

I tied my robe, glad in the chill of even the thin warmth of the velvet. 'Yes,' I said. 'She has decided to make trial of me.'

We recovered our swords, left our clothes for the servants and made our way back to the sleeping house. On a chest our chamber-candles stood ready. We lit them from the hall sconce. As he pinched the wicks, leaving the hall in darkness, Antony said: 'There is a public bath off the square, but the attendants there are known as catamites. You'll find few prostitutes. Married women often say yes.'

I shrugged. 'I loathe to covet what I cannot have for my own.'

We mounted the stairs: our candles cast soft golden shadows in the wood. 'Then there is a courtesan named Sabina Korytowska – pretty, skilled and young, like all the best of her profession. *Pan* Zamoyski enjoys her occasionally. You will find her in' – he grinned – 'Reformacka Street, if you can afford her. Take a retinue: her kitchen-staff are well used to feeding them while they wait for you. She might cost you the price of that sapphire there.' He gestured to a ring I wore.

I grimaced. 'For a night's entertainment? I'd sooner use my hands. Or dream of—'

Of Yolanta. Antony's bright gaze did not interrogate me.

At his door we hesitated; then I embraced him. 'May God be good to you both tomorrow. Good night.'

Outside my own room I halted. 'Master Philip!' Ambrose Hyde, in shirt and hose, was coming out of the chamber he shared with Ludovic Briskett.

'Ambrose? Are you not well?'

'Briskett is asleep, sir. Come with me into your room.'

I did so; he closed the door behind me. 'Put out the candle.' I obeyed. Ambrose moved to the window and pulled aside one corner of the curtain. 'Look there, sir, in the shadow of the cage. A man has been standing there for two hours; and if he's a drunkard with nowhere else to go, then he's sleeping damned upright.'

'Where? I cannot see him.'

I gazed out over the huge square. In the moonlight its cobbles shone grey with the patina of feet, of horses' hooves and cartwheels; centuries of voices lay suspended in its silence. Yet now it was empty, its furthest houses black on the edge of an expanse so great that London has nothing to equal it, nor even, I think, the great square at Florence. At the limit of my vision I saw, standing isolated in the square, a graceful tower and, nearer, a building with a colonnade.

We were looking down from the topmost corner window of Antony's house. Across from me and rising high above, the uneven towers of the Church of Sancta Maria had gone dark; the colours of stained glass had faded to lead and ash.

I could see the cage. It bulged from the left-hand wall of the church: a patterned web of ironwork that protected a table-tomb, the whole forming a kind of chapel open to the weather. In its complex shadows nothing stirred.

Then I focused a figure that was not grille or effigy, and detected the gleam in the dark of metal that was not iron.

'What shall we do? Who are they?' whispered Ambrose.

'The Ambassador may have enemies. The lord Zamoyski obviously has many. The man may not be watching *us*.'

'You believe that no more than I do, sir.'

I nodded, and gently clapped him on the shoulder. 'Thank you, Ambrose, and good night. Sleep all tomorrow if you can. Sleep is the best thing for a cold – that and mulled wine.'

'I'll get them both, then. Good night, sir.'

When he had gone I stripped naked and lay down. The goosedown pillows smelt of lavender; someone had run a copper pan full of fire-coals over the sheets to warm them.

Yolanta – the name I had not said to Antony. Suddenly her face, with its privacy, its quality of resistance, sprang full into my memory; and with it came appetite.

Such imaginings, rising to our need, are vivid, crude and brief. I kissed her throat and pulled down folds of cloth. Her armpit smelt delicately of fresh sweat, her skin, fine as talc to my lips, was moist with it. The white translucence of her breasts retained the print of my fingers. I bore her down on to the floor, ripped fabric and, crushing her cry of shame, exposed and held her down.

Beauty, music, sweetness, love, while she doth against me prove . . .

My cry was audible. I crushed my face into the pillow and shuddered, emptying.

When I woke in the morning I was lying as I had fallen. I had been too exhausted even to move.

Three

I have never been to a pleasant wedding. Usually the principals are distracted, the parents strained, and the guests vulnerable to the disasters that threaten a festival where enjoyment is stringently required of them, and their hosts hurry away for whispered conferences, or jump at sudden noises. Our modern customs, of course, allow a modest retreat for the bride and groom – she first, to be undressed and put to bed by her women, he following after an interval, unattended by practical jokers if his friends are wise. For Antony and Dorotea their return to the Embassy, though well guarded, was to be even more subdued: they would bid their friends good night at the door, and then give themselves into the care of their own servants. To my embarrassment, I would be sleeping down the corridor: I did not yet know anyone in Kraków whom I could have asked to invite me for the night.

In addition, after the wedding at eleven in the morning, there would be a meal, and then several barren hours to get through before the evening's feast. Antony was to be the guest of the Princess Anna at the Castle, and I wanted to see the Wawel, so I intended to be punctual that evening. I hoped that, while their guests watched the masques the Princess had arranged for their entertainment, Antony and Dorotea might be allowed a couple of hours' sleep.

At eleven therefore, dressed in green taffeta and sighing with stifled yawns, I stood (there were no pews) with several hundred other people in the echoes and incense-smoke of

Sancta Maria. Frankincense mingled with the scent of the yellow roses that had come from Zamoyski's glasshouses. Pressing my upper lip against a sneeze, I glanced around. Far above me the vaulting was painted with gold stars. They had shut the doors, and the church glowed with the rich shadows of stained glass, and with the light of beeswax candles whose honey-scent I now identified as a third element in the sweetness I disliked. On the walls and in side-chapels monuments guarded their dead; citizens in the dress of three hundred years ago gazed down from above the Latin of their epitaphs. Every cough rustled in the heights above us.

I had heard of the famous triptych. It rose behind the altar, its tiers of huge saints clad in sheet-gold, their bodies sinuous, their faces worked with colour and white enamel.

The wedding-party stood directly in front of me: Zamoyski in black, Antony in blue, the two girls dressed in yellow velvet with a bloom of white, and Dorotea in white cloth-of-gold that cast off a pale shimmer when she moved.

They had finished. Dorotea turned; her sisters bent with rehearsed alacrity to scoop up her train. I saw Yolanta's frown of concentration. Maria was wearing a square cap trimmed with silver; as she bent down a lock of hair fell over her shoulder, and I saw her tuck it back. The sisters exchanged a glance of confirmation, the great velvet folds came up, and to the music of the choir the married pair moved towards the door. With a single impulse the crowd relaxed, and I, as Antony had instructed me to do, fell in with the retreating party.

Because I was walking behind her I saw what Maria did next. She had worn a yellow rose tucked into her bodice between her breasts: I had noted this because Yolanta had chosen no matching ornament. I remembered wondering, during the service, whether the rose possessed thorns, and then had suddenly and unwillingly found myself imagining the odour of Maria's breasts. Emptied, too tired for lust, I had cursed and gone on with my prayer.

I did not see her make any ungainly motion, though she must have shifted the weight of her sister's train for an instant on to her right arm. But she did not inconvenience Dorotea or break the smoothness of her gait as, with a flick neat as a boy's, she tossed the rose to her left.

It fell on the flags in an area of shadow where no one stood; I dropped out and stepped quietly aside. Possibly only I had noticed a motion whose deliberateness puzzled me.

Where I now stood, in a shallow side-chapel, votive candles flickered like jewels in their cups of red and blue glass. The rose had fallen on a gravestone – a slab laid flat into the floor. On it I read the words:

Helena Poniatowska Zamoyska
1530–1564

'Blessed are they whose iniquities are forgiven, and whose sins are covered. Blessed is the man to whom the Lord will not impute sin.'

'Master Sidney?'

I started and looked up, to confront my friend from the rooftiles of the night before. The ugly, intelligent face that smiled at me could only have been English: white-skinned and freckled, with a shock of pink-blond hair. He was taller than me by an inch or two, and probably older than he looked. 'I'm Robert Sellier, sir. I hope you took no hurt last night, and that you got some sleep.'

'A little, thank you, Sellier.' I held out my hand. 'And thank you for your good company last night.'

'It may relieve you to know that *Pan* Balinski has retired to the country. It relieves *me*, at any rate.'

'I wish it did me.' But it left the slasher of packs, the man in the shadows, and now the obscurely disturbing inscription I had just discovered. 'Tell me' (his eyes followed my gesture) 'do you happen to know whether there was a fourth sister?'

'A fourth? Oh no, sir: this was the mother of the ladies – *Pan* Zamoyski's sister-in-law. The father died while travelling abroad, so I have heard.'

'It seems strange wording for an epitaph. Of what *sins* and *iniquities* was the poor lady so lucky to consider herself absolved?'

'She committed suicide, sir.'

The bridal party had paused in a grey glare of light on the steps. I saw Antony glance over his shoulder, seeking me. Sellier and I had stepped back into the body of the church. At my expression I saw Antony's eyes linger on my face, startled and inquiring. I blew him a kiss of congratulation: with a comic shrug he turned away. 'What did you say?'

'She died a suicide.'

'Then why does she rest in holy ground?'

'You understand, this was before my coming to Kraków, and the family never talk of it – or not to strangers.' I nodded. 'The Church found its usual compassionate excuse: that self-murder is a sin no one would sanely incur, and therefore that her very commission of it proved her to be of unsound mind.'

We had begun to move towards the door. I saw Briskett approaching us. 'And was it true?'

'That she was not sane? I have heard it was true.'

Ludovic's arrival gave me no choice but to say, 'This is my servant, Ludovic Briskett.' The two men shook hands. 'Master Sellier, I mean to let the wedding-party take care of itself for three hours. If you have nothing else to do, will you walk with us through the town?'

And so for that afternoon we wandered deep in the walled city, while the wind blew about us a rain of yellow leaves. Radiating from the hub of Market Square, where the arcades of Drapers' Hall still smelt of new cement, Mariacki Close led into Butcher's Market, while on another side a slope took one down into the lanes of the University; and in a third direction other streets led upward to the height of Castle Hill.

I saw half-timbered houses with windows whose panes refracted glittering light; and some houses of ancient stone; and others whose façades were surmounted by scrollwork or by toothed patterns blacked with tar. I remember Turkish cannon piled in a colonnade, ten-foot cylinders engraved with a script that seemed one beautiful, single line, calling down indecipherable blessings. I remember a red door studded with silver nails, a wrought-iron cross above another door, and over another still the inscription 'God is my Judge and my Protector'.

A solid, closed-in city, ancient and elusive, it smelt of people who were not my own and of a history from which I felt shut out. The red, purple and orange of autumn flowers was blowing into tatters; when rain spattered us, beech-leaves stuck to the cobbles, whose dark patina now shone pink with sunset.

The place must be very ancient, I thought: perhaps originally, in Roman times, it had been a hunting-camp, with a hill, a ford and a river. Probably the earliest settlement had spread down from the vantage offered by Castle Hill. Everywhere I saw traces of lives lived and forgotten: buildings demolished, their foundations brimming with gardens of late marigolds or weed-patches where women bent, gleaning herbs; buildings engulfed, the stones of a five-hundred-year-old house crumbling into the grain of the brick house built over and around it, with a Florentine loggia and gargoyle drainpipes and a fish-scale roof of green bronze tiles.

In later months faces were to gather fellowship and buildings individuality for me; but from that first day I chiefly remember texture, and the feel of something alien. And I remember walls: walls of pebble and dressed stone and brick sifting into powder; walls stained with time and war; walls battered and tumbled and forgotten.

And down the walled lanes flowed the crowds. They were blond but not English-blond (for we English like to think of ourselves as a fair-haired people, though in fact most of us are dark). I saw no redheads, and few white-blondes like Maria: every head was dark-gold or straw-colour. I know it insults any people to describe them from the outside, but what more can a stranger do? For they were not *my* people, these handsome men with their straight narrow features, and the women with their broad graceful bodies, fine teeth and clear, ivory-yellow skin. All seemed dressed for the cold, in velvets lined with fur; velvet veils covered the women's hair, embroidered with vine-like patterns of bird-headed snakes in gold and silver thread.

I remember two girls laughing arm-in-arm in front of us, while we walked behind with respectful interest. I remember the full curve of one girl's cheek, the sheaf of her hair bound by its coif and veil, and the gold rings on her fingers. And with that memory comes its immediate context: two nuns hurrying past us; a vendor with his tray of hot sausage-patties and cheese-custard pies; a man in a belted gown leading a horse, which was yoked to a boat-shaped farm-cart loaded with turnips and pears. I remember noting the beauty of the women's voices and of their speech, with its complex, supple consonants. A beggar on crutches held out his hand. The girls gave him money with gentle, unlingering courtesy; I gave him more.

'The Turks value these women,' said Robert Sellier.

'As slaves?'

He nodded. 'For their fair colouring and their beauty. Every now and again one hears of Turkish raiding-parties taking women and young boys for slaves in the south, to be sold in Constantinople.'

'They look brave enough,' remarked Ludovic Briskett.

'Perhaps they're used to it,' I said. 'War with Swedes, Tartars, Danes, Russians, Turks – war all around them as far back as they can remember. How could one live with such constant fear, except by becoming hardy and cheerful?'

'And cruel,' said Robert Sellier. 'In one skirmish Balinski won last year, word got out that one Turkish general had swallowed his gold for safekeeping. So every Turk the Poles caught they slit open, to examine his bowels for gold or muck; and some they left alive thus, telling them they were free to crawl homeward if they could. May God forgive them.' He crossed himself. To my shame, my expression moved him to add, 'Yes, I am a Catholic, sir.'

'I beg your pardon, Master Sellier.'

He shrugged, and yielded right-of-way to a servant walking two greyhounds. Four men rolled past us a huge cask of wine. 'There's no harm done.'

Above us from the direction of Sancta Maria rang a high and broken melody – a trumpet, I thought, but the sound ended too suddenly for me to identify it. Sellier grinned. 'The alarm. They say the Tartars came once, and one man climbed to the top of Sancta Maria and tried to rouse the town to arms. A Tartar arrow took him with his tune unfinished. Ever since, every hour of every day of every month for five hundred years, they have had a trumpeter play that same alarm from the spire of Sancta Maria: *and never once have they let him finish it.*'

'Let me see,' I said. 'There are twenty-four hours to a day; three hundred and sixty-five days to a year; that means . . .'

'That means,' said Ludovic Briskett thoughtfully, 'approximately four million, three hundred and eighty thousand unfinished trumpet-calls.'

'My God,' I murmured; and the reflection brought us to a halt.

Bathed and changed into blue canvas striped with silver, I found myself, at nine o'clock that night, seeing the state rooms of the Wawel through the short temper of a headache. Nothing, neither moderate food nor a cautious use of wine, could rid me of it. Nonetheless I hoped no one, from the Princess Anna to my newly met acquaintances across the table, had noticed anything unusual. Our conversation, between French and Latin, had gone pleasantly if not volubly; and now a consort of viols, lutes and pipes was tuning for the dance.

I could glimpse the Princess from where I sat. On her right she had placed Dorotea, and then Jan Zamoyski – on her left, Antony Marshall and myself. I guessed the Princess to be even older than Adam Kózmian had estimated, perhaps forty-five – a pleasant sharp-faced woman with thin lips, reddish hair under a coronet of baroque pearls, and grey eyes of extreme intensity. Her voice was a sweet alto, and her manner masterful and gracious. She had greeted me and asked after my teacher Hubert Languet, with whom she corresponded; and I was able to give her news of him. After that she let me go.

Around me stretched a room whose coffered ceiling resembled a chessboard of gold boxes, each frame enclosing a golden rose. The floor was tiled in diamonds of red, white and black agate; on the tapestries, Adam and Eve were created, sinned and suffered expulsion from a garden of rich fruits. We might have been in Paris, except for a fifteen-foot-high edifice in one corner. It was built of blue faience tile, and shone with that peacock-green that resembles turquoise gemstones. I assumed it was a stove.

'Antony, does your housekeeper have any remedy for headache?'

'Why, do you have one?' My godfather's eyes were grey-ringed with fatigue. 'Well, so have I. My God,' he whispered, leaning towards me, 'how can anyone expect a man to make love with his wife after a day like this?'

'No one does.' I tapped his arm: in its comic solicitude it resembled (I realized suddenly) a gesture my mother often made. 'If I were you I'd slip a strong sleeping-dram into the wedding-posset, and have her wake at noon tomorrow.'

'On one condition: that I drink half the posset. There now, they're going to dance. Do you want to go home?'

'I'll try a dance or two, and then perhaps yes. Is it too dangerous without guards?'

He frowned. 'I'll detach twenty of my own servants to go

with you. May Christ damn this city, it's only a ten-minute ride! And they've mended the gate.'

I patted his shoulder and grinned, pushing back my chair. 'Noon tomorrow.' My godfather groaned.

Half an hour later I found myself going down the dance with the hand of Maria Zamoyska lying cool and light on my own. She had changed into a gown of rich dark blue taffeta, and wore black ribbons plaited in her hair. We drew apart, parted and came back together for another slow, ceremonial progress down the line. 'Master Sidney, my sister asked me to apologize for her absence. She felt ill and has gone to bed.'

The dance separated us: rosettes of four people touched hands, circled, and swirled into a pattern that brought partner against partner again. I raised Maria's hand with mine, on which, I noted, she was laying two fingers only, with the utmost lightness. It occurred to me that she did not want to touch me. 'It was kind of your sister to remember me. Please tell her I hope she feels well tomorrow.'

'I will.' She bowed again; the taffeta of her gown made a delicate crisp sound as she moved.

It was the final motion. The music ended. As the dancers applauded the musicians and each other, I said, 'Mistress Maria, I thought last night that you disliked me. Have I displeased you in some way? I confess, considering we have known each other only a few hours, I can see no chance I had to offend you, nor any just reason.'

I should not have named 'just reason': it seemed a complaint, and put me in the wrong. 'You were mistaken, Master Sidney,' replied Maria with civility, and with a calm stare that was very close, I thought, to insolence. 'I was weary last night – as I am now. Please excuse me.' She saluted me, swirled and dipped in a curtsey, and left me.

I had deserved her abruptness, but her composure and her courtesy challenged me to disbelieve her words. I found I did disbelieve them, leaving my puzzlement no less than before. In any case the heat on my skin was anger, and I felt my heart beating too hard.

It was enough: I made my duty to the Princess Anna and prepared to go. Jan Zamoyski looked up from his wine. 'Master Sidney, will you come to us – my family and some few friends – tomorrow night at eight for supper?'

'Yes, my lord, that would please me very much. Thank you,' I said. 'Good night.'

At home I took a Turkish bath, which helped. I wished to avoid the bridal party and any reminder that Antony had a guest, but nevertheless I dressed and settled in the library. There I read for two hours by bright candlelight, and found my headache neither worse nor better. The quiet had helped, however, and I felt calmed.

At last I heard singing in the courtyard, then good wishes and good nights, and the door opening, and the soft welcome of the servants. Antony's voice said, 'Has Master Sidney come home safe?'

Since I could not avoid them, I opened the library door. 'Yes indeed, sir. I feel better, and have been reading.'

'I'm glad.' Antony looked tired and eager for privacy. Dorotea turned on me brown eyes made brilliant by fatigue, and held out her hand.

I kissed it, then gathered her in my arms. 'God bless you, both of you; and from Father and Mother too.'

'I wish they were here.' Antony's smile dismissed me. 'Come, my dear, they'll have prepared a bath.'

'One with lavender-oil, I hope.'

She laid her hand on his arm, and as they mounted the stairs I heard him say, 'I told them specially.'

So they went up to bed together; and I wished them gentle sport or gentle sleep – whichever would give them joy – and went back into the library.

It must have been two-thirty when I mounted the stairs to

my room. My reading had not affected the headache, and had helped in every other way. Behind Antony's door lay darkness and silence; my two servants were sleeping (Ambrose's day in bed had done him good).

In my own room, considering the events of the past few days, I had decided to leave a candle burning. I had placed it in the centre of a protective pewter tray, so that it could not fall except on to metal where the flame would gutter out harmlessly. And across the candlelight beneath the door, as I approached it silently, I saw a shadow pass.

I went to my servants' room, and eased the door open and then shut it behind me. 'Sir?' came Ambrose's whisper in the dark.

'Get up, both of you, and bring your daggers. There is someone in my room.'

Each man was wearing his shirt; each slid his dagger from beneath his pillow, and without a sound we moved down the corridor. When I opened my door, a man I did not recognize was slitting cushions, cutting open mattresses, ransacking chests.

He fought us, and we mastered him, noiselessly. 'Tie him and get him out in *silence*,' I whispered. 'I want that poor man to have no more misery on his wedding-night.' Briskett nodded, sucking a cut hand.

We tied him with strips torn from the sheets and bundled him, trussed, down the stairs and out into the cold of the courtyard. 'There's the porter at the gate,' said Briskett.

'Then we'll tell him we're tossing out a thief, and he can tell the Ambassador in the morning.'

In the shadow of the tomb-cage, where the stones of Sancta Maria cast a cold that made our prisoner's teeth chatter, I seized his jaw and forced him to look at me, and laid my dagger against his throat. 'Who is your master?' I demanded.

I had spoken French, but the frantic eyes told me even before Ludovic's guess. 'I suspect he speaks only Polish, sir. It might be a wise precaution in the man who hired him. He could recognize and seize all written material, whether or not he could read it. He would not, in any case, have had time to choose among your papers. And letters from your father, your uncle, perhaps even from Her Grace, might interest the man who sent him.'

Our prisoner shifted. My knife bloodied him, though not deeply: he gasped and lay still. 'Her Grace gave me a licence to travel abroad, no more written word than that,' I said, in case, despite our guess, the man understood me. 'Whom could my father's letters interest? This French observer Antony mentioned? And as for my uncle—'

'He could give news of Her Grace's Court,' replied Ludovic softly.

Zamoyski? I glanced at Ludovic in the dark, and received a shrug for answer.

I said in French and Latin to our prisoner: 'I will let you live to take a message. Tell the man who sent you that there is no letter. If he wants to know more he must come to me. In the morning I will kill you if I find you here; and since we intend to leave you bound, I hope someone will take pity on you.'

And so we left him and, as my room was filled with a drift of goose-feathers and mattress-ticking, I collapsed between Ludovic and Ambrose on the bed my servants shared.

Four

I had ridden to Kraków, in part at least, to cheer Antony's wedding with my family's greetings. I had not yet been forty-eight hours in the house, and had so far contributed some share in the attack on the embassy; in the trapping of a thief during what I hoped had been the undisturbed consummation of my godfather's marriage; and in the wrecking of my bedroom. Add to this that Maria seemed to dislike me, that I could seldom distract my thoughts from Yolanta, and that the whole matter of the Privy Council's message to Caspar Laurence had yet to be attempted, and it seemed a fair two days' work. Antony must be told about the bedroom; but his gatekeeper beat me to telling him.

However tired they had been, I think something had gone well for them; for Antony in his robe, and Dorotea in a green peignoir with her hair loose on her shoulders, absently slipped their arms around each other's waists as they gazed at my ripped mattress and at the snow of goose-down. 'My own men will do the cleaning,' I said, 'and I'll pay for every penny of the furniture. Christ, Antony, I'm sorry.'

He looked at me, and decided not to refuse the payment, or at least not then (actually I had already settled the matter with his steward). Dorotea said, 'May I call you Philip?'

'Please – Dorotea?'

'That would be excellent,' replied Jan Zamoyski's eldest niece. 'My uncle, Philip, hears much, and sometimes he tells us what rumours come to him. Perhaps he should not: he has a vein of indiscretion surprising in so wise a man. Now, I have heard that someone slashed open your packs in the inn at Torún, and that a man tried to drag you from your horse during your ride from Saint Florian's Gate. It seems to me these three men were looking for the same thing. Perhaps you know what it is. In any case, Antony, I think it would be dangerous now to go to Vienna. Could you bear to leave our wedding-journey till the spring?'

Antony raised her hand and kissed it. 'Dorotea, thank you for sparing me: I had dreaded to disappoint you. No, we will find the embassy a shambles if we leave it in Philip's care. We believe the thieves want a letter which does not exist, whereas a spoken message does.' She nodded. 'Philip will deliver that message,' said Antony.

'I must,' I replied. 'Lectures at Collegium Maius begin in just a few more days.'

'They have reserved a room,' said Antony, 'in the unmarried professors' quarters; but your man must be still on the road. In any case my friends cannot find him in the city.'

'Then I'll attend his first lecture as a student. Dorotea, it is Caspar Laurence.'

'The Jesuit surgeon? Ah. You need not have told me.'

'No, but you have been so kind to me – and my ineptitude is beginning,' I said softly, 'to shame and frighten me.'

'You told no one in Vienna?' demanded Antony.

I shook my head. 'And the message came by courier from Sir Francis Walsingham – a rider I presume he could vouch for.'

'Yet it seems someone knows. I must write to Francis and tell him.'

'Yes, of course. And my uncle of Leicester, Antony?'

For a moment Antony considered. 'Philip, I see no reason to inform your uncle Robert: you have done nothing inept and nothing wrong. Hear your lectures and perform your errand, and perhaps between us we can discover who has alerted this enemy, and why.'

* * *

What Dangers Deep

At the foot of Castle Hill stood a little cobbled rise – a spur of Castle Hill itself. A wall pierced by a single gate ringed its base; and rising above that battlement I could see the lights, roofs and lattices of a structure so fantastic in the dark that it reminded me of some edifice – Castle Chariot, Castle Senaudon or Dolorous Garde – of which Malory has written in his book *Le Morte D'Arthur*. As far as I could judge in the darkness, roofs of tile and slate rose at crazy angles up the slope to a single, lighted summit.

The guards admitted us into the first courtyard, and I began to guess the plan that had wound a spiral round the hill. All around the court lay buildings – stables, kennels, latrines, storehouses. Private staircases led up to houses with lit windows, and the road wound upward to a second courtyard. Here we found lodgings of timber, brick, split stone; the roofs of the first level lay below us, and again steps led to doorways flanked by stripped rosebushes – houses where, I supposed, lived Jan Zamoyski's servants and dependants. Here and there I saw cords of wood lying piled; padlocked doors let into storehouses inside the rock; and I noticed a small court, set at odd levels, where the hill had proved intractable, and the cobbles cracked like piecrust around an outcrop ten feet high.

All the windows we saw were barred. We rode on, moving around and up. Now below me I could see the roofs and chimneys of a dozen buildings, with smoke hanging pale as steam under the stars.

We had come to the final court and to the topmost house: a timber building that incorporated and leaned against a gatehouse so ancient it seemed like a fragment of a Roman aqueduct. But no, I remembered that no Legion had penetrated this far north: the gate belonged, I guessed, to some earlier structure on the site. But a staircase still bored down through its thickness and let into the useless arch, which opened now only on the plunge of roofs below; and judging by the wicker railing and potted rose-trees I could glimpse, I suspected Zamoyski had turned the gatehouse roof into a sun-terrace.

Impregnable, Zamoyski had called it. So Yolanta and Maria lived here. What mood, I thought, must that induce in their suitors – for surely they had many?

But the house before which we dismounted was an undefended structure of half-timber and slate. Its front door opened, without steps, directly off the flags of the court. It had many windows, each bubbled pane so set into the leads that none refracted the light uniformly. In sunlight they would have sparkled; lit, as now, with fire- and candlelight, they showed glimmering depths of orange, yellow-rose, and blue-shadowed, colder light.

They led me up three flights of stairs. In a little room panelled with caramel-coloured wood, Jan Zamoyski held out his hand. 'Master Sidney! I hoped we might take wine and talk a little before we join my guests.'

'Gladly, my lord. Is this your study?'

'Yes; and, I think, except for the Castle, the highest window in Kraków. Come and see.'

He led me to one casement. I noticed it had no cage of bars.

'We have a garden, by the way,' said Zamoyski, 'straight below.' He smiled, his face vivid with amusement. Of Dorotea's eyes I should have said that they were brilliant; of Zamoyski's I should have said only that they were bright, small, and that they had been (I realized abruptly) studying me for several seconds. It came to me that this big, ugly man was successful with women; and also that I had never before, except I think in Her Grace Queen Elizabeth, confronted an excellence so self-aware.

'I cannot see, sir,' I said: 'the candlelight dazzles everything.'

'Then come here instead and let me show you some things I value. This book was sent me by Doctor John Dee. You have met him?'

'Yes, my lord. He is Her Grace's astrologer.'

'And cartographer. Look: maps of the coasts of Newfoundland and Labrador.'

And so for half an hour we moved from object to object: the

distillation-vessels with their blown-glass arms; the celestial and terrestrial globes, where near the South Pole I saw marked the name *Terra Australis noviter reperta*; an armillary sphere made of intermeshing rings; a Roman silver cup with double handles; and an exquisite marble girl, naked except for gold lace painted around her breasts, who was bending down to unbuckle her sandal. 'She was found on Capri,' remarked Zamoyski, 'and may have belonged, so I hope, to Tiberius. Now come sit with me: I have made you wait too long for that wine.'

He was wearing a sleeveless robe of brown velvet over a fine shirt with blackwork at the cuffs and throat. He took a chair, gestured me to another and, as he poured wine, remarked, 'I shall now be witty, subtle and truthful all at once – a rare combination. Someone, Master Sidney, once asked Prince Willem the Silent *why* he was so silent. The Prince considered for a long moment, and then replied, "Because."'

I grinned.

Zamoyski handed me a full goblet. 'Are you to be his son-in-law, Master Sidney?'

'Is all Kraków asking?' I replied, the complacency of my question revealing the answer I expected.

One discards these moments as they pass, valuing them only when one has learned they will not come again. Now, aged twenty, I felt descend on me Fortune's most malicious gift: the self-importance that comes so naturally to the young. But Fortune, who seldom laughs kindly, had tossed that flattery to thousands of young men like me; for she has seen us come and go.

The bright brown eyes assessed me. The experienced voice, adjusting tone, informed me precisely of my significance. 'Half Kraków is asking the other half. So, for this week, are Paris, Vienna, London . . .'

I set down my cup. I should be lucky if I ever confronted this man in intimacy again; and not even Antony could help me more truly if he chose. 'Tell me, my lord Zamoyski: will I ever get a better chance than this?'

I had expected to be liked for my honesty. But the clever face, amused, chose not to praise me, or not yet. Zamoyski's brows rose. 'Chance for what, Master Sidney?'

This was the man whose saying all Europe knew: 'I would give half my life to bring back to Catholicism those who have abandoned it; but I would give my whole life to prevent them from being brought back by violence.'

France had not learned this lesson; Spain had hated and earned hate for it; we in England had scarcely begun to study it. Knowing this, I looked at him and said steadily: 'To acquire political power for the help of the Protestant cause.'

'But what is the Protestant cause, Master Sidney? To convert, for example, me and all my co-religionists to your Faith, with or without force?'

'I did not speak of conversion, sir. I spoke, at least in intent, of defending the New Religion from King Philip's generals in the Netherlands, and from those who instigated, in Paris, atrocities against the Huguenots which I have seen and you, in this happy country, have not.'

'True. That is my work and King Zygmunt's, may God have pity on him; and without a new king of similar excellence we will go the way of France.' He gestured to the window, and to the city that lay below us – to the night with its latent threat of motion. 'Have you heard of Stefan Bathóry?'

'The Prince of Transylvania? I know he is a formidable general, and that the Turks respect him.'

'He is the only king the Diet must elect,' said Jan Zamoyski. 'Any other man will lose our fight against Russia – and our fight, in Poland, for humanity of religion. As to Protestantism . . . A cause, Master Sidney, is most dramatically defended by a war. Prince Willem *has* a war.'

'So has France,' I replied. 'Religious civil war.'

'Ah, but no one is going, I believe, to offer you a Protestant

What Dangers Deep

princess there.' He refilled his goblet – gestured a question. I covered my cup in answer, and he settled back, his fingers interlaced. 'By marriage with Willem's daughter you would inherit generalship in the Dutch war, which, by being a war against Spain, *is* the conflict of the New Religion against the Old. Whether you could best serve your Faith, or serve us all, by *making* war is a question I think you too young to answer – for which I pity you, since an answer is demanded of you now. But for two or three weeks – until other affairs distract us – many of us are asking ourselves whether we see in you the next leader of Protestantism militant. I do not know, Master Sidney, whether Nature has made you a superlative soldier. If she has not, save lives by sparing men your generalship: it takes more than birth to make a soldier. Within six months Prince Willem will find another husband for his daughter, and then your hope of achieving importance in the eyes of men will once again depend on whether Queen Elizabeth chooses to advance you.'

'Do you think she will, my lord?'

Zamoyski smiled faintly. 'I would give a great deal to meet Her Grace. Now, my guess from what I have heard of her is that she finds fervour dangerous.'

'But everyone knows her troops and money sustain the rebellion in the Netherlands!'

'Of course. But you cannot have grown up under your father's tutelage without realizing that English *complicity* can always be denied, even while it drains Spanish attention and resources from turning on heretic England. If you are a fervent Protestant, sir, it is my guess Her Grace will advance you only with great caution. Are you a fervent Protestant?'

'I hate the cruelties I have seen.'

'You would make war to prevent cruelty?'

'If I must.'

Zamoyski nodded. 'It is a cruel question, and has no answer that is not cruel: I apologize, Master Sidney. Would you obey the Queen if she commanded you to deceive, to act with caution, to temporize or to lie? Keep in mind that Spain is rich with New World gold, while Queen Elizabeth has her poverty and her cunning.'

I thought. 'I would obey her as far as my conscience allowed.'

'Precisely. Therefore, lest your conscience distort your advocacy of her policies, or force her into a proxy commitment, she will hesitate to give you power.'

'And therefore I had better seize another patron: Prince Willem?'

'Exactly so. You cannot love his daughter?' I shook my head. 'And you will not marry without love. We have talked together for twenty minutes, and I have discovered you to be a man of conscience and affection, stubborn in both. How much more clearly must the Queen see this, who has known you from your cradle? For these few weeks, Master Sidney, you matter in the affairs of Europe. Lose this chance, and if you matter again it will be for some other achievement, or for some other gift of luck.'

If you matter again. Cautiously I clenched my hands against my mouth, and saw him mark that they were trembling. Zamoyski said: 'I will tell you one thing more. You are beautiful, like most young people; you have intellect and rectitude, and no doubt courage. In addition, you have the power to elicit love. There is no more potent magic – or not in the eyes of your elders who will judge you. But remember this: *magic is not capacity*.'

I rose and walked to the window. Gazing straight down, I could make out the leaves of the lilac bushes, tarnished as pewter in the light of the waning moon. I said: 'Every man longs to matter in his time. It frightens me when I see in my elders' eyes the knowledge of their smallness. *I* do not think them small: it is a judgement they have reached, each one upon his own life.'

Chin on his hand, he watched me peacefully. 'Death takes us all, but our Faith tells us it does not make us nothing. May I call you Philip?'

'You are the second person who has asked me that today. Of course, my lord Zamoyski.'

His gaze on mine was friendly. 'Your family are desperate –

What Dangers Deep

as they have rendered you desperate – to re-achieve power. But have you, Philip, a gift for power that is distinct from arrogance or from the wish to serve? You have gifts, I can see. But you should *want* to do what you *can* do. Each of us has limited time. Understand your gift correctly, and you may not judge your life small when it is ended.'

At that moment Antony Marshall, frowning through his spectacles, was writing in cypher to the First Secretary of the Council:

> My dear Francis,
> Philip has arrived, and has three times been attacked or had his bags rifled. I gather he has spoken of your message to no one but me – and that because I guessed. I cannot believe that – here so far from England – anyone hates him for the actions of his grandfather, his father or his uncle. They all, as you know, offended in some eyes. The Duke of Northumberland profited by the plundering of the monasteries, and then aroused contempt by turning Catholic in terror at the end. And of course the Irish detest Philip's father, while many in England feel an envious hate towards Robert of Leicester.
> Still, this country looks towards the East, towards Russia or Constantinople; and I cannot believe revenge has pursued Philip here, or that anyone can hate him for himself.
> Caspar Laurence has not yet arrived. If he receives Philip, I trust the boy will write to you immediately. In the meanwhile I suggest we investigate the actions of Cardinal William Allen and of Father Robert Parsons. I know Laurence saw them both at Rome after his return from Turkey. It occurs to me that Philip's enemy may be Caspar Laurence's friend . . .

* * *

My evening had begun arduously. There was worse to come.

Zamoyski had a senior guest that night: the Catholic statesman Pavel Zborowski, who had played a rôle in enforcing religious tolerance on the fugitive King Henri. Naturally this man sat at my host's right hand. Beside Zborowski and to his right again sat Yolanta, then myself, then Maria.

So I found myself between the two girls. For the rest, I could see ranged down the long table about two dozen other faces: faces Slavic blond – kindly and literate, and distinguished from French or Italians of the same rank by the long belted robes the men wore, and by the women's autumn-warmth of apricot, cinnamon or cramoisy velvet lined with lynx or red fox-fur. I found them kind and voluble, and meticulous to include me in a conversation I would gladly have avoided, caught as I was between Yolanta and Maria.

I recall that we ate a broth of ginger. For the rest there were the usual meats and fowls in almond-milk or plum sauce, and, for dessert, dumplings fried in honey and marchpane fantasies. All the vegetables came pickled in brine, and I felt the lack of something fresh; and after supper there was sweet wine and also a steaming hot, colourless liquor flavoured with pepper and cinnamon. A consort played: the music was French and Italian as far as I could judge.

Maria had dressed in black, with her hair woven in a coil of tiny plaits to reveal a neck whose white firmness distracted me from her sister. Yolanta wore golden-yellow velvet, and had let her hair fall brushed and shining about her shoulders. I had learned how to use a fork in Italy; the one I found beside my knife and spoon had two prongs and was made of gold, and as Yolanta used hers I noticed, on her finger, a ring of white jade. She wore, I saw, one other ornament: an enamelled brooch that appeared to bear a coat-of-arms. She had touched her skin with violet scent, which I dislike – a strange flower that has a tone (to my senses, at least) of fruit, wood and autumn leaves, too richly mingled. Now I can never smell oil of violets without recalling her – and without remembering all that came after.

Yolanta seemed recovered from whatever illness (a woman's complaint, I supposed) had troubled her the night before. She smiled at me with a contraction of the brows and a thinning of the

What Dangers Deep

lips that gave her smile a quality of ruefulness, of private amusement. Maria greeted me and, chatting softly, we began our meal.

I ate lightly, for the stiffening in my groin awakened by Yolanta's scent would mix (I knew from experience) abominably with food. We had got to the marchpane fruits; people were shelling nuts with silver crackers, and I was beginning to realize I had underestimated the potency of the hot wine when I caught, in a flow of Polish between my host and *Pan* Zborowski, a few words of Italian: *Il Principe* and *Il Cortegiano*. I recognized both titles, and Yolanta, seeing this, raised her brows. 'Have you read Baldassare Castiglione, Master Sidney?'

'Yes, of course.' Castiglione is the author of *Il Cortegiano*, which we call in English *The Book of the Courtier*.

'I think his conclusion very beautiful,' she said.

'The speech he puts in the mouth of Pietro Bembo? Yes, it is beautiful, I agree. It has such a feeling of *dawn*.'

She nodded, apparently pleased. 'Of dawn when all the night's talk is over, and their ardour and their wit fade into weariness, and as day rises they talk gently of God's love. Yes, it is very fine. And Machiavelli, have you read him?'

'In Italy, yes. In England the book passes from hand to hand in secret.'

I noticed Maria was listening to us.

'And what do you think of him, Master Sidney?' said Yolanta.

'Machiavelli? That he teaches evil. He tutored Queen Catherine de' Medici, so it is rumoured.'

'Teaches *evil*?' Maria's voice, too self-assured, interrupted me, and its challenge distracted me, not pleasantly, from her sister. 'In what way does he teach evil?'

'We have a saying in English,' I replied, '"to call a spade a spade". Machiavelli calls a spade by its true name, and the spade is evil conduct everywhere: in tyrants, in their subjects, in their sycophants. Men as he describes them never *try* to be good. I believe that is one human motive he never sees; and yet it exists, and is powerful.'

Her eyes, with their blonde lashes and clear grey irises, met my own with impertinent equality. '"Whether it is better,"' she quoted softly, '"to be loved than feared. It is far better to be feared than loved, if you cannot be both. For one can make this generalization about men: they are ungrateful, fickle, liars and deceivers, they shun danger and are greedy for profit. While you treat them well, they are yours."'

I stared at her. 'Do you believe this?'

'I find, sir, that Machiavelli speaks the truth, and men are hypocrites to hate him for it.'

Now, twelve years later, I would agree with her; but then I barely stopped myself from uttering an intimacy to which she had no right: *Every day since I was born I have laboured to do what was good. I cannot remember a single day, from the time I was five years old, that I did not try.*

Instead I turned to her sister, and said with utter discourtesy: 'Mistress, what is that brooch you wear? A coat-of-arms? I thought I recognized it.'

Yolanta leaned her brow on her hand; hair whose shine fell and parted like a curtain hid her face. Then she shook it back, straightened, and said, 'It is the arms of Coligny, sir. Two years ago I went to France, and there I became a Protestant. I was in Paris when the mobs murdered the Admiral Gaspard de Coligny.'

'So was I,' I said. Beside me Maria had gone still.

We were speaking in private, normal tones; around us the conversation flowed almost unimpeded. Yolanta's eyes slid towards me, but all at once I knew she was speaking not to me at all, but past me to Maria. 'I wear this,' she said, 'to honour his martyrdom. Madame Marguerite, whose waiting-woman I was, let me come home only two months ago.' (The household of Madame Marguerite, sister of King Henri, included among its several notorieties a flirtation with the Protestant Reform.)

'*Martyrdom!*' whispered Maria, with a face that said *liar*. 'Coligny was a traitor to his king; and where the king falls the State will fall. Remember the tracts you have read, my sister, because I know you have read them: remember "Franco-Gallia" and the "Reveille-Matin des Français", which say that, when the king no longer serves his subjects, it is their right to destroy him. Your martyrs are advocates for chaos. Everywhere the Protestant Reform has come it has created civil war: everywhere.'

Yolanta's eyes remained downcast. But I was gazing at her sister. I have never looked at a woman with so vehement a dislike. 'Madam, in Paris I saw Catholic order enforced on children and on women, and I will not describe it.'

'Describe it. Do not spare me.' Maria's voice had risen. I did not notice that around us the other voices were stilling.

'Very well,' I said softly, speaking straight to her. 'We were hiding in the embassy. Outside the gates, on the second day we hid there, two men laid down a pregnant woman in the road, and squatted down and watched her as she lay. I saw, from the window behind which I was crouching, that she was weeping but not screaming. And then I saw that she was in labour; and, being Christian men, they had tied her legs together so she would rip herself apart.' The table had gone silent. Maria sat straight; her stare did not flinch from mine. 'I leapt over the wall and killed one, before the Ambassador's men killed the other and dragged her and me inside. There the Ambassador's surgeon cut her open in an attempt to save the child. The shock murdered her; and killed the babe too.'

The silence lasted, I think, a hundred seconds. Then Maria crossed herself and said with icy softness: 'Before God I am sorry. Do you think I am *glad*?'

'No. I think you are a fool.'

Twenty faces were staring at us. I looked at Zamoyski. 'Sir—'

'Stay where you are, Master Sidney. Maria, my child, come here.'

She rose, so did he; and like a winding clock-spring the conversation around the table resumed. Yolanta remained with her head bowed, her hair shielding her face. Zamoyski led Maria to the fireplace, in which burned a huge log, and sat down in a chair. Maria knelt beside him and, his hand stroking her hair, they talked out of our hearing.

Yolanta raised her head. 'Master Sidney, forgive us. My change of religion has greatly hurt my sister.'

'Such things have hurt many families,' I said.

She nodded. 'I know.'

I think fifteen minutes passed before Zamoyski returned to the table, and Maria came back to us smiling. As she passed Yolanta she laid her hand on her sister's shoulder; the hand with the white jade ring came up to clasp it. Then Maria appalled me by kneeling beside *my* chair.

I pushed back my seat, caught her hands and raised her. 'Mistress, do not kneel! Forgive me!' In my shame and my concern for her, I was almost babbling.

Her hands rested on my own, for unconsciously I had lifted them in the dance-gallantry of the night before; and their lightness and the white translucency of her skin reminded me, suddenly, how young she was to have suffered from me such an appalling rebuke.

She said, 'Master Sidney, we have hurt you sufficiently for one night. Forgive us. My uncle begs you to help us rescue your visit to Kraków. Will you join us for a four-day hunt? The countryside is beautiful in the autumn; and we have a salt mine and a holy well that we could show you.'

'A salt-mine?' I inquired, feeling my way back to any normal tone.

She nodded. 'Not so bad as it sounds. Wait and see.' Then she curtseyed and left me.

'Will you help me, Master Sidney?' The voice of Yolanta distracted me.

The others were rising from the meal. I pulled back Yolanta's chair and, as she thanked me, I reflected that I could either leave Kraków in the shame I deserved, or accept the invitation to four days more of their company.

Five

But the four days stretched to a week, and never in that week did I catch a trace of my enemy. We rode away from the city with its angled double belt of walls; from the Vistula with its rivercraft and rafts of roped timber; from the fields of stubble and new-harrowed earth.

Instead we plunged with joy into a countryside of brick-orange bracken, crisp by day and iced or dripping in the dawn. Mottled lemon-coloured leaves still hung thickly on the trees; crab-apples showed pink as roses where the birds clung pecking at the fruit. The rowan-berries had swollen fat and tight within their skins, and among all the rustling yellow and brown, pine-trees perfumed sunsets whose mint-green coldness already promised winter.

Even before the attack on the embassy I doubt Zamoyski would have permitted us to move unguarded. As it was, our company numbered about a hundred, with men-at-arms, cooks, body-servants (including three women for Yolanta and Maria), and grooms for the horses and the hounds. We would have been numerous enough to kill bandits or slave-traders had we met them; and this company deployed itself with trained skill around us, sparing us both inconvenience and the dirt with which so many men and animals foul their camping-grounds. Horses and dogs were cleanly dealt with, and each evening – surrounding our own tents in a distant protective ring – would rise the tents of our company, so that hot bath-water and picnic-meals waited for us every night. Also at each campsite latrines were dug in orderly fashion, and filled with earth and obliterated by the time we moved on.

'What about your holy well?' I demanded of Maria as I rode beside her. The day was pungent, Maria's cheeks were red with cold, and I, an hour after the midday meal, already felt pleasantly ravenous: in short, I liked her that day.

She smiled at me. 'We call it the Ancient Mass. That translates an archaic dialect name–' here she spoke it – 'Old Polish, if indeed it does not preserve some even more ancient tongue. Tribes of our ancestors hunted these forests when Tacitus was writing his Histories. It is a spring-fed pool, not a well in fact, and we call it the Ancient Mass because the priests – the holy wise men – used to perform their rites there.'

'The wise men?'

'They were priests of the people who carved the stone axes we still find sometimes on Wawel Hill.'

'And what were these rites? Human sacrifice? A sacrifice of virgins?'

It was a callous joke, and it relieved me that she missed it, and only frowned with thought – a furrow in the brow that I find so mock-fierce and so touching in young skin matte as velvet. 'Not virgins, Master Philip: bears.'

'Bears?'

Yolanta was riding on my other side; she wore a habit of green cloth, and her hair shone soft and dark against her frost-chapped cheeks. 'Great bears with teeth as long as my thumb.' She held one up, quirking it like a claw. I grimaced. 'About eighty years ago some farmers found beside the spring a pit filled with bear-skulls. Whoever put them there had piled them in a pyramid, layer upon layer in a pit five feet deep.'

'Did he mean them for guardians? What did they guard?'

'The sacred spring,' said Maria. 'And people near there tell a story I do not believe: that in our great-grandfathers' day a young man vanished in the woods, and that the magic of the place transformed him into a man-bear who is still seen from time to time.'

I had now encountered the people who told these stories; had seen them wielding their sickles or gleaning windfall pears or carrying home loads of sticks; had seen the boat-shaped carts in which they brought their roots and apples to market, and the dirty thatched cottages, their walls stained in beautiful pastels – yellow, blue, pink, violet. Most of these people were slaves bound to their lord's fields. They left their babies naked until the fifth month of life, and those who survived were so hardy they could walk barefoot on ice; but only the young girls were pretty, and everywhere I saw bodies coarsened and exhausted, old with work by the age of forty years.

'Are these the people you seek to relieve, my lord?' I said to Zamoyski one day.

He nodded. 'As I may. Some lords are better, some worse. First of all I want that they shall not starve; and for that they must have peace – must have a King who can enforce the peace. Our history is old and alien to you, Master Sidney: judge it with humility. I do not know when serfdom in this country will cease, but in my time I can at least seek to spare them starvation, Turkish raiders and religious civil war.'

Now, recalling this conversation, I glanced once again at Maria. 'And the salt-mine? Excuse me, but why in God's name show me a salt-mine?'

Maria laughed. 'I thought ancient things interested you.'

'They do.'

'The first salt from these workings went to the tables of Antonine Rome. And there are . . . things you should see: one especially.'

'Our uncle has found a treasure there,' explained Yolanta, 'or the miners found it and reported it to him. We ourselves have not seen it. We do not even know what it may be.' I saw the salt-mine could not be escaped, and turned the conversation to something else.

Not even what came after has destroyed, in memory, the joy of those five days. I was always hungry, always aching with exercise; and at night the roast meat had that tinge of smoke which I find as potent as a spice. At night, too, we once heard the astonishingly musical song of the wolves, each note a cry of wavering sadness; and by day we sometimes heard the baying, almost retching challenge of the stags.

We rode in silence through forests where leaves lay pressed into a cake of moist, tannic brown, and groves where orange shelves of fungus grew from trees. We found marshes where kingfishers swooped for perch among the reeds. Once – across a meadow's distance, because the beasts are dangerous – we saw blue-tongued bison feeding, and I heard of – but despite my longing did not see – the *tarpan*, the shaggy thick-legged wild horse whose back bears a single slate-grey stripe. To me it sounds a little like the Iceland pony (in spite of our preference for Arabs the sturdy ancient horses have a real beauty, or so I think) and Yolanta said they are so hardy she had once seen a *tarpan* rolling in a snowbank, apparently just for the delight of it.

On the fourth night out from Kraków we camped a short walk from the spring called the Ancient Mass, and less than an hour's ride from the salt-mine at Wieliczka. Of these two attractions I felt, if any interest, a slight preference for the former; but Zamoyski suggested we might take a day for the mine, and then the two girls could conduct me to the spring before our next (and final) day's hunt. 'I suspect dawn is the best time for such places,' he said to me with a smile. 'You'll take armed servants, of course. A pity: any holy place, however ancient, deserves the honour of silence. In any case it is only a short walk through the trees.'

And so we came after a forty-minute ride to the huts and workings of the miners, and to a doorway cut into the hill and hazed with vines. Unpromising, I thought, looking at the modest arch. But from it sighed an air I had never breathed before: a profound and alien scent. And I had never seen any

What Dangers Deep

night like the blackness beyond the arch. 'Does the passageway slope down?' I asked Zamoyski.

'Yes. There will be torches: here they come.'

'Excuse me, sir, but it seems unwise, after last week, to corner yourself in a hole from which you cannot escape. What if *Pan* Balinski, or some other enemy, should have occupied the tunnels? Or what if, coming out this evening, we find the doorway blocked?'

'Master Philip, my men have combed and occupied this square mile of land – more people of mine than you have seen. We checked all the tunnels for gunpowder or poisoned air, marked all the side-borings with white paint, sent every miner home with three days' pay, paid a week's wages to those who will conduct us through, and have detained the owner, a charming man who informed me of the treasure we are going to see, and to whom my librarian is at this moment presenting a terrestrial globe which also functions as a clock, made by Benvenuto Cellini. My men will accompany us; many more will guard the doorway.'

'Excuse me, *Pan* Zamoyski, but when we go down a mine in *England*—'

'A man of your rank would never go down a mine in England. If one did, you think he need take no men-at-arms. True; but then *you* have not had a civil war for – what, three years now?'

I blushed: only three years had passed since Her Grace had put down the Catholic North in what we hoped would be its final rebellion. Zamoyski bowed, and gestured me through the curtain of vines. Followed by the girls and by Ludovic Briskett, I entered the mine of Wieliczka, whose blocks of green-salt, together with waggons of pine-logs and grain and amber, had once travelled south to furnish the Rome of Pius and Aurelius.

'I will not trouble you with much talk,' whispered Zamoyski in the blackness; and the multiplication of his whisper from walls and floor made me jump. 'But I think, whatever Genesis may say, that you are descending here through the salt-residue of a primordial sea. Deeper still below us lie its limestone sediments.'

'What sea can have left,' I whispered, as men struck more torches, 'pure salt, miles deep?'

'One ancient and long-enduring, and, I should guess, very concentrated. Over aeons the waters would have dried and vanished. Below lie the ancient lime-muds, compressed into rock, and above them the salt-residue. So this once was ocean where now we stand.'

'I have never heard a silence so deep,' I said.

We stopped and listened to it. The tunnel, cut into what looked like black rock, sloped down; and already Earth enfolded us, sucking out all sound. We descended, moving softly. Here and there we passed a side-tunnel whose lintel Zamoyski's servants had marked with white paint. At these points I felt eyes watching us. I stared into the blackness, challenging the watchers, but saw nothing.

'Who are the ghosts?' I whispered to Zamoyski.

In the dull grey-orange torchlight I saw him cross himself. 'Hush: no words of ill-omen. Men hear tapping here that is not made by their own hammers. And as for the eyes, I feel them too. For fifteen hundred years, when a new passage had to be opened and the poisoned air burned off at the risk of explosion, the foremen would select for that work the weak, the mischief-makers, the husbands whose wives some other men coveted. If they are watching us, honour them. And pray for them: we will come to the Miners' Chapel soon. Here, Yolanta.' For his niece, with an anxious smile, had slipped her hand into her uncle's. Maria, her hair gathered into a hood, her white ruff showing blue in the dark, came circumspectly behind us.

Now the cutting widened, while keeping its downward slope. Forty feet above us the roof was invisible; but the floor descended, a flat, artificial slope from which rose trees of timber. Each trunk of planks branched into a crown of supporting timbers, so that as we descended steps cut into the

What Dangers Deep

green-black salt, we moved through a lifeless, sculptured forest. 'These planks are seven hundred years old,' murmured Zamoyski. 'In this air they do not decay. So they grew leaves in the forest, Master Philip, when your country was just a patchwork of Danish ruins and half-Christian fiefs.'

But the ancientry of the wood did not move me: it looked so new, its grain so raw and pale, that I found myself unable to feel its age. We left the geometrical forest, and came by an archway into a little room. 'The Miners' Chapel,' said Jan Zamoyski.

Above us rose a small dome hewn from the rock-salt; beneath our feet stretched a pavement of the same dreary colour. The torchlight caught fallow sparkles in a chandelier with pendants of carven salt – doves, apples, pears, clustered grapes. Someone long ago had hewn an altar and had left saints to guard it. The figures, mantled with salt as though they had reared up out of it, were noseless and eyeless with the ages in which they had knelt there, watching over a sanctity of black stillness and unmoving air – a place of no escape. Most of the party crossed themselves; I doffed my cap, praying only to leave the Miners' Chapel.

We did, by another descending tunnel. Here the air was fresh and cold: there must, I reflected, be vents to the surface. Yolanta still held her uncle's hand. I fell behind with Maria, and murmured to Ludovic in English: 'I do not like the feel of the place.' He nodded.

The mass of rock above us was porous to all sound, producing a stillness of aching intensity. I hoped nothing would put out the torches. I remembered that, even if our lights went out, our miner-guides would be able to lead us back to the surface by touch; but it had been a mistake to bring the women down. Maria was holding well, but I saw the tight grasp Zamoyski had taken on Yolanta's hand, as if to reassure or warn her. I knew a mistake when all the subtler senses warned me of it, even though I could feel no exact unease, nor any sense that registered actual discomfort. What treasure (for so Yolanta had called it) could have drawn Zamoyki here?

And then, with a sigh of wonder, we were out into an expanse so vast it might have been the nave of Sancta Maria. And here Zamoyski had already stationed men with torches whose cold blue-orange light flickered upwards into shadow. Around us as we descended further steps, stretched a chamber huge as a ballroom, its floor polished to the shine of dirty glass.

And in its centre, on-edge like a giant gamesboard, stood a slab of stone thirty feet high. The miners who excavated it had rimmed and shored it with timber; torches burned around it. Zamoyski led us towards it; and when we stood before it he said, *'Behold now Behemoth: he is the chief of the ways of God. Upon earth there is not his like, who is made without fear.'*

The monster in the rock had lain there for uncounted ages: a carcass, bloated perhaps and ragged with torn flesh, settling through the thick green water of the primordial sea. A rain of rotting particles must have filtered the light of the ancient sun, and he had sunk, compressed as the mud hardened into a cage of bones. But each crushed rib was twice my own length, and his fins – diamonds of archaic bone – were articulated like mosaic. Some force had bent his neck, twisting it backwards over his spine with the anguished grace of a huge swan. Crushed – silvered in stone – he rose before us, his bones shining. Contorted by death and by the postures of decay, he still exceeded any beast, any whale of which I had ever heard.

'There *were* archaic animals,' said Jan Zamoyski. 'This proves it.'

And Yolanta, looking up at the stone panel, began to scream.

Of us all it was Zamoyski who moved most quickly to embrace, to comfort, to stifle her cries, which had turned into a shuddering weeping. One man spoke to him in Polish and looked at the roof; Zamoyski nodded an agreement which I needed no Polish to share. 'Yolanta, my dear, you must be *quiet*, the walls may not be stable. Christ forgive me for bringing you here. Here, my cloak – we'll make a litter of it. Yolanta, what is wrong? Can you tell me?'

But she could only sob words in Polish. Maria softly translated: 'She keeps saying it is dead,' as men, myself among them, gently swathed her in one cloak and formed a sling out of Zamoyski's robe. So, bound and carried, four of us bore her away; and when she could not stop weeping Zamoyski removed one of his gloves and gently thrust it between her teeth, holding it there with a hand whose warmth seemed to still her.

Our torchlight slipped and glimmered down the panel, leaving bones that glittered like mica for an instant, then sank back into the dark. *Let them lie buried*, I thought. I was shuddering with disgust, and had to re-catch my grip on the sling. The girl, heavy in her binding of fur and velvet robes, lay quietly.

Zamoyski rode with her in his arms back to the tent she shared with Maria; and there, after some useless questioning, ordered his surgeon to dose her into sleep for several hours. Presently he came to me. 'Philip, it will do Maria no good to stay here. The women and I will watch Yolanta; so will Doctor Solniecki, and letters have come for me that I must read, even here. It seems I have a busy and anxious afternoon to face. Will you take Maria to the hunt, or at least to ride? Come back for the evening meal: Yolanta will be awake, and I hope will have forgotten this strange fit of horror. Poor child, how selfish I was to take her there.'

'I will try to entertain Maria,' I said.

He clapped me on the shoulder. 'Thank you. Let us hope by evening Yolanta will be better, and well enough to share supper with you.'

We hunted through the woods all that afternoon, not talking much. Maria accepted my company with gentle courtesy, and I wanted only to think. The mother a suicide; kindred embittered by the New Religion – what other secrets did this family keep? As I rode with Maria I longed – and she seemed to understand it – only for silence in which to digest the questions, and to ask myself whether I wanted to know the answers, or deliberately to refuse them.

When we rode back into camp, a cold green sky was smudging upward into rose. Frost edged the oak leaves, two early stars were shining, and men moved quietly around cooking-fires whose coals smouldered like late marigolds, and whose smoke mingled with the savours of broth and roasting meat.

We found our table set with a white cloth. Beside it burned a bonfire, around which someone had made a ring – three seats of logs. Yolanta sat at the table; before her lay a lute in its case. She rose to greet us.

'Forgive me,' she said. 'I slept well and bathed, and feel hungry. Maria, forgive me for this morning. My uncle is too busy to join us. I hoped we might eat, and then share some talk and music. I *can* play.' She gestured to the lute in rueful atonement.

We left her for the half-hour it took to bathe ourselves and change, and then joined her for supper. I did not find her sullen, and if she felt ill she concealed it adroitly. Indeed, her charm held such an urgency to entertain us that the memory of it hurts me, even now.

When the blue dark lay all around us I called for my cloak and the women for mantles of velvet lined with sable, and we sat on the three logs and talked. Yolanta tuned the lute, leaning back with grace to keep it from the heat of the embers; and our talk turned, as it should not have done, to the Ancient Mass and the transformed bear, to ghost-nuns and black dogs.

I protested that we should not linger on such things, but Yolanta, laughing, insisted. 'Maria saw something once. Tell him, Maria.'

Maria leaned forward, hands cupping her chin; her exquisite, sharp-featured face was troubled. The firelight cast a pink sheen into her hair, which fell in thick crimped wings to mask her cheeks. 'Play something, Yolanta. I cannot sing, Master Philip: I draw. Play him something.'

What Dangers Deep

'When you have told him your story.' The morning, it seemed, was over: she had referred to it the single time.

Tented in her folds of sable, Maria's shoulders were too weighed down to sketch the shrug her face conveyed. 'But I do not know what it was I saw.'

'Tell me,' I said.

She frowned. 'One night about two years ago – a November night – I was lying in bed reading. A whole sconce of candles was burning, so the room was brightly lit. I think the hour was about eleven.' I nodded. 'Suddenly,' she said, 'a flicker of motion attracted me, and I looked up. What followed lasted while I could count *one . . . two . . . three*' (her fingers measured it) 'no more. I saw a transparent white veil moving across the room towards the far wall, about five feet above the floor. It was beautiful and moved very fast; I felt no fear. It flickered and crackled and flowed – not even the most skilled conjuror could have flicked a veil that quickly. And then it moved into the wall and vanished.' This time she did shrug. 'And that is all.'

Yolanta had tuned her lute and was playing softly, watching me.

'I also saw something once,' I said. 'In the dusk in the upstairs corridor. My mother had been sewing downstairs, and sent me to her room for some silks she needed. I ran upstairs in the dark. The month was August, and very hot. At the head of the stairs I realized a man was standing outside my parents' door. I confronted him in the bright moonlight: a monk dressed in grey homespun with a cowl over his head. His face was very round, his features coarse, and he wore a two-day stubble of beard. He appeared to be looking past me, not at me.'

'What did you do?' asked Yolanta. 'Were you afraid?'

'No. He appeared wholly solid. But I did not want to pass him to get my mother's sewing-silks, so I retreated down the stairs. At the landing I stopped, changed my mind and ran back up; but he had gone. I remember the corridor felt cold.'

'What was it he wanted?' wondered Maria softly.

To my relief Yolanta began to play. She played well, with a firm nimble competence, and the instrument's delicacy and her soft, trained voice blended in my senses with the smoke and the orange coals with their wincing, shadowed light.

She sang '*Mignonne, allons voir si la rose*' and '*Quand vous serez bien vieille au soir à la chandelle*'; and one song I heard for the first and the last time that night.

> *Si notre vie est moins qu'une journée*
> *En L'eternel – si l'an qui fait le tour*
> *Chasse nos jours sans espoir de retour,*
> *Si périssable est toute chose née –*
> *Que songes-tu, mon Ame emprisonnée?*
>
> *Là, ô mon Ame, au plus haut ciel guidée,*
> *Tu y pourras reconnaître l'Idée*
> *De la Beauté qu'en ce monde j'adore.*

(If our life is less than one Eternal day; if each year only hunts us down into oblivion; if each thing is born to die – why linger here, O my captive soul? Brought to the highest Heaven, there shalt thou know the essence of that Truth – while I, benighted here, can only yearn.)

> *Que songes-tu, mon Ame emprisonnée?*

'Master Sidney?'

I started. 'I beg your pardon, Mistress.'

'Do you play?' Yolanta handed me the lute, whose neck bore a weightless knot of satin ribbons.

'Yes, of course.' I play and sing well (I remember being beaten into both skills at school). I took the lute from her with a slight, troubled smile, and tuned it to my liking; then I said, 'In this song the lover defends himself, assuring his lady that he did not speak a certain slander.' Beyond that I did not translate; and perhaps I had my reasons.

> Perdie, I said it not,
> Nor ever thought to do:
> As well as I ye wot
> I have no power thereto.
> And if I did, the lot
> That first did me enchain
> Do never slack the knot,
> But strait it to my pain.
>
> And if I did, each star
> That is in heaven above
> May frown on me to mar
> The hope I have in love:
> And if I did, such war
> As they brought out of Troy
> Bring all my life afar
> From all this lust and joy.

And so memory strains back to recover both women. Clouds, dim grey masses, were rolling above us softening the stars. The embers fried and hissed, fluorescent beneath their mantle of ash; and opposite me the two sisters sat unmoving. Their pointed faces were alike, as strongly structured as the broad shoulders they also shared; but Maria's face seemed gentle and elusive, while Yolanta, with her dark boy's brows, had gone graceless for the moment. She was frowning over some thought; the hand with the white jade ring cupped her chin, and I noticed she had used the Coligny brooch to clasp her cloak. Two women – solid, restive, inward-turned on their fatigue: memory can get no more from them.

> And as I have deservèd,
> So grant me now my hire:
> Ye know I never swervèd –
> Ye never found me liar.
> For Rachel have I servèd

> (For Leah cared I never),
> And her I have reservèd
> Within my heart forever.

I stilled the strings with my palm. For a moment there was silence. 'Ladies, it is cold. Do we not hunt at dawn?'

Yolanta stirred. 'Yes, and we promised to take you to the spring. It is only a short walk through the trees, and it might interest an antiquarian like yourself.' I nodded. As she took the lute from me she said, 'What a pretty melody. Who made it, do you know?'

'The music?' I grinned. 'My mother, while I worked the harmony. It gave us a pleasant afternoon.'

She swirled the ribbons into a protective coil; the music-case snapped shut. 'You have told us twice about your mother tonight, sir. When you write her next, will you tell her that a Polish lady whom she will never meet has loved her music, and sends her a gift in thanks?' To my astonishment she drew off the ring and held it out to me: the long fingers curled around it were, I noticed, shaking.

The jewel lay in her palm, an oval with the warm pallor and translucency of flesh. I glanced from Yolanta to Maria, and saw in the latter's face a stare of unbelieving accusation.

'Take it.' Yolanta jingled her hand a little, converting the tremor into a motion of impatience.

I glanced again from sister to sister. 'No, mistress, I must not. I beg you keep it. Your praise will give her delight enough; and that I promise to convey.'

'Very well.' She slid the ring back on to her middle finger, 'We will come for you at first light.'

Maria rose, gathering her robe about her. By her sister's seat she paused and said softly, 'I will ask the men to set up an extra tent for me.'

'As you choose.' Yolanta stared straight at the embers.

Maria turned her head, cameo-clear against the circle of her hood. 'Thank you for the music, Master Sidney. What did the monk want, do you think, that he appeared to you?'

'Mistress, with all my heart *I do not care.*'

Posed so, three-quarters turned away, she considered. At last she said: 'Yes, that is safest. Good night. We will come for you just before the hunt.'

In my tent, with Ludovic and Ambrose asleep on their pallet-beds, I lay and listened. The silence of a country night is drowsy beyond any drug, any wine. I felt the night's awareness of me: a scrutiny inhuman but also not unkind; a power that seemed to search out my exhausted body, and to will that it should sleep.

And, obeying it, I ceased to be aware of my own consciousness. Thoughts bent with the rhythm of an inner logic and became dreams. I started, woke, and again succumbed; then crossed the frontier no man can identify.

It was to be my last untroubled sleep for many hundred nights.

Six

It is not easy to take one's morning bath in a tent in mid-October, still less out of the two or three helmetsful of hot water Ambrose had managed to procure for me. Still, I had done it, eaten breakfast and dressed for hunting in the dark of pre-dawn: I did not want lights in the tent to exhibit me to the ladies. Outside, the world lay frosted in blue silence. The Morning Star, clear and constant as an opal, hung above pine woods where even the wind had gone still.

I stepped outside. This was to be our last full day. I would miss the woodsmoke and the food, killed to our need as if we had been ancient hunters, and cooked in the open. In Kraków waited the enemy who had chosen to bide his time this past week, or who had been unable to penetrate Zamoyski's ring – or who had accomplished his objective? Stretching my shoulders in the dawn cold, I reflected cheerfully that I would never make a diplomat. But I must do the Privy Council's errand and contact Caspar Laurence; and his lectures interested me. A soldier should know about wounds and about anatomy; and this great surgeon . . .

. . . And this great surgeon might soon be dead. For in England a Jesuit, by preaching in secret, committed treason – so involved has our Faith become with obedience or disobedience to the law. Caspar Laurence insisted he wanted to go home; but there – unless he abjured his religion, his friends and his career – the law would hang him, disembowel him while he was alive to watch it, and cut him into quarters.

Woodsmoke stung my eyes. Yes, Caspar Laurence had arrived in Kraków by now: I felt his presence there, searching for me as I for him. How old had Sir Francis called him? Forty-two. *Abjure*, I thought: *abjure or do not come home. Be content to die in exile: no sane man invites that death*.

All around me people and animals were stirring. The Morning Star faded in a glow of rose; above us hung an indigo sky. Frost furred the grass, which rustled crisply against my boots. Horses were stamping; grooms were feeding them hot mash and harnessing them. Some tents had become bells brimming with candlelight; from others came the whispers of people who know the walls are made of cloth. Grooms knelt to feed the dogs the hot sops that would let them hunt keen and leisurely, not ravenous. Someone struck flint; I heard a dog silenced, and saw a man pull down a horse's head, gentling it and talking to it.

Zamoyski's tent was lit, but from the hazed shadows I guessed his servants had brought portable frames hung with tapestry to thicken his privacy. Now all around me a ring of hearths held crackling yellow fire or the orange-pink of coals. All that was not yellow or fluorescent coral had gone blue. Light extinguished the last stars in the heights of the sky.

It was a pale blue, cold morning when Yolanta and Maria came to me. Both wore brown velvet for hunting, and gauntlets and velvet caps that tied beneath the chin. Behind them came three menservants carrying torches.

'Good morning.' Yolanta held out her hand. 'You shall not escape our only other local wonder, however dreary you may find it.'

'Not at all. Tell me, did they leave the bear-skulls in the pit where they were found?'

Yolanta shrugged, and glanced a question at her sister. Maria said, 'I believe they left them undisturbed, Master Sidney, or if not quite that, they put them back and covered them over. People here are afraid of holy things.'

What Dangers Deep

'That was wise and, I think, kindly of them. How far? Is there a path?'

Yolanta gestured. She carried her riding-whip; the brooch she seemed to use with every costume and, under her gauntlet, I thought I saw the misshapen protuberance of the ring. 'A clear path, as I remember. Our father brought us here when we were – what, Maria? – eight and nine years old?'

Maria nodded. *(The father died while travelling abroad, so I have heard.)* 'A strangely clear path,' she said with a smile. 'I suspect lovers come here on Midsummer Night.'

'And other nights,' said Yolanta. 'This way, I am almost certain; and once we find the path, a ten-minute walk.'

We moved through the shadowed, stirring camp. 'Will three men be enough?' I asked. 'They have swords, of course? – ah yes. Let them come close behind.'

'We'll be within hail of the camp,' said Yolanta.

The first colour touched the grass. Why does wind come with dawn? I do not know, but all at once a delicate gust rustled the rowan sprays, and clattered berries that frost had shrunk overnight. The frozen gorse rustled, glassy and fibrous to the touch; and within the forest – behind the emerging dappled shadows of beech, birch, rowan and wild pear – we sensed the pines, with their perfume and their power to hold the shadows.

'Here is the path,' announced Yolanta, 'so clearly marked that I fear it has become a common walk for the people here. What a pity if nothing is left to show you.'

'What will I see anyway in this dim light?' I answered with a shrug. I did not care, and so was prepared to be pleased.

'Only a pool among the trees,' answered Maria's alto voice. 'The spring feeds it from beneath, and a little stream flows out. Behind it rises a low cliff with, if I remember well, some pine-trees on the crest; and all around are rowans and apple-trees my father believed the ancient people planted. And of course underneath it all lies the limestone.'

'And therefore caves?'

She nodded. 'Yes, and many underground streams. As for the pool, it will be choked with leaves; but I remember the water was fresh to drink.'

We moved forward. Occasionally, more for high spirits than (I thought) to clear a way for us, Yolanta would switch the bushes, and they leapt back rustling. The servants' torches cast in front of us shadows with which a warmer yellow daylight was at last beginning to blend. I heard birdsong – a single sweet note.

The forest closed behind us, tattered and mottled but still full-leaved enough to add to the gusts of morning sound: birdcalls and bracken and wind and human voices. The camp sounded near, but we could no longer see it. I broke off from a tree-trunk an apron of white fungus, its texture solid and appetizing as bread – then threw it where its fall caused something to thread rustling through the bushes.

'I think,' said Maria, 'it is light enough now to put out the torches.' Her servants obeyed. Without our lights the colours around us still lay coolly latent – blue-greens, cold yellows touched with grey.

And so, through a brush of evergreen, birch and rowan, we came to the Ancient Mass.

'Wait,' said Yolanta. 'Let the men stay behind.' She gestured them back, speaking a few words in Polish. One answered her, and was silenced. Yolanta glanced at me. 'It is a place for stillness,' she explained.

I patted my sword-hilt and exchanged with the servants a glance of masculine fellowship. They shrugged and grinned, but with the air of men who do not intend to retreat far. I left them, following the girls.

The young light was melting the ice-crystals on the grass when we came to a change: a stillness both felt and seen. Our servants had by now vanished from sight behind us. Now the ground, bare of bracken, sloped downwards towards a rock-face. On its top I could see the blue dark of pines; wall and boulders were quilted deep with moss. A pool lay before it, and the pool was ringed with trees.

Yolanta stopped at the first of the great trees, looked at me and said, 'I feel very happy today.'

She had moved on ahead of me when I forced myself to loosen my fingers from my sword-hilt. One must not draw steel here. I let my other hand fall from my hunting-knife and went forward with open palms.

Beneath my feet lay a fragrant resiliency of leaves dappled yellow – of windfall apples and rowan sprays. For the trees the Bear People had planted long ago were exclusively rowan or apple. The sweat-smell of fermented fruit came to me, tinged with the acridity of leaf-cake. In the centuries of their growing the trees had killed all undergrowth; yet they must be, I guessed, the great-great-grandchildren of trees whose crumbled substance lay deep beneath the leaves. Softness, stillness, fragrance: all these compounded, in the blue shadow and amber light, into a peace that seduced the mind like sleep.

The water of the pool looked brown. Its moisture had crusted everything nearby – rocks, logs, living trunks – with a moss into which one could plunge the fingers – moss whose fronds would have seemed coarse had they not been so soft. My fingers came away from it touched with a pure, sweet scent. Cushions of moss quilted the rocks; its colour was a green intense as emerald.

We had broken apart, and now wandered separately, in utter leisure, towards the pool among trunks that must have been five hundred years old. Some of the apples, seeded in the grass and never tended, had grown into giants thirty feet high. Their branches twined above our heads with the yellow, palm-like fronds of rowan, which hung under their burden of shrivelled, lacquer-red berries. I remember passing an apple-tree that the centuries had broken open under its own weight. One huge arm lay in the grass, split from the trunk; and the moss encrusted every surface.

I remember now that I heard no birds, that the wind had stopped, that I no longer heard our servants' voices. To my right, caught in a trough between the slope and the rock-face, the stream laced boulders from which green weed flowed like hair. Before us rose the little cliff, damascened with the moss whose scent – mingled with loam, autumn fruit and leaves – was a delight of delicacy and freshness.

I found the pool and knelt. The brown water shone when I brushed the leaves away. Of the spring that gave it life I saw nothing beyond the evident freshness of the water. I remember the toothed shape of a leaf, one on which my eyes lingered I do not know how long – recall precisely its saw-edge and its butter-yellow gloss. Around it lay a mat of berries and sodden rowan sprays. I brushed, found clear water, and drank from my cupped hand.

I will never know how long these motions took, nor will the living witnesses ever now agree. But as I knelt there, warmed and drowsy in the light which was now full day, I heard a *hum* that I cannot compare to anything, except perhaps to a sudden sonority of male voices. At that instant a pain went through my head, and I felt a rolling within my mind, a shuddering and destabilization of inner structures, as though ideas could spin like marbles on a floor. It exceeded any bodily pain, any anguish of mind I can describe. I clutched my head, certain that here – without warning, without help – was insanity.

I think I screamed, *'Maria!'*

The buzzing sound had stopped. Now the rolling – like the heave of great solid bubbles – also re-concreted, stabilized and ceased.

I was alone in the glade.

Seven

No. Let this not be.

The human mind has reflexes that apply to the deep and the rare: the laughter of shock, for one. Now, as I stared around me at the Ancient Mass, body and mind gathered in one primitive rejection.

I was still on my knees. A bird's song broke the silence. My mind surrendered its refusal; and at that instant I heard the servants' shouting, which had a strange note. I rose to my feet: I was shaking as though I had not eaten in forty-eight hours. At that moment it occurred to me that the servants did not seem, by their noise, to be coming *towards* me. Then I forgot the impression, for the three men came running down through the trees.

For a second, as the sunlight melted the rime on the grass, they stood silent, their eyes seeking my companions. But Maria and Yolanta had vanished from the glade.

I knew by the servants' faces that I was an Englishman alone, guilty of my foreignness. One man struck my shoulder with the heel of his hand. 'Sir, where are the women?'

I hit his fist away. 'Don't handle me. I do not know. I had a moment of dizziness. When I looked up, they were gone.'

I saw them hesitate towards rage. But we were men together. More – in that sunny silence, looking each other in the face, we abandoned in one common instant anger, manhood and courage. We ran like children from the green humid glade, where the year's last brightness was lending suppleness to the moss; where squirrels and birds were stirring to feed on the rowan-berries; and where the stream soothed all fear with its ancient, delicate music.

The hunting-party had mounted, and Lord Zamoyski was looking towards the path – I suppose seeking the latecomers – even before we came crashing out of the trees. When he saw me he swung his leg neatly over his horse's back, dismounted and came towards me. 'Philip, what is wrong?'

'My lord, I do not know what has happened. Your nieces disappeared virtually before my eyes. Virtually, but not quite: I felt faint and looked down, I do not know for how long. When I raised my head, both girls were gone.'

'*How?* Without a sound?'

'I heard a sound: a humming.'

'Are you wounded? Can someone have come from the edge of the glade? Were you shot at?' His hands grasped my shoulders.

I shook my head. 'I heard no shot, sir; I feel no wound.'

'Sometimes one does not feel even a knife-thrust at once.' His hands still gripped me: his power was so great I would find bruises on my shoulders later. The three servants spoke to him in Polish; Zamoyski grimaced acknowledgement and, without explaining this exchange to me, called, 'Bring my doctor! Philip, my men will strip you and tend any wound they may find. You are under arrest. We will cordon the forest. Any thieves, any Turkish slave-traders, any village-people I want found and brought to me. A sink-hole may have opened beneath their feet: the limestone is full of holes. The villagers know the caverns in this area. We will search every cave, every sink-hole, every underground stream. My nieces must be physically present in the forest or beneath it. We will find every hidden place – find everything that moves.'

Men were already in motion around him. As Zamoyski gave me into the doctor's hands he said, 'Philip, let Doctor Solniecki do what he must. The humming sound may have been a shot, or the impact of a shot. Give my servants no trouble, and I will find the girls.' I nodded, and let a group of men take me, with a kindness whose latent force I saw no reason to tempt. As we went, Zamoyski added an instruction to the doctor in Polish. Later I guessed what he had meant.

In a tent with brown walls Solniecki and his assistants dealt with me with a firm, hard gentleness, ignoring the noise of crisis all around us. I knew Solniecki slightly: he did not hunt, and had spent the days of his idleness sketching and making notes. 'Get him hot brandy,' he ordered. 'But not at once: poor soul, he is shaking. You may swallow, sir, when I know that you are whole.' I nodded and sank down on a stool while they stripped off my doublet and shirt. Hands whose warmth calmed me seemed to find no wound, and their touch somehow also made clear that the sounds outside need not frighten me.

'Good news so far. You'll have that brandy soon,' murmured the doctor. 'Stand up, sir. No, let him do it without help. Does your abdomen hurt?'

I shook my head. A ripple of shuddering contracted my muscles.

Solniecki's hands had not ceased to move. 'It's too cold for this. We'll have a blanket on you in a moment.' I nodded again, my teeth chattering. He unfastened my points. 'I must pull this down, sir, and your smallclothes, to make sure there is no wound to the belly.'

'But I would *feel* it,' I protested. From behind me four men's hands had slid round my arms; and as their grip hardened and Solniecki stripped me to the naked skin, I understood what Zamoyski had ordered. I lunged at them, weeping with anguish. Even so they held me; and afterwards had the decency to reclothe me in my own things before they wrapped a blanket around me and put a mug of hot spirits into my hands.

'You have no internal wound, and nothing has struck you. Lie down, sir. Here, lift his feet.' Now I was on my back, and a man was piling cushions so I could drink safely. Doctor

Solniecki sat beside me. 'Drink that, and all of it: I dare give you only one, or the shock may bring it up again. So, slowly.'

I steadied, realizing I might otherwise vomit the spiced grain-spirit, whose warmth I needed. Solniecki took out his handkerchief and wiped my cheeks and my closed eyes of the tears I did not remember shedding. 'I will tell my lord Zamoyski that I found no sign of semen or of penetration. If the women are alive he will find them, and you cannot help. Remember your own parents who look for your return, and the English Ambassador, who will think first of you when he hears this news. Therefore lie still: otherwise I must drug you or tie you.'

'I will be still. You put something in this,' I said. For the release on my muscles and my mind, carried by the hot alcohol, was not only drink.

'Alas, yes.' Solniecki shrugged. 'Sleep if you can: it is better than fearing. My lord Zamoyski will come to question you, but not, I guess, for some hours.'

I nodded, and sank with gratitude into a chemical calm. As the horror in my mind let go, I noticed that it was a form of pain. The drug took the pain away: and I lay with half-open eyes, gazing at the candlelight.

Hours passed. Through the weave of the tent I saw the day go smoke-blue, then cobalt, then black; and then the oiled cloth threw back a sheen of candlelight. As the cold deepened, people to whom I paid no attention laid more blankets on me. Once they sat me up and gently eased on to my arms a jacket lined with fur.

By the time they brought me my supper Doctor Solniecki's potion had worn off. I felt grateful that he had let me prepare to face Zamoyski with an undrugged mind. Outside I could glimpse cooking-fires, and hear the subdued sounds of some returning men. Servants brought me sausages, boiled cabbage and a compôte of apples, all very hot. Solniecki looked up from his notepad. 'Eat it, even if you feel no appetite. He is coming to interrogate you, and you will not find him easy to deal with if you are weak in body.'

'Have they found Yolanta and Maria?' I demanded.

The doctor shook his head. 'I gather they have not.'

I ate; washed face and hands and combed my hair, and cleansed my mouth with a brush and tooth-powder I had them retrieve from my gear. Neither Ludovic nor Ambrose had been allowed to wait on me. It did not surprise me when Solniecki mentioned that they too were under guard, lest they desert the party and ride back to the English Ambassador, my protector, at Kraków.

Presently the door-flap lifted and Jan Zamoyski came in. His eyes were bright with exhaustion, but he had changed and shaved and, I supposed, taken food. He motioned me back on to my couch. 'They tell me you have no wound. I'm glad.'

'Have you found them?' I had begun to tremble again, and had no choice but to obey him, much as I would have preferred to face him standing.

'No. Therefore we have not found them dead: let us thank God.'

I sought for the place in my mind where the awareness of Yolanta and Maria should have been; but instead of the clarity where, sometimes, I could feel the love or the thoughts of others, I found only turmoil.

Jan Zamoyski drew up the doctor's stool. We were alone – he had motioned the others to go. 'No new sink-hole has opened in the glade. Of course the ground underfoot is utterly untrustworthy – soft lime riddled with the workings of water. On the other hand, the place and its dangers are well known to the people here. They have searched every known cave, and have found several dead animals, some of which must have fallen in very long ago; but no human bodies. They are tapping the cave-walls in case we have missed any hidden chambers. No mounted party has been found in the area, and none on foot. I do not believe any abductors *could* have escaped in the time before I sent my searchers out. But our own party has filled the forest with prints over the past days: there is no denying that all the tracks are ruined.'

'Someone has taken Maria and Yolanta, then?' I said. 'Why?'

He counted on his fingers. 'What reasons apply? Three: rape, money or power – power, in this case, I presume in the form of influence. Or revenge.'

I controlled my voice, mastering a childish desire to weep. 'I was with them for five minutes, sir: five minutes unobserved.'

Zamoyski crossed his arms, hugging himself, and met my stare. The plain face, with its small virile mouth and extraordinary eyes, held no warmth, only skill and judgement withheld. 'I know it. But that makes you, by a small elapse of time, the last human being to have seen my nieces; perhaps to have seen them alive.'

'That, sir, I understand. But do you believe I would have attacked them in that time? Or, if I attacked one, that the other would not have cried out?'

'Philip, when Kraków comes to know of this – if my nieces are not found at all – the mob will suspect you simply because you are not one of us. For that and for Doctor Solniecki's examination of you I apologize. But I cannot protect you unless I feel confident of your innocence. The point is not that you had time to commit rape: of course you did not. But you might have been party to their abduction by accomplices waiting, let us say, among the trees.'

I said, 'I utterly repudiate the accusation you imply.' He nodded, shading the motion towards respectful seriousness, not towards mockery or doubt. 'Any pleasure my flesh betrayed I got, sir, from your nieces' company, as innocently and chastely as any man may do. You can prove by my body only that I felt something.'

'I know,' he said gently. 'But the truth remains that you were the last man to see them. Until we find them alive I cannot formally exonerate you of some suspicion in this matter. I

What Dangers Deep

intend to place you under loose house-arrest in the custody of Sir Antony Marshall, and you may not leave Kraków until we have found Maria and Yolanta, or their bodies.'

'I *will* not leave Kraków until that time, sir. They are my friends.'

'Then tell me about the humming in the wood. Tell me it all.'

So, carding it over and over, we examined every action, every word I could retrieve from memory. At one point Zamoyski said, 'What were the last words Maria spoke to you – the very last?'

'I cannot remember, sir.'

'Yolanta, then?'

I thought. 'As we went down towards the stream, she smiled at me and said, "I feel very happy today."' Zamoyski's brows rose. 'After that I do not remember that she spoke, or that – or that I saw her again. Sir, do you know the place has an evil reputation?'

'Yes. But God did not strike this place today, Philip. My nieces have been kidnapped for rape and ransom, or are lying, perhaps still alive, in some underground cave where their bodies may be discovered, perhaps hundreds of years from now. We must find them soon, before cold and starvation kill them. I almost hope—' He hesitated, then concluded softly, 'I almost hope they are in human company tonight, however cruel.'

Human company can be cruel indeed, I thought, and said, 'Sir, what was it Yolanta's servants said to you?'

'Oh. That *was* odd. You heard them calling?'

'Yes, and thought there was some strange note in it, in their tone or the direction of the voices. But I had no time to think about it.'

'They say they got lost.'

'*Lost?* But I left them—'

'You left them a few paces behind you, barely out of sight among the trees. They decided you were unwise, and made up their minds to follow you. Yet they also say that for several minutes they could not find the path or the direction in which you had gone. None seems certain how many minutes: one man guesses five, another fifteen.'

'Fifteen? That seems impossible.' With dread I touched, in memory, the rolling and destabilization within my mind. Then I looked up into the face of the man who would, I knew, destroy me if he concluded I had done harm to the women; and with a gasp uttered the question I most feared. 'Sir, do you think I went mad and killed them?'

Jan Zamoyski gazed down at me. 'No. Sane men can go mad, Philip; but such states do not last long. If you had done what you just had the courage to name to me, you would have awakened to find their bodies at your feet. There was no place to hide two bodies; no time; no hiding-place that you knew of. And there are no corpses. No, you did not kill them.'

He dropped to his knees beside me and took me in a brief, hard embrace – as much, I thought, for his own comfort as for mine. 'Let us pray they are safe tonight – at least that they are alive, and that they know we will come for them.'

'Amen,' I said.

He let me go and stood. 'Try to sleep. No–' at my motion of entreaty – 'you may not join the searchers tomorrow. I can vouch for you better if I have you under guard. You will naturally wish to punish or to prove yourself by ignoring your own safety, Philip; but do not forget that I must answer for you to Her Grace Queen Elizabeth. The terrain is too dangerous by dark: I have stopped the search till dawn, guessing that the slavers or soldiers who have taken them will also have to stop for the same reason. Tomorrow we will search again. After that you and I must return to Kraków: you to Collegium Maius' (with a shock of disgust I remembered this duty) 'and I because, if my nieces' disappearance is intended to be a diversion, I should not be absent from the city for much longer. Let us hope we will find them by sunset tomorrow, and all this fear is for nothing.'

At the doorway he stopped and looked back at me. 'About the time. The groom's fifteen minutes *is* impossible, I think. I

What Dangers Deep

have walked the route, and even allowing for some loss of time, the whole adventure from its beginning to its end cannot have taken more than twenty minutes. And one man of the three – only one – did hear something unusual. It was not the buzz or hum you describe. He said it was more like a sudden rush of wind.'

Next morning they drugged my food. I slept all day, involved earnestly in intricate dream-adventures. When I drifted into waking I could not recall them, but as consciousness inverted its terms and stretched and became dream again, I returned to sleep as if to a form of labour.

That evening when I woke, Ambrose and Ludovic sat beside me. I noticed, as Ambrose helped me upright, that he appeared to have slept little: bruises of exhaustion formed blue half-moons beneath his eyes. In answer to my gaze he shook his head. Ludovic said, 'They are gone, Philip. The searchers found nothing again today.'

Twenty-four hours, I thought. No: nearer thirty-six. Were they dead? How many men could have raped them in that time? The feel of a man in a woman's belly was something I could not imagine, though I had often tried; and for a virgin . . . They said a woman could die from seventy rapes, a hundred. Why? Did her heart stop? Did all the organs haemorrhage?

My mind fell back from the words, from the cruel and lascivious ideas. *Should* I wish they were dead? Whatever state Yolanta and Maria had entered yesterday, it had now held them in its secrecy for thirty-six hours: they were becoming part of its secrecy.

'We haven't been able to send to the Ambassador,' said Ambrose. 'Here, sir, eat. You may groom yourself before my lord Zamoyski comes in. I gather they bathed you earlier today.'

'That was kind of them.' I took my hands away from shielding my face. *They are not going to come back*. I accepted a bowl of broth from Ambrose. *Maria and Yolanta are not coming back, and we shall be left alone with that – and with each other.*

'I can tell you one thing for certain.' Ludovic steadied my hand around the spoon. 'Her Grace gave you a licence to travel and study decorously abroad. She does not want your uncle's nephew at the centre of a scandal in Kraków. As soon as we return, the Ambassador will send you back to Vienna.'

So he would, I thought. With the concurrence of Sir Francis Walsingham; and my uncle of Leicester; and of Her Grace, who had decided to make trial of me.

Late that evening Zamoyski called on me. 'Philip, the caves are empty. We have sent men down each sink-hole: nothing. We have dragged the pool: nothing. As far as I can determine, we ourselves have been the only party on horse or on foot in this square mile these past four days. We have found no smaller groups either, such as thieves or charcoal-burners. I have sent scouts riding southward, begging my friends for help and looking for parties who may try to cross the border. Each girl left plenty of clothing in her tent: we have given our hounds the scent of each, but the trail brings us only to the edge of the pool, then, in both cases, a few steps back and leftward – then nothing. I must station fifty of the searchers here, and take you back to Kraków.'

'Leaving them here–' I gestured to the forest – 'to endure the first frost: perhaps the first snowfall?'

'If they have been raped they are at least in shelter, and have probably been given food. I will send another party here from Kraków. We will scour every place again: an unconscious woman could be missed among all the underbrush and shifting light.'

'Unless,' I said, 'God did strike the Ancient Mass yesterday at dawn.'

For a long moment Jan Zamoyski stared at me. Then he said, 'The Church commands me to believe that Christ performed miracles, Philip; therefore perhaps I believe it. But what has happened here is no miracle: it is an accident or a trick. More: at this moment my people have enemies, but no king. We are leaderless; the French prince this summer exposed us to ridicule; we are beginning to quarrel among ourselves. My nation is Catholic, but its Protestants are the soldiers and scholars who can afford a spiritual luxury like the New Religion. Many of them are fighters already; therefore they will fight if the Catholics turn on them. If my nieces have been ravished or murdered, the Catholics will conclude this work was done by Protestants, who lust for rape and anarchy. If the Protestants can blame the Catholics, they will cry brutality and superstition. Or if the girls are found dead, then all, without evidence, may to their souls' harm turn to lynching the Jews.'

He lifted the tent-flap, and glanced back over his shoulder. 'No miracle has occurred here, Philip; for if it did it was a miracle of destruction, and that outrages reason. More: a miracle *must* not have happened here – nor must Kraków be allowed to imagine that it did.'

Eight

Four days now remained before I must present myself at Collegium Maius. I would do so under guard; for I returned to Kraków, if not in bonds, as Zamoyski's prisoner.

The sky was a flow of grey running clouds. Stubble stood bleaching in the fields; horses, their breath blue in the dawn, had dragged the shallow-biting ploughs through the autumn harrowing. They made us wait for a moment as they opened Saint Florian's Gate. I patted my horse's neck to tell it the halt would be a short one and, glancing aside, caught sight of an apricot-tree that had seeded itself against the wall – a sapling whose leaves trembled like a tree of golden coins. Then the gate opened, the air stirred, and wind stripped the yellow leaves; hurled them rustling against the wall and left the branches bare.

We rode forward. Would I escape Kraków this winter? Did I want to? Winter here was half a year long.

I do not know who had preceded us with the news. But we rode down an avenue of faces – of passers-by and of heads thronged at windows. Women peered down, leaning idly on each other's shoulders; men flattened themselves to avoid our horses, for we cantered the length of Florianska Street, staring straight before us. Heads tow-coloured, blond, light brown; faces whose narrow-featured handsomeness and alert compassion now concealed other emotions whose weight I could feel. I glanced up – saw a woman dressed in green leaning from a window, in her face a frown of pure, warm pity. The rawness of novelty lay on us all, glimpsed as a grin of distress on several faces. I saw one man smile with malice, his gaze on Zamoyski.

No voice called an indecency. As we turned our cavalcade by Sancta Maria I realized the omission surprised me: for, among the crowds going about their commerce in the packed and shock-stopped square, lust hung as evident as though we had all spoken the word. Trouble to a great man gives many people pleasure; and who dared hope that, dead or living, the girls had not been raped?

We rode through the barrel-arch that bore no trace of the turmoil of only eight days ago, and into the courtyard where three figures – two dressed in black, one in grey – stood surrounded by their households. We dismounted; and Zamoyski, his eyes on Dorotea, dropped quickly to one knee and kissed the hand of the Princess Anna.

The ash-grey satin she wore proclaimed half-mourning only – and therefore half-hope, I thought, and liked her for it as she nodded to me and I bowed. Zamoyski had already risen and gathered both Antony and Dorotea into his arms. *'Where are they?'* demanded Dorotea.

'I do not know.'

'Then the Turks have taken them.'

'There were no Turks, Dorotea. We found no slave-party; but remember Turkish raiders would probably keep them virgin.'

'To sell them in Hungary,' cried Dorotea, her voice cutting across Zamoyski's greeting to Antony. The latter glanced at me: distress puckered his eyelids and brows upward in an inverted V, and I felt the depth of his glance.

Zamoyski was speaking again. 'Their disappearance, Dorotea, gives a clever effect of supernatural horror and *therefore*–' folding her hands hard in both his own – 'and therefore is a trick. I think our abductor is a Pole, and that the horror is one success he intended and has achieved. When I find him I will kill him.'

What Dangers Deep

'Have you,' said the Princess, 'a candidate, *Pan* Zamoyski?'

'I have, madam.'

'Then bring Dorotea inside.'

Dorotea moved half-crouching, her arms clasped across her belly in a gesture that made Zamoyski exchange a glance with Antony, and Antony shake his head. 'My lady's cloak, for God's sake,' he called; and Robert Sellier, with a nod to me, wrapped the garment round her and helped Antony shepherd her into the house.

There, in a room where a fire burned and the walls were hung with carpets, Antony lowered his wife's swathed body into a chair. She was weeping with unconscious clarity, making no grimace, as though the tears belonged to someone else. '*All* my family?' she whispered. 'My father, my mother and both my sisters *too*?'

The Princess Anna sank to her knees beside the chair, and clasping Dorotea's arm, gazed up at Zamoyski. 'Jan, whom do you suspect?'

'Madam, whom else should I suspect but Daniel Balinski?'

'Have you any proof?'

To my astonishment he did not answer her, but raised his voice. '*Jozef!*' His roar made Dorotea shake, and Antony grip her shoulders.

'My lord, I am here.' Jozef Petrycy, his steward, had been standing close by.

'Arrest Daniel Balinski and bring him to me. Take as many men as you require to search his house in the city. Explain our need and beg permission, then force them if you must. I want every house he owns searched to the cellars, and Balinski found no matter where he is.'

'My lord—' began the steward.

The Princess Anna rose. 'Jan, no! I forbid this.'

'Madam, had your *brother* lived to forbid me I would not have obeyed him. Go, Jozef.'

'My lord—'

'Go.'

In the silence that followed, Zamoyski turned again to Dorotea. 'My dear, I have sent messengers riding south to Sultan Selim and, since he lies ill, to his heir Prince Murad as well. They carry a description of both girls, and an offer of reward and friendship if they are found unharmed.' Dorotea nodded; she had stopped weeping.

'My lord Zamoyski.'

Anna's voice was gentle, but it brought her, with a hostile and exhausted courtesy, his attention. 'Madam?'

'All of us wish my brother were alive to command you: to command–' she crossed herself – 'to command us all. If you are wrong your household and Balinski's will form two rival mobs. The Holy Roman Emperor has begun to muster an army to attack us; and the Diet asks me to inform you that you will, with the other electors, cast your vote on the plain outside Warsaw on the thirtieth of May next year.'

'When spring opens the roads,' said Zamoyski, gazing down at her.

She nodded. 'I have no authority, Jan; and who *will* have authority in this country when the Emperor comes against us, and commanders like you and Balinski indulge this luxury of private hate? I love Maria and Yolanta, but lacking a king we must have a confederacy, or we will lose, and our conqueror will choose both this king and all the kings who follow.'

'Jan,' said Antony, 'I hear distressing news of Philip's part in this.'

Zamoyski glanced round at me, his eyes haggard. 'I have arrested Philip, and place him in your care, Antony: but for no act – only because he had the ill-luck to be there.'

'Where? With the girls when they were captured?'

'With the girls when they vanished. He heard a strange sound, experienced some dizziness, and may have entered, I think, a form of waking unconsciousness.' He stopped me with a gesture. 'I know he will not agree. I believe his word, and think whoever stole the girls contrived to practise some deception on him; but until this question is resolved I cannot allow him to leave.'

'Do you charge him with any crime?' demanded Antony.

'No.'

'Then Her Grace's Council will wish him to return to Vienna. You cannot hold him without a charge and without evidence.'

'But I can, Antony. Forgive me. I will let Philip go as soon as I may.'

I said, 'Antony, if you will not trust Ludovic or Ambrose, may I have Sellier to wait on me?'

Antony's eyes consulted Sellier's alert impassivity, then Zamoyski's gaze, from which he seemed to interpret a refusal. 'No, Philip. Ludovic and Ambrose seem almost equally suspect–?' His intonation made it a question: Zamoyski shrugged – 'and therefore you may have them for your comfort. I think Kraków would be best pleased if my Polish servants waited on you otherwise.'

'Be patient with me, Philip,' said Jan Zamoyski. 'And forgive me. Let us hope it will not be many days. Antony, I will do all I can to keep our people from turning on the three Englishmen who were near my nieces: that is, your godson and his two servants.'

'Are your people so unjust?' demanded Antony.

'All mobs are unjust and to be feared. When Philip goes to Collegium Maius, Polish servants must surround him and vouch for him.'

'Why: will he be in such danger at the University?'

'That depends,' replied Zamoyski, 'on the mood of the University. Collegium Maius is Catholic, Antony, but it dislikes the Pope, likes Papal Councils and theological arguments, likes demagogues and alchemists and riots and pretty girls. Its opinions have tutored the mob before this. Therefore the Rector has created something called the Small Dark Cell, of which I trust Philip will learn no more. Collegium Maius educated both Nicholas Copernicus and Doctor Faustus: we hope the first achievement expunges the second.'

'They say the black arts are practised at Collegium Maius,' said Dorotea.

Antony glanced down at her, frowning. 'I repeat, Jan: will Philip be in danger there?'

'Not if he can make them respect him. Surround him with servants they can accept, and they will forget the novelty – perhaps even like him. *I* liked them in my time. We broke down the door of the Small Dark Cell five times in my case: once from the inside, and four from the outside with the help of fifty friends. And we filed off the lock eight times that I remember . . . Antony, I should like to stay near Dorotea for a few hours. May I bathe and change, sleep for a while, and then have supper with you?'

'Of course.'

'And Balinski?' said the Princess Anna. But Zamoyski, with an obeisance, had turned his back on her and gone.

Servants spread mats before my bedroom fire, set towels to warm and filled a copper bath. I asked them to leave me alone. Outside the window the short November day was darkening: flames sparkled in the panes, and the sky beyond had gone a deep lint-blue.

All my muscles ached as though someone had beaten me. I let my body go loose. *Thank God I am safe*, I thought, loving the human kindness that protected me at this moment. In an ecstasy of gratitude I closed my eyes, then opened them, and thought, *They are gone*.

Fresh astonishment brought fresh agony, clenching the muscles of my belly into a spasm emphatic as vomiting. I remembered skin translucent as snow in the light of another fire, Yolanta's frown of fatigue, Maria's small fist shadowed by its bones. Ivory and snow and light: sweet normal chemistry of breath, the irritation of normal anger. What quarrel between them had death interrupted? *Were* they dead? I felt my mind recoil from them – felt the cowardice that rejects another human being because, in our fear, betrayal has already become easier.

I had covered myself and was towelling my hair when Antony knocked. 'Philip, may I come in?'

'Yes.' He entered and sat down on the bed. 'How is Dorotea?'

'Jan and the Princess have her: I thought I could risk half an hour. Philip, did you touch either girl to harm her?'

'I did not.'

'Did you touch either one at all?'

'Not that I remember. In fact I begged–' my breath caught – 'I begged Yolanta, I think it was, to see her servants were well-armed, and to keep them with us. I disliked the risk of leaving the men. I can't remember which girl made that decision.'

He nodded. 'You approached neither carnally?'

'In five minutes, Antony? No.' I slung the towel on to a stool and sat down beside him.

His hand covered mine. 'You are clear, then, before your own conscience?'

'Yes.'

'Good. Because I must write to your uncle Robert and to the Council. They will want you out as soon as possible.'

'I will not leave,' I said.

He frowned, his mouth pursing in the grimace of concern that had made me, as a child before I learned to value him, find his face so comical. 'You understand that your implication in – at a guess – the rape and killing of the nieces of the Chancellor of Poland will equal the scandal of Amy Robsart's murder. I beg your pardon, it was *not* a murder, the coroners found your uncle innocent. Already pamphleteers like Robert Parsons accuse him of poisoning, of incest, of getting bastards on the Queen.' I made a sound between a laugh and a sob. His hand bore hard on mine. 'Your uncle's disgrace *is* the Queen's, Philip. I know you care for these girls. They are my sisters-in-law: I care for them too. But unless they are wandering lost in the forest, which I do not believe, this business can have no outcome that is not grossly ugly. I want you far from such contamination, and from such pain.'

'I will not go, Antony. Had I somehow succeeded in protecting them, they might be here – might be safe. My uncle trusts me and will believe me. I will not betray them further by running away.'

Antony got up and went to hunker by the fire. 'I know.'

'Give me two weeks,' I said. 'Surely in that time something will become clear. The abductors have had their sport with us. They cannot terrify us further unless they declare themselves, either by revealing an outrage or by demanding ransom. They cannot get whatever else they want unless they speak or move. Give me two weeks to get to Caspar Laurence. If I run away lord Zamoyski will assume my guilt, and my uncle's distress will be increased.'

'That is probably true; and it would also destroy my position here, since it will be I who must get you out.' Antony frowned into the fire. 'Perhaps we *can* best preserve your credit in Kraków by holding fast, at least for a few weeks. Tell me about the dizziness. Can someone have drugged your food?'

'Only if he got to the servants' food too: it all came from the common pot.'

He hunched his shoulders, rocking very slightly. 'If each individual *bowl* had been drugged . . . It could be done. Every man is accessible in a camp of a hundred souls.'

'Has Zamoyski thought of this?'

'Yes.'

'Doctor Solniecki?' I said. The thought angered me, for I liked Solniecki.

'I doubt it,' replied Antony. 'I don't know; probably not. Someone might have plundered his medicine-chest, though.' I nodded. 'There seems to be some real doubt about the *time* during which you and one of the servants experienced confusion.' I nodded. 'If someone *had* drugged you, events could have occurred before your eyes without your seeing them.'

'A sink-hole seems more likely. The ground is riddled with pits.'

'But there is no new sink-hole in the glade; and all known pits, chambers, river-paths are clean and empty. And yes, they are investigating the possibility that an underground stream might have carried them down-river. They are taking the dogs over the trails again – another party left this evening.' Antony stood, moving with a care and difficulty I had never seen in him before. 'All we can do now is wait, Philip. I want to get Dorotea with child. My heart tells me I must give her someone new to love, as one must always do to replace the dead.'

We stood facing each other. I remembered when I had come only to his shoulder; now I was the taller by an inch. 'Antony, I'm sorry. You've had nothing but misery ever since I came into the house.'

'Do you know, I suspect your coming was not the cause. It has been, I admit, a most wretched beginning.' He took me in his arms – then, to my appalled pity, wept while I held him.

At last he shook his head to indicate it was over. I let him go; he wiped his face with my towel. 'Well, better here than in Dorotea's arms. Good night, Philip.'

When he had gone I walked to the window. Full dark had now fallen, and though windows rimmed the square with frosty light, no one crossed its shadowed, sparkling stones. Not even a drunkard lay sleeping on the church steps; and no watcher, so far as I could see, stood in the shadows of the cage.

Had that same enemy pursued me to the Ancient Mass? I shook my head, dismissing the possibility: it felt wrong.

They were holding late Mass in Sancta Maria. The church's bulk with its uneven spires showed windows shadowed by moving lights: candle-glow glimmered ruby, emerald and honey-colour in panels of stained glass. A dog barked on the far side of the square. Within our house I heard a door close.

Was the Princess still downstairs, I wondered? And Zamoyski, whose nieces I had failed to save? Fragile and troubling as my acquaintance with them had been, I owed them now whatever atonement loyalty could give.

For this city – ancient and inimical, indifferent and dangerous – had taken me as the Grove had taken Maria and Yolanta. Behind the house-windows waited men and women with whom I now shared something human. I could feel their restlessness, their puzzlement, their pity – and, latent beneath it all, their fear.

I must be loyal to them all: to Antony, his marriage so pitiably begun; to Zamoyski, whom I admired; to Her Grace my distant Queen; to my uncle who trusted me. I rubbed my palms across my eyes. I must be loyal to Caspar Laurence, at least to the extent of my commission. I must keep the Council's trust. I must preserve my family's credit. I must obey – obey everyone: Zamoyski, Antony, my uncle, the Privy Council and its Lord Secretary. All these could demand my obedience, and yet I must not run away. Disobedience could cost me the career I hoped for.

And I would disobey.

Discovering that certainty, I shook my head and drew the curtain. I would care for them all if I could, but most for those I loved; and most of all I must be loyal to Yolanta and Maria.

For whatever had destroyed them in the Grove had bound me to them as long as I might live, in the revealed simplicity of my human love for them.

Nine

Next day the Princess (who had in this matter, I think, consulted with Antony) required Dorotea to attend her at the Wawel where, before her marriage, she had been one of Anna's ladies-in-waiting. With the message came a second, addressed to me.

> Philip,
> If Antony is occupied, as I seem to recall he will be today, I should be glad for all our sakes if you could escort Dorotea to the Castle. I can offer you a game of chess with *Pan* Pavel Zborowski, who wishes, if you are willing, to ask you about your father's campaigns in Ireland. Sober amusements, but the Princess adds her invitation to my own.
>
> Zamoyski.

'I seem to be free on my parole,' I remarked to Antony.

'Then go. You have not yet met Her Highness informally, and that I think you might enjoy. I *must* be busy all afternoon: an English merchant, Richard Saltonstall, has come north out of Turkey with letters from my friends, and I hope also with the news they dared not write down. I hear, by the way, that Sultan Selim is dying.'

'Will Murad be better?'

Antony shrugged. 'What king would not be better than a man nicknamed Selim the Drunkard? Had Sultan Suleiman let Prince Mustapha live, now, we might have cause to fear that Suleiman's genius had descended to his successor.'

'Mustapha was his favourite, so I hear.'

'The eldest and most gifted, but falsely suspected of treason on the accusation of the Sultan's wife Roxelana.'

'And Suleiman had him strangled with a bowstring?'

'While he himself watched from behind a curtain. And then he sent the eunuchs to kill the man's wife and little son. I wonder if it haunted him. And all for nothing, since the least able and most vicious son only was left to succeed him. In any case Murad will inherit the administrative and military structures built by his grandfather Suleiman. Do you remember the fortune our eighth Henry inherited from his father's thrift – the fortune he squandered?' I nodded. 'Well, Suleiman's bequest will prove, I think, more durable. The Turks have a standing army, Philip, while England, France and even Poland have levies or hired troops – mercenaries. The Turks tax their people to finance this army, while Her Grace begs Parliament for subsidies, and the King of France dares not surrender the revenues of the Catholic Church because he has no other. And the Turks are just and skilful administrators of their conquered lands.'

I frowned. 'Religious war in Europe has torn us all apart. We have not had the unity to learn these skills.'

'That is one excuse. In fact the Turks have created a united empire, while we in Europe still prove unable to unify even a single state. Until Suleiman's achievement sinks into utter decadence, we must fear them.'

'I hear he even besieged Vienna.'

'For a few days, yes. That will, I think, prove the northward limit of their ambition. But when you see the Wawel, remember that the castle at Budapest has been reduced by the Turks to an empty shell; and that castle lies eight days' ride from the room in which you are now standing.'

Queen Bona, mother of the late King Zygmunt, had been a Sforza; and had redecorated and (I think) partly rebuilt the palace to which the road led up the hill. The early northern dusk had already fallen on the fortress that now opened its courtyards before me. I have seen nothing more impeccably splendid, not even in Italy. A huge court with a loggia led us, up shallow steps, through galleries floored with agate tiles; and in the soft light of torches and candles our steps gave that echo redolent of hollowness and dust – a sound so delicate that it connects with an equivalent perfume in my mind: the smell of rain on stone.

'Why is it so empty?' I asked Dorotea. Behind us pattered the steps of our escort.

She had thrown back her hood. Her good hand on my arm was steady, her face pleasant. 'King Zygmunt's Court has disbanded: all the nobles have gone back to their lands to defend them and to wait for war. The place gives a sad impression, doesn't it? Many government officials have their offices here, but they live down in the city. A small Court surrounds the Princess Anna.'

Half an hour later I sat in a window-seat watching *Pan* Pavel Zborowski play with Jan Zamoyski the chess-game I had declined. Her Highness sat watching them, and attendants of all three were talking or playing board-games out of earshot of their masters. Dorotea, for whose composure I felt afraid, had agreed to sing with the other ladies-in-waiting. With quietness and grace the women moved to set stools beside the fire, to tune lutes and exchange music-sheets.

The chamber in which we sat was small enough to be warm. Its elegance incorporated the superb timber which, varnished or very simply adorned, the Poles love to display. A spiral staircase wound down from the Princess's bedroom, its steps turning round a barley-twist post. The timbers shone burnt-caramel; wooden Turks with spears and gilt turbans formed the newel-posts, their bodies sinuous in carven drapery. Above us hung the warm brown timbers, massive beyond anything an Englishman can imagine, that needed no ornament but a stripe of gold where the workmen had squared each log. Beneath my feet stretched an intricately worked parquet, and pillars of crannied, cream-coloured stone flanked my window-seat.

The women had tuned their instruments. Dorotea, with her single good arm, could take only a singing part. I could see her in profile, straight-backed on the stool, her velvet caul hanging down to her shoulder-blades above the crossed laces of her bodice. As I watched, she tossed back her head and sang in a voice that startlingly resembled Yolanta's:

> *Mignonne, allons voir si la rose*
> *Qui ce matin avait déclose*
> *Sa robe de pourpre au soleil,*
> *A point perdu cette vêprée*
> *Les plis de sa robe pourprée,*
> *Et son teint au vôtre pareil.*
>
> My dear, let us see if the rose
> that opened petals to the sun
> has not by night lost her soft robes
> and colour equal to your own.

'Master Sidney?' The Princess Anna had come up to me.

'Madam.' I rose. She wore a plum-coloured velvet which did not flatter her pallor; a cap of stiff lace covered her hair; and on her hands, as she seated herself beside me, I noticed several emerald rings.

'Please sit down,' she said.

I obeyed. 'Madam, Antony says the Sultan is dying.'

'Of drink, I suppose.'

'So everyone seems to assume. Please tell me: what interest have the Turks in this—' my gesture encompassed the room – 'in this election?'

'I suspect they think, like most of us, that the King of Spain and his cousin the Emperor have power enough already. They will prove friendly to any good King here, at least for the present . . . Have you met Monsieur de Monluc, the French Ambassador?'

'Not yet, Madam.'

'Or the Sultan's ambassador?'

'No.'

'Well, *Pan* Nemet Josef is a Hungarian: do not be surprised when you come across him.' Her face, with its long chin and prominent eyes, gazed shrewdly at me.

I said, 'A renegade?'

She shrugged. 'Renegade against what? Christendom? His masters are also his friends and his protectors. There are Christians in Hungary; the Turks tax them and leave them alone. *Pan* Nemet Josef, however, is a Muslim and, I believe, devout.'

'Madam, these ambassadors, as you call them, cannot be accredited, at least to the King. To whom, then, do they come?'

'To me. They are my guests.'

Anna studied me. I, leaning forward, sat watching Dorotea. Calmly the Princess said, 'I think that, among us, we can help her.'

'What happened to them all, madam – to all that family? Why has *Pan* Zamoyski no wife, no kin?'

'Oh, he has kin: a brother near Warsaw, who must stay there to keep order until the election is safely over; and his sister Teofila. She married Prince Stefan Báthóry's Chamberlain.'

I nodded towards Dorotea. 'And the father of these girls.'

'Yes: Jan's youngest brother Tomász, who died while travelling abroad. As for a wife, he will take one someday. He is not old, you know.'

'And how long has he been Chancellor?'

'He *was* Chancellor for twenty-two years. The next King will make him so again.'

I stared at her. 'Twenty-two years? Then he must have been—'

She nodded. 'Seventeen years old.'

We both gazed at the big powerful man who over-filled his chair, his eyes on the chessboard, his hand shielding his mouth. He glanced up, rested on us, in salute, eyes bright with intelligent pleasure, and moved a piece. We heard him curse; *Pan* Zborowski laughed.

Anna said softly, 'The thought of a Hungarian Muslim distresses you, Master Sidney?'

I turned and measured her. 'Madam, what right have you to ask?'

'No right.'

I thought; rejected words in which I recognized a young, a dangerous arrogance; then said, 'The Protestant cause contents my heart.'

'Forgive me,' she said gently. 'Why?'

It occurred to me to rise and leave her; but I remembered courtesy, and also my arrest. I said, 'First, because it keeps England safe from Popes and Catholic powers. King Philip of Spain was my godfather.' She nodded. 'Four years was too much. He has no right to be King in England again. The Queen of Scots, whom we have in prison, is Catholic, and wants to call Spanish infantry into England to establish her right. I hate, I suppose, two women. Mary Stuart is one. Queen Catherine de' Medici is the other.'

'Mary of Scotland is a bad woman: a proven murderer who would murder again; a queen ungifted with love for others, yet avid for power over them. She is treacherous, a liar, self-enthralled, and not intelligent. All this she is,' said Anna, 'but it is not her Catholicism that makes her so.'

I stared at her in a complex distress. '*My* faith, madam – forgive me – needs no priest-intercessors, but leaves us alone with God.'

The Princess Anna said softly, 'And so we are . . . How old are you?'

'Turned twenty.'

I met her gaze, and there astonished me a pang of that

physical excitement which I expected only with young women. I had been leaning forward; now pride and doubt drew me upright. I saw amusement in her eyes. I was staring at her as a man looks at a woman, and being assessed in my turn. I thought: *Why has she not married? Did she not wish it until it was too late? Does she long for children?* I was breathing too fast: I think I hid it. 'Tell me,' I said, 'about Prince Stefan Bathóry.'

'He is my friend and Jan's,' she replied, 'and the only equal to Jan that I have ever met. Both men know this, of course.'

'Has *he* agents here, madam?'

'Yes, he has agents here, Master Sidney.'

At that instant we heard a noise from the outer room. The Princess's Chamberlain came in. 'Madam, *Pan* Daniel Balinski asks if he may speak with you and *Pan* Zamoyski.'

Zamoyski put the chessboard from him and rose with careful leisure. Anna said, 'Please let him come in. Master Sidney—?' With a nod she excused herself; I rose and bowed. By the fireplace alto, lute, soprano fell into silence.

Into this stillness walked the man I had not seen since his eyes acknowledged me in the torchlight. Now I saw him mark my presence again without seeming to, for he moved with a quick light grace to the Princess and made his obeisance. He wore a leather coat that reached to his ankles, and in his hat I saw the three white feathers that distinguish the Polish cavalryman. His sword was not a rapier like my own, but a scimitar, its scabbard worked with turquoises and moonstones and Arab script. From whom, I thought, had he plundered it?

One expects beautiful men and women to prove intelligent, and this man, I suspected, was so; but in his eyes, as they flicked over us again, I saw nothing beyond a certain hard amusement. He bowed to Zamoyski. 'My lord, in my great sorrow at your trouble you will find me eager to help you in every way I can. Some people of yours came to my house searching for your nieces. I welcomed them and let them examine every room, even into the attics and the cellars. I swear before God I have not harmed your ladies, nor did I take them.'

Then he is perfectly secure, I thought, *which means he has sent the women to a hiding-place we cannot discover; or else—*

Or else he does not have them.

I saw Zamoyski reach the second conclusion, or appear to reach it. Slowly he held out his hand. 'My lord, forgive me the anger of my great distress.'

Perhaps now Zamoyski's people can, in any case, search better by stealth, I thought. Concession and apology would spare us all a war between their households. *Was* Balinski indeed, as I had assumed, the Chancellor's enemy – or did I simply hate him for Adam Kózmian? Had the two men any purpose, any history in common? Might a cruel trick on the night of my arrival have seemed fair to Balinski, leaving him genuinely innocent of whatever had happened in the wood?

Again I remembered the Grove, rich with the life the ancient people had planted there: a place they had furnished, as if in emblem or in warning, with beautiful things of power – water, fruit, living creatures, the centuries-old trees. *What do rowan and apple mean?* I thought. Memory of my nurses' rhymes brought me only one charm in English, something the country-folk used to say:

> Rowan-tree, red thread
> All the witches hold in dread.

The rowan then was holy – at least in the eyes of my own ancestors. Had they too piled bear-skulls in pits and linked their bear-guardians with the sacred rowan? Why? Ancient and delicate, the original clues had faded from the Grove, leaving only – what?

All this passed through my mind while Jan Zamoyski and his adversary measured each other. Had they once been friends? What calculation, hate or doubt, what real innocence now moved these two men twenty years senior to myself?

And then my consciousness dismissed them; because suddenly I knew where I had felt or met the Ancient Mass before.

Near Penshurst, my father's house, stands a ring of stones raised by our most remote ancestors – people about whom I know little, for they faded into the past before the Romans came. These monoliths of granite stamped with bosses of lichen are weathered soft and gentle, and it seemed obvious they marked the limit of some old temple, or so I remember my father's telling me.

One night's truancy when I was twelve years old (I had climbed from my bedroom window down the elm tree – my usual route when my nurse had left me safe in bed) I rode there under the humid stars of August. A truant needs a goal for his adventure. And he needs an errand. On this night I had invented an errand – part prank, part debt of conscience, and (so I now know) wholly dangerous.

In the present, in the Princess Anna's chamber, I sank back down on to the window-seat. The three Polish noblemen were talking softly. Anna glanced at me, then away, drawn by the Polish speech I could not understand.

My visit to the Standing Stones, that night when I was twelve, had really begun, I reflected, a year earlier, when a tenant of ours brought to my father an object he had dug up within the Ring. Though he tore up the ground afterwards to find more gold (and got none), still it was honest of him to bring this piece to us. Father had his jeweller clean it, then showed it to me and my mother, who had then just recovered from the smallpox. I remember the treasure as it lay in my father's palm: an axe three inches long, made of dark yellow, almost wheat-coloured gold. A Janus-headed axe; for its two crescent blades faced opposite ways from a central haft that had obviously once held a wooden handle.

I touched it with my fingertip. 'It feels oily,' I said.

'That is because it is *pure* gold, Philip – purer than any we fashion now. Do you know how old this thing must be?'

'No, sir.' I shook my head.

My father held it up. My mother moved nearer; I remember the rustle of her black taffeta skirt. 'Philip, this came – God knows how – from Hellas: from the land of the Trojan War. They say Irish merchant-vessels used to carry precious things so far, in Rome's time and even before. Perhaps someone fashioned this axe when Achilles was a living man. Think of it, the Trojan princesses then still lived unharmed and honoured: Cassandra served at the altar of Apollo, the god whose desire for her drove her insane; and no Greek victor had yet slaughtered her sister Polyxena, to be Achilles' slave in the underworld. Have you heard of Daedalus and the Labyrinth he built?'

'Yes, Father.'

'Roger Ascham used to tell me – I cannot vouch whether it is true – that Labyrinthos means House of Labrys: House of the Double Axe. This is Labrys, Philip, and sacred to Minotauros, Lord of the Labyrinth.'

'Then why, sir,' I said, 'did someone bury it in the Ring?'

'I think,' replied my father softly, 'as a sacrifice.'

'Then Master Taberner should not have dug it up.'

'No, he should not, but his finding it was an accident.'

'Then he should put it back.'

'I think not,' replied my father. 'We are wealthy, Philip, and should be kind. Why should gold slumber in the dark when poor people could use it to buy food? I paid Master Taberner its worth. But it is old and holy; we will keep it.'

'Father,' I said, 'will you give it to me?'

My mother spoke. The scars had healed and I had learned to look at her without weeping; but only her grey eyes, their irises ringed with green, and her calm voice remained unchanged. The first time I saw her after her sickness (may I, in Heaven at least, heal her of this hurt), I had run away from her and wept while my brother Robert held me. She did not follow me.

What Dangers Deep

No comfort existed; and I never let her see me weep for her again.

Leave me, O Love, which reachest but to dust. So I wrote much later. But it was from my mother I first learned that our flesh is no more to be trusted than the trees and flowers to which it is kin. The Bible says we are dust; but only when one has seen a woman's beauty vanish in a destruction as natural as its birth – only when one has sounded, as I did into my pillow that year, the long whispered word *dust* – does one confront the Nature that made and that will destroy us. There are deaths without dying; my mother was the first to teach me that.

'Father,' I said, 'will you give it to me?'

He shrugged refusal, his face troubled: not only was it gold, but its antiquity gave it a value with which, I think, he did not trust a child, not even me.

'Philip,' said my mother, 'I wonder if you remember a thing that happened when you were five years old: because it impressed me – disturbed me, perhaps I should say.'

I frowned at her. 'Madam?'

She smiled. 'No, I think you were three, in fact – very small. I used to find you kneeling on your bed, your hands cupped in prayer, your bedsheets draped over your head in the fashion of an ancient Roman – for when they made sacrifice or prayed, you know, they covered their heads, as we still do in church out of reverence to God.'

'Why did I do this, Mother? I don't remember.'

She glanced at the dusk beyond the window, and pointed. Above the trees was rising that globe of disturbing gold, swimming in a colour and immensity borrowed (so Doctor Dee claims) from the earth's own atmosphere. I dislike the golden Hunter's Moon, I do not know why: I always feel glad when it shrinks to a cold white circle among the stars. 'You were worshipping the full moon. I think, Henry, that so old a Roman will value your token as it deserves. Please give it to him.'

'Very well,' said my father. 'Remember she is a holy thing, Philip. Her name is Labrys, the Double Axe.'

And it was therefore with Labrys in my pocket that I rode to the Ring of Stones.

I had brought no tinderbox, but the stars cast faint blue shadows from the monoliths, their shapes abraded by three thousand seasons of rain and snow. I stepped within the Ring and walked to that tumble of stones which was all that remained, so my father believed, of an original altar. I must dig deep, because Master Taberner might return, so I had brought my pocket-knife and a spoon from the table; and I must put the stones back once I had finished. I knelt and moved one rock from another; I remember the soft, gritty, scraping sound. All around me the stillness grew more alert.

The place was watching me – concentrating on me a thought clear and dense and merciless – but merciless without cruelty, like the coldness of stars or running water. I remember I began to shudder: contractions that rippled through my body, wringing my stomach and even my arms so that they hurt next morning. And yet it was August, and at the same time the sweat of heat stood on my skin.

At last I had a hole deep enough. I placed in it the little golden axe, its shine gone grey-dull in the starlight, and thought: 'It is a sacrifice: I should pray.' As I laboured – for I knew now I had been impudent to come here, and that I must get out – I panicked so far as to whisper a prayer my nurse had taught me:

> The time it draweth near
> Of bitter painful throes:
> How long I must the same
> Endure, alone God knows . . .

This, God help me, was a prayer meant for women in childbirth.

With such ludicrous ceremonies was Labrys laid back into

the earth. I ran from the Ring, jumped on to my pony and fled towards home. That night I slept hard, and remembered no dreams.

'*My lord!*' Doctor Solniecki's cry returned me with a shock to the Princess's room. The door opened: Solniecki ran towards us, holding something laid on tissue-paper, and dropped to his knees before Zamoyski. 'The searchers found this yesterday afternoon.'

Displayed on the tissue-paper lay a woman's brown velvet cap, stained with damp, but not rotted or wholly ruined. It had no strings. I saw Balinski cross himself. Dorotea, laying down her music-sheets, rose with dangerous care; I saw another woman clutch her arm. Dorotea shook her off with a clean, simple fury, as Maria would have done.

Zamoyski touched the thing. 'This is relatively dry – that is, it is not soaked through.'

'No, my lord.'

'And the strings – didn't these caps tie beneath the chin? Philip—?' He glanced at me: I nodded. Zamoyski said: 'The strings have been–' he examined the object – 'cut off. No, not cut off: ripped clean.'

'I know, my lord.' Solniecki was still on his knees.

Gently Zamoyski turned the cap inside-out, studying the damp but unrotted velvet. 'Wait. Look.' On the inside surface lay curled a single hair, shining like silver.

'Maria,' said the Princess Anna softly.

Zamoyski looked down at the doctor. 'Where did they find this?'

'In the cleft of an apple-tree, my lord, some height above the ground.'

'An *apple-tree*?'

'Yes.'

Zamoyski laid down the cap. 'Doctor Solniecki, how tall is my niece Maria?'

'Five feet tall, my lord.'
'And my niece Yolanta?'
'The lady Yolanta is about five feet six inches tall.'
'And you found this cap – in a tree – at what height?'
'Seven feet eight inches, my lord,' replied Doctor Solniecki.

Ten

The deep, steep-roofed square of Collegium Maius enclosed a courtyard with colonnades on every side. I noted colours: the grey of cobbles and of gothic doors; the green of copper fish-scale roofs; black marble of the well, into which placards prohibited students from throwing coins; the grass-green of the Library door, studded with gilt nails shaped like flowers. Above me, from a square of soft grey sky, fell snowflakes that melted on the cheek.

Like my servants I had surrendered my sword to the porter at the entry-lodge. Nor were the young men who surrounded me permitted, in this place, to arm themselves, so they made do with their hands and with whatever makeshifts they could seize. I wondered, as I glanced at the crowd, whether I had ever seen so handsome a nation – no wonder the Turks prized them. Of course there were no girls here, but their brothers had the straight features and brown or dark yellow hair I had come to expect in these comely people. In the whole court I glimpsed not one head of black hair, nor a single redhead.

My progress across the court, leading my suite of six men, had gone, I hoped, with modesty; certainly without announcement. But as we proceeded to the staircase – up which the porter had told me I must go to find Caspar Laurence's lecture-room – the noise around us died to an aggressive hush. No one challenged me: I might, I thought, reach the lecture-hall without a fight, although my appearance and my protectors had obviously identified me.

Someone barred the staircase. A voice said in Latin, 'Master Philip Sidney?'

I sighed. 'Yes, sir, I am he.'

One hand on the rail, one propped against the wall – blocking the whole staircase unless I chose to fight – there stood, two steps above me, a man of about twenty-three: brown-haired, with grey eyes and Tartar cheekbones, and a voice extraordinarily rich and deep for someone little older than myself. He said, 'I am Adrian Firlei, son of Stanislas Firlei, a Protestant noble of this city. I must ask you to tell us what happened to the ladies Maria and Yolanta.'

The silence had become intense. Gazing up at my antagonist, I said with a gentleness that excluded all the watchers: 'Which was it – Yolanta or Maria?'

I saw his hands relax. After several seconds' pause he answered, 'Maria.'

'It was both for me, I think.'

The crowd had heard; some moved hesitantly, but now there was uncertainty in the sound. From the gallery above a voice said suddenly, 'My lord Adrian!'

Both of us looked up. Gazing down at us, his hand on the balustrade, stood a professor in a black gown barred with velvet – a handsome man with a moustache but no beard, a fashion we seldom see in England. Adrian said, 'Yes, Doctor Pasek?'

'You have half an hour to quarrel in; bring Master Sidney–' he smiled at me – 'and his servants up to my room, where we can give them some wine. And you, the rest of you, disperse.' To my surprise the students obeyed, falling back from me; and I was urged up to Doctor Pasek's quarters with Adrian Firlei's hand under my elbow.

There the professor served wine to my men, who thanked him, and then he said to me, 'I'll leave you alone with Adrian. Forgive us our discourtesy, Master Sidney: we hear from Italy that you are a most excellent scholar. Enjoy Father Laurence, and speak with Adrian. Good day.' I shook his hand and found myself, except for my servants, who kept their distance, alone with Adrian Firlei.

My new acquaintance filled for me one of the professor's pewter goblets (doctors at the University did not live rich, though I remembered having heard that King Zygmunt the First had made them at least nominal noblemen). 'Please, Master Sidney, come and sit down.'

The room was simple, with dark wood furniture and white-washed walls, its windows set with roundels of alternating clear and yellow glass. Cut into the wall beneath one window was a seat – a stepped alcove where one sat on the top step and rested one's feet on the bottom one, while one's friend on the opposite side did the same. Nothing is better for conversation, or simpler or more gracious for reading. Here, accordingly, we settled, and Adrian said: 'Tell me, I beg you, about the ladies.'

Although these repetitions by now exhausted me, I told him all the truth – because I saw how, in his place, I should have hungered for it.

At last he bowed his head into his hands. 'Ah God. God help us and them.'

I let him alone for several minutes. Then I said, 'My lord Adrian, there are questions I dare not ask of Dorotea or my lord Zamoyski. I wonder whether you could help me.'

He settled back, wiping tears from his eyes, and stared at me, arms folded. His voice was perfectly steady. 'I'll try.'

'When Helena – the girls' mother – died, you were how old?'

He glanced away, calculating. 'About twelve.'

'Then you may know nothing. I have heard Helena became sick in mind.'

'I did not know Helena, Master Sidney; I only remember rumour.' I nodded. 'And grown people, you understand, let children hear some things, but they conceal others.'

'I know.'

'I do not remember that anyone ever called her ill in mind

until the year that elapsed between her husband's death and her own. And then I should think *insane* was, at all events, the wrong word. Some lunatics are violent, some quiet. I believe she was . . . the latter kind.'

'Was there any rumour of such aberrations earlier – in her girlhood? Was she eccentric?'

'Oh, one of the most famous eccentrics we have ever had. She was the only girl to attend the University in the – I don't know how many hundred years since it was founded. She did so in disguise as a boy, with the connivance of friends; among them they even deceived the aunt with whom she lived – not about her sex, of course, but about how she spent the day. I know it sounds improbable, but the rest of the family lived near Warsaw, and the girl was not adequately controlled. We do not, of course, permit women at Collegium Maius.'

'Nor do we at Oxford. I think it an atrocious pity. How hungry for learning she must have been.'

Adrian shrugged. 'Perhaps; but at home our sisters can learn as much as they want from the finest tutors – and Helena's family were noble and could have afforded teachers. When the Rector discovered her he had her imprisoned in a convent.' I made an exclamation of compassion. Adrian said, 'Well, King Zygmunt thought it a shame. Though he could not make the University take her back, he sent an emissary to free her and offer her the gift of a dowry. And his emissary bettered him, for His Grace had chosen the scholar Tomaśz Zamoyski, who was already a widower with one daughter, Dorotea; and Tomaśz fell in love with Helena and married her.'

I felt a shock of truth. No one had before thought to tell me – it had not, I supposed, occurred to Antony to mention it – that Dorotea was not the full blood-sister of Maria and Yolanta. *They make a pair*, I thought of the two younger – and imagined Dorotea at ten or eleven years old. What had she thought of her father's marriage to a girl perhaps eight years her senior? And I realized that, outside the pair of demi-twins that was Yolanta and Maria, Dorotea stood alone: beautiful, stoical, still a maiden at thirty – and less than her sisters, even in my own unconscious estimation. And she knew it: of that I suddenly felt certain.

I said, 'It was a happy marriage, then, between Tomaśz and Helena?'

'I believe so. My father says she was not pretty, but that she had much intelligence and charm. I believe she tried, poor lady, and that she loved Tomaśz, but there were rumours of her temper – of her rages. When Tomaśz died she endured it well, so I have heard, for several months. Then one day she began to weep and could not stop. After several weeks of this she curled her legs up to her chest, and never stirred or spoke another word.'

'And she killed herself – how?'

Up to that moment he seemed to have been honest, even impulsively honest, moved by the grief we shared. But the loyalty that surrounds a suicide often forbids, in its compassion, the single answer, *how*. Adrian gazed at me with distress, and said, 'Now that, Master Sidney, my father never told me.'

I sighed and nodded, and saw his look of gratitude, though I think that too escaped him without his knowing. 'Who found her, then?' I said.

Another, longer hesitation. 'Yolanta,' said Adrian.

My servants sat talking quietly in Polish; I do not think they noticed our silence. In the courtyard down below us an undergraduate, his notebooks under his arm, ran past the well, slipping from amber glass into a daylit roundel, and then out of my vision.

'And Tomaśz,' I said at last, 'how and where did he die? Travelling abroad?'

'About that I know less, because it took place so far away; but yes, in a country with which I believe your family has some connection: Ireland.'

'Yes, my father is Lord Deputy of Ireland.'

'So I believe I have heard *my* father mention.' Adrian's voice implied an indifference so profound it would, on another day, have made me smile. 'A manuscript came on the market and was offered, by the Irish nobleman who had inherited it, to the highest bidder. I do not know whether he also offered this treasure to Queen Elizabeth: probably not.'

I grimaced. 'I wish my father had heard of this thing. What was it?'

'A Gospel illuminated on parchment, made, I believe, about six hundred years ago.' I whistled. 'Yes: very precious, and made more so by gemstones set into the binding, and by some cursive notes in the margin describing, if I remember what King Zygmunt once told me, some Viking raids on the coast. You may have gathered that King Zygmunt was a man who treasured such things.'

'I hear nothing but good of him.'

'We loved him,' said Adrian. 'And we miss him. Well, His Grace, my father and Tomaśz – all scholars – thought this object had unique value; and, to be frank, they wanted to get it out of Ireland before – I must assume – your father's troops destroyed it.'

I felt my skin go hot with shame. 'So King Zygmunt sent Tomaśz to Ireland?'

'Yes. Journeys are dangerous; I gather the sweating-sickness took him that summer. He was buried there.'

'So he vanished utterly: at least his daughters must have thought so.'

'Perhaps. They still speak – spoke – of him.'

'I know. Can you remember any names? The monks who created the manuscript, did they work at a place called Iona? And where in Ireland did Tomaśz die?'

'Iona?' For a speaker of Polish and Latin he reproduced the syllables with excellent clarity. 'Is that Gaelic? Of course the monks made it, but I know no more, except–' he hesitated – 'forgive me: that the English have set out to destroy the native Irish culture, with its language and all its monuments.' I made no reply, for shame allowed none. 'As for where he died, it was a castle with an Irish name.'

'And what became of the book he was sent to find?'

'No one knows,' said Adrian. 'Good God, there's the bell. You mean to hear Father Laurence? Because so do I.'

'Yes, I mean to hear Father Laurence. Thank you, my lord Adrian.'

'You need not thank me.' Someone had begun to ring a handbell. My servants in cheerful panic set down their cups; students were running in the halls. Adrian Firlei looked at me. For one second more his eyes expressed pure doubt. 'Forgive me, Master Sidney. The city has concluded you did not hurt them.'

'I did not harm them,' I said softly. 'Nor do I know what happened to them.'

The *lectorium* where we settled on our benches had a vaulted, whitewashed ceiling, and offered the teacher a choice of desk, lectern or step-alcove. Someone had painted the ceiling with patterns of geometrical figures; and Time had faded their intricate circles until the design looked like an old map of the world – a rhythm of complex and gentle pastels. A group of professors sat round the walls. I noticed Doctor Pasek. I rose and bowed to him; he waved a kind dismissal. Then around me, with a rustling and scraping the whole crowd – including spectators come up from the town – rose too, and Caspar Laurence entered the room.

He carried nothing in his hands, and wore a black gown over an ordinary doublet, also black. Nothing distinguished him as a priest, but much, I thought, distinguished him as a Yorkshireman. He stood over six feet, broad-shouldered and strong. His hair, which had been yellow, was beginning to go white, and I saw that his eyebrows were also blond, which is unusual. The rubicund skin and blue eyes traced, I thought, from the Danish raids on our own North. His lower jaw protruded, and his underlip was slightly pouched: I suspect a woman would have thought him a plain man. His smile pinched his lips together and down at the corners, which gave it a wry, frowning quality.

He sat down at the desk and surveyed us. 'Good afternoon,

gentlemen. How many of you have passed three courses in basic anatomy?'

Most hands went up, including Doctor Pasek's. I kept my own arms folded and, as for my skin, I had given up hoping it would cool to a less betraying colour. Father Laurence noted with a smile the gallants from the town; dwelt, for an explicit second, on myself; and passed to the colleagues ranged against the wall. 'I cannot teach you what you should already know. My regrets, therefore, to those of you who will not attend my second lecture. That said, I thank your lord Rector for inviting me to teach you in this famous place.

'Our subject is the treatment of wounds, as practised by the physicians of Islam – treatment both by surgery and by drugs. You must know at once that I passionately oppose one of our own crudities: the searing of any wound with a hot iron, which cleanses the flesh by destroying it, and kills the patient with shock. Never employ this practice.'

His voice was rich and soft and carrying. Some of my fellow-pupils were already taking notes. Laurence resumed. 'But first let me tell you something that happened when I was travelling down to Constantinople in the train of Monsieur de Busbecq, the Imperial Ambassador – a charming man who gardened in his spare hours, and who kept a menagerie of tame animals. He had a pet lynx. It happened that this creature fell in love with me: it used to prevent me from leaving its company by gently pinning the hem of my robe to the floor with its claws. There was also a crane, which fell in love with the Ambassador himself. It used to wake him in the morning by tapping on his door with its beak. It finally insisted on sleeping under his bed, where it laid an egg.'

Everyone laughed. And so Laurence went on speaking, and when I could master myself enough to listen to him I found that he was confirming, from his experience, stories I had heard of the Turks' indifference to Greek antiquities – statues fed into the lime-kilns, Roman coins melted down for blacksmithing. But my thoughts would not come under my control. My palms were as cold as my skin was hot. I had already had enough; there was more to come, since I must, today, at least contrive to introduce myself. And when I became aware that he had begun to deal with treatment of the wounded, I admitted I could not force my understanding to follow him.

The lecture lasted ninety minutes, and left me exhausted but slightly calmed. At last the speaker finished; Pasek and others came up to congratulate him, and Laurence and I lingered in each other's vicinity, I talking to Adrian, whose sponsorship I now seemed to have.

A moment came when Adrian shook my hand and turned to go; when Pasek's speech had come to a natural end, and at an opening in the crowd and in the noise around us, Laurence looked at me and said: 'Master Sidney, good-day. I am glad you have acquired a sponsor; but still I think you would be in less danger of lynching if you accepted an invitation and let me give you coffee in my room.'

I came to him, holding my hat in my hand. 'If it is Turkish coffee, Father Laurence, I should like that very much: I haven't tasted it since Vienna.'

'Then you cannot,' replied Laurence, 'have made the right friends in Kraków. Come along.' And so, convoyed out of the room by this second protector, I walked along the gallery to a whitewashed chamber much like Pasek's, with a fire burning on the hearth.

There I obeyed an order to sit down. Laurence must expect a courier from the Council; because of my name and family, and in spite of my age, he must suspect I was this courier; but he gave me no help, nor any signal of curiosity. To prepare our coffee he detached a key from his belt and removed from a small locked chest a bag of roasted coffee-beans. These he ground by hand, then mixed coffee, water and pounded sugar in a brass pot with a long spout. He set this to boil over the fire, and sat down beside it. 'One must watch it every second, then drink it as soon as it boils, or it will burn. Forgive my impertinence down there. You look like your father: I saw him once.'

I smiled. 'How can you tell, behind all that beard he wears?'

He glanced at me. 'By the nose and eyes.'

We sat in a silence whose quality of repose I recognized with grateful surprise. I had left my servants in the corridor at Laurence's suggestion: he had remarked on our way up that they would gossip there and satisfy the University. And indeed, judging by their noise, they were discussing me with several dozen strangers.

Caspar Laurence said, 'I am sorry about *Pan* Zamoyski's ladies; and deeply sorry this scandal should trouble him at this time.'

'Do you also,' I demanded, 'want to ask me if I raped one of them?'

'No. Here, drink this.' He gave me a pottery cup, without handles and scarcely larger than one of my mother's thimbles. I sipped the bittersweet stimulative liquor, frowning as it burnt my lips. 'I want to ask,' said my host, 'whether you have heard the legend of the Children of Hamelin.'

'No, Father Laurence, I have not.'

'Hamelin is a town in the principality of Brunswick. About ten years ago my superiors sent me there on an errand, and I had an opportunity to search through the town records. Although I had other business, I remember feeling curious and noting what little evidence I could find.'

'Evidence of what, Father Laurence?'

He poured more coffee. 'Of the vanishing, about three hundred years ago, of a large number of children.'

I spilled scalding coffee, wiped it with my hands. 'How many? *All* the children of the town?'

'Tradition mentions a single survivor: a little boy. The accounts did not make the matter clear. I think I remember a carved chimney-piece inscribed: "Made in the sixth year from the vanishing of the children"; and one line in the town records

– "Thirty-four years after the disappearance of the children".'

My hands had gone steady with anger. 'Children die in epidemics. And there was a Children's Crusade which took thousands of them southward to slavery and the Turks. No doubt the people of Hamelin remember a symbol of some such event.'

'I do not think so,' said Caspar Laurence gently. 'Because, you see, on the road outside the town gate stands a marker I have seen with my own eyes. On it are carved the words: "At this place the children vanished".'

'*At this place?*' I whispered.

Laurence nodded. 'I think the stonemason meant precisely what he said. I think the children, drawn by some power or some beguilement, trouped out of the town, and that, at a particular spot on the road, they were seen to vanish. Not to die, not to go away – but to become unmanifest.'

'And you think the Ancient Mass is such a place?'

I almost whispered it. His gaze held mine. 'Perhaps.'

At that instant a knock came at the door. A voice called softly, 'Caspar.'

Caspar Laurence went still. Then he glanced at me. 'Master Sidney, whatever happens, do not leave.'

'I will not.' I was almost stammering with rage, and as I spoke I wondered what claim of his could justly elicit my promise.

Laurence called, 'Come in.'

A man, dressed in black gown and cloak, entered the room, and gazed from Laurence to myself. 'Caspar, good evening. I see you have a pupil with you. Master Philip Sidney, I know you by sight. I am Robert Parsons.'

This, then, was the famous rebel whom my father or any other of the Queen's officers would have hanged without hesitation – probably without trial. A fat, strong, ugly man with a virile presence and a voice of extraordinary literate power. I had guessed that some women might find themselves attracted to Caspar Laurence despite his plainness. I knew at once that the ugly priest who stood before me could have fascinated any woman he chose.

He said to Laurence, 'Send the child away.'

Laurence shook his head. 'No, let him stay.'

'If my host wishes it, Father Parsons.' I rose but did not offer him my hand. When he strode past me I sat down again, lacing my fingers hard together.

My uncle, according to this liar whom I ought perhaps to kill, had begotten five bastard children on Queen Elizabeth. Sir Francis had showed me the pamphlet, confiscated from a man whose right hand the Privy Council had ordered cut off for possessing it: a pamphlet that named midwives, secret refuges, times to the hour and minute. But he was Caspar Laurence's friend; and I had business with Caspar Laurence.

'No, Master Sidney, not in these—' Parsons cast his eyes upwards – 'not in these sacred rooms. Murder me some other time.' He had gone to the window, and stood there with one elbow on the sill, the other hand on his hip.

'I do not know, Father Parsons,' I replied, 'whether English law kills a man guilty of slander.' Since then I have regretted I offered him so transparent an opening; but anger and sarcasm is a mix that requires experience, and it suits young men badly.

'Kills a man for slander?' said Parsons. 'Why not? It kills for everything else. Shall I tell you how English law, and the chief maker of English law at that time – King Henry – destroyed an uncle of mine? He was a monk at Glastonbury. When the King's men tortured the Abbot to death and turned the monks out as beggars from the home they loved – a place where they served the poor as Queen Elizabeth's almshouses will never do – he found his way to us, and there lived out his days, observing his Rule in secret till he died. But before that, the law branded him on the forehead, since it abhors the class King Henry so foolishly impoverished and then enraged: the class of *able-bodied beggars*. Your grandfather, I think, got part of the Abbey lands.'

'That is true,' I said.

'I am glad to see you admit it unashamed.'

'I *am* unashamed, Father Parsons, but sorry.'

'Let me make you more so. I said my uncle had been a monk at Glastonbury. After he came to us I used, at night, to listen to him weeping. By day he would tell us of the Abbey's beauty, all vanished, all destroyed: the gardens, the carvings, the organ and the bells, the clock-tower raised to the glory of God; the fosterage of scholarship, the Brothers' charity to the poor. He told us how the Abbot, those last years, spent every penny the Abbey possessed in order to punish the King by giving him a bankrupt shell. And he told us the names of his Brothers – some hanged, some reduced to starving, some abandoned to die in prison. Even now, Master Sidney, the country-people say you can hear the ghost-monks chanting on summer nights among the ruins Henry and your grandfather and the other plunderers left us: their very souls could conceive no other home. Many of us, sir, can give such bitter thanks for the Reformation of the Church in England.'

'And on this country that you say you love,' I replied, 'you would bring the Spanish infantry? I am sorry about the Abbeys: they were beautiful, and a succour to the poor; I wish I had seen them. I myself would not choose to plunder anything. But you have lied about a woman whose capacities surpass your own; and now you are lying about love.'

'How impudent of you,' said Parsons. 'You speak of Spanish infantry. Tell me, Master Sidney, how your own father pleaded when, in order to offer their submission, he made Irish chieftains approach him down an avenue of pikes on which he had speared two thousand Irish heads.'

'That was Humphrey Gilbert, not my father.' I forced my back to straighten, my head not to bow: forced my eyes not to waver. 'My father reprimanded him.'

'Reprimanded him,' echoed Parsons. 'Tell me, sir. You were born to be Lord Deputy of Ireland: some day Her Grace may give you your father's work. Would you do what Humphrey Gilbert ordered and your father reprimanded?'

My hands closed hard on the back of my chair. 'No. Human beings hate those who terrorize them. Such a course leads only to defeat.'

'It fascinates me,' said Robert Parsons, 'that the unkindness of Gilbert's act is not what occurs to you first.'

'I hate unkindness,' I replied. 'And I hate those who impute bastards to a virgin lady. No, I would not do what Humphrey Gilbert did.'

'Then, sir,' said Robert Parsons, 'you will no more conquer Ireland than your father has.'

'Master Sidney,' said Father Laurence, 'if you kill Father Parsons, as upon further provocation you might rather naturally do, the authorities here will treat you like any other student, and exclude you from the University for life. I therefore advise you against it.' I nodded. 'Robert, if you continue to insult my guest in my own chamber I shall have to put you out – you know I can – before I can even ask how many days you have been in Kraków.'

'Since before your arrival. William sent me.'

'Ah.' Laurence steepled his hands against his face, then quickly shielded his eyes. 'Ah.' His voice held no surprise.

Robert Parsons assessed me with one final glance; then, dismissing me because he could not rid himself of me, came and drew up a stool. He leaned forward; I saw him reach for his friend's hand, then respect Laurence's nod of refusal. 'Caspar, when we saw you at Rome William and I concluded you were ill. The soul has its sicknesses, and this despair is one. All such diseases have their course. You will not believe me; you cannot believe me, I know. But William implores you to come back to Rome – to the English College, where we can nurse you.'

The coffee burnt and hissed. Laurence dived to rescue it; the smell of its charred sweetness filled the room. 'Excuse me, Master Philip, I was not attending to it.'

'Thank you, Father Laurence, I had had enough.'

Robert Parsons, hands folded in his lap, had withdrawn into a stillness whose power I could feel. Before this love, respecting it, I drew back. Parsons raised his head. 'Despair has its inner course, so our Fathers have told us; and even within it we progress without knowing it. "Thy fury is confirmed upon me, and all thy waves hast thou brought in upon me; my skin and my flesh hast thou made old; thou art become to me a lion in a secret place."'

'And in the core of death?' said Caspar Laurence.

Parsons appeared to understand him, though I did not; but he made no reply, except that suddenly he looked at me and said, with a mockery whose gentleness surprised me: 'Poor boy.'

'You need not fear me, Robert,' said Caspar Laurence.

'Then,' replied his friend, 'I do fear you indeed.'

I think the silence lasted three or four minutes. At last Parsons stirred. 'I will be in Kraków until you leave. We want you to come to the English College, where we will cheer you with kindness if we can.' Laurence nodded. 'I will wait with you; I will wait for you. Today, however, I will leave you with your–' he stubbed a thumb at me – 'with your child-ambassador.'

When a clever man makes a mistake there is no excuse, and in the silence that suddenly appalled us, Parsons made none. He stood up. 'Yes, you have here your messenger from the Council.'

'Even though there was no letter, Father Parsons?' I said.

'Robert,' demanded Laurence, 'what have you done?'

'We would not have hurt him. He carries a verbal message. I cannot now prevent him from delivering it. May God give you peace, Caspar. And on you–' he smiled at me – 'on you, sir, I wish the sound of ghost-monks chanting at night among the ruins your grandfather helped to make.'

'If I hear them, Father Parsons, I will bless them and bid them go into the past; for they belong there.'

'Have you not noticed, Master Sidney? In twelve years, perhaps in twenty – so will you.' He grinned and left us.

When he had gone Father Laurence said, 'Philip, I am sorry for whatever violence he has practised. Give me the message.'

'Sir Francis Walsingham instructs me to offer you Ulmerstead if you will turn renegade and tell the Privy Council what you know.' It was his home in Yorkshire; and I pronounced the name as I had heard Sir Francis do, with the accent on the first syllable. 'We think your own people there – your family's people – remember you kindly and will keep you safe.'

'Ulmerstead,' he said softly. 'Yes, that was clever of him.' He blinked hard; I saw his cheeks were wet. 'Well: how long do you stay in this city?'

I rose. 'Until your lectures finish, and until – this other thing is finished too.'

'And am I to answer Walsingham through you?'

'You may: I hope to get back to Vienna by Christmas. It might be safer to entrust a letter to *Pan* Jan Zamoyski, under seal. Or use both means: one may fail.'

'Indeed. We'll talk again, then. Good day, Master Philip.'

In the corridor my servants straightened from their slouch against walls, palmed their dice in the hope I had not seen them, and formed a group around me. I did not speak to them. I now knew Parsons had sent the slasher of packs and the watcher by the cage. But I doubted that Caspar Laurence's misery had driven him to confide his dangerous plan to Parsons or to Cardinal William Allen: if he had spoken to them in Rome they would not have left him free, but would have imprisoned him in the English College, for his protection and their own. Whatever despair they had seen, therefore, and whatever they had deduced of its cause, they had taken some time to connect it with a message to Walsingham.

Then how had Parsons learned of Laurence's offer to the Privy Council? And who had told him I was the messenger?

Eleven

The ninth day passed since the disappearance at the Ancient Mass; then the tenth; then the eleventh.

Though Zamoyski had placed me under house-arrest, his kindness and Antony's (I was to abuse that kindness later) allowed me to move about the streets well-guarded. I did not attend Caspar Laurence's second lecture, though I meant to go to the third; but during the restless days I walked a good deal. Eight Polish servants surrounded me, and the crowds in Market Square did not molest me.

So far no riots had occurred in the city, although its mood was shifting. Though the streets were ill-policed – at dusk the Watch closed each thoroughfare with a chain as thick as a man's forearm, which would, I thought, stop a horse if not a thief – other business went on as usual. When I woke in the frosty dawns I would see the scavengers, sweeping with brooms of twigs and piling into carts the dung, animal and human, and the offal from Butcher's Market that had accumulated during the previous day. They had finished by the time the shops opened; so the streets were fairly clean for walking. Pigs and chickens did escape from private yards, and a day's traffic left horse-droppings that crossing-sweepers would sweep away for you for a penny. I saw no packs of feral dogs such as trouble most cities: if wild dogs bred, a patrol went out and killed them, so the streets of Kraków were free at least from this danger.

From my window also I could see the long arcaded block of

Cloth Hall, which smelt of new cement and stone-dust that made me sneeze. Masons balanced on top of ladders had begun the fifty-year labour of creating the gargoyle carvings: setting in stone, as is their privilege, their jokes at the expense of living citizens (among the caricatures sculpted thirty feet above me I thought I saw more than one Jan Zamoyski). Stone flowers and palm-fronds mixed with those demons the Poles believe in – Undines, basilisks, the knocker-spirits they say infest the mines – and with tiny, suspiciously vivid figures from the street outside: little bakers, monks, butchers and farmers, all in stone. Granite vines curled down the pillars that separated stall from stall.

In these shops I found the cloth for which the city was famous, and bought for my mother a black veiling damascened with gold and silver roses, and for my sister Mary a cramoisy velvet patterned with interweaving rings of gold. Antony had passed to me a packet of letters from home, as well as money from my father. My tale to Ludovic of having had no Court clothes as a boy was near enough true, though of course it does not mean we were ever really poor; but my father's service in Ireland *had* impoverished him, and even when my allowance had just arrived, I was never wealthy in those years. As for the letters, I could not bear to answer them except briefly and coolly. I hoped the gifts would make clear how much I still loved them.

Behind Mariacki Close lay Butcher's Market, where sides of new-killed pork hung in the frost, and pigs' heads lay displayed on trenchers. And all around me moved the crowd that used the square during the day: farmers selling the last of the autumn fruit from the back of their carts; the collapsible stalls of spice-vendors, the wheelbarrows of men who sold rags and old boots; the vendors of flour and vegetables and nuts. And the costers who carried their trays above the crowd's heads – trays of hot fruit pies, spiced sausage pies, or new bread wrapped in cloths. Around the square's edges stood the better or more necessary establishments – smithies and barber-shops, public roast-houses, jewellers and the sellers of fine weapons.

I possessed a few fine jewels that I could turn into money; and a pressure unwelcome to me, since in my unhappiness I grudged even the five minutes' work needed to relieve it, had begun to trouble me. From those days when we all waited – a suspense that, even in memory, stops the commotion in the square in a frozen succession of images – I remember women. All had dark yellow or brown hair and ivory skin reddened by the cold, and those clear intelligent eyes that show, in Polish women, so many shades of hazel – grey or green or topaz.

I remember one pretty woman of about thirty: a jeweller, whom I saw displaying a clock shaped like a little golden ship. When one turned the key, sailors climbed the rigging and tiny soldiers stood to their cannon. She was laughing over this toy with a customer. She had, I remember, a charming little broken nose, and paused in her laughter to cast me a shrewd glance.

I passed by her window, only to stop at the sight of a barefoot girl frying bread which she sold to passers-by. Next it was an exquisitely strong and graceful brunette who glanced at me over her father's gate as she threw barley to the hens; and after that a girl kneading bread behind a bake-shop window. She had caught back her hair in a square of white linen twisted into a knot, and she was thinking about someone else. I could tell by her smile; for there are some smiles so intimate they are like a kind of nakedness. I caught her at it, this smile. Startled by the intimacy she had let me see, she raised to me eyes of a clear pale green, and dropped them again when I could not help smiling back.

I must sound like a spy through windows. I did not mean to spy; and yet I glimpsed, through unshuttered windows, girls in the depths of their own houses, sweeping or spinning or reading. And one cold blue evening I passed a house where two women were nursing a sick old man. The square of brightness caught my eye, for it was full of a subtle, gentle light. On the settle the patient lay dozing on his pillows, his nurse beside him. The woman-apothecary had lit the fire and was grinding medicine in a mortar held between her knees. Fire cast its taffeta-shine into the dark, a cat glanced at me, its eyes winking like green jewels, and the woman's profile seemed so tender in its gravity that I winced away, disturbed by the privacy on which I had intruded.

When a young woman is outraged, our pity is mixed with lust; and I felt in all this crowd, those first days while we waited, this compassion mixed with lewd curiosity. No one uttered it aloud; and in retrospect I know that this excitement, foul as it was, gave us some reprieve. The nights wore by – nights of silence lit only by fire and stars; and days when the first ice rimed the windows. Necessity weaned us from shock: the need to live, to work, to eat, moved us again. Days passed in labour and in silence, and a chill appalled us. It was not shock this time, more like exhaustion.

Zamoyski's searchers found the cap. Excitement clenched us all and flung us down; for we knew – thousands of people knew – that there would be no further evidence. At first, I reflected, we had feared to find the skeletons of Maria and Yolanta. But as the days passed and frost curled the oak leaves, we had begun to *hope* they were, however damaged, yet fed and sheltered and alive.

After the finding of the cap no further word came. Endurance now enforced its own peculiar terror: the grief of knowing there will be no more. I thought: *The river is dragging us past it*. I could no longer remember Yolanta's face. The world closes itself over such sorrows every day.

A day came – about the tenth – when we all knew they were dead. I heard a choir practising in Sancta Maria, and saw two nuns dragging sheaves of pine-boughs through the doors. In the dimness beyond them, the triptych raised its great gold

What Dangers Deep

angels over Maria's mother's grave, and over the place where Maria had stood.

On the eleventh day I came home to find Dorotea in the solar. Antony, Ludovic told me, was in his study – I guessed, waiting till Dorotea should speak with me. If so it was by her choice, I thought, not Antony's. I pulled off my cap and greeted her.

She turned from the window: a beautiful crippled woman, the wholeness God had broken in her shining richly in the fall of her hair and in her great, brilliant eyes. 'Philip, my uncle has called off the search. There are no bodies, no tracks, no witnesses, no evidence beyond the cap; and there will be no more. They are dead. We will say Mass for them in Sancta Maria.'

I came to her and laid both hands on her shoulders. 'Dorotea, Adrian Firlei told me some things.' She closed her eyes, but opened them at the pressure of my hands. 'What will happen,' I said softly, 'if you *cannot* break?'

'Then I will break at last. When my stepmother used to weep, when Father died, I took both my sisters into my bed and held them through the nights. When Helena died in her turn I sat sleepless with Yolanta for, I think, sixty-eight hours. I loved our father; and with my sisters I am their flesh, as I am their death. I will live and conceive to Antony, since the living need us too. I will try, Philip. But when all we loved in our childhood has vanished into death, on that day we ourselves begin to die; and from that day there is never any returning. I expect to live some years. I will try to make Antony happy. Pray with me for a child.'

All this she had spoken too low for anyone to overhear. 'What can I do?' I demanded. 'For Antony's sake, Dorotea, do not conceive his child in despair.'

'I will live,' said her vehement soft voice. 'God will destroy me as he destroyed my father: impeccable in service, obedient to endure and love. For in this, Philip, we are God's betters, and can mock him and hate him. For the human mind can conceive of simple mercy, but the mind of God cannot. Let me go.' Gently she struck my hand aside, for Antony had come into the room.

In the courtyard where Adam Kózmian had died I saw a boy sweeping the cobbles. A woman who smiled at me bent to draw water from the well; and a party of men with buckets was attempting to reach the top-storey windows to wash them. Late afternoon had turned the sky a cold blue-violet. Smoke white as steam rose from the bath-house chimney.

A group of servants' children, boys and girls, were squatting over a game of marbles; a few adults had joined them to watch. I saw Robert Sellier, on one knee, his hands bare and his face almost as ruddy as his hair, shooting marbles with them. He looked up: I saluted him, and said to one of the Polish servants whom I found it difficult to avoid, 'Would you please bring a change of clothes to the bath-house for me?'

'Of course, sir.'

I thanked him and crossed the court towards the children, followed by my solitary guard.

Beside Sellier I hunkered down. 'How,' I said in the English my guard did not understand, 'does one get to join the game?'

In Polish he responded (a simple sentence, one I could follow if not speak it): 'Only if Mila here lends you some of her marbles.' The little girl giggled and shook her head doughtily; I grinned at her. The marbles were fine heavy ones, big enough to fill a child's palm – some blue, some green, some claret-coloured, and some clear with whorls of colour inside. The children had drawn a chalk-ring on the flagstones; one boy, flat on his belly, lay measuring his shot at the king-marble that sat in the centre.

In English I said, 'They have ended the search.'

'Then they had reason,' replied Sellier. '*Hey!*' This rebuked the boy's shot, and was ignored.

'Ambrose and Ludovic are watched. I must entreat your help.'

Sellier shrugged. Mila, who was about eight years old, relented and slipped into my hand a globe of yellow glass that shocked the skin like ice. 'Christ, these things are cold.' I blew a kiss at her. 'If the Ambassador dismisses you for this I will take you into my own service, or, if you choose to return home, I will engage to get you a place in my parents' house at a good wage. They can pay better than I, and they will do as I ask them.'

Over the musical, shrill voices of Polish children Sellier asked softly, 'And for what service is Sir Antony likely to dismiss me? You want to get out of the city?'

'Could you meet me about two in the morning at the flagpole on the other side of the river, with money, warm clothes and an extra horse?'

'If I had money, yes.'

'Be there. Getting across the city and out of it is my concern.' My guard was grinning at a girl across the court. Sellier's turn had come round. I corrected his shot, and he shook off my touch, having palmed the ring I had held closed in my fingers.

Sellier said something in Polish to the children. One girl objected, in the tone children reserve for adults they like, and subsided as he took his turn. Again the king-marble shot out of the circle. Behind us an extensible ladder stretched fragilely to its full height, and the man who was going to have to climb it expressed his doubts. Buckets of soapy water stood steaming on the cobbles.

'Robbers will cut your throat before you get half-way,' said Sellier, straightening.

I shrugged. 'I cannot abandon the women.'

'Then the Ambassador might dismiss me for letting you go alone. What will you need?'

'Two coils of rope, strong but supple, hidden in my room tonight.'

'You will find them. You know that, however little they have troubled you, *Pan* Zamoyski's spies have followed you ever since you came back to Kraków; that they are watching us now;

that you will be followed across town; and that they will track us to the Ancient Mass.'

'We may need them.' I smiled as my servant approached with the bundle of clothes. 'Turn the ring into money for food and fresh horses: we cannot risk sleeping at inns. Thank you, Sellier.'

He ignored me. His hand on Mila's shoulder, he was arguing with one of the boys. I went on into the bath.

That night when I lay down to sleep I found beneath my pillow the lumpy bulk of two coils of rope. For several hours I lay open-eyed, listening to the silence. My being guarded did not, I thanked God, extend to my own room. At last I judged it to be about one o'clock. I got up, dressed very warmly, and wrote to Antony:

> Forgive me. To keep faith with you I must accept that we will never find Yolanta and Maria. I cannot believe it: not unless I myself search again at the Ancient Mass. I owe them whatever service I can still give. If I live, I will come back to Kraków and bear whatever punishment you and my lord Zamoyski think good. Please pardon also the servant whose defection, done to protect me, is my fault, not his. I beg *Pan* Zamoyski to understand that my disobedience is my own act, and that I alone will answer for it.
>
> Farewell – I hope, only for a few days.
>
> Philip.
Forgive me.

I put this note where no one would find it for several hours. I filled two purses with money. One I hung around my neck inside my shirt; the other I clipped by a chain to my belt. I armed myself with sword and dagger, then knotted the shorter rope to the bedpost. The remaining coil I slung around my neck, along with my boots, tied together by their laces. Then I went in my stockinged feet to look down into the Close.

I saw no watchers; and in the well of darkness below me I hoped they might not see me if no light in my room gave me away. I returned to damp the fire, then put on my riding-gauntlets.

My window consisted of a transom set with clear glass roundels and, below that, of two panes that opened outwards. If I unlatched them I could get through. Cautiously I flung the window open and paid the rope down into the dark. Then – barefoot, my gauntlets taking the burn – I slid in one motion down on to the stone.

The moon, which had been full when I arrived at Kraków, was now in its first quarter: only the winter stars lit with their icy sparkle a darkness unrelieved, at this hour, even by house-lights. I could feel no one in the blackness immediately around me. Softly I drew my sword and stepped away from the rope. My feet were already aching with cold, but I moved without sound, and in so dense a blackness I might hope to get, unobserved and unhurt, to the city wall.

I began to run from black to black, dodging the blurs of starlight, and the primrose-and-crocus flicker of candles before roadside Madonnas. I slipped under a street-chain; from some niche above me doves called sleepily. The dark smelt of frost, of cooking, of ordure and clean hay.

From street to street I ran soundlessly, invisible in the strips of dark. Here and there a human being lay sleeping – homeless or drunk or dead, I would never know. A beggar-child, dozing with his mother in a doorway, lifted his head and stared at me. Half a street further on a man lay sprawled, spreadeagled in the starlight. I guessed the Watch would find him dead at first light, but I saw no sign of them now. Occasionally light still showed around the cracks of shuttered windows. Once I heard a man and woman screaming hate at each other, and shivered with casual dislike.

Two things almost detained me. I had won past the Church of Corpus Christi, and the Wawel rose palely-lit on my right, when I saw a glow: the flaring ruddy brightness of torches glimpsed from a distance. There was no fear of this group's noticing me, however. Surrounded by a ring of friends who held the torches, two men grappled, fighting on the ground. This was no prank, no challenge to the Watch. Not one voice called a jest or an encouragement, and the two enemies strained against each other in the silence of men who meant to kill. I slipped by around the edge of the light, and never knew the end of it.

I could now see the wall, and the tree that grew too close to it. Because Turkish raiders might do precisely what I intended, the city authorities had marked it with a whitewashed X for felling. I had noticed it some days before, for I had always guessed I might have to find my own way out of Kraków. If I could climb the tree, the second coil of rope would take me over the wall and on to the river-verge.

You will be followed across town, had said Robert Sellier. Undoubtedly Zamoyski maintained a spy among Antony's staff; had I chosen that spy to help me? I did need Sellier: without at least one helper, my survival outside the walls depended largely on passing unnoticed in the dark. If Sellier had turned informer and I found it necessary to kill him, I might travel at night and hide by day; but at that rate I would find Zamoyski's men at the Ancient Mass to welcome me.

A soft growl came out of the darkness. I stopped. Gradually, black from black, there emerged the shape of a dog five feet high: a hunting-beast that must have leapt a gate or otherwise escaped its kennel. I could scarcely see him, but could distinguish a huge head with cropped ears. This creature could kill.

I backed slowly. He did not move. If he followed me or attacked me I could use my sword, but I hoped to step gently out of whatever limit he was guarding, and so leave him satisfied. I faded back into the dark, and he proved content to watch me.

So I had to cut round by another street to get to the tree. Yes, it still stood. I climbed it easily. From the crook of its two main trunks I gazed for a few seconds out over the city, which maintained a meticulous silence.

My gauntlets took me from the tree down the wall. I landed on ground as hard as fired clay, but bare of snow or ice. Above me now rose the great sparkling courses of the wall which, on my right, turned at an angle into the full starlight. There I could see the nearest city-gate; from it came a sense of watchfulness. Trees clacked and hushed in the wind. Behind me lay a city of roofs and towers; above me the stars clustered, blinding white.

I stole a fishing-boat and crossed the river, crouching as low as I could. On the far bank I tied up my boat, so the owner would not have far to search for it. A hummock covered by bracken would lead me up a slope to the flagpole (or so I assumed it to be, though I had never seen it used for any purpose: a thirty-foot post that rose from a timber brace in the middle of the field). I began to run.

Twenty paces from the flagpole I stopped, my sword held ready. Out of the dark came a man leading two horses, and Sellier's voice said, 'Master Sidney?'

'Sellier?'

'I'm alone, sir. I've been walking the horses.' He came closer; I did not move. 'And I will not draw on you. You've noticed how rash you were to choose me? Never mind: the spy, I think, was Adam Kózmian. Here's your bridle. The bedroll also contains two changes of clothes. We'll get thinner, I promise you, on the rations I've packed.'

I mounted. For a moment we considered each other. 'I'm grateful, Master Sellier,' I said. 'I admit I *was* afraid of you; but it was a bad run across the city. I met Padfoot, and I'm still shaking.'

His horse sidled. 'Truly, sir?' he demanded seriously. Padfoot, whom we also call Black Shuck, haunts our English roads in the form of a black dog. The man who sees him need not hope to live long.

I grinned. 'No, *not* truly – not yet. I've an idea I was allowed to leave the city.'

'Why?'

'So we can lead Zamoyski to the evidence of my guilt.'

'Then let's ride. We'll find decent change of horses at the inns, but I think we should gallop straight through. Going hard enough, we could reach the Ancient Mass by late tomorrow.'

'I'd like to beat Zamoyski's men who will come to arrest me for breaking my parole. As for the Ancient Mass, I want to be alone there. I think I must dare the place, if I can do nothing more.' (Labrys, glimmering as I laid her in the earth.) 'And I want to go over the ground.'

'If bandits don't kill us we may beat out the lord Zamoyski, but you'll get nothing from it, sir: nothing but a quieting of your conscience.'

We settled into a canter, heading for the road. 'I think,' I said, 'I am seeking an end to it.'

Twelve

The sky rose bright and cold above us. From it fell snowflakes so puffed they were almost transparent. There was no wind.

Sellier frowned. 'The light's too high for my liking. An hour's search will bring us out at dusk.'

'Shall we wait another day, then?' I demanded.

It was not a question. Sellier's silence acknowledged the answer.

Frost had destroyed the colour and richness of the wood. Around us stretched the field where we had camped, its ruts and footprints frozen into such a barren chaos that I could only approximately guess where my tent had stood. But one thing, I saw, did remain. I drew my sword and walked towards it, Sellier following. The mud was mixed with trampled ash: horses and men had destroyed all our little hearths. With one exception: in all that desolation one core of cold ash remained, protected by a barrier: three logs set as benches in a circle.

Sellier and I stood staring at them. At last I said, 'Let us go to work.'

Frost crisped the leaves, which lay in drifts beneath our feet as we approached the path. Nor did we find the track difficult to follow. Beneath the delicate grey shadow of the trees the pathway to the Ancient Mass lay grooved by the searchers six inches deeper than when I had last seen it. It too was an obstacle-course of ruts and prints. Above us hissed a few yellow leaves. The trees that had on that first day closed us off so abruptly from the camp had gone bare – trunks and branches laced into a smoky tangle of dun and grey and silver. The place was quiet: one could feel that many men had been there, and had departed.

'Dusk will fall earlier in here,' said Robert Sellier. I nodded. 'How long will it take us to search the Grove?'

'That depends on how minutely we choose to look. They have dragged the pool: I have no thought of meddling with that. To look about may take us only a few minutes.'

'Very well; but there is nothing lord Zamoyski's men have not touched, have not searched. They even climbed the cliff and looked among the pines at the top.'

'I know.'

'And Sir Antony was telling me – perhaps he did not mention it to you – that the Abbot of the Bernardine monastery that lies a mile down the road even sent his own search-party to investigate.'

'Did he perform an exorcism?'

Sellier smiled slightly. 'Would you believe in a Romish exorcism, sir?'

'That's not what I asked you,' I replied. He did not flinch at my tone. 'I'm sorry, Sellier. I would feel much better if he *had*.'

'Well, I don't know whether he did. But there's no need, sir: there is no one here.' We had come within sight of the apple-trees and the rowans. 'The place is empty,' said Robert Sellier.

And indeed it seemed so. The after-feel of the searchers soured the quietness. Wind woke small normal sounds around us; the air had grown colder. In the bright, remote light of late afternoon we gazed down among the ancient trees into the dell. Here too the leaves had fallen, and small creatures had sunk into their winter sleep. The water lapped cold brown, and shadow fell from the height of the cliff; but the pines were still dark green, and the moss, though a little yellowed, still smouldered with colour.

'Let's go down,' I said.

'As you wish.' Sellier, like me, held his drawn sword.

What Dangers Deep

We descended warily, moving among the trunks. Here lay the apple-tree with the split-off arm. 'It was here they found the cap, sir,' remarked Sellier.

'This tree?'

'Yes, sir.'

I stared up into its branches. Of all the trees in the Grove, it alone had emerged with delicate naturalness from my first impression of the place; it alone I had remembered as an individual. I saw Sellier's startled, questioning eyes, but I shrugged. 'I suppose we can do little but walk among the trees and observe whatever we can. Will you go that way, towards the stream?' He nodded. 'I agree, dusk will fall early here. It seems after all there is little we can do. Let's walk a bit, and then we must go back.'

'Back to our reckoning at Kraków.' Sellier frowned. 'Yes, I'll scout towards the stream. You know that all the original prints you made, you and the ladies – all traces you left have been destroyed.'

'Yes, the searchers have torn the ground apart.' The resonance troubled me: I remembered my father's voice saying: *Why should gold slumber in the dark, when poor people could use it to buy food?* 'We'll meet back here, and unless I cut into the undergrowth over there–' I pointed to the left, where a tangle of bushes obscured the far side of the pool – 'I'll not be out of sight or call. Take good care.'

'And you also.' And so we parted.

I strolled through the trees. Shadow now slanted further up the trunks: the light was moving. Here was the spot where I had knelt. The water looked cold. Someone had cleared away the wrack of leaves, leaving visible the brown slimed stones. Of course: Zamoyski's party had dragged the pool.

'Nothing here, sir,' came Sellier's voice.

'Nor here.' I raised my voice the little that was necessary – the place was small and quiet. 'Did they search the far edge of the pool – that bank between the water and the cliff?'

'I told you: they climbed the cliff. As for the trees above, we won't have enough light for that – not today.'

'No, there I agree with you. Well, I'll press through the bushes and search the far rim. Then I'll come back.'

'You'll find me sitting under a tree, Master Sidney: I've found nothing.'

I had reached the leftmost tip of the crescent-thickness of the Grove. Here the trees whose ancestors the Bear People had planted came to an end, fading into undergrowth towards the cliff. I waded into the bushes, swearing as some wand lashed my hand. I sucked blood from my fingers. The haze around me was turning blue.

The bushes yielded to the slight rise of moss-encrusted boulders – most of them, it occurred to me, probably fallen from the cliff-wall – which formed the margin between the pool and the rock-face. The precipice rose on my left, its quilting of fragrant green torn by the feet of the searchers. The wall, I realized now, swelled a little outwards about fifteen feet above the ground; and yes, the boulders, though settled and softened by vegetation, had clearly fallen. The scooped rock cast a shadow whose cool, as I climbed up over the stones, preserved a faint summer sweetness.

The snowflakes began again. I squinted upwards, wondering a little, for the sky was clear.

And so I found her almost at my feet, as still as one of the boulders: a shape marmoreal, natural and, in the first dusk, almost impossible to see. A woman, her arms and hair outflung, her knees doubled up against her chest.

I suppose I had expected it. With the little gasp one gives at the actual presence of what one has dreaded, I knelt beside her. Snow had fallen on her hair; her skin shone like a pearl through the blue-green shadows.

I succeeded at the third effort in calling calmly, 'Sellier!'

'Sir? I'm coming.'

'Then run. I have found the lady Maria.'

What Dangers Deep

* * *

'Oh, Christ's mercy,' whispered Robert Sellier. 'Is she alive?'

'There is a pulse at her throat, but her skin is very cold. Give me your cloak and help me lift her.'

He tore off his cloak, as I had already done with my own, and with them we made a layered blanket. Maria's limbs flexed when we touched her. Her skin, it distressed me to see, did not contract into gooseflesh at the cold. Her clothes were gone: she wore only a white voile shift; beneath it I could see that she was naked.

Working gently and with speed, we lifted her and wrapped her in the cloaks, both of which were lined with fur. Her head I covered as much as I could, swathing the cold hair into folds of velvet still warm from my own body. Her lips were pink, her eyes closed into the privacy of profound unconsciousness.

I rose with her in my arms; she and the cloaks together made a bulky, heavy bundle. 'Now the twilight is coming down, and we must move. We will ride with her to the Bernardine monastery: surely the Brother Infirmarer will care for her if she can be saved. Then you must go for my lord Zamoyski.'

And so we carried Maria from the Grove – and found, waiting mounted in the field, thirty cavalry dressed in Jan Zamoyski's colours.

I called across to them. Their captain dismounted and came running towards me, his errand and my arrest abrogated by what he saw. 'Help me take her to the monastery,' I said to him. 'I will stay with her while the Brothers care for her. Then take Sellier with you and ride back to Kraków. Tell my lord Zamoyski to come himself, and to bring Caspar Laurence – and Doctor Solniecki, of course.'

'Why Caspar Laurence, my lord?' demanded the captain.

'Because he is the best doctor presently in Kraków, and a witness I hope many people will believe. Doctor Solniecki may be glad to have him there.' I mounted; the man lifted Maria up into my arms.

She did not wake during the ride. I dreaded that the jolting would force her deeper into unconsciousness; but she was still breathing when the monks took her from us. Sellier shook my hand and, with the captain and fifteen men, rode back to Jan Zamoyski at Kraków.

In a whitewashed room whose windows showed ultramarine with dusk, the Abbot and the Infirmarer shut out everyone but me. 'Stay with us, Master Sidney,' said the Abbot. 'You are the only available representative of *Pan* Zamoyski her guardian, and we must all stand witness for each other as a precaution. Markus–' to the Infirmarer – 'make your examination quickly. I'll build up the fire; we must keep her warm.'

'I'll have her under blankets as quickly as possible,' replied Brother Markus. 'Master Sidney, come close: I shall require your corroboration.' He lifted one of Maria's hands. 'Her hands have suffered scratches. Her pulse is strong, and she does not seem wasted by hunger. Good God, what can have happened to her clothes? Her hair is untangled, and her face is clean.'

'So is the shift,' I said. I noticed now that it was unstained and untorn.

'No blisters on her feet,' continued the Infirmarer. 'She has not been wandering in the forest – not walking at all, I should guess, since someone took her shoes. There are no cuts on her feet.'

Warmth flared behind us; the Abbot returned. The Infirmarer said, 'Master Sidney, gently lift her shoulders, please. I must strip off the shift and preserve it exactly as we have found it. It grieves me for her sake that we have no woman here to help us, but let us simply be quick. One thing, however, I cannot determine until my lord Zamoyski arrives. There.'

I lifted Maria. Softly he pulled off the garment and handed it to the Abbot, who folded it and observed, 'No earth, no blood. And it is not torn. Strange. I will lock this in the chest in my office until I can give it to *Pan* Zamoyski.'

Her naked body was unmarked. 'No one has bruised her

breasts. Poor lady,' murmured Brother Markus. 'There, let us turn her gently. Her back and buttocks are unmarked. At a cursory examination I see no blood between her thighs. Yes, thus, lay her on her back.' The flesh I handled was chilled, but solid with unwasted muscle and not, I thought, profoundly cold.

The Infirmarer with great gentleness palpated her belly: she gave no sign of feeling it. 'Poor child. She seems not to be in pain. I cannot tell whether anyone has raped her. There are no gross signs.'

'That is for my lord Zamoyski and the doctors he may appoint,' said the Abbot. 'Let us keep her very warm. I am glad Caspar Laurence is coming.'

And so we finished. The Abbot took me, unwilling though I was, to a bath and supper; and then I returned to Maria's room, to nurse her through the night with Brother Markus.

In the huge expanse of the Princess Anna's bedchamber, with its tiles of red and white agate and its roundels of clear glass, Maria lay with her hands bandaged. On the ceiling above our heads the carver had stamped the letters IHS and a cross in gold into every beam. I saw little furniture: a hold-all cabinet, its teak-wood doors inlaid with roses and tulips made of lemon-yellow woods. For the rest, I noticed a fireplace in which the servants had set three great logs to burn. A carpet of indigo and green, soft as coarse velvet to the touch, covered the only table.

The bed rose from its pineapple-carved posts to a tester of blue velvet worked with bullion; the quilt that covered Maria was made of ivory brocade. And I had watched – crying as casually and unstoppably as a child – while Anna and Dorotea had eased her into a white velvet nightgown. They combed out over the pillow the hair they dared not yet wash, and added, for warmth, a cap of ermine, its strings knotted lightly beneath her chin.

So Maria lay, ignoring us in an unconsciousness so vehement that occasionally I saw her forehead crease in a frown – turned from us utterly into some dialogue of the soul against which, with grimaces and slight motions of the head, she seemed occasionally to protest. The frown would deepen to distress; then smooth, as though someone had touched her forehead; and her flare of relief, of comprehension – still guarded from us by the tight-shut eyes – would blend into a converse more remote, and thence, I thought sometimes, into sleep.

'Is it coma?' demanded Antony.

'No.' Caspar Laurence drew his stool closer to his patient's bed. 'Or I should hesitate to call it so with certainty. I think it is exhaustion, combined with some deep dream. She is *working*, can you not see? But working at what, and with whom? Dreams so deep can shade into coma and death. But she swallowed the last drops of broth I gave her. Over the next twenty-four hours I want her fed meat-broth, not too hot, out of a baby's cup – can you find one? A clay cup with a pipe for the child to suck from.'

Zamoyski nodded. 'You can get them in the market-place.'

'Send a servant to find one or two. I want them in half an hour. And coffee, which I will boil myself, must be fed gently into her as long as she can swallow it safely. She can last without food, and coffee and broth will give her water, and keep her perhaps from slipping deeper.'

'And her condition, Father Laurence?' said Jan Zamoyski.

We moved away from the bed – Caspar Laurence, Antony, Solniecki and I. Laurence said: 'Her condition was competently noted by the Brother Infirmarer. The marks on her hands are indeed scratches – as if she had fought something, or had had to tear her way through a thornbush. Her feet bear no such marks. She is not wasted from twelve days' lack of food, and she bears little trace of exposure to the elements. She has not fallen or been thrown from the top of the cliff: both bones and internal organs seem to be intact. No one appears to have handled her breasts – at least they were not crushed; and the womb is sound as far as I can judge. She has not been beaten.'

What Dangers Deep

After that he shut us out of the room, keeping only Dorotea and the Princess as witnesses.

Presently Laurence came out to us. 'My lord Zamoyski, she is virgin intact, and no one has wounded her womanly parts, either externally or internally.'

'God be thanked, at least, for that.' Zamoyski crossed himself. 'Philip, I release you from your arrest.'

Down in the city a clangour had begun: brass and silver softened by distance stammered out what was, what must be joy. The bells of Saint Stanislas, of Sancta Maria; the bells of the Bernardines, of King Zygmunt's Chapel, of Corpus Christi and Sanct' Anna had begun to ring out their exultation at the rescue of Maria. Today men and women had tossed bouquets over the walls of the Princess's garden. And in Sancta Maria and in the Chapel Royal, candles of thanksgiving glowed in cups of ruby and emerald glass, and citizens plaited wreaths out of pine-boughs and vines and brown winter flowers – everything they could offer at the altars.

And then, during the hour we watched by her bedside, it changed. None of us, Zamoyski's and Antony's households included, had yet dared to leave the Wawel. They had given me a chamber where I could bathe and eat the food I did not want; for servants had brought up my things from Antony's house.

Among them came Robert Sellier. 'He's keeping me on, sir. He is not angry: he thinks I did rightly.'

'I'm glad,' I said. 'But remember my promise: it still stands. I'll talk with you when she is well. And tell me what the city thinks, if you can.' We shook hands again, and parted for that time.

Maria was now swallowing both broth and coffee, though she seemed as unconscious of this as a baby suckling in its sleep. Laurence watched her constantly, and as the water and nourishment and heat began to reach her, her cheeks changed from tallow-colour to a clear ivory. Still she did not wake; and we could only wait for her.

I heard the bells stop, and knew what it meant. *Yolanta has not been found. Only one? Only Maria?* Over the first day the ragged clangour died, and I could feel the violence of the city's disappointment. The crowd moved below Castle Hill – talking in small groups in the market-place; gate-wardens giving the news to farmers come with their carts from the country; artisans conversing quietly, with greater sophistication; and, behind shuttered windows, colloquies we could not hear.

Where was Robert Parsons, I wondered – and had he appealed to Caspar Laurence a second time? Certainly Laurence's new commitment to Maria would hold him here, safe for a while from the English College and from the Privy Council.

On the second day Daniel Balinski rode southwards towards the mountains with two thousand cavalry: Turkish and Hungarian raiders – also some masterless men – had been taking slaves on the border. Kraków cheered him as he passed by, and then settled towards Advent.

I heard the bells cease, and knew why. 'They will turn angry,' I said to Zamoyski. 'If she can tell them nothing, then they may turn on her.'

'Or on each other,' replied the Chancellor. 'I will not fear for Maria until she has wakened, if she does, and we have searched her memory. But last night five men were knifed in a brawl in the square; a dormitory for poor scholars was set on fire – a loss to the University that I will make good out of my own purse; and in a cellar at Collegium Maius thirteen men – I have their names – drew a pentagram and invoked the dead Yolanta, and when she did not manifest to them, they bricked up a cat alive into a wall.'

'Can nothing be done?' I demanded. 'Is not the Cardinal-Archbishop the *interrex*: the king when there is no king?'

'The Cardinal-Archbishop is old and timid, and no one obeys him. Each great family – Zborowski, Firlei, Balinski – will keep order as we can. But Poland, Philip, lies huge and unguarded beyond the capital. Someday I want you to see the mountains –

the wild country we must patrol. Make no mistake: Balinski does this well. And I want you to look out over Hungary, into the world – Islam – that believes *we* are the infidel. Daniel Balinski, like most men, desires a world in which he will get all the power he can. Islam has not only its Faith, but appetite and means: it too will take all that it can get. Sultan Selim died four days ago.'

'Will Murad not want peace to the north?'

'Yes – under an experienced soldier with whom he can deal.'

'Then take the kingship for yourself.'

'No. There is one better man; and–' he turned away from me with a faint, frowning smile – 'only a lunatic would attempt to rule five million Poles alone, Philip. Some men long for colleagues – for fellowship. If I could find such a man, I would serve him. Understand me: Kraków is shaken, not only by the events at the Ancient Mass, but by the wars we can perhaps win but never end: against Russia, Denmark, Islam. The King must work: he must teach us to believe we can take up the burden of war again. He must police, he must tax, he must administer. He must dominate the nobles. But above all he must secure us against war; and he must do it soon.'

When Maria had lain for four days in a profound but stable sleep, Zamoyski said, 'Will she come back to consciousness, Father Laurence, or turn away from us, and sink more deeply into it and die?'

'I think her body has its own desire to live,' said Laurence. 'Food – even such as I have given – and rest, cleanliness and love may hold her here. It seems a restless, unbreakable sleep, unlike any other condition I have seen.'

'Then I want to remove her most gently, after dusk, in a litter to my house. She has only one sister now. Let her wake or die in her own room.'

'The mob may attack her, even if they mean no harm,' said Antony. 'If they want to touch her, to see her—'

'My pikemen will not let them near, and a cordon of cavalry will flank the men on foot. I can make a safe route for her.'

'Then let me ride in the litter with her,' said Caspar Laurence. 'It is not good to move her yet; but if she wakes, it should indeed be in a room she knows.'

It was therefore with a line of Zamoyski's cavalry on either side, and with pikemen pressed against the watchers, that we carried shoulder-high a silent bed. The cold rich colour of evening had come down. I could not interpret the muted sounds of the crowd, or their faces in the torchlight. Respect and tenderness for the unconscious woman – this I felt in them; and something else: the change that had stopped the ringing of the bells.

Suddenly Dorotea exclaimed, 'The shift: Antony, I forgot the shift.'

'Where did you leave it?' demanded my godfather.

'Wrapped in silver paper on the chest at the foot of the Princess's bed.'

'I'll ride back and get it,' I said.

Zamoyski nodded. 'Do so, Philip, please.'

I turned, taking care to show no haste, out of the cavalcade, rode back up the alley of pikemen, and took the path up Castle Hill. Shapes rose in the darkness: the greenly-glowing windows of the Chapel Royal; a courtyard where servants and men-at-arms still moved by torchlight; and the huge main court with its three-tiered loggia. Here the Princess Anna had bidden us good-bye. 'I will come to see her tomorrow, if you will let me,' she had said to Zamoyski, and, with a smile of explanation to me, 'Now I cannot, for I have promised to talk with a friend.'

Up, then, through halls tiled with black and white marble, among the echoes, past lines of halberdiers to whose captains (they had seen me leave only a while before, and under Zamoyski's patronage) I stated my errand. All of them let me pass up the shallow steps that led to the Princess's apartments on this level.

The guards in the first antechamber let me by. In the second antechamber a woman-in-waiting, pressed up against the wall, was kissing a man who did not see me.

And so – soothed by my haste – with inexcusable discourtesy I walked into the Princess Anna's bedroom. For days we had come and gone as we needed to; and she had said she would be busy.

She was there, seated on the bed, across from a man I had never seen before. Between them lay spread Maria's shift, which the man was touching and examining. No sensuality linked them: only the arrogance of startled eyes, and the fact of their being there at all. I had surprised them in a privacy whose depth lay thus inadvertently exposed; and they had, I saw, been talking about Maria.

'Master Sidney?' said the Princess.

'Madam, I came for the shift. I thought from what you said you would be elsewhere. Please do not be angry with me.'

'I'm not angry. Here is the paper; I'll wrap it for you.'

'Thank you, madam.'

'And now, I think,' said the Princess, 'I must introduce you to my friend.'

The man wore a black robe lined with wolf-fur, and now rose to his full height of six feet five inches. He was younger by a decade than the Princess, and wore his yellow-blond hair cut short. That and his clean-shaven cheeks (Alexander the Great once remarked that a beard only offers a handhold to the enemy) and his trained grace made it clear he was a soldier. I already knew before he said in an easy, literate Latin, 'Master Sidney, I am Stefan Bathóry.' I dropped to one knee. 'No, rise, please. You have noticed the Castle's river-entrance?'

'The escape-door, sir, known as the Dragon's Cave?' I remembered it: a grilled door flush with the stone of Wawel Hill, several hundred feet from the Castle's summit. A shallow grotto hid it in shadow; it might have been the door to a cellar or a storage-room; and it let directly on the river.

'Yes,' said Bathóry: 'Passages cut down to it through the hill.'

'It's well-hidden, sir: everyone can see it.'

'There are other tunnels also, that bore under the city walls and emerge in the fields. I came in by one such way last night; I will be gone in several hours. Yes, the people in the palace have seen me: a rumour in the city will not displease me, but I must ask that it not come from you.'

'Of course not, sir.' He had been here, then, some part of twenty-four hours. When – all our attention focused on Maria, and all my exhausted feelings on my own affairs – my elders on the periphery came and went, it must have been not to sleep, but – at least for Zamoyski and Anna – to confer with this man.

'My own people brought me word ten days ago about the Ancient Mass,' said the Prince. 'And I received the news of Maria's rescue two days ago. I know her, of course, though not well – her uncle is my friend.'

He was the biggest man I have ever seen, taller even than my uncle Robert of Leicester; and the handsomest, with a large-boned, comely face. The eyes of most fair-skinned people are in fact blue-grey, but his were a warm actual blue, and conveyed an intense, intelligent kindness. Yet he seemed to me neither simple nor accessible, and I should have feared to face his anger.

He said softly, '*"Then shall two be in the field: the one shall be taken, and the other left. Two women shall be grinding at the mill: the one shall be taken, and the other left."*'

I felt gooseflesh contract my skin. Stefan Bathóry gazed down at me, as if he could not decide whether to spend more time on me; then abruptly he said, 'Will you sit down, Master Sidney, and talk with me a while?'

'If you want them not to grow suspicious, my lord, I cannot stay long. But yes, most gladly.'

He sat down on Anna's bed. Ruffling her skirts in a gesture that conveyed she would be further from us if she could, she settled on the far side. I again sank on one knee before the

What Dangers Deep

Prince. He smiled. 'I said please sit, Master Philip: I am not King of Poland.' I obeyed. 'Who sent you back for the shift? Was it Jan?'

'Yes, my lord.'

'Excuse my asking. It simply occurs to me that, with getting Maria safely through the crowds and settling her into bed, they will not even think of you for an hour. I doubt they remember you have gone.'

I nodded. 'That's likely enough.'

Báthory glanced sidelong at me. 'I have heard King Philip of Spain speak of you.'

'How could he, sir? I cannot have been more than three years old when he saw me last.'

Prince Stefan smiled. 'I always find it interesting when an adult remembers so slight a meeting with a child. It implies something unusual about both. And the late Queen Mary Tudor loved you too.' (Had King Philip told him this? Certainly my mother has said the same.) 'I have heard she longed for a son, poor lady; and it occurs to me, seeing you now, that her friend – your mother – *bore* that son, and called him Philip. I suspect Queen Mary chose your name.'

'They called her Merciful Mary when she first rode into London. Four years later they were calling her Bloody, and so she will always be remembered. Need you burden me with my godparents, sir? I like neither.'

'No: it is impertinent to lay that burden on the young, I agree.' He smiled faintly: I suppose my own gaze was, at best, impatient and puzzled. 'And yet you are part of stories you do not know. In many ways, I think, our parents have lived most of their lives by the time they engender us, and they see us in terms of a dialogue they never describe to us – with their own childhood and with the dead.' I straightened my shoulders: I saw Báthory note the motion. He said, 'Does your soul tell you Yolanta is dead?'

'Yes, my lord.'

'Do you know the story of Cassandra, Master Sidney?'

I nodded. 'She was the Trojan princess whom Apollo loved, and who refused to lie with him. To punish her he gave her the gift of prophecy, but condemned her never to be believed. King Agamemnon took her as his slave and prize of war, and carried her back to Greece, where his wife killed her.'

'That is the common understanding of the ancient sources, yes. But you know, I find I cannot agree with it.'

'How is that, my lord?'

'Because it seems to me that the secret about Cassandra is not that Apollo condemned her never to be believed: Cassandra should never expect to be believed. The secret is that the god *did* love her.'

'*I* should not trust such love,' I said.

'It helped to kill Cassandra, I think,' replied Prince Stefan. Princess Anna bowed her head. The Prince resumed. 'Yolanta has gone beyond our help. I shall not be here when Maria recovers enough to understand what life she must live, every day of her life henceforward.'

'*What* life, sir?' I said. 'I know she will grieve for her sister. Can she not survive that? Others must.'

His gaze assessed me, though mildly. 'Do you truly not understand me?' he demanded. I did not answer, but held my eyes steady on his. 'Let us say the informal tribunal evolving in Kraków – for there is a court of judgement here – acquits her of lying if she cannot remember. Most of us hate what denies us satisfaction. She must give them satisfaction if she can.'

'So *Pan* Zamoyski and I have feared – if she wakes.'

'It might be better if she died. If she wakes and survives interrogation, then a memory – even of brutality – would be more endurable than whatever touched you and the servingman in the Grove.'

Fifteen minutes, had guessed a man not thirty yards from me: *for fifteen minutes we could not find the path*.

What Dangers Deep

'I know the Grove was holy to the ancient people,' I said. 'But what power they left there must be unlawful to a Christian.'

'What does Yolanta care?' replied Stefan Báthory.

'My lord Prince, do you mean to terrify me? Why render this thing into its most impossible and most suspect form?'

'Because I am probably wrong. I should simply be happier if only *you* had experienced an aberration of Time, and not the groom as well. If Turkish raiders came, they vanished strangely. Most likely the culprit was the land itself: limestone and water make for treacherous ground.'

'How can I help her?' I demanded.

Prince Stefan shrugged. 'I doubt you will be in Poland long enough to help her, Master Sidney. Crowds are volatile, but they have short memories. Nothing has yet been certainly broken here – except, perhaps, Maria. I hope I meet you again, Master Sidney. If I never do, I wish you scope for your gifts, and happiness.' He held out his hand. 'Goodbye.'

He had finished with me. I accepted the parcel for which I had come; bowed to Her Highness, and more deeply to the Prince; and left them alone together.

And I did not succeed in isolating until later the second impression they had left in my mind: of a man and a woman standing together, their hands arrested in a motion of touching, for fear that I should see. And I thought: *She is in love with him; and only through her can her brother's royalty descend. If Poland gives him the Kingship, he will marry her.*

Thirteen

After Zamoyski released me from my arrest I went home to the Embassy and slept for nineteen hours. Then I rose, ate, bathed and wrote – to my own astonishment and without conscious plan – a letter to my mother telling her all that had led me to the Ancient Mass, and in what state Maria now lay. I asked her please to tell my father and my uncle of Leicester, as I had not the strength. The letter left me empty: not the vital, exhilarated emptiness of release, but a stoic and ominous coldness.

I had never before confronted, even in intimation, the price of maturity. As I finished dressing I looked at my face in the mirror. The barber had combed my hair forward in the ragged points then fashionable; I had shaved off months ago the young moustache whose stubble Veronese had the unkindness to record when he painted me in Venice. But beneath my cheekbones the flesh had sunk, and weariness or sorrow had dragged the mouth downwards at the corners.

Will my face set like this? I thought. Secretive and severe it gazed out at me. In the double shadow of glass and candlelight there hovered, confronting me, a man it shocked me to think I might become.

Before I went to see whether Maria had wakened, I walked to the Jesuit College where Ambrose had told me Father Parsons was staying. I wanted, simply and without hope, to ask a question.

The Fathers received me courteously; and presently into the parlour came the ugly, vital man I had last seen in Caspar

Laurence's room. 'Master Sidney,' he said, with a geniality I had not expected. 'How can I serve you? Will you take wine?'

'Of course, Father Parsons. Thank you.' He poured for us both, and gestured me to a chair by the fire. 'I doubt,' I said, 'whether you will wish to serve me, Father Parsons. I can offer you only a gift of information, and that has now no value. I *am* the Privy Council's courier.' He nodded. 'I want to know who informed you of that fact.'

'Assuming William and I did not guess in Rome?'

'If you guessed Father Laurence's intent when you saw him in Rome, you acted strangely slowly.'

'So we did; so we did.' One hand, white and freckled, rasped his upper lip. 'It appears, then, that you have a second enemy. You will naturally wish to defend yourself. I will give you the information, Master Sidney, although it violates confidence to a degree I do not like, if you will do one thing for me. You have delivered your message. Do not make a friend of Caspar Laurence.'

It violates confidence. Not a hired enemy, then: someone had confided in this priest. I said, 'Father Laurence has not offered me his friendship. I doubt he would wish to befriend a man so young, and one confessedly estranged from him in religion.'

'Probably not; but he is lonely and afraid. He need not fear *me*, though you will not believe it.'

'Of what, then, Father Parsons,' I said, 'is he afraid?'

Parsons sighed. Once again – as though Laurence, not I, sat before him – I saw him frown with a sort of haggard tenderness. 'Master Sidney, let us say you held a rock – one cracked by a hairline fault the eye can scarcely see. Now strike that stone with a hammer. Where will it break open?'

'Along the hidden fault, Father Parsons.'

'And so it is with men.' He set his wine-cup delicately aside.

'I do not understand you,' I said.

'Master Sidney, some Christian men have no hope, no joy in God. For a man who loves God, this state is a great torment.' I nodded cautiously. 'And yet,' Parsons resumed, 'and yet it is not a sin. To be joyless and hopeless in the yearning of love is an affliction of God's giving: it is not our fault.'

'Does Father Laurence, then, somehow believe himself to be in sin?'

'I am not sure. Leave him to me: I mean him only good. If William and I take him by force, which I do not want to do, it will be to comfort and protect him while he heals. Your errand being discharged, do not frequent him, sir.'

'In short,' I said, 'you want him reserved to your influence – not to mine? Nor to the influence of those who offer him his manor-house and the right to die in the place where he was born?'

'If that is the true bargain, yes. Leave him alone and I will tell you the name of the man who informed me of Caspar's correspondence with the Privy Council, and of your part in this.'

I rose. 'I cannot give you what you want, Father Parsons. I intend to see Father Laurence again: he knows something that may help Maria Zamoyska.'

Parsons nodded and pushed back his chair. 'Then I regret I cannot help you. Good day, Master Sidney.'

I have a good memory, and on my walk home (my Polish servants still moving in a protective group around me), I rehearsed this conversation. It seemed Parsons had not paid for his information: to barter it would *violate confidence*. Confidences given to a Roman priest, I knew, were sacred within the confessional. Yet he had offered barter, if on terms I could not meet. A confidence, then, that was human, not confessional.

Who in Kraków had means to know much about me? Jan Zamoyski. Startled, I realized that I had assumed his complete awareness of my secrets from some point before Sellier had spoken of his spies. Sellier too had taken for granted Zamoyski's access to such information.

Yet I could form no link between Zamoyski and Robert Parsons – no link I could understand.

My uncle has a vein of indiscretion strange in so wise a man. Suddenly the rich, controlled voice of Dorotea occurred to my memory. And with it came the unobtrusive precision of the clue Parsons had tried to deny me. 'Leave him alone and I will tell you the name of the man who informed me.'

No direct link need connect any indiscretion of Jan Zamoyski's to Father Parsons. A go-between had chosen to repeat something intercepted, overheard, or read by stealth. And that person had been – Parsons' unstressed precision suddenly inverted itself with the relief of certainty – no man at all, but a woman.

A woman, then, whom Zamoyski trusted, with whom he might be less than cautious: a member of his household; a friend often there.

His niece Dorotea Marshall.

Or his niece Maria Zamoyska.

I did attend Father Laurence's next lecture. It amused me to see that the gallants from the town had vanished, that all the professors, including Doctor Pasek, persevered, and that the number of students had diminished by about one-third. On this occasion Laurence did not single me out for special notice; nor, I think, did the reduced size of the class surprise him.

Once again Adrian sat beside me. Beyond greeting me, he made no other comment until, leaning towards me, he whispered, 'I rescued the cat.'

'The cat?' Abruptly I remembered. I had once seen, taken from the wall of an ancient cottage my father had ordered demolished, the three-hundred-year-old mummy of such a sacrificial beast: a chicken, its beak open wide, its claws locked, and its skin desiccated into identity with the eggs it had expelled in the terror of its dying I do not know why people used to brick living animals into the foundations of houses: I suppose so their poor ghosts could protect their tormentors.

'I took two men I trust, and unbricked the wall. We set the

poor thing free next night, after feeding it and warming it by the fire.'

'That was kind,' I said. 'Were you afraid?'

'Of *them*?' He indicated with a thumb the students rustling their notes. 'I'd like a fight, if it comes to that. They've begun to bait me – about men whose priests are lechers that bed with nuns.' (Martin Luther, the German reformer and hero of our Faith, repudiated the celibacy of clergy and married, I think, a former nun.) 'And magic doesn't frighten me, or not much. I saw no demons as I unbricked the wall.'

'I hate cruelty to creatures that have no voice to cry with. To torture them is sinful and ignoble,' I said.

'Whereas there is no pleasure more permissible than punishing a man who differs from oneself. There are more Catholics than Protestants here today.'

'And down in the city?'

'The same. All Poles loathe all other Poles, Philip, until a common enemy forces unity upon them. There is no king, no rule. The Protestant minority are beginning to be afraid. And Yolanta's death means,' said Adrian, 'that someone killed her.'

'Gentlemen . . .' Caspar Laurence's voice ended our conversation. I glanced around, and happened to see one young man, his face watchful with a defensive arrogance. Something had scored his cheek open, covering the right one with four raking parallel scabs.

Antony, returning exhausted with Dorotea, told me that night that Maria seemed stable and in no present danger, and that she had not wakened.

'May I go to see her?' I demanded.

'Yes. Her Highness said to tell you. She and Dorotea, Doctor Solniecki and Father Laurence all take turns around the bed; but I *must* go back to my work, and we must watch Maria all through the twenty-four hours, in case she wakes. Yes, the Princess asked if you would help.'

'Most gladly.'

'Thank you, Philip,' said Dorotea, and gave me her hand. Then she went upstairs, she and Antony supporting each other, her head on her husband's shoulder.

From the moment of her sisters' disappearance, I reflected, she had taken care not to neglect Antony or any duty in her new home. Neither – though I seldom glimpsed their effort – had they let this grief tear apart the union they were labouring to build. I found Dorotea busy, courteous, controlled and warm. Sometimes, however, I noticed she had been crying; and Antony's hand on her shoulder, on the evenings when we shared supper at home, would sometimes stop her in the shadows for an exchange of words I could not hear, or for a kiss that seemed to delight them both. Whatever Maria's need, Antony insisted that Dorotea come back each night to the relief and comfort of his bed; and there I hoped he did not spare her.

In her own bedroom Maria lay surrounded by the possessions she could not see.

She collected everything, I saw. A buffet in one corner lay piled with books, from many of which stuck paper markers; on a table lay boxes crowded with shells, bits of glass, old coins and river-stones. On the window-sill a lap-desk stood locked; and tucked beside it I saw a doll, her wooden face red-cheeked, her ruff and farthingale embroidered with minute flowers. Her cap covered a wig made, to judge by its delicacy, of baby's hair. Yes: it was infant-blonde, and it must have taken some nurse months of cardings and combings – but I recognized the hair for Maria's own.

Princess Anna rose to greet me; Doctor Solniecki remained seated, gazing at the woman who slept unmoving in the bed. In a glance I assessed the room. Less magnificent than Anna's and smaller, and filled with cool white winter sunlight. The furniture was finely made, its air of shabbiness somehow worn into it, I thought, by a child's hard-driven games and by a young woman's work and study: for it smelt of all these as gently as a girl's body will smell of her natural perfume.

On the settle lay cushions of dark red velvet. The bed had four posts, and was made of some wood palely varnished to show the grain; and from its canopy hung curtains that must, like the doll, have been the work of nurse or mother – for someone had embroidered cream-coloured cloth with wildflowers: daisies, violets, eglantine, carnations and yellow pansies.

Anna said: 'Philip, welcome. She has sucked down some broth.'

'Should one whisper, madam?'

'I think we should speak softly. I dread that she might hear, and we not know it: sometimes people do half-wake. There, take a seat.'

I drew up a stool. 'What shall I do, madam? Good day, Doctor Solniecki.' The doctor nodded, frowning. 'If I am simply to wait through the hours, would she mind if I touched her books?'

'I think you may.'

'Thank you. I – *Oh.*'

On either side of the door by which I had entered glowed two large framed pictures, one above the other, making a panel of four. Each must have measured three feet by two, and each, I saw, represented the same scene. There – detailed and coloured like an illuminist's border – I saw, four times repeated, the view of Kraków on which I had looked down that first night.

I rose and went closer. Yes: the artist had worked from that same hill – had probably placed his easel almost where Ludovic and I had waited for Adam Kózmian. Four times, identical, I recognized the pebbled downsweep of the road, the field with its flagstaff, the river where a barge lay mirrored in its own shadow and two fishermen walked, carrying poles over their shoulders. There was the place where the wall broke and curved; there, the very tree by which I had climbed over; and there, smaller than my thumbnail, were fifty roofs I knew. Among them rose spires – Sanct' Anna, Saint Stanislas, Sancta Maria – and beyond them all, the hills as they looked in four different seasons.

For each panel, though identical even to the fishermen, was unique in this: each took some moment of a certain season. Here I saw autumn with grain standing yellow on the hills, while clouds in a cold green sky made one smell the spice of evening. Below it lay a scene set in the spring dawn. A primrose sky glowed over a landscape still lost in blue, and only the river had caught the light, reflecting it in an iridescence of apricot and rose.

Next came a Christmas scene where the fields showed frozen earth, snow shawled the roofs of the great churches, and delicate black trees cast shadows colder than themselves. Above the spire of Sancta Maria shone the Christmas Star, spiky and haloed and casting, to my delight, a lane of gold in the river.

And last and most beautiful, a night-scene. Every stalk, every stone cast silver shadow; Kraków shone like a heap of crystal jewels; and in the blackness above it clustered hundreds of stars.

'Maria made them,' said the Princess, 'and Jan had them framed. The draughtsmanship, the watercolour, everything is hers. I believe she said it was a mixture of pencil and gouache.' She shrugged. 'I wanted them for the Castle, but she and Jan refused.'

'They are astonishingly beautiful,' I said.

We moved softly to the bed. Doctor Solniecki sighed. 'Last night she turned her head and made a sound like a half-formed word. There has been nothing since.'

'And my lord Zamoyski?'

'Has been here as often as his work permits. No doubt you will see him soon.'

What Dangers Deep

Maria lay almost plain in her serenity. Her spiteful liveliness had faded, leaving me to wonder why I had disliked the too-pretty face whose big bones and delicate straight features now suggested neither beauty nor even adulthood. I should have guessed her, in the humility of her helplessness, to be about thirteen. Her hair lay brushed over the pillow, skin and hair respectively a matte and a shining ivory.

'No news has come from the Turkish border?' I said to Solniecki.

'Yes, news has come: a message from *Pan* Balinski. He has caught one party of slave-raiders. Yolanta was not among the women he recovered.'

At dusk Zamoyski came. Solniecki sat dozing in his chair; the Princess had excused herself to change her clothes for supper. Zamoyski greeted me and, sitting down on the bed, took his niece's hand. 'Maria.' His voice was imperative, though gentle. 'Maria.'

She did not move. He straightened. 'Her Highness tells me you praised the pictures.'

'I did: I think them extraordinary.'

'Of course they are beautiful. But why so *exact*, I thought. Their minuteness disturbed me, and the way she would go to that same place and set up her boards and tools and ignore her guard for hours. Sometimes I think there is reborn in her the soul of some old limner – some monk-illuminator who consecrated his whole life to copying texts and working miniatures in gold leaf.'

Together we moved through the twilight to the panels of colour that flanked the door. Each picture now gathered an individual dusk, through which stars and primrose sky were fading differently. 'Yes,' said Zamoyski, 'they are beautiful . . . Here come Maria's women with the lamps; we'll wake the Doctor for supper, and at ten Father Laurence promised to come. What joy they gave me, my children, my daughters.

There is no wit like the wit of an intelligent young girl. Did you ever see Yolanta dance?'

'No, my lord: she was sick on that one night.'

'Poor child. They are alike–' I do not think he noticed he had used the present verb – 'in that fierce love of excellence: Yolanta in her music, her playing and dancing and composing, and Maria in her scholarship. I loved to talk with them.'

Three women curtseyed to him, lamps in their hands. He smiled at them, and guided me onwards to the small room, close to Maria's, that we had adapted for these late suppers.

What I said next I cannot excuse, except by its genuineness. 'I wish you had children of your own, my lord.'

'I do.' His smile reassured me. 'Two sons, aged fourteen and three. They live with their mothers, though.'

'I beg your pardon, sir,' I said, as lightly as I could.

'No matter. And I have a dear friend, as no doubt gossip has already told you?'

'It had not, sir.'

Zamoyski grinned. 'Well, what a strange neglect.'

Sabina Korytowska, I thought, recalling the courtesan Antony had said would cost me my sapphire ring. In that guess I was right but not wholly so, as I learned some weeks after; and only once did I glimpse Isabella, Adrian's sister, whose lover Zamoyski had been since her marriage fifteen years before.

The Princess joined us, and Doctor Solniecki, yawning and apologizing. We ate in quiet, watching the white flames that licked around the fire-logs. The cooks had taken care to feed us for cold weather: even dessert, I remember, was a hot compôte of last year's apricots stewed with almonds, cream and brandy. I ate it hungrily – I always craved fruit in winter – and heard the Princess begin, 'Jan, I must go home . . .'

The door opened. Caspar Laurence entered, followed by Dorotea, and by Antony who looked haggard with interrupted sleep. My godfather said, 'We were in bed. Father Laurence insisted on bringing us here, on what business I do not know. Be quick, Father: my wife is tired, and so am I.'

'He had a reason.' Dorotea had not pulled off her hood. Wrapped in her cloak of dark blue velvet, she bowed slightly to the Princess. Anna reached up her hand and drew Dorotea down beside her on the settle.

Father Laurence held up a scroll made, as far as I could see, of cheap paper through which, as though the ink had soaked, red and black capitals showed in reverse. 'I tore this from the gate of Collegium Maius and, on reading it, looked out for others and ripped down such as I could find. No doubt I missed many. These bills were printed today: the ink is fresh. All Kraków will have read them by morning.'

'Then,' said Jan Zamoyski with great gentleness, 'let us anticipate them.'

Laurence unrolled the paper.

Gentlemen of Kraków:
They say the lady Yolanta died pregnant. And of what should she be pregnant, save of her uncle's seed?

Over all the days of nursing, of pacing, of destructive leisure; through all the nights when sleeplessness sharpens fear, I thought I had imagined every shock that could come upon us. Now, during a silence that lasted perhaps two minutes, I discovered the one shock I had missed.

Zamoyski lowered his head into his hands. When he straightened his nose had gone that unseemly red that means drunkenness or tears. In a voice empty of all surprise he said softly, 'Oh, how cruel.'

After that we waited for him. He rose, made for the window, then halted and, without looking at Father Laurence, held out his hand for the papers. Laurence gave them to him. 'Burn them, my lord,' he said.

Zamoyski thumbed them through, counting six, and said mildly, 'After I have identified the press.'

I noticed Dorotea was sitting rigid, her good hand clenched on the arm of the settle. Her eyes, brilliant with some private calculation, stared straight before her. The Princess clasped her hand with, I thought, a cautionary firmness.

Antony glanced at the two women, stroked his lower lip with his steepled thumbs and said, 'Jan, I can scarcely imagine a more wicked harmful lie – or a shrewder one.'

Zamoyski stared at him. For an instant his face showed a more startled surprise than I had, somehow, expected. 'Yes, of course,' he said. 'No one can prove an incest; but the rumour will scarcely help me or my candidate.'

Antony glanced again at his wife. 'Jan, I will soon have no position here to lose – indeed, I am in truth already merely Her Grace's observer. Dorotea, shall I leave it alone, my dear?'

'No. Say it.'

'Very well,' replied Antony. 'Can you prove an incest untrue?'

'Without Yolanta?' Zamoysi tapped the roll of papers softly from hand to hand. I shrugged away the memory of Robert Parsons' cruel, amused voice: *It fascinates me that the unkindness of Gilbert's act is not what occurs to you first.*

'Another thing,' said Antony. 'Father Laurence, is it your opinion that these posters are student work?'

'That is my opinion, yes. The Watch surprised a club of students working a secret press in the cellar of one of the dormitories last year, as my lord Zamoyski will know.'

'And this is pure student mischief, then?' said Antony.

'Mmmm, no.' Laurence took his time. 'Children of twenty love to lecture their elders, God knows, but they seldom identify their vices accurately. Something here savours of adult malice.'

'Are you suggesting,' demanded the Princess, 'that someone *paid* the students to start this rumour?'

Laurence shrugged. 'Does the University not lead the mob?'

'So it likes to think,' said Zamoyski.

What Dangers Deep

'Then where better to start, if someone wished to destroy your good name and your power to help your candidate?'

'This rumour seems–' Antony hesitated – 'somehow an intricate tool.'

'Not,' said Dorotea softly, 'if Yolanta did die pregnant.'

There was a long silence. 'And did she, my dear?' demanded the Princess Anna.

Dorotea shook her head. 'Not that I know. But it occurs to me now that I would *not* know. She came back from France only three months ago; and I am so much older, and since Uncle Jan began to take care of my sisters—'

'You had borne enough,' said Zamoyski gently.

She nodded. 'Thank you, sir: for that I have always been grateful. In fact Uncle Jan took them in, freeing me to serve Your Highness and – and to seek a husband. It occurs to me now that I have not seen my sisters naked, not as women will who live together; that I have lived with Your Highness, then with Antony, now for several years; in fact, that I know neither Yolanta nor Maria. We have become grown women, and strangers.'

'And yet you *feel*,' insisted the Princess with meticulous gentleness, 'that Yolanta did die, if she has died, pregnant?'

'I feel it, yes. But for God's sake, madam, remember I have no evidence.'

'Would Maria know?' wondered Antony.

Zamoski shrugged. 'They did not share a chamber or a bed, as sisters sometimes will. Each of us likes privacy and solitude, and Maria and Yolanta, though they loved each other, were not warmly intimate.' I remembered the ring held out to me in fingers for whose shaking I knew no reason, and Maria's stare of disbelieving rage. 'It is possible Maria does *not* know. In any case she is not going to tell us.'

Doctor Solniecki cleared his throat. 'Then, my lord,' he said, 'since Her Highness is in presence here, may I speak?'

Zamoyski bowed.

Solniecki turned to the Princess. 'Madam, a week before the disappearance at the Ancient Mass, the lady Yolanta, with obvious reluctance, let me examine her for two women's complaints.' (I remembered with a shock her plea of sickness on the night Maria danced with me.) 'One was a lump in her left breast, which did distress me: I hoped it was benign and that it would subside with time, so I tried to reassure her while we waited. She was frightened and wept, poor lady.' Anna nodded. 'The second – I had to insist when she told me – was an ordinary infection of the female parts, but neglected, or rather mistreated, because she had used some ointment from the stillroom instead of coming to me as she ought to have done. I pretended not to have noticed the reason for her having avoided me: indeed, I hope she died believing she had deceived me. From the condition of her breasts and from the pigmentation of her inward parts, I judged her to be some three months pregnant of a child conceived in France.'

'Uncle,' demanded Dorotea, 'do you think this is why Madame Marguerite sent her home?'

(Madame Marguerite, whom I have met, is sister to King Henri of France, and therefore daughter to Queen Catherine de' Medici – and, as if that were not trouble enough for her, has also married her brother's chief rival, the Protestant King of Navarre. Despite my dislike of her family, she delighted me when I was in Paris, I admit. I remember her as a plump little lady with a husky voice and an air of vehement charm. But the household of the Queen of Navarre is known for its wit, not for its chastity.)

Zamoyski frowned. 'I suspect this is the reason Madame Marguerite sent her away; but the reason she wrote to me was that Yolanta was exhausted and pining for home.'

'Therefore,' struck in the deep confident voice of Father Laurence, 'if you knew of her pregnancy, sir, it was not the Queen of Navarre who told you?'

'No. Nor Yolanta, nor Maria. Doctor Solniecki came straight to me.'

'I felt disloyal to the lady, but still I thought it best,' said Solniecki.

'You did well, whatever came of it.' Zamoyski still held the rolled papers, and stood in front of the window-seat – a distance from us which he made no attempt to diminish.

'Had you confronted the lady Yolanta?' demanded Laurence.

'No. But it was coming, by her initiative or by mine. It shames me to guess, now, how much she seems to have feared me. She need not: I would have helped her.'

So nothing was as it seemed, I thought, remembering wild horses rolling in the snow; remembering a flight of kingfishers; remembering a shelf of fungus, fragrant as new bread, snapped off and tossed away.

'Then I think we must ask,' said Antony, 'who else knew of Yolanta's pregnancy, and who would wish to turn that knowledge against you.'

'Queen Catherine de' Medici,' suggested Anna, without, I thought, much interest. 'Or her son, our erstwhile King.'

To my surprise Zamoyski turned to me. 'Master Philip, you have met Queen Catherine, as I have not. What is your opinion?'

I considered. 'I dislike Queen Catherine, my lord, but one feels she wastes nothing, neither strength nor malice. No one doubts her intelligence, and few seem to doubt her practicality. She cannot get Poland for her sons: why should she punish any Pole for that? It is lost: my impression is that she would shrug and let it go. And King Henri, now King of France, has notoriously never looked back at this country, so why should he meddle here? I think you can dismiss them.'

'I agree,' said Antony. 'And if your candidate, Jan – I mean Prince Stefan – were to lose, then the Hapsburg family – the Emperor and his son the Archduke Ernst – may win. Queen Catherine will not want to help a Hapsburg king to any throne on earth: she would prefer, if necessary, to leave even you and your candidate unharmed.'

'This is likely not French mischief-making, then,' remarked Laurence. 'May I suggest the Emperor Maximilian or his son?'

Now I did, as it happened, know both these men from my months in Vienna. I could remember the first time I saw them in procession (later on I was to meet both at Court as well). On that day, I remembered, a friend had let us use his house as a gallery to look down upon the royal route. A consort of lutes had been struggling to make itself heard above our voices, and a pretty girl, I recalled, had been crowding me on my left. I remembered jostling her gently – so delighted by her that, when the crowd in the street below cleared for an instant and offered me a glimpse of the Emperor and the Archduke, I gave them little conscious attention.

I could see nothing remarkable in Maximilian, with his workman's face and subtle eyes. Rumour made him kinder to Protestantism than his kinsman the King of Spain. But Ernst glanced up at me: for an instant I confronted him.

He was blond, not much above thirty, and wore an elegant spade-shaped little beard, beneath which I could see a pink pouting underlip.

'Philip?' had said my companion: for I had gone suddenly still. Surely I had seen Ernst before, but where? No, not the Archduke himself, but another face so like his . . .

My companion twined her hand in mine; I kissed her fingers. Yes, now I had it.

At Hampton Court there hangs a portrait of Philip of Spain as Titian painted him to arouse the desperate love of Queen Mary Tudor. Could I have kept some latent memory of the man who held me at the font? That might account for the shock I now felt. As the crowd moved and the instant dissolved, I had a sensation inexplicable in ordinary terms: the sensation of seeing back across twenty years. For Ernst resembled his kinsman King Philip when, long ago, he came from Spain for Mary

What Dangers Deep

Tudor to fall into her pitiable passion for him. That love had killed her; had ignited the torture by burning which destroyed the Protestants, my co-religionists, at Smithfield; had filled my nation with fear and hate of Spain; had committed me to preventing any marriage Queen Elizabeth might seek to make with any Spanish or Catholic prince. And that marriage had brought Philip and Mary – he a slight, correct, impatient man, she a little, dowdy, flustered woman with sad eyes: both more human than the old coins show them – to be godfather and godmother to me.

'May I suggest,' said Laurence in the present, 'the Emperor Maximilian or his son?'

'Would Ernst use such a tool as this rumour?' demanded the Princess.

'He is a candidate,' replied Antony with a shrug. 'And his father is, though cautiously, mustering an army. And both have agents here who might act without seeking the permission of those who pay them. The Archduke might prefer nominal ignorance, and nominal innocence.'

'Excuse me,' I said. 'Antony has already asked, of course. My lord Zamoyski, do you think Maria knew of her sister's pregnancy?'

'It was not Maria who told me, Philip.'

'I ask because on the night before – before the Ancient Mass, I was distressed to notice some quarrel between them. It may not matter now.'

Zamoyski shrugged. 'Maria and Yolanta were intimate friends only as children, if in truth then. Since they came into my care I have noticed their estrangement. Sisters can both love and quarrel though, Philip. No, I do not think Yolanta would have confided in Maria as a matter of course; but I *do* think loneliness may have forced her to it, and that Maria would have helped her, not betrayed her. I do not know the answer to your question.'

Laurence said, 'And, discounting private enemies, you agree that agents of the Archduke Ernst could have seeded this rumour, or this part-truth, among the University?'

'It seems possible.'

'Then we must find and punish the slanderers,' said Anna. 'And someone must say it: Jan, I must ask you whether you *were* the father of Yolanta's child.'

Zamoyski sank to his knees and crossed his breast. 'Madam, as I hope in the Redemption I was not Yolanta's lover. I never touched my nieces except as a father should, and I loved them honestly.'

Anna bowed her head – a mixture of assent and apology. Zamoyski rose and started towards us. To my relief, it was in this motion of normalcy that Maria's tirewoman found us an instant later.

The door opened crisply. The woman held a candle; her hand shook as it shielded the flame. 'My lord, please come at once. The lady Maria is waking.'

Fourteen

So often in my imagination have I looked through Maria's eyes that night that the memory seems to be my own. The pupils dilating on a familiar room, on candlelight, on faces exhausted with their watching. I saw her glance at Father Laurence, and remembered she had never seen him before. Then her attention, absorptive as an infant's, fastened on her uncle's face as Zamoyski sat down on the bed. He took her hand, and when she gave back the pressure, covered it with his other hand as well. 'My child, can you speak? Just softly?'

'Where—' She coughed: cleared her throat. 'Where is Yolanta?'

'In her bed asleep,' said Jan Zamoyski, 'as you will be soon again. You have lain here for several days, Maria.'

Her eyes counted us all. I saw her acknowledge Dorotea; saw her salute me, though impersonally, with recognition. 'You are lying,' she whispered. 'Yolanta is gone.'

'Gone where, Maria?' demanded Zamoyski softly. Caspar Laurence started forward. Zamoyski's gesture stopped him. 'Where were you last, do you remember?'

'Yes: in the Grove. I—' Her brow creased with concentration. 'Yolanta is not here, is she?' she demanded.

'No. Can you feel her?'

'Yes.' The grey eyes sought inward.

'My lord, you risk everything by this.' Caspar Laurence pulled up his stool, without attempting to order Zamoyski away. 'Maria, I am Father Laurence. Doctor Solniecki has asked me to help care for you. Do you feel hungry?'

Her head turned on the pillow. 'Of course, I have heard of you. No, Father, I don't want any food.'

'Nevertheless I shall hold you up while your uncle feeds you broth, and then I will put you to sleep for a while.' He slipped an arm around her and eased her upright.

Maria frowned with surprise at her own weakness. 'The room is ringing,' she said.

'I don't wonder,' replied Father Laurence. A spoon clinked against a mug: Zamoyski accepted the broth and began to feed her. When she had finished half, on some excuse the mug passed to Father Laurence, who added to it some clear drops from a phial. As Maria finished this, she frowned again and remarked, 'Bitter.'

'Does your throat hurt?' asked Zamoyski.

She shook her head and whispered, 'It feels dry.'

Sleep was visibly claiming her. As she sank from his hands Zamoyski bent close and said, 'Maria, was there anyone else in the Grove?'

'Only Philip. Hello, Philip.' I knelt beside her; she took my hand and cuddled it to her cheek, where her tears fell on it.

'Hello, Maria,' I said softly. 'Maria, *where did Yolanta go?*'

'She fell down,' said Maria, and slept.

Zamoyski plunged away from the bed and, arresting the motion, stood still, his hands on his hips. With his back to us he said, 'Get the lord Rector out of his bed. The students responsible shall be flogged and expelled.'

'My lord Zamoyski,' I said, 'this slander need not be true for you to act as badly as your enemies desire.'

'Bravo,' murmured Caspar Laurence.

Zamoyski turned to me: if he frightened me I do not think my eyes showed it. 'Then let the lord Rector discipline his students. Because when Kraków reads those posters it will say aloud what before people only asked each other in secret: whether, if Yolanta was pregnant with my child, I killed her to destroy the evidence; and whether I did not simply *fail* to kill Maria.'

What Dangers Deep

* * *

I was not at Collegium Maius when the Rector's search-parties tore apart the dormitories and traced informers' leads to find the illicit press. I did not follow the crowd to see the cellar where they located it. I did not see Zamoyski's men dismember the press, to make a bonfire of the wooden frames and throw the type into the Vistula. I passed the next day in Maria's room; and from it I twice heard rise from the city the roar that is not any single voice, but the voice of a monster I intensely fear: the mob.

'They have found their culprits,' said Caspar Laurence in midafternoon. 'Since the lord Zamoyski is not cruel enough to torture students to find who paid them, they will suffer expulsion merely. And they are to be flogged in the square tonight.'

'I wish there were a king,' I said.

Her women had bathed Maria and washed her hair: it fell in damp strands of gilt-silver over her shoulders when they sat her up in bed to attempt her first solid meal. Her interval of exposure in the forest had left her unwasted, but the liquid diet had fined blue hollows beneath her cheekbones. In its delicate severity her face, by a paradox which the changes in her effortlessly sustained, now seemed to look five years older than her age. I had not seen her greet Dorotea, but whatever passed between the two sisters was over by the time they let me in.

Maria smiled at me and gave me her hand to hold. It felt smallboned and delicate in my grasp. I drew up a stool, thinking: You informed Father Parsons so he might rip my baggage open – you, not Dorotea – of that I now feel certain. Did you know of your sister's pregnancy? Did you know (suddenly I realized none of us had stopped to ask) the real identity of its father? You have wakened. For what calculations are you too weak? What secrets must you marshal your wits to hide?

'I cannot see anything,' remarked Antony, drawing aside the curtain but remaining in its shadow.

Dorotea joined him at the window. 'God, it is unwise of him.

I cannot remember a public flogging here – not since I was a girl.'

Then your customs are gentler than our own, I thought. The Embassy gates stood barred; crossbowmen, Robert Sellier among them, manned the roof. Perhaps they could see more than we from our hiding-place. I did not care about the flogging – the students deserved it, and God knows we do worse than that in England; and I pitied Zamoyski in the agony of his rage.

As we waited for the crowd, which seethed and roared in the umber light, to turn and loot the houses, I thought, *Why such anguish in a clever man? Can it be the rumour contains some actual, essential truth – some temptation refused?* I have seen adult men troubled by the womanhood of their daughters. I think it a natural and innocent distress, provided it leads to no sinful action.

He says he has done no sin, and I believe him. In the torchlight the distant figures quieted, waited; then, moved by some stimulus we could not see, roared with a fresh fury of pity. Horsemen were now riding through the crowd, pushing gently, as if under orders to do no harm. 'Perhaps they've finished. Perhaps they've come to take the children away,' said Dorotea. By 'children' she meant the young men who had, I reflected, slandered a dead girl with an apparent wantonness to which I wished Zamoyski had not shown himself so vulnerable.

No sin, I thought: *but a guilt? If a guilt, one innocent of action. Does he know?*

'I think it is over,' said Antony. A few women had begun to break away from the edges of the crowd, carrying tired children in their arms. I saw one man – a handsome bearded Pole with a gentle face – hesitate, then walk away with his arms folded.

'Wait,' said Dorotea. 'We cannot be secure till the soldiers have cleared the cobbles round the gibbet.'

And so we waited on into the night. And I thought: *Yes, he knows*.

* * *

What Dangers Deep

The next afternoon came cold and snowless, with an iron glare of light, and frost that sparkled on the cobbles. I did not like the feel of the city, and did not go out. About two o'clock, to my surprise, Caspar Laurence called on me. 'Philip, I have put up a notice postponing my lecture. I came to tell you because I do not want you to go to the University today. Instead will you walk with me to my lord Zamoyski's house?'

'Willingly,' I replied, and escaped before Antony could send any guards with me.

We walked along quiet streets, our footsteps ringing among the frozen horse-dung on the road. A smith, his pincers grasping a cherry-red bar of metal, glanced at me from the depths of his forge. Through another window we glimpsed the bakeshop-girl, her eyes lowered, her neck bent in a posture of burden. I saw her straighten with an effort, and glance around at me and away. A gingerbread manger, its eaves daggered with sugar icicles, stood on display beside her.

'Advent is coming,' remarked Father Laurence. 'They'll be carving the crèches soon: wonderful things, so I hear, with a prize awarded each year for the best.'

We had entered Jana Street, which lay totally silent. On our left a tavern door stood open; to our right rose the three grey storeys of the Protestant Chapel, with its lattices, its modest adornments of carved stone, and its tall, cap-like, red-tile roof. 'I do not like the quiet,' I said.

Once, while on a visit to the North Country, I saw a dam crack open, and a single deadly breaker roll in silence along the canal. Neat as a comber, silvered, quiet, that wave was still a destroyer unparalleled. It gutted the house of the friend with whom I was staying, slimed the floors with mud and left the walls a shell.

The wave that rolled behind us now was as dangerous, but it brought a single warning.

'Gentlemen!'

We stopped. A rider, the only man in the street, seemed to have noticed us, and, turning about, trotted towards us. He wore a turban and a coat of brown brocade; the face that smiled down at us was Slav, and its broad jaw and high cheekbones gave him an air of calm as well as of vindictive amusement. His French was excellent. 'A mob of students has broken out from the University and is coming, so I believe, for the Protestant Chapel.' He nodded towards the tavern. 'Buy yourselves a drink behind a barred door, Father, and quickly.'

'Come with us, sir,' I exclaimed.

He laughed. 'Thank you, no. I'll watch your Protestants and your Catholics tear one another apart from a safer distance, and in greater comfort – or so a lady has promised me. Take care: they have axes.'

Laurence plunged into the tavern and, while I barred the door, warned the innkeeper to bolt his shutters from the inside. I remember the man's startled thanks, and the *clack* of bolts in uneven rhythm that followed us as we climbed the stairs. 'He'll bring us something hot,' said Laurence. 'Well, God help us. Let us hide and watch from here, and pray they do not take to demolishing taverns too.'

They still recall that evening, the people of Kraków. I did not know, when we locked ourselves into a room with a fire and a bowl of hot rum-punch (our host proved grateful, despite his haste), that I would not leave it till next morning. And ten years later a friend sent me a placard only recently printed in the city. It commemorates the demolition of the Protestant Chapel in Jana Street, and shows stick-men wielding axes, wielding picks – throwing stones, ripping tiles from roofs. A doggerel verse in Latin boasts how it was done.

It is true that soldiers armed with halberds came, dressed, I think, in the green and white of the House of Firlei; but in the picture they stand to one side, and I do not remember any help they gave. As dusk grew richer, the street more deeply black with shadow, torches, candles and lamps in pierced tin cages cast a mixed radiance on the mob which was destroying the building twenty yards from our hiding-place. Boys in gowns and hoods and leggings – were they drunk, I wondered? I have never seen so systematic a fury.

At first they worked shouting and fighting – screaming, faces distorted, at the halberdiers while others stripped tiles, scaled the tower, ripped out gratings from windows. They axed open the door; more lattices fell, pushed from inside, and furniture for the bonfire. I saw books flutter down into the flames. The halberdiers hung on the edge of the crowd, able to defend themselves but not to enforce authority.

Now I felt certain the students were drinking. I saw no obvious ringleaders. Around ten o'clock they grew quiet, and in methodical silence attacked the fabric of the church. The stone mouldings had gone, tumbled into the street. Exhaustion, boredom, hours of persistence should have stopped them: I have seen these things stop other mobs. But at midnight, lit by taffeta-yellow flame that grew paler toward the tower's peak, they began to demolish the shell of the spire itself. They had torn the slates from the wooden substructure. Now they stripped boards down to lath, exposing the tower for a latticework of fragile timber. Still more attackers manhandled another grating on to the flames, too tired to remember it would not burn. And still the axemen attacked the roof.

'You saw Saint Bartholomew's?' said Caspar Laurence's gentle voice behind me.

'Yes. It was worse than this.'

In the street below me a man, his face tranced with exhaustion, ripped a prayer-book up its spine and threw it into the fire. I found in me at that moment the need to pray – for safety, for forgiveness on our human barbarity: found in me, nearest to my memory, words I myself had turned into verse.

> Mercy, Lord: let mercy thine descend,
>   For I am weak, and in my weakness languish.
> Lord, help: for even my very bones their marrow spend
>   In cruel anguish.

Nay, even my soul fell troubles do appal.
    Alas, how long, my God, wilt thou delay thee?
Turn thee, sweet Lord, and from this ugly thrall
    My dear God, stay me.

Mercy: oh mercy, Lord, for mercy's sake –
    For death doth kill the witness of thy glory.
Can of thy praise the souls *entombèd* make
    A heavenly story?

'That was the sixth Psalm,' said Laurence. 'Did you verse it?'

I shrugged. 'As I could.'

The punch had grown cold, the house sunk to a wary quiet. From the street twenty feet below came the bonfire's crisping sound; the chunk of axes; an occasional voice, truculent with fatigue. The crowd, still very numerous, was circulating restlessly.

I came across to Father Laurence, who had sat down. 'Father, do not go back to England. Live and die in peace here in exile. Do not betray them. I have known you now perhaps a fortnight, and knowing you I can find no sense in the message you sent the Privy Council. What will you have in England but the landscape of your boyhood, stripped bare of the human love that gave that home its worth? For you will have left that love here, with Robert Parsons and the others your defection would destroy.'

The magnificent virile head lifted to confront me: the hair Viking-white, the mouth thinned, the eyes naked in their tenderness and their intelligence. In that instant it came to me whole: that Caspar Laurence had never meant to betray his friends.

I whispered, 'Do you seek death, then? And do you know to what death you go?'

'I know.'

'Why?'

'Because I fear it. I admit nothing, Philip. My offer to the Council stands. Any guess you make I will not confirm: I will deny it as the lie and fantasy of a child.'

'You will compound with Walsingham for information you never intended to give! And then they will kill you for it.'

'That may be.' Laughter and anguish, I had noticed, both pulled his mouth into the same sour, down-twisted smile.

'Why?' I demanded again.

'Because since I was eight years old I have known that we must die. And now that I am forty, I shake with fear of it. I wake in thought of death; I search my body for it; I cannot let myself faint into sleep without pulling up in terror, as though my will could conquer my death. I am a coward, Philip. I want to walk *towards* death. I want not to wait any longer. And if I wake afterwards – and I will not, for we are creatures of earth and perish as earth – then perhaps God, who has never shown me mercy, may give me peace.' He shrugged. 'What incense have I to burn before him, Philip? Only my cowardice. We must give God what we have.'

He leaned back, glanced at the window, considering some sound. 'Five years ago I began to feel a pain in the centre of my mind. Not in the muscle or the brain, but an agony so pure it has no characteristics, and no cause that I know. I tell you one thing, and you will not understand it. That pain shall not find me again: I will seek it at the torturers' knives, and go, through the cleanness of agony, into the presence of God. Or into annihilation. Let me alone. Let me seek the purest rage of anguish, the most exquisite extreme, the nearest state to my creator's presence that has ever come to me.'

'I will not let you.'

'You cannot stop me.'

'I can. I can impugn your honesty to the Council – even your sanity.'

'Do you truly think that, in the Council's presence, I cannot convince them I am sane? Give me to them: enact your commission. Do not destroy your career at its beginning for a man who has chosen, using the only means he knows, to be in solitude with God. That is my right, Philip, as much as it is yours. And now sleep: I do not think the crowd will turn on us here, but it'll not be safe to go out before morning.'

'I know.' I was trembling, and wished I had eaten supper to steady me. 'I'd like to get a message across town to Antony.'

'It's too late, it must be one o'clock, and neither you nor a messenger could leave the house safely. Antony knows you went out with me. And our friend–' he gestured downwards towards the street where we had met the horseman – 'may do us a service, though it seems unlikely. It is possible he recognized me, at least, of the two of us.'

'I'll thank him for his kindness if I see him again,' I said.

Laurence nodded.

For sleep he pretended to prefer the settle, which was too short for him; and I, mistrusting innkeepers' mattresses, made a pallet out of the cleanest blankets and set it by the window. This I kept shuttered for safety, but still it gave me some feeling of escape.

But the sleep of my boyhood, avid and easy, had begun to desert me in the past year; and on this night it would, in any case, have been impossible. I lay angrily longing for oblivion, while the residues of panic in my body kept me so tense I could not even doze.

Once or twice during the night I glanced at Caspar Laurence, and saw him also awake, the firelight reflected like topaz in his eyes.

For warmth her attendants had dressed Maria in at least three gowns: cambric and ribbed scarlet silk lay under the outermost robe of grey velvet, and all three were caught in a thick frill at her wrists. From her sheets came the sharp herbal smell of rosemary. Two women sat sewing in the window-seat; and Doctor Solniecki from his sketch-board said, 'Hand my lady Maria this book, please, sir, she has just asked for it. The lady Dorotea stayed on watch throughout the night. I made her go home to bed just now.'

'I know, I saw her come in. Good day, Maria.'

What Dangers Deep

She accepted the book from me. Her skin was still too white; but they had crimped her hair, and the heart-shaped face with its delicate symmetrical features had regained some of its attraction. Her voice today was normal. 'Philip, they tell me you found me. Thank you.'

'I only wish . . .' I said. *I only wish I had found Yolanta too.*

Without raising his head from his work Doctor Solniecki controlled me. 'I have found my lady does not remember her first waking. You will, of course, not tire her, sir.' *Or you will go*, I thought.

Unlikely, then, that Zamoyski dared press her yet either. 'I am glad to have served you, Maria. Have you walked yet? Can you stand?'

'I tried. My legs feel like new bread-dough. I hate the weakness: it frightens me.'

'I suppose it would.' I did not know how to entertain her, here where my service and (I suspected) my being Maria's contemporary had at last won me the right to come. Did Zamoyski hope she would tell me what she might not tell someone she feared – an elder who might punish her?

Maria bowed her head, shielding her face in wings of fresh-washed hair. When she looked up at me I saw what colour there was in her mouth and eyes – the young delicacy in the curve of her upper lip, chap-marks on the lower one, and eyes like freshly broken agate.

'Philip, I have a sin to confess to you.'

'How can that be?' I demanded.

Again the weight bowed her down; again she forced her head upright. 'Many weeks ago, before you came to Kraków, I overheard my uncle discussing you with his secretary. Do not be angry with him: I listened at a door where I had no right to be, and the fault is mine. A message had come to him concerning you and Father Laurence.'

I nodded. 'I understand.'

'Then,' said Maria steadily, 'I will not shame myself by

repeating what I heard. Please do not think of me as a spy who listens at doors: I had a reason. I wrote to Father Parsons and told him to come here.'

'To interfere in the delivery of my message?'

'To do you any harm he could. I am ashamed and sorry.'

The book rested on her knees; she folded over it hands capable and strong in spite of their thinness. I said, 'I have twice seen Father Parsons, and we have talked together. I do not think he will harm me, Maria.'

'I'm glad.'

'What reason had you to hurt me? We had not even met.'

She started, and opened her mouth to speak, but Doctor Solniecki rose and, with a clatter of rings, drew her bedcurtains shut against the winter sun. 'That will keep, my lord Philip. We all share Maria's gratitude, and *Pan* Zamoyski has asked me to tell you that you may come to us at any time, if my lady's strength and willingness permit.'

Get out, said his look. I wished Maria good day, and went gladly enough; for I meant not to leave Kraków until I had extorted from her everything she remembered – everything she guessed or knew. For some weeks she might be too frail, and I did not want to forfeit my privilege of access to her room. But the need to demand, if necessary to force her, filled me now with a patient anger.

She is alive and silent, I thought. *She is alive and silent, but I will wait*. And Zamoyski, I now suspected, might want – in case she responded neither to love nor to authority – to give her a friend, to entrap her with an equal.

I will befriend her patiently; and if she hides any knowledge of how Yolanta died, she shall not escape her memories.

Antony's courier had called that afternoon and had left letters for me. They were, of course, some three weeks old, even when carried without shipwreck or robbery by the fastest riders. Therefore they contained no response to the events in

Kraków, which in any case I had kept from friends my own age. After supper I settled in the library to read them. One came from Fulke Greville, who was, with Ned Dyer, my closest friend from school.

> Damn you, Philip, I have written five letters to your every single one. Ned and I play dice for your head when we contemplate the couriers' empty packets. Here are his latest verses, by the way: he asked me to include them. I think them less bad than the last. When are you coming home to us? Do you remember the dinner when you explained to us, by deductive logic, historical precedent and the usage of the common law, why there are no wolves in England? Must we now relapse into our ignorance? Ned swears he *saw* a wolf on his way home the other night. And this was in Conduit Street. You had better talk to him.

I grinned and set the letter aside, to turn to one from Hubert Languet.

> My beloved pupil,
> A baseless rumour ascribes to me a knowledge of the Q'abalah. Since I do *not* know these arcana, I do *not* cast on you the following curse: that someday, to atone to me and your other friends in Italy, you must write a letter three hundred pages long. Do you care for me so little, truly, Philip? I remember that gift you have, of making your listener feel loved. *Do* you love, or are you only supple beyond your years? You did not charm me heartlessly, in wanton awareness of your gifts, I am sure? Yet your neglect of our friendship since you left Italy . . .

I sighed, and wrote, '*My beloved Master* . . .'

'My lord Philip,' said a woman servant. '*Pan* Nemet Josef.'

I rose. The man who came towards me, holding out his hand, wore a brown cloak lined with fox-fur; beneath it I could see a gown of silver brocade that fell to his calves. He wore (it is not the

Polish fashion) high boots, and carried a mace crowned by a steel globe. The cap he swept off as he came towards me had a high cone, with a band of fur and four tall feathers. He was handsome, burly, balding, and definitely our rescuer from Jana Street.

'Master Sidney!' he said. 'I am Nemet Josef, Her Highness's guest from Hungary.'

'Then you give me the chance to thank you, sir. Will you sit down? What can I offer you? I wish we had coffee.'

'No need.' He sank into a chair and crossed his legs. 'I'll have wine, please. And I will not, like the old man in the anecdote, shout to warn my soul that I am about to commit the sin of drinking it.'

'That relieves me, of course,' I said, smiling. 'Wine, please, Marta, for us both. How did you discover who I am?'

'By telling Jan I saw a young man with Father Laurence. It occurred to me afterwards that the tavern was a dangerous refuge: I felt truly badly about suggesting it. By the way, the lord Rector is at this moment waiting on *Pan* Zamoyski with the University's apology for the libel.'

'Will the students like that?'

He shrugged. 'I suspect some of them feel ashamed. And it will give *Pan* Zamoyski a public reason to turn kind. I hope both sides will apologize and retreat: I think they will. *Pan* Zamoyski loves Collegium Maius because of his own youth there, and the Rector will suggest to him that there is a poor students' dormitory that needs renovation and a patron. Thank you.' He took a cup of wine from Marta, and I saw her smile and blush.

His voice was beautiful: ironic, friendly and controlled, and well sustained by the muscular resonance of a body more powerful than tall. European, Tartar, Slav – I guessed all three crossed in him, for the broad square balance of his face seemed oriental, and his cheekbones were so high that laughter closed his eyes into half-moons. They were grey-blue eyes; his hair was brown, his chin cleft. I did not doubt a woman had been waiting for him.

I said, '*Pan* Nemet, who is the Sultan's choice for King of Poland?'

What Dangers Deep

He shrugged. 'I cannot speak for the Sultan, but my friends would prefer Prince Stefan Bathóry. I think it was Jenghiz Khan who said, Master Sidney, that there are two best gifts in the hand of God. The greatest gift is a noble friend; the next greatest is a noble enemy.'

'And you would prefer a noble enemy to the north?'

Nemet Josef sighed. 'A pity you missed the late King Henri, or you would understand how dangerous, sir, is a base and unstable enemy. If Zamoyski will not take the Crown, we want Prince Stefan.'

'Then who has set this slander on Zamoyski?'

'Almost certainly agents of the Archduke Ernst. This is a vile opportunity, but finding it in their hands they would use it. I believe *Pan* Zamoyski will regain his self-command. It was a cruel accident that struck at him through his love for these girls; and more cruel than any man could bear that he may yet find Yolanta's skeleton, or a body and sanity degraded beyond endurance if her captors have kept her alive. I think he will try to earn back what power the floggings have cost him. But until Yolanta's death is confirmed—' I nodded. I liked Nemet Josef, and had trusted him at once. He said, 'You have seen Maria. Can she help her uncle, do you think?'

'Doctor Solniecki says she has forgotten what slight admission she made.' He cocked an eyebrow. I searched my instinct of disloyalty, then, ignoring what it told me, continued, 'She said of Yolanta: "She fell down."'

Nemet Josef exclaimed with exasperation.

'I can understand Maria's forgetting the words,' I continued. 'Father Laurence's opium was already in her blood. Since then she has said nothing more, and no one dares question her.'

'It must come.' He saluted me with his cup. 'She must in a sense *feed* the crowd, Master Sidney; and I pity her for that. Any memory she has must be recovered, to help her uncle and to placate those who would prefer to see silence as guilt, rather than as a mystery they cannot bear.'

'Then we cannot let her go among the crowds,' I said.

He set down his cup. '*Pan* Zamoyski knows that. I think, Master Philip, that for your safety here someone must tell you certain things. One is that Tomász Zamoyski died in the massacre at Castle Doyle, killed by your own father's troops. That is why Maria hated you before she saw you.'

'Castle Doyle!' I exclaimed. 'I think I remember the name. But why has no one told me this? Why did *Pan* Zamoyski not tell me? And why did they give out Tomász died of the sweating-sickness?'

He shrugged. 'A private matter, perhaps, gentled down to comfort the children; perhaps he told them the truth when he thought them old enough to bear it. And as for you, events overwhelmed the inevitable indiscretion. Someone *would* have told you. But I can believe Jan thought it an old and a personal event, for which you must not be made wretched; and I can believe his enforcing this silence on his nieces. It is a poor host who welcomes his guest with a story of old guilt. He thought it no grief of yours, and no business of yours.'

'Yet Maria would not obey him.'

'No. It was a mistaken compassion, I think now, in that its breaking was likely to prove a shock to you worse than honesty. And another thing. Remember that the servants who wash the ladies' linen can be bribed. Yolanta's pregnancy was rumoured in the city by its second month.' He rose to go. 'Someday I will take you to see a monastery that *Pan* Zamoyski has generously endowed. In its churchyard you will find a grave. That also I want you to see; but not yet.'

'Why?' I rose too: I was four inches the taller. 'Because Prince Stefan has not yet instructed you?'

Nemet Josef smiled, his gaze arrested on my face, but when he replied, it was as if I had not spoken. 'On that stone you will find a very beautiful quotation from the Christian Scriptures: "Man comes forth like a flower, and is cut down." Good day, Master Sidney.'

Fifteen

This time when I sought out Robert Sellier I found him in his small, decent room. Dressed in shirt and hose, he sat in the window-seat, his legs crossed, reading a pamphlet bound in marbled paper. He would have risen when I came in, but I motioned him to stay where he was.

'Sir!' he said. 'Please take the stool or the bed, as you prefer. Or there's the chest to sit on.'

'That will do well.' The chest was solid and, like many of its kind, could also double as a hard bed. I sank down on it.

Sellier said, 'It's time you called me Rob, sir.'

'Only if you'll call me Philip.'

'I'll try, but not where my betters can hear me.'

I nodded. 'What's the book?'

'Well, not a book exactly: a pamphlet hot off the stalls. Kraków prints treason and heresy in five languages.'

'And someone is selling off the stock of the late illicit press?'

He laughed and watched me, his arms crossed, his eyes bright with a quizzical reserve that might, perhaps, have been part fear. The booklet was in French. Its title ran: 'On the Duty of Sovereigns to their Subjects.' I flipped a page and read:

> The King is the creation and servant of his subjects. In old times, so the histories tell us, the ancient peoples *elected* kings capable of leading them in war and of governing them in peace. In short, each leader was gifted *in himself* to fulfil the functions of a king. Our ancestors had not yet

fallen into the degenerate modern use which has made kingship merely hereditary. The People are greater than the King; and if the King cannot or will not serve the People for whose good alone he exists, then to depose him is their duty and their right.

'You read the Protestant firebrands, then?' I inquired, handing the thing back to him.

Sellier shrugged. 'To know what they say. Let me be honest, Master Philip: Luther *was* right, and so were many of the critics who followed him, and who created the Reformed Religion because the Church of Peter *is* corrupt. Not all of us who love the Church deny the reformers' charges. I hated the business in Jana Street, and I am sorry for it.' I nodded acknowledgement, startled to feel tears prickle in my eyes. 'I hope,' said Sellier, 'that this factional bloodletting may pass, and that someday the Church may win back souls because she has deserved them. And as an Englishman I hate the opinions of Robert Parsons, and I no more want Philip of Spain – or any Hapsburg like Ernst or Maximilian – for Her Grace's husband than you do.'

'Queens must marry, and their husbands become master in their houses,' I said. 'That is what happened to Her Grace's predecessor, Queen Mary Tudor; and so her people's love for her was destroyed.'

'I know.'

'And Queen Elizabeth may still marry. She must be stopped from marrying a Catholic.'

'That also I know,' said Robert Sellier. 'How can I serve you?'

'By getting me some money.'

Sellier straightened carefully. 'A pawn shop?'

'Not precisely. I have several jewels: five rings and a chain of considerable worth. If you can sell them discreetly and without letting the buyer rob me, you may have one-fifth of the money as your fee.'

Sellier whistled. 'An inducement to honesty.'

What Dangers Deep

'Yes. What *does* matter is that, in addition to realizing money, no jewel known to be mine reappear, unaltered or unmelted, in the shops of Kraków.' I handed him a ring: a ruby this time. It shames me to admit that my uncle had given it to me. My reasons for this piece of ingratitude I will tell later on.

Sellier took the ring and tucked it into his hanging purse. 'I'll see to it, Master Philip. You need money: does that mean you also need help?'

I sighed, knowing I did not have to tell him. But he was the nearest thing I had to an English friend in this city. 'No. I need a base pleasure.'

'Ah. Well, every man does, sir, some days.'

'Knock at my door when you have the money,' I said. 'I'll send Ambrose away.'

'I will. Would tomorrow night be good enough?'

'Of course.' I shook his hand, and he let me out.

I cannot call my lust an appetite, for that would imply that it involved my wishes. At this time I would not have agreed I desired anything but freedom from the pressure that made me dread to touch my loins, or that filled my mind, as I lay trying to sleep, with indecent images.

Even at fifteen or sixteen, when lust gives a boy most trouble, the idea of a loose unchastity had bored and distressed me. I did what I had to then, and did not come away harmed, as some young men seem to be, by intimacy with bodies so different from our own – so lubricious in their secretions, so shocking when dirty, and rousing so genital a lust. In any case I liked women, and by eighteen I had steadied enough to think of lust as a form of skilled friendship – a union of gifts and competence that fascinated me, and that turned my desire not towards prostitutes but to ardent, frequent loves. Of course the girls were older (by which I mean twenty-five) and married, and most said no; and if I discovered that a beautiful woman can lack intelligence and honour, at least I never fell into that foolishness of woman-hatred that is still fashionable among our philosophers, and that makes these pretentious gentlemen sound, I think, like so many jeering schoolboys. I always had my mistresses and my women friends; and very rarely had I felt the need for bodily service, for a simple skilled relief, that moved me to write that evening to Sabina Korytowska.

Madam,
If I dared I would address to you the words the poet wrote to the lady from whom he stole three kisses:

> *Thénot sur ce bord ici,*
> *A Vénus sacre et ordonne*
> *Ce myrte, et lui donne aussi*
> *Ses troupeaux et sa personne.*

With the note I despatched – using Ludovic as messenger, because I trusted him though I hated to employ him on such an errand – a brooch I had bought with the money Sellier had paid over to me: a rose in tourmaline with grey pearls pendant, the carved flower shimmering from green to lilac-pink.

An hour later Ludovic brought back a note written on unscented paper, in a serious, precise handwriting.

Sir,
I am not skilled at these games, and can answer you only in the words of another poet:

> *Mais je n'suis pas déesse, et si ne le puis être:*
> *Le ciel pour vous servir seulement m'a fait naître.*
> *De vous seul je prends mon sort aventureux.*

Will you honour me by accepting an invitation to supper tomorrow night at eight o'clock?

Your servant,
Sabina Korytowska.

What Dangers Deep

Heaven gave me life only to serve you: my hazardous fate depends on you alone.

I left Ludovic and Ambrose out of it, but took the fifteen servants Antony had originally chosen out as my bodyguard. When I reached the house in Reformacka Street I found, from the courtesy of Mademoiselle Korytowska's servants, that they expected bodyguard as well as master. *So much for privacy*, I thought as I climbed the stairs. It seemed the lovers of Kraków seldom moved except in the middle of an army; I suspected the gossips of Kraków were bound to notice these assignations *en masse*.

She opened the door to me herself. Beyond lay a candlelit room with a small table set with food and flowers, and a bed, its covers closed. Perhaps, as Antony had guessed, she was as old as eighteen; in any case her face, a round oval, was as innocent, as full of courteous comradeship as if she had been one of my sister's friends. Her hair was brown, her eyes of some light colour; someone skilful had plucked her eyebrows and her hairline, which made her look even younger. She had strained her hair back into a tight chignon, and her bodice of green figured velvet plunged low enough to show me nipples as delicate as hedge-roses, and to emphasize the purity of neck, shoulders and breasts. Like every Polish woman I ever met, she had a sweet voice. She said with literate assurance, 'Master Sidney, you honour my house. Will you come in and take some supper?'

'Thank you, Mademoiselle, yes.' (We had begun in French and continued so.) I had already eaten, since I hate to combine food and love; but I needed an hour to assess her, and I intended to come away satisfied. So we sat and I let her serve me, which she did with an apparent liking and an impersonal courtesy. 'I saw you once,' she said. 'On the day *Pan* Zamoyski brought you back into Kraków. I was so very sorry for you all that day.' With a shock I remembered: the girl in green.

'Yes, I do recall you,' I said.

'So I saw you first on that sad day,' remarked Sabina, serving herself frugally (I guessed she too had in truth already eaten) and sitting down. 'And I thought then that I would like to meet you. I hoped you might hear of me and write.'

'Mademoiselle—'

'Sabina.' She shelled a walnut for me. Some have unusually hard shells. This one did, and it amused me to see her frown at it severely, though briefly. Then very strong hands dealt with it with a *crack*, and she handed me the walnut-meat.

'Sabina, you speak of that day. Tell me, what do the women think?'

She frowned again. 'About the lady Maria?'

'Yes.'

Her face showed a sort of plain goodwill, like a schoolgirl talking of a friend. 'Well, you are not asking me about those who like her.' I shook my head. 'And many do. But some say she is lying: that she *does* remember—' she crossed herself – 'what happened to her sister: remembers but refuses to confess. And some say worse: that she was party to Yolanta's murder.'

'My God, on what evidence?'

'On none. They need none. *I* do not believe it: I think it a terrifying thing to forget where one has been – truly to forget. And I wonder, you know, whether she may not begin to ask herself if the accusers are right. You know her, sir?'

'A little.'

'Then protect her from her guilt,' said Sabina, 'for she will invent it.'

We had descended from desire with such chilling abruptness that Sabina decided, to my gratitude, on continued sobriety. She led the talk to other subjects – to Paris and Madame Marguerite, and whether we English, as rumour says, customarily kiss strangers on the mouth as a first greeting (we do: the only one of our customs the Italians envy), and whether the virgins at our Court wear necklines cut so low they expose the full breast (they do: even Her Grace at forty-one still shocked the Puritans by wearing this fashion).

When we had eaten, Sabina rose and, her face grave, slipped the ribbon-knots that tied her sleeves to her bodice. The sleeves slid off; she laid them on her chair, and, with the warm muscular curves of her arms thus bared in contrast to the green velvet dress, went to pick up her lute. Then she simply sat down on the bed.

She played the lute well, and for a while I listened. Then I removed my doublet and, sitting down beside her, took the instrument away.

Her mouth tasted of fresh wine. When she slid her arms around me I said, 'No, do not move: I will do it all.'

Her bodice unlaced down the front, and the voile shift beneath it pulled down to expose her breasts. I handled them hard (the next time I enjoyed her I saw the marks of my fingers fading yellowed from her breasts, and paid her extra for the custom I feared I had cost her). I did not undress her, but bore her down, crushing her, and marvelling as I always do at the fragility and muscular resilience of the body beneath me. She obeyed me and made no sound. I took her with her skirts around her waist; and remember almost screaming with the joy that wrings our inmost nerves with absolute sensual accuracy.

The second time Sabina pressed it from me, seeing that I needed it. The third I worked hard for, and grew almost bored until – freed by some thought or some motion of the woman beneath me – the power seized me again, and wrung out of me the utmost ecstasy with the most profound and searching pang.

Afterwards I said, 'I'll be kinder next time, if you'll let me come to you again.'

'Whenever you wish, only give me a day's warning,' she answered. I let her cradle me; and then slept, defenceless, the brief sleep that Nature exacts from us after such work.

* * *

I returned home from Reformacka Street at four in the morning, sent my servants to bed, and went straight to the Turkish bath. There I lingered only long enough to get clean, for I already felt sleepy enough. Afterwards I had to pull back on a shirt that still smelt of the sweat of rutting, and faintly of a stranger's body. These traces of odour oppressed me, for (I was young enough not to have noticed it before) I was exhausted, and the sadness and overfastidiousness that sometimes succeed intercourse had begun to irritate me. It was therefore in quietness of spirit that I lit my chamber-candle and climbed the stairs to bed.

Thank God I remembered, out of habit, to quench the candle, for I was sleeping as I fell back upon the pillow. *Pan Zamoyski sometimes enjoys her*, said Antony's voice, as clearly as if he were in the room. *But she looks like Yolanta*, replied my own voice, detached and audible.

Only sleep could have freed me to make the association. I sat straight up, sweating, broad awake, my eyes open in the dark. I remembered Sabina as she walked away from me to pick up the lute: the set of her strong youthful back; the dancer's neck and shoulders; hair precisely similar, not in its style but in its colouring. Only my dreaming mind had recognized it. Had another man done so, dreaming or awake? For from certain angles, with a melting elusiveness, Sabina Korytowska did indeed resemble the vanished Yolanta.

Fourteen days before Christmas *Pan* Zamoyski brought Dorotea home from her sister's room and stayed with us for supper. I had not seen Maria in two days; it seemed she was sleeping a great deal. Over supper we talked mainly about events in France, and about a recent Protestant rally broken up by the King's troops in Paris. Apparently the bystanders had included, to the embarrassment of everyone, the King's brother-in-law Henri de Navarre, whose proximity to the procession had arisen, he said, from innocent curiosity.

What Dangers Deep

'If he ever becomes King, do you think he will take France towards his religion?' I asked Zamoyski, assuming, like everyone else in Europe, that the King of Navarre was in fact a Protestant.

Zamoyski shook his head. 'No. The Reformed Faith has not taken root in France as it has, say, in Scotland or in the Netherlands. I think France is somehow Catholic at its root, and that if Monsieur de Navarre were ever to come to the throne he must revert to the Old Religion. For one thing, the Church will finance him only if he does. But truthfully, Philip, I think Protestantism in France will prove to have been only a toy for the rich man and the scholar.'

Dorotea, smiling, cleared her throat. 'Excuse me, Uncle. Perhaps since it is nearly Christmas God will forgive me for tempting Fortune by telling you.' Antony looked up from his wine-cup. 'I know it has been only a few weeks, but I hope – I think – I am with child. And you are all my family. I could no longer bear my joy alone.'

'Bravo!' said Zamoyski, and rose and kissed her.

But Antony laid his hand over his wife's. 'Dorotea, let us hope with caution. Nothing could give me more joy, but let us wait eight more weeks to be sure. And by *next* Christmas I *promise* you a child!'

She nodded, laughing and blushing.

That led to more conversation; and an hour passed before I had the chance to say, 'Antony, may I talk with *Pan* Zamoyski for a few moments in your study?'

'Of course,' replied Antony. 'In fact . . .'

'We know, you want to speak with her alone.' Zamoyski glanced at me with a certain hard shrewdness: his voice was amiable. 'Come along, Philip.'

In the study I faced him and said: 'My lord, I have learned what you must have known could not be kept from me: that my family owes your family a blood-debt.'

'Oh, God *spare* us, boy!' The voice was a bellow: the anger instant and appallingly controlled. Zamoyski struck the table with his cup. 'Go to France if you want blood-debt; go halfway up Castle Hill if you want to stumble on one. Is this world not full enough of blood? Let me tell you one thing about men: they enjoy shedding the blood of others, and they have a hunger to kill and die. What blasphemous lunacy can make blood a coin of barter between you and me?' I did not move; he was shaking. In a normal voice he said, 'My brother Tomaśz, whom I loved and love, went on a scholar's errand, as was his duty to his King. At Castle Doyle troops under your father's command, in a mutiny for which I am told your father punished them, murdered everyone, including my brother. And this was ten years ago, when you were a child. I have forgiven; nor will I ever know what man slew him. My brother is earth and spirit now; and we must live together.'

I fell to one knee. 'My lord, there is nothing I can give you. If Tomaśz had not died, then perhaps Helena might have lived, and . . .' *And, somehow, Yolanta.* Zamoyski nodded, gazing down at me. 'I tell you formally that my family owes your family what atonement lies within human power; nor will I accept a rescission of that debt. In the meanwhile I offer you apology: a word that may sound impudent, but I can find no better.'

'It does not seem impudent,' said Zamoyski gently. 'Rise, Philip. We must get back to our hosts.'

'They won't want us yet. Please tell me why you concealed the *manner* of Tomaśz's death.'

'And so explain, in passing, why a man reputed to be intelligent seems to make nothing but cloddish errors in dealing with men and women? Or so it has begun to appear to me. I *did* tell Helena and Dorotea the truth; and even that I regret. His very loss hurt them so much, and the girls were so little. I told Yolanta and Maria the truth about five years later. You must understand, Philip: Ireland seems as remote from us as New Spain. Kraków was fascinated by *Helena*'s death, but they knew little about the death of Tomaśz. For the children's sake and for the sake of our privacy I gave out a gentler story. I know now that no lie of that sort *can* succeed; but if I had to tell children of nine and ten, not only that they would never see their father again, but that he died in his blood, then I would lie to them again.'

Zamoyski motioned me down beside him on the window-seat. 'Next week the artisans will set up their carved crèches in the Square, and the Princess Anna will judge among them. Please be there: we have given you little gaiety and beauty . . . You have seen Sabina Korytowska.'

'Yes, my lord.'

Zamoyski smiled, more with a reflective kindness than with amusement. 'Does it trouble you to share a woman's body – as if it were somehow a commerce between man and man?'

'I've never liked sharing, my lord. But she is a courtesan, free to choose.'

He nodded. 'I think it is time I gave Sabina a dowry and a kiss for friendship's sake. While you are in Kraków I judge it best that we not be rivals. When you are with her think, if jealousy tempts you, of other men, but not of me.'

'My lord, you need not be so generous,' I said, and did not say: *I will not take your charity*. 'I cannot support Sabina. You are a more lucrative lover to her than I, and you will be here longer. She will not thank me for losing you.'

'Sabina will not lack lovers, nor will she lack money,' said Zamoyski. 'This is not charity, as you are thinking, but simply prudence. I am an imprudent man in many things, and also impulsive. In a statesman, both are atrocious faults.' He tapped my shoulder, indicating that we must both rise. 'Let me hone my virtues for my soul's sake. As for this pregnancy–' he gestured towards the door that concealed our hosts – 'I pray she may carry, but it is the first time, and she is not young. I wish I felt less fear for her. I think she will lose it; and in a way I should be glad. An early miscarriage is easier than the loss of a fuller hope. Come, we must join them, and somehow explain my shouting.'

Sixteen

Since I now saw so much of him at Zamoyski's house, I had ceased even pretending to go to Father Laurence's lectures. Collegium Maius had become, at least for the present, a place a Protestant and a foreigner should avoid; and attendance in Maria's chamber replaced it in the structure of my days.

I now had two people to watch and to protect: Laurence and Maria. Waiting is a form of action, and one of the most difficult. The grey sky was filled with cold smoky clouds, but brought no snow; and as artisans, in the back-rooms of the shops, shaped their manger fantasies out of paint and gold leaf and carved wood and spangles, I made myself gently useful, and watched Maria and Caspar Laurence befriend each other.

He would not, I now knew, try to force her mind. 'The Arab doctors have an art,' he said, 'of making the patient look into a flame or at a moving, shining object – say a pendant on a chain. This soothes the mind and renders it, within limits, obedient to the doctor. Some memories blanked out by terror can be recovered from a mind so reassured. But I think this method, which is fallible and limited when dealing with profound memory, to be dangerous in Maria's case. I know her friends want the content of her memory; but not at the price of her stability. Let her healing grow in wholesome balance first. That will take more time than any public curiosity will tolerate. But I think she wants to tell us when she can.'

'And if she can truly remember nothing?' I demanded.

Laurence shrugged. 'Then she will need a different kind of healing – and need it desperately.'

Zamoyski's house consisted of four wings that enclosed not a courtyard, but the garden on which he had made me look down that first night from his study. Given that it was built on a hill, this square of lawns and flowerbeds had a charming rustic slope, for which the rise of the house compensated on the far side. On the second storey of the house a gallery ran all round the rectangle: sparsely furnished, with tapestries on whitewashed walls, beamed ceilings and floors that smelt of beeswax polish. From there I could look down on the patterns of green with which Zamoyski's gardeners tried to tempt our interest in winter: evergreen topiary and mazes of some hard-wintering hedge-plant.

Here we began to walk Maria gently once she could stand. She liked my company for these walks; the two doctors and a waiting-woman followed behind, close enough to help but not to hear.

'Rain again,' Maria said, looking at the panes streaming with grey water. 'We do not usually have a Christmas thaw. It makes the light in here so changeable and dull.'

She had tucked her hand through my arm, though she leaned on me only a little. I said, 'How do you feel today?'

Maria gasped and replied, 'Like someone cut in half.' If it was a plea, I took it up too slowly. We walked on. 'I miss her, Philip,' said Maria. 'She is not coming back.'

'No,' I said softly, 'I think she is not.'

'They all want it from me,' she said, 'the secret they think I contain. And the secret is that I can give them nothing. My memory ends in the Grove, and resumes in bed, at home. They tell me there was a time when they could not find me. And I search backwards, and *I cannot find myself.* Do you think,' she demanded suddenly, 'that I killed my sister?'

'How could you have done so? Sit down.' She took one of the

benches that were all the gallery offered. Our *doyens* hesitated, then sat down to wait for us on another. I said, 'Maria, why did it anger you that last night when Yolanta offered me her ring?'

'Because I gave it to her.' She smiled, tears streaking her cheeks. 'She often gave my presents away, and always saw to it that I knew. When we were small she used to destroy my toys. She would smear my clothes with ashes from the fire; leave fragile gifts outside, to be melted in the sun. When my clothes hung drying on the line she would tear them down and trample them in the dirt.' I offered her my handkerchief, folded so our elders need not see it; she used it with quick discretion. 'During the two years she was in France I wrote her a letter every week. She never answered one. She mocked and repeated every secret I ever told her.'

'Why did you let her treat you so?'

'I did not have skill to stop her. I hate to hurt others: Yolanta seemed to find relief in hurting me. I hated her, and oh Philip, I loved her so!' An agony of weeping – strangled, almost silent – took her; I enfolded her, and saw Father Laurence rise warily, then obey my gesture. 'I want her *back*! Oh, give her back to me! Let her come *home*!' Into my shoulder, stifled by the pressure of my hold, Maria screamed her entreaties, while the doctors watched, wondering when to intervene.

At last, when she seemed empty of anguish, I held her away, gripping her firmly. Her face was scarlet, hot and streaked with weeping. 'Maria, what reason had Yolanta to dislike you?'

'None that I knew. I loved her, praised her, gave her gifts–' she stumbled a little – 'I served her, was loyal to her. I believe she hated me because I existed. Do you think I killed her?'

'I know you did not.'

'How?'

'You loved your sister, Maria. Consult your own heart's knowledge.'

Maria stared at me with eyes so dilated I thought their blackness might have penetrated night itself. 'Yes, I did love her. Then,' she whispered, 'in the time I do not remember, where was I? Did I cease to exist – *and then begin again?*'

Winter's cold came back to us just before the Feast of the Holy Manger. I had not realized Kraków celebrated this festival at night, and that we would inspect the crèches – some hundred of them, I think – not only with torches, but by the light of lamps dancing and trembling on lines of cable, or hung from poles.

The Market Square at Kraków is huge: in the night, through which for this one evening of the year we could wander in safety, it seemed to stretch to the edges of vision. The isolated buildings – Cloth Hall, the Tower – stood dark, lest their windows eclipse the lanterns; but the doors of Sancta Maria had been flung open. From them flooded candlelight, with the odour of pine and the burnt-rose smell of incense. Reduced to doll-size by distance I could see the closed doors of the triptych, a shield of matte gold. They would be opened only when the litter-bearers carried in the winning crèche, shoulder-high, and set it down before the altar.

Vendors sold food at stalls in the Square – sausages on wooden prongs, heavy slices of honey-cake, and confections in almond-paste. In the lantern-shadows gentle, voluble crowds ate and sauntered and criticized each crèche mounted on its table – each table-cloth having been donated, with canny generosity, from the middle-value stock at Cloth Hall. I do not think anyone in Kraków would have dreamt of violence on this night; and as Antony and Dorotea and I moved among the crowds I noticed that pleasant characteristic of the Poles, the delicate courtesy they can assume in public towards strangers. The crowd had its drunkards and its beggars, and people treated them with a gentleness that delighted me.

I did not care for the crèches: some small as toys, some confections five feet high, each representing every possible variation on stable, infant, Virgin, beasts and Eastern Kings. Some were all silver and hung with icicles of glass; some laid with real straw and painted in peasant colours – red and blue, yellow and gold and orange, all streaked together like oriental clouds. One represented the entire inn from which the holy couple had been shut out, with all its little carved guests feasting or sleeping four to a bed. I even noticed a tiny figure using a chamber-pot in a corner, pissing a minute stream of silver wire.

These fantasies did not interest me. The truest beauty lay in the darkness and the lamps; for on the cables above me hundreds of candles burned in blown-glass bells, and, by some tradition, the colours were invariably pale. And so there wavered over the Square an exquisite mixed light of honey-colour, of violet, of radiant white-green; of pink and orange and cool, strange blue. I have never – even later at Kenilworth, when my uncle made his famous festival in Her Grace's honour, and I wrote for her the play called *The Lady of May* – seen anything more beautiful. Of course it made it harder to judge the crèches, and I saw the Princess Anna, surrounded by no visible guards, peering at them conscientiously, obviously dreading the responsibility of disappointing the losers. Someone spoke to her: she laughed, and I lost sight of her, while Dorotea's face beside me swam from blue to primrose light, and then into a band of soft orange.

Antony, calling apology to us, had fallen behind to squire a woman friend. Dorotea said, 'Philip, what is wrong?'

I smiled down at her. 'You are with child and therefore to be cherished, and the night is beautiful. Nothing is wrong.'

'Then why have you ignored me the last three times I spoke to you?'

'Good God, have I? I beg your pardon.'

'You had better tell me. I will not cast the child, you know.'

I frowned. 'What did Helena look like?'

We paused before a crèche, one of the peasant ones done in brilliant blues and greens and reds. 'Very slender. Pretty-plain, with thin lips and hair the colour of Yolanta's. In her adolescence she might have passed for a boy: she had flat breasts, and she loathed the childbirths, I remember. I liked her: she was a wit. I think she hated the men who had cast her out from the University: they had humiliated her before us all. And it is a dangerous thing, I suspect,' said Dorotea with apparent serenity, 'to have a mother who hates: unforgivingly hates.'

'And Yolanta and Maria, did they love each other?'

'Yes.'

'Would you have said either one tyrannized over the other?'

Dorotea stopped, gazing up at me. 'She has told you, then. What Maria says is true; but I think Yolanta believed that *Maria* was the stronger. She is prettier: that matters between women. And my father preferred Maria because of her scholarship: she loved what he loved, and was intelligent and teachable and gentle. It makes me weep, now none of us can embrace her, to think how Yolanta laboured to equal her sister. She fought with Maria; she fought with my father; she even attacked herself. After Helena died I found Yolanta's arms bruised black, with circles of teeth-marks where she had bitten herself.'

'That is pitiable,' I said.

'*I* pity her,' replied Dorotea. 'But believe Maria: she tried to placate Yolanta, and would not defend herself. And even as a small child Yolanta could rule us all by her rages. I think she found anger easiest.'

'Did Helena prefer either daughter?'

We paused before a silver fantasy: lace and icicles and a Virgin huddled in a silver robe, and the breath of the beasts blowing white. Dorotea shook her head. 'No, she did not prefer, but she tried to protect Yolanta from the quarrels with our father. And Yolanta deeply loved her mother – that I know.'

A cheer, with some groans, arose at a distance from us; then applause. 'They have chosen a winner,' I said. Men were hoisting one crèche on to the victor's litter. 'Then,' replied Dorotea, 'let us follow them into the church.'

Seventeen

Advent and Christmas and the New Year's Feast were all to be consumed by the experience I must now describe; and if my story returns to other aspects of Advent, of Christmas, of the New Year, my reader must remember that this experience never spared me. Through all other events of that season I never forgot that with nightfall I must go where I was driven.

For two years of my boyhood it had been like this: fourteen and fifteen, I think, had been the worst. My steadying towards twenty had made me confident it would never happen again. I had been wrong. In Kraków that winter there opened on me a desire against which no exhaustion, no boredom, no longing for private dignity had any power. I would relieve myself at night; lie still, hoping for peace for twenty minutes; and then realize that lust must be served again. Of necessity I would do this, sometimes straining for the final risible indecency that would empty me; and then wash off the sweat, so that I began to make the servants leave an extra ewer of water in my room. Had they smiled I would have struck them: servants know everything, and certainly the house knew this.

As for Sabina, I sold every jewel I had to pay for her twice a week. I have found that other human beings are often compassionate to a young man's lust; and because I went often (and, with my guard, in necessary publicity) to Sabina, the laughter in which I was too distressed to recognize liking spread beyond our household: spread to the crowds in Market Square.

For strangers indulging their mirth at the expense of a foreigner, they were subtle, even kind. No one so much as winked; and if the shopkeepers began to treat me with a certain mocking admiration, I think now it held an element of gentleness. No one provoked me to knock him down, which was fortunate since I would have quarrelled with almost anyone; and months passed before I realized that their mockery had hidden a good-natured reversal of judgement. Ever since I came to Kraków I had run a certain danger from the mob. I am glad their admiration did not reveal the humiliating source of my new safety.

I suppose the soul somehow feeds desire into our loins: I remember one of the Saints remarks that our genitals can only take joy according to their nature. This leads to the charming, and I think true, implication that the presence of God might induce in us the climax of love.

But it was not love that drove me to Sabina. She never abated her prices for me, and I tried to repay her by giving pleasure. We came to like each other. I admit I thriftily made all the use of her I could, and by Christmastide was staying with her for several hours at a time, returning home only a couple of hours before dawn. Frowning at my exhaustion, she would re-arouse desire when she knew I was not empty, and help me to the ultimate profound pang of emptying that would release me for twenty-four hours.

Desiring nought but how to kill desire – so I wrote ten years later, after the single other time. I could have shed tears of shame – did shed them once, punching my fists against the walls – when lust insulted my tired, disinterested mind, and again forced on me its relief.

No illusion of love drove me: no connection, then, to help me link my longings with this hunger. And then I would go to Sabina, ashamed that another human being should see me in this helplessness; and I would take from her, or she would give me, that delicate racking of the nerves that in the end empties us into a triumph so exhausting that sometimes, pausing on that height, I have wondered whether this *was* joy: whether it was even pleasure.

Sabina's servants always kept a fire burning; and we had worked so hard that night that even in the Polish winter (outside snow was falling) we lay naked on top of the sheets. Propped on several pillows, I studied Sabina. She lay on her belly, her face cushioned, with lounging comfort, on her arms. Hair stiffening with sweat streamed in tendrils over her back, down to haunches tense and shapely, and to legs as limber as those of an athletic boy. 'Philip?' she said.

'Yes?'

'My lord Zamoyski has stopped coming to me.'

'I'm sorry,' I replied, not knowing what else, or how much, to say.

Sabina raised herself on her elbows and smiled at me. 'He made me a large gift at our leave-taking, so you needn't frown. And he explained the reason.' Her hand, used with skill, beseeched me. 'No, do not be angry: he spoke of you only very briefly. He did not pay me to do anything for you, nor ask me to do anything for you.' She rolled on to her back. 'I wonder whether you have noticed: he has eliminated me as a source of new information about his household. Not that he ever talked of his family to me: it would have been improper, and I do not want the anger of such a lord. Philip, do you come here to learn about Yolanta and Maria?'

'How often have I asked?' I too had rolled on to my elbows, so that we faced each other.

'Once,' said Sabina.

'Then you do know something more.'

She frowned. 'But you see, *Pan* Zamoyski has taken care that I shall know only gossip.'

I nodded. 'And he fears that gossip? What risk would you run by telling me?'

'Within limits, and since the news is old, none. He is kind.

And great though he is among us, this scandal in his household is fundamentally a private thing, and cannot influence the election, either against Prince Bathóry or for the Archduke Ernst. Ernst's factors in Kraków have used it viciously, but I doubt it will change much.'

'Then you think the election is resuming its course?'

Sabina shrugged. 'I think May is tardy for an election and then for a muster; and I thank God spring comes late in the mountains.'

'What gossip,' I said, 'does *Pan* Zamoyski hope is the last I shall hear from you? And why should you tell it to me?'

'To help you,' said Sabina. 'Listen. Certain people suspected Yolanta was pregnant when she came back from France late last summer. And I can tell you one thing more. The tryst that begot the child left her so bruised it shocked the maids who saw her naked.'

'Did someone beat her or rape her, then?'

'I do not know. I tell you: *She came back from France that way*, so it was not her uncle who beat her when he found out. A man who raped her might have been punished in France, I do not know; I have heard no such rumour.'

Softly I said, 'You think, then, that she solicited violence against her own body?'

Sighing, Sabina drew up the sheet. 'Again I do not know.'

I swore.

'What?' said my companion.

'Sabina, do you think Yolanta is dead?'

'Yes.'

'Lord Zamoyski resisted it, but I believe he now thinks so too. At last they have planned a Mass for the Dead in Sancta Maria on January sixteenth.' Sabina crossed herself. 'Have you heard of Minotauros, Lord of the Labyrinth?'

'Prince Theseus and the maze? Of course I have. He found his way to the centre.'

'And so must I. There must be a centre that explains all this.

What Dangers Deep

For weeks I have sought out the past of strangers I never knew – dead people about whom I care nothing. We cannot live by seeking the motives of the dead.'

'Then forget the dead,' said Sabina, 'and Yolanta too. What makes you think there is a centre, Philip? And why, and what, should it explain?'

After the English fashion, Antony's household ate its first meal of the day at noon. When we had finished it my godfather said, 'Philip, will you attend me in my study for a moment? Dorotea, will you excuse us?'

'Yes, of course,' replied his wife. 'You know I'm going to the Castle this afternoon. Maria is beginning to hate the house. *I* should, if I were a prisoner there.'

'Nevertheless it is for her uncle to say when she shall leave it. Philip—?'

'At once, sir.' I bowed to Dorotea; she made a *moue* of sympathy, and I could not help grinning back.

We settled in Antony's study. 'Wine?' said my godfather after a pause.

'I've just had some, sir. Have letters come from my uncle of Leicester? Is that the reason for this?'

'Letters have not yet come, but I expect the courier by Christmas. I hear *Pan* Nemet Josef has invited you to go hawking with him tomorrow.'

'Yes, Antony. Do you object?'

'Not at all, he's an excellent man. You'll have poor enough sport at this season, I don't doubt, but at least the roads are frozen, not thigh-deep in snow. The New Year makes up for that, I promise you: I've been in Poland long enough to know.'

'I'll remember,' I said. 'Excuse my short temper, Antony. Can I serve you?'

'I want you to know that my household staff, Market Square, Mariacki Close, Butcher's Market – in short, everyone from Collegium Maius to the top of Wawel Hill – approves of your manhood as proven on Sabina Korytowska. And that is the fault of your inexcusable imprudence.'

'Then Market Square, Mariacki Close, and the University up to the top of Wawel Hill can all be damned.'

'Since two-thirds are Catholic and the other third Protestant,' observed my godfather with serenity, 'that is indeed the general contention. You've done well not to pick fights. Never fight a man who congratulates you over a woman here: laugh and pass it by. Philip, you may still have a year on the Continent before you get back to England. I cannot watch you strip yourself of money without asking if I can help.'

I stretched out my legs and shrugged. 'I'm grateful, Antony, but no, I need no help.' He steepled his fingers, considering me with an expression so transparently duplicitous that I added, 'And if my banker tells me someone has made a large deposit to my account, I will ask him to trace it back to the source.'

'Then what,' demanded Antony gently, 'can I do?'

'Pray for it to stop,' I said.

'Have you fallen in love with Mademoiselle Korytowska? You know – forgive me – she is not worthy of your rank.'

'Whatever is driving me, Antony, it is not love for Sabina.'

'Love for whom, then?' said Antony.

It came to me then in simplicity. Irritation always carping; criticism that sought out quarrels; comparison that deliberately wounded: one whom I would grasp and hold to force her memory – such possessive right had I extorted from her helplessness.

I had held her naked in my arms, there on the rocks in the green light.

Maria.

We had left our escort across the road to fly their falcons for hare and other worthless winter game over the hard-crusted snow. We opened the cemetery gate. All around us, and especially over the graves, trees raised a whispering and a shadow of smoke.

'It is very beautiful in summer. The Abbey gardens are famous,' said Nemet Josef. I glanced back to where a timber Hall, as great as the palaces of our Anglo-Saxon kings, raised its buttresses above the trees. 'And there,' said *Pan* Nemet, 'unless I am mistaken, is the gardener. I have seen him here once or twice before. A gardener in winter seems to me so *sad*.' He clucked compassion a little mockingly, and bowed to the handsome, thin young monk who appeared, indeed, to have been inspecting the frozen flower-beds. The Brother had drawn up his hood and tucked his hands into the black sleeves of his habit. He turned on us dark eyes in a dark-bearded face, bowed, and continued his walking.

'What can he be doing?' I wondered.

'God alone knows what a gardener does in December. Watch over his bulbs? Sing them lullabies? This way.' Today we wore leather and furs; our gear creaked in the frost and gave off that animal smell I have always found disturbing. Over his arm Nemet carried looped one of the vine-wreaths one could buy in the market, its stems twined with ribbons instead of flowers.

'I have brought him something,' he said softly. 'I wish I could bring him life, or make him speak to me.' I glanced at him: his eyes were bright with tears controlled.

We passed among the trunks, and came to a grave with a new stone. In deep, crisp-edged letters the mason had carved in Latin the words:

> 'Man comes forth like a flower and is cut down.'

Nemet knelt and gently placed the wreath, then remained hunkered down, gazing at the stone. I sank on my knees beside him.

'Why,' I said, 'does it bear no name?'

'Because Jan Zamoyski thought it safest not to acknowledge who is buried here. A secretary of my own, a most gifted man, whom I recommended to Jan's service. Three months ago Jan, as he briefly wrote me, found reason to discharge the man. The boy died on his way home to France – of a fall from his horse, the monks told me; and they added that it was Jan who brought him here. One can only guess why Jan should happen to be on the road in the company of a servant he had discharged. Since then, I know, he has had many Masses said for his own soul and for that of the man who lies buried here: Jean Palmette.'

'Then you think Zamoyski killed this man?' I said.

Nemet shrugged. 'I think nothing: I only ask. Jean Palmette was half French, half Italian. He had curly hair, and his eyes were darker than the Brother-gardener's over there. He was a little man – I suppose he stood no more than five foot four – and he had vivacity, intelligence and wit. He wrote for me one poem for which I shall always feel gratitude and love; and he died when he was twenty-nine.'

'But Yolanta's child was conceived in Paris,' I said softly. The gardener was bending over a flower-bed.

Nemet Josef rocked on his heels; folds of fur and leather creaked with his motion. 'I bribe servants, Master Philip: despise me for it if you choose. But this man was mine, and I gave him to Jan – as I thought – for Jan's good and his own. I am to blame for whatever he may have done; and Jan, who is my friend, would not persist in lying to me about this matter unless, as I fear, the boy had somehow offended deeply. No: at the time Yolanta's child was conceived, Jean Palmette was still a servant in my house. As you see, a pattern emerges here if we detect or invent it. I need more information than I have.'

'And to whom,' I said, 'will that information ultimately go?'

He stared at me. The square face seemed impassive; the narrow eyes were hard. 'What, Master Philip, is holy to us both?'

I thought a moment. 'Truth,' I said.

'Then by God's truth and by his mercy I will not repeat any information I may learn through you. I want to know the truth about my friend. If you hear anything more from any source, I beg you to tell me.'

'I take your oath,' I said. He nodded. For several minutes we knelt silent beside the grave.

Presently Nemet said very softly, 'I *have* learned this. Sometime last September, about six weeks before you came to Kraków, Jean Palmette slept with Yolanta in Maria's room, because someone saw him leave before dawn. The two girls had, they said, intended to keep each other company that night, as women often do. But Maria served as doorkeeper to a tryst that somehow so harmed Yolanta that her lover fled from the house at daybreak. I think he ran away from *Pan* Zamoyski, and that he did not run far or quickly enough.'

'Had he ever mistreated a woman?'

'Not that I knew, or why would I have commended him to a family with daughters?'

I nodded. 'Yet you think he harmed Yolanta that night?'

'I know he did.'

'But what would elicit such violence from a decent man?'

Nemet shrugged. 'What would make a woman seduce a man to her own physical destruction?'

Christmas now lay two days away. People curtained their windows with streamers of red and green ribbon; tinsel Stars of Bethlehem had gone up over the lintels, and on every door hung a wreath of pine-boughs adorned with its own resinous, aromatic cones. The weather, however, continued not to help us. One slipped on frozen puddles everywhere, and icicles hung from the eaves, to be cracked off by children and sucked like sweets, or used as brittle swords. No snow fell to soften the grey of cobbles, of house-stone, and of the cloud-thronged sky.

Deliberately I had not seen Maria since my conversation with *Pan* Nemet. She was almost twenty years old: I had known many girls to be married at fourteen. It shocked me with surprise but not with abhorrence to imagine her guarding a door within sound of her sister's lovemaking. If anything it suggested complexity, not unnaturalness: I knew she had loved Yolanta. My own sport with Sabina must be, I thought, the sort of delight girls longed to share, if the danger of pregnancy did not deter them. Still, I needed to calm myself, and not to show Maria my knowledge.

So I stayed away. Weeks ago I had despatched Christmas gifts to home, but I needed something special for Dorotea – and had not found it by the time a need for supper brought me back to the Embassy on December twenty-third. In the hallway where the bridal party had hidden from Balinski's attack, I stopped to pull off my gloves. From two rooms away Antony's voice called, 'Philip!'

'I'm coming.' I crossed the dining-room and found the door to his study open. 'Good evening, Antony.'

'Good evening. We're bidden to Christmas at the Castle,' (I frowned) 'and I think we had better go. The Princess intends, with Jan's agreement, to make it Maria's first appearance in public since—' Antony shrugged. 'A small Court, but enough to test her composure gently, for her own good. Her doctors will both be there.'

'Then I'll go.'

'The courier came,' said Antony. 'Which would you rather have first: the letter from Robert, or the one from Her Grace the Queen?'

I held out a hand whose shaking shamed me. 'I may as well have both. May I sit down?'

'Please. Shall I stay?'

'I wish you would.'

'Steady, then,' said Antony. 'No rebuke can have power over you when it is so many weeks stale.' I accepted a cup of wine, acknowledging it with a grimace of thanks.

My uncle Robert's hand was more than usually illegible.

Philip, get out. Your mother is most bitterly distressed. In your father's absence I must ask you to get back at once to Vienna, and thence, I think, to Italy and England. What if the Emperor Maximilian attacks Poland, as they say here he may do? It is time we had you home. No duty to your friends abroad can supersede your obedience to us.

Your loving uncle,
Robert of Leicester

The other I opened carefully. On the page before me I saw the handwriting Roger Ascham had trained, as formal in its composure as her cool, pure voice with its drawling 'a's'. *Madam*, I thought, *it is not for lack of my grandfather's effort, or of my uncle's, that you are not simply our creature – one of us.*

Master Philip,
Robin tells me strange news of you. You will not continue to burden the lord Zamoyski with your presence: I think your safety too great an imposition, when private grief and his concern for the election both distress him. I am sorry for the young women, but I think it best that you return to Vienna. Your wisdom, if not your kindness, will tell you the truth – that there is nothing you can do. In honesty, therefore, decide in favour of those who love you, and come home to us by autumn.

Tell me what hope we have of Father Laurence: Antony wrote that you had talked with him.

At the bottom of the page I saw the weaving loops, calculated as a draughtsman's design, of her signature.

With such casual composure had she ordered me to desert Maria, and to deliver to her a man whose intention – to deceive her – torture could cure. She was not, I thought, as cruel as her father: she hated waste, and Laurence's hunger for martyrdom would have angered her. But what fortitude gave him such confidence against her? Young though I was, I did not presume to imagine that Laurence's belief in his own bodily courage was foolish or unfounded. However, no torturer can fail, given only time. Had Laurence chosen to forget the truth that physical possession of him, and not his intent, would determine what he told the Privy Council?

Or did he seek – I thought suddenly – not only to die, but to fail?

On one thing I wasted no doubt: I would not be dishonest with Her Grace. I knew I lacked both subtlety and experience. She had given me work to do: surely I could tell her a limited but honest story, and let her use the truth to judge against me if she must.

'Madam,' I therefore wrote that night:

> I have indeed talked with Father Laurence. I find him intelligent and good, but, so I believe, somehow disturbed in his judgement. I think that, because of some sickness of the mind, his intention is not sound, and that he seeks to destroy himself, using us as his instruments. My conscience will not let me despatch to the Privy Council a man I think to be ill: if his intention is self-murder – and I believe it is – then I cannot abet it. I beg you for more time, and also entreat your understanding on my remaining here for the present. I myself, by searching at the place where the two young ladies disappeared, recently found Maria Zamoyska – yes, found her – but not her sister, who has vanished utterly.
>
> Some propose a natural solution to this mystery, and some, as Your Grace may imagine in this priest-ridden country, a miraculous solution. But whatever happened to Mistress Yolanta, I cannot leave Kraków until I feel certain that her sister is not only alive, but sane and safe.

In one of the State rooms of the Wawel we celebrated a laborious Christmas feast. Princess Anna had chosen her

What Dangers Deep

guests with care: maturity, stability and kindness enfolded Maria, and the quiet sounds of adult pleasure. She sat in a chair surrounded by her uncle, the Princess, Dorotea and Antony, with her doctors a little behind. Father Laurence wore secular dress, and nursed a goblet of wine, from which I noticed he drank little. Solniecki sat beside him. Maria had gently declined my invitation to dance.

I wanted to dance that evening, though few of my partners were young. The room itself was an elegant delight – a floor of agate tiled in cream-colour, red and brown, and a golden chessboard-ceiling studded with carven roses. On the walls hung tapestries which the Princess said her father, the first King Zygmunt, had brought from Paris fifty years ago. In their faded reds and greens, courtiers in the dress of King Henry's day hawked and hunted among wildflowers woven with such art that I could identify each bloom – and sometimes, by guess, the face of a courtier or a lady my grandfather might have known.

We had eaten well; cloths had been folded, the trestles dismantled, and the floor cleared for dancing. Since Maria did not want me, and since a performance of La Volta had left me panting, I sat down beside Doctor Solniecki. 'Merry Christmas, Doctor. And you, Father.'

Laurence saluted me with his cup; Solniecki shook my hand. 'Merry Christmas, my lord Philip.'

'Doctor, a friend has written me from Paris and asked me to pass a letter to a cousin of his who serves my lord Zamoyski. He seems uncertain where the cousin is, and asked me to make sure. I do not know the man myself, but it does seem the matter is urgent: it concerns a lawsuit.'

'Ah well, when the French take to litigation . . .' The Doctor shrugged. 'And you want me to introduce you?'

'If you know the man. His name is Jean Palmette.' We were speaking, I took care, far too low for the people in front of us to hear.

I saw Zamoyski speak to Maria. She bent to her right to hear him, and the silken shawl of hair that masked her shoulders parted, its sheen altering in the candlelight. I was truly staring at her when Solniecki demanded, 'Why have you not asked my lord?'

'I will,' I said, 'but not now.'

'No, there you are right.' Laurence too appeared to be gazing at Maria, but I felt his listening. 'Jean Palmette,' said Doctor Solniecki, 'was a secretary who proved a thief, and so you may tell his cousin. A Book of Hours painted on Vellum disappeared from my lord Zamoyski's study, and was located in the man's baggage. So *Pan* Zamoyski set him on the road to France. If Palmette has a cousin in Paris, I am surprised he has not come knocking at the man's door. In any case you may send the letter back.'

'I will, and thank you. Perhaps he went elsewhere.' I shrugged. 'Father Laurence, might I come and talk with you this week?'

'I have no lecture tomorrow.' The subtle eyes rebuked me with his amusement. 'About two in the afternoon, perhaps?'

'Thank you, yes,' I said. Laurence nodded.

Again I studied Maria. Her elders had dressed her simply, in a pastel, peach-coloured velvet that was gentle to her pallor. The skirt and bodice were narrow, rising to a ruff edged with silver wire. The tire-woman had snipped the sleeves with little slashes, and had plucked through them the puffed folds of a gauze underdress.

The sheen of light in a young woman's hair arouses in us, I think, a profound animal tenderness – an admiration so primitive that Adam himself must have felt it. Maria's face was calm. Every once in a while I saw her ease her back into a straighter posture, as though it hurt her.

She had not danced this evening. Now I saw Zamoyski make a signal to the musicians and, rising, bow to her. The other guests fell back; Maria, with a troubled smile, took her uncle's

What Dangers Deep

hand and followed him alone into the middle of the floor.

Zamoyski had chosen a country-dance for her, lively and playful – the sort they start children on when they first begin to teach them. She must have known it all her life: it did not exhaust her as La Volta would have done, or expose her to the grave emotion of the Pavane. And as he drew her in – smiling as they bowed, circled and parted, only to rejoin – I saw Maria laugh and utter some protest that made him grin and shake his head. He moved well for so big a man, and when he caught her waist for the whirling motion that dissolved into a final bow, I saw with what careful gentleness he was touching her.

The music ended. Zamoyski held high Maria's hand. She drew away and, in homage to him, sank into a deep Court curtsey. Father Laurence set down his cup and led us in applause.

Servants offered wine to the musicians; and they brought in a troupe of tumblers who bored me for half an hour. Then the carollers came in carrying a silver star held aloft on a staff, and sang in French, in Polish, in German, the melodies all Christian nations share. They sang *'Illuminare Ierusalem'*, *'Christum wir sollen loben shon'*, and two we know in English to the words 'There stood in heaven a linden tree' and 'Our Blessèd Lady's Lullaby'.

People sank down on stools to listen, or on cushions on the floor. I remember one woman leaning against her husband's shoulder; and the faces – gentle, watchful, quiet. Of all melodies the Christmas songs, I think, speak most of kindness. In Europe we have chosen the Birth for our great festival, and not, like the Greek Church, the Resurrection. A birth unsullied, cold as silver: a promise in the ringing purity of its manifestation – not in the sorrow of its fulfilment.

The choristers sang, now, in Polish; but the words that came to me, unshared with anyone, were words to this same music that my nurses had taught me long ago.

> Iesu, sweet son dear!
>   On poorful bed thou lyest here,
> And that me grieveth sore;
> For thy cradle is but a byre,
> Ox and ass they be thy fere:
>   Weep I much therefore.
>
> Iesu sweet, be nothing wroth,
> Though I have ne clout ne cloth
>   On thee for to fold –
>   On thee to folden ne to wrap,
> Yet can I rock thee on my lap:
> So lie thou sweetly to my pap,
>   And keep thee from the cold.

'Very well,' said Father Caspar Laurence, laying the coffee-pot on the fire. 'Very well: you have found a grave in which, according to *Pan* Nemet, there lies a man called Jean Palmette; and Doctor Solniecki has verified that such a man existed. What if *Pan* Nemet is wholly lying?'

'Why should he lie?' I demanded.

Laurence shrugged. 'I have no idea. He says *Pan* Zamoyski brought the man to be confirmed dead – I believe you implied? – at the Abbey's infirmary, and then to be buried there.'

'That is what he said.'

'Why do you think Zamoyski buried the man, and in such secrecy?'

'Because he killed him,' I said.

The coffee frothed up the spout: Laurence deftly rescued it. 'Murder?'

'Or manslaughter. If he discharged the man, and then waylaid him on the road – if he had reason to be that angry – they might have fought, and Palmette could perhaps have been killed by accident. And Zamoyski had a reason for rage, as I have told you.'

What Dangers Deep

Laurence handed me my cup. 'Take care, it's hot . . . Listen: *Pan* Nemet has contrived, apparently in innocent human distress, both to slander Yolanta, whom we believe to be dead, and to arouse a suspicion of murder against *Pan* Zamoyski. Has he acted the part of a friend to either one? In truth, Philip?'

I sipped the hot liquid. 'I have verified the existence and disappearance of Jean Palmette. And I have from another source a rumour that Yolanta was not a virgin, and that she used violent practices. From a third source – Dorotea – I have heard very old evidence that Yolanta was capable even in her childhood of attacking herself in whatever anguish drove her. I believe that *Pan* Nemet's distress and puzzlement are real, and that Yolanta solicited Palmette to do something which may have given her uncle reason to kill him.'

'What are you going to do?'

'I mean to go back and learn what I can from the Brothers – if possible from the Infirmarer.'

'With the Grand Chancellor of Poland paying them to say Masses? You cannot be so simple. His gift to the Abbey will have been huge, and their obligation understood.'

'I know.'

'And Maria? Did you notice that *Pan* Nemet, in his seeming innocence, also contrived to slander her?'

This time I took longer to answer. 'Yes. But what little evidence I have been able to get still supports his statement about Yolanta's practices. What if she loved Palmette? I cannot believe he came to that tryst knowing what he was to do there – not to judge by his panicked flight. I think that as Yolanta prevailed on him, so she may also have prevailed on Maria. If one's sister were in love, it must be hard to know what loyalty would do; but to betray her would, I should think, have been impossible. If Yolanta begged her, what *could* Maria do? Tell her uncle? Tell her sister to find another bed?'

'That depends on the nature of Maria's loyalty. Do you notice how *convenient* Yolanta has become to us all? How the weight of blame has come to rest on a girl who is probably lying dead in a cave, or who has been raped and sold to the Turk? Dead or living, need we hurt her memory further without proof?'

'This is private talk, not slander,' I said. 'Or do you forbid me to make *sense* of what I hear, even if it is a wrong and wounding sense? Yolanta must have longed for peace from whatever anguish tormented her.' Laurence nodded. I said, 'What *was* that anguish? What could make sense of the bruises on her arms; of a virginity violently lost; of whatever she begged or induced Palmette to do?'

Laurence shrugged; his face was sad. 'If a woman longs for peace from being, then she is desperate; and I cannot with certainty understand her. She is gone, Philip, and we should be tender of her good name, and humble in our presumption of understanding.'

'But you are a doctor,' I said. 'Can you tell me nothing to make sense of the three things I know?'

'Why should a woman solicit others to destroy her?' inquired Laurence softly. 'Who can know? I cannot. But one destroys what is worthless. Or one enacts one's rage at others, inverted upon oneself. Or one is suffering and needs help; and only the cry of death has power to make them hear.'

Eighteen

The courier departed with my letter. Her Grace would receive it, I judged, some time in February.

When Anne Boleyn, Queen Elizabeth's mother, was beheaded for adultery many years before I was born, King Henry persuaded himself that this daughter was not his own, but the get of some other man: the lute-player Mark Smeaton with whom her mother was accused, or perhaps even of George Rochford, Anne's own blood-brother.

But in middle age Her Grace's cheeks have hollowed, and her face – while feminine in its oval planes and in the white translucency of her skin – has matured until she resembles her supposed grandfather by the paternal line, King Henry the Seventh (so think those who saw that King; and so even I think, who know of him only the Torrigiano bust, and the funeral-effigy which that same artist made for his tomb in Westminster Abbey). There is now no doubt that Her Grace *is* descended of both King Henrys. More, she came to the throne because the people loved her – while they hated my great-grandfather because (let us be frank) he fleeced them, and my grandfather because he was rebel, apostate and executed traitor. Her Grace is Queen by right; and my ancestors lie like Anne Boleyn, beneath the paving-stones of Saint Peter-ad-Vincula in the Tower, with their heads between their knees.

My family had worked hard to prosper under Queen Elizabeth. My mother took smallpox while nursing her, and so my mother was destroyed, while Her Grace's skin carries no mark she cannot conceal with rice-powder. I had seen my father worn out by the endless wrong we do in Ireland. I had seen my uncle Robert age, caught between devotion and cupidity, until he provoked the Queen's fury by longing for a consummated love in which to be beloved, like any other man.

And I too, I now began to understand, longed for her patronage, her trust, her approval – and for the gifts she could give. I, a twenty-year-old student who had written to her that I would not obey her order to come home – that the Privy Council had a purpose which *I could not abet*.

I who must look each day in the living face of Father Caspar Laurence.

I whom my mother had once comforted when I woke screaming, because I had dreamt of my grandfather lying dead with his head between his knees.

Her Grace would not receive my letter for weeks yet. But, in the days while we waited for Yolanta's funeral Mass, I felt descend on me an anger as certainly hers as though I had succeeded in piercing the near future. I could see her read my letter, her hand across her brow, her eyes serious with attention. I could see the hand stray down to press her mouth; could see the nearsighted eyes go cold. My uncle once admitted to me that she never spoke to him in a certain tone but that it made him tremble, although he had known her since she was five. Now I felt in my own flesh the fear he must dissemble as she turned on him her astonishment at my impudence.

You may lose her, you who have not even gained her, I thought. *What if you lose her? How to be loyal to Father Laurence then? How to be loyal to Maria?* Should I leave Kraków, and merit, by this human desertion, never to know how their stories ended? My grandfather had found life short. And who ought to accompany us, in this brief time that birth draws out to death, but those we have freely chosen in love – those to whom respect, pity and duty bind us?

These are the things I was thinking while we gathered in the gallery of Zamoyski's house, to proceed in a group to Sancta Maria for the Mass that would admit three months had passed since Yolanta vanished from the earth.

In the grey light from the windows I saw Dorotea, her hair cauled in black, go up to Maria and speak to her; then saw Maria hug the taller woman, kissing her on both cheeks. She was not smiling: her face had a tender gravity. Dorotea passed me, and I approached Maria. 'So she has told you?'

'That Doctor Solniecki has confirmed she is with child? Yes.' She wore black taffeta; a veil of black velvet hid her hair. 'Yes, I am glad,' she said.

It occurred to me that I had not visited Sabina in eight days. And this last week had frozen into stillness too my desire for Maria. Most likely, I thought, her women had told her about my mistress. 'Well?' she said abruptly. 'What do you see, Philip?'

'I beg your pardon?'

'I said, what do you see? The doll they all dress, comfort and pity? The daughter who repays them with cheer – with healing as best she may?'

'Be quiet, they may hear us.' I moved with her to lean on the window-sill. She had asked me a question, but the answer I discovered was different. 'Two of my sisters died when they were small.'

'Then tell me,' said Maria. 'How does one cease to grieve?'

It came to me that she did not deserve a lie. I said, 'I do not know, because I never ceased. I think some people cannot. I am sorry, Maria.'

'No, I am grateful for your honesty. *God*, how I want to be out of here.' In its soft violence the oath was savage – almost coarse. 'Do you think Madame Marguerite would take me in Paris?'

I should have expected it; but my silence held so unskilled a shock that Maria, staring at me, saw, I think, all the truth.

Behind us Solniecki had come through the door and was

explaining his lateness to *Pan* Zamoyski. Maria stayed still, her gaze arrested. The past weeks had added to her beauty a plainness that I liked. The hands she rested on the window-sill were long-fingered, deft, disproportionately large, and the double of Yolanta's. In them and in her eyes I saw suddenly a woman who was not young: a woman whose solitude mocked us with her despair and her charity on our suffering.

How long, I thought, could she sustain the appearance of recovery – even of composure?

'Ah,' she said softly. 'Yes, she was pregnant. *I should guess she is not now.*'

'Oh, Maria, have pity on yourself,' I whispered.

'I have been left to live,' she said. 'My whole body aches, every limb of it, as if I had the rheumatism.'

'You are too young for rheumatism,' I said, finding, in my distress, the least thing she had said.

'I know. Father Laurence says it is fear.'

'Maria,' called Jan Zamoyski.

My companion gathered up her skirts. 'Then,' she said, 'let us go mourn my sister.'

Three months had worn away the novelty of Yolanta's disappearance. The rhythms of life had begun – uncertainly at first and then with increasing confidence – to usurp our grief. The mind cannot retain shock: that is, I believe, impossible in Nature. And if Yolanta had entered Eternity, a quality of Eternity seemed now to touch us when we thought of her. Yolanta had always been gone, and we were sick of nonsense and mystery. To its relief, Kraków discovered in its midst a liar.

A stir greeted Maria's progress up the aisle clinging to her uncle's arm. All were here who could crowd into the church, and the Square too was half-filled with spectators and with Zamoyski's pikemen. I had felt, I thought, something like that stirring before; where? We filed into the front row of chairs – these were for the mourners; others stood, or had brought their own cushions – and I identified my fear. The head of a mastiff in the dark, and the ancient apparition that pads along our English roads, seen only by those whose destiny is to see and to contend with it.

The great gold angels of the triptych hung above us, shining in the candlelight. And so, to the polyphony of the choir, with pine-boughs and incense we celebrated our grief and surrendered the dead to God. For surely the dead need comfort as much as do the living.

It began when we turned to go. The choir was singing a recessional – 'It is my part, Lord, to keep thy commandments' – but their plangency covered more than the sounds of our retreat down the aisle. People gave way for us indeed; but above the choir, above our footsteps I heard a shouting in the Square; and then the crowd closed in front of us.

They were Maria's people; even now, made bold by their numbers, I think they were not precisely angry. But a mob when it finds its voice ceases to consist of men and women, and becomes a beast whose collective cruelty exceeds that of each individual. The faces that surged around us were ordinary and kindly in themselves; some Maria must have known. The roar of questioning, of accusation was for her; and she bore it with her head held erect and her eyes open – focused, I saw, on nothing.

Zamoyski, his arm about her waist, was dragging her. Our servants had drawn their swords. *'Let us through!'* Zamoyski's bellow could have shivered walls. From outside came shouting: the crowd in the Square seemed, by their tones, to be fighting among themselves.

They had battled Zamoyski's guard away from the steps, but not without resistance. We emerged into the grey, bright sun, and saw, for perhaps thirty seconds, what Maria's tormentors had prepared, and what some of the shouting had protested against. For not everyone liked the dumb-show that now stood on a wheeled platform just below the steps; and not everyone disliked Maria. For a moment we wavered, the party on the steps, as hundreds of minds considered her – pitying, angry, and trembling towards the laughter of ribaldry. For public suffering rouses lust in all of us.

On the platform, which measured no more than a yard square, someone had fixed a stake made out of a young tree. To it they had bound a cloth doll, its humanity sketched five feet tall, with limbs of sewn sacking and a featureless head stuffed, I suppose, with straw. Limp as an unconscious woman, this doll drooped from the ropes that held it to the stake. They had piled loose straw up to its knees. It wore a black dress like Maria's; and over one detail its makers had taken extreme care. The wig of hair it wore shone, combed loose, and blew in the wind like a veil; and it was made of pale yellow silk.

Utter silence fell. There was motion at the edges of the crowd: Zamoyski's pikemen were forcing their way back to us; and Maria stood staring – a pretty girl, intelligent and solidly made, marked only by the bruises of exhaustion around her eyes. Zamoyski tugged her forward, down one step towards protection. His captain shouted to him and he called back; and someone we never caught stepped forward and laid a torch to the straw at the dummy's feet. There was a billowing crackle. Straw, stake and effigy all flared in transparent orange flame.

Maria shook away her uncle's hold and plunged down the steps – as I was the first to realize – *into* the fire.

She moved quickly, reaching out to it, the better to catch it – with hands, veil, hair, before we could rescue her. If her hair should catch she was a dead woman.

In half a pulse we were after her; and I, tearing off my cloak, threw it over her, not then knowing whether she had actually been burned. She fought me, blinded, terrified, as I deliberately stifled her; and Zamoyski flung her over his horse. His guards converging on him and the blinded Maria slung before him, he began to force his way through the crowd.

I think they did not want to stop us: half of them were

fighting the other half. In any case we reached Zamoyski's gate. Later we learned that the priests had barricaded the church door with the Princess Anna safe inside, and that Antony, breaking away from us and dragging Dorotea, had escaped through the vestry to his own house across the Close. We had lost Doctor Solniecki on our ride across the town; next day we learned he had taken shelter and got away safely.

In the room where Yolanta had shown me the Coligny brooch Laurence tore away my cloak from Maria. Her head-dress had come off: hair freed from its pins spilled over her shoulders in a tangle. She was shuddering. She said, 'Father—'

Her teeth locked. Her eyes rolled up to show the whites, and she fell, caught by Laurence's hands.

'Get me a spoon, for God's sake, or a nail-file – a blunt edge!' shouted Laurence. 'Philip, bundle your cloak into a pillow, so. Good. Now help me lay her down.'

Her eyes were open; she was both rigid and shuddering. I saw white spittle foam at the corners of her mouth. 'Is it *grand mal*?' I said to Laurence as we knelt beside her.

'Has she any history of epilepsy?' demanded Laurence.

Zamoyski was also on his knees. 'None.'

'Well, it is a seizure of some kind. Ah, thank God.' One of the women had found a nail-file in her hanging pocket. I watched as Laurence tried to work it between Maria's teeth.

At last her eyes focused and – abruptly, without transition – the shaking stopped. 'Father,' she whispered, 'I – what happened? Did I faint?'

'Yes, I think so,' said Laurence. 'Do you hurt anywhere, Maria?' Zamoyski made to lay his cloak over her, but obeyed Laurence's gesture of forbidding.

Maria's smile was haggard, but her hand, when her uncle took it, folded over his. 'No, it felt quite pleasant, only I am confused. And what is burning?'

'Nothing, Maria.'

She moved her head in protest and was stilled. 'No, something *is* burning: something acrid and rotten.'

'That will go away,' replied Father Laurence. 'Now, do you feel queasy?'

'A little.'

'Well, I am going to risk lifting you gently, and we'll carry you up to bed. Yes, put your arm around my neck.'

He rose with her in his arms as smoothly as though she had been a ten-year-old. The serving-women fled before us up the stairs. 'No warming-pan,' called Laurence to the woman who was pulling down the sheets, 'no heat.'

'What was it?' demanded Zamoyski softly, sitting down beside Maria on the bed.

Laurence shrugged. 'Not, I think, epilepsy. A paroxysm of some kind. It will come back soon if it comes at all. An hour from now she should be safe; and if it does not recur within twenty-four hours, then I suspect it never will.' He too sat down beside Maria and lifted her wrist, pressing it hard. 'Her pulse is good, though a little fast. No, give her nothing to drink.' The woman bowed and took the cup away.

'The rheumatism is gone,' murmured Maria, 'but my back feels hard as a board.'

'And no wonder,' replied Laurence. 'Next time get rid of your rheumatism some easier way.'

She laughed, exhaustion in her voice, and lay still. Her eyes closed, then opened suddenly. She said, 'I remember now.'

Her uncle glanced at Laurence. 'And what,' said Zamoyski with caution, 'do you remember, Maria?'

'After the Grove. I remember falling.'

'Falling how far?' Laurence, his face averted, seemed to be taking her pulse again.

She frowned. 'Perhaps five feet. And it did not hurt me to land. And then I can feel my feet standing on marble – sugar-white marble: I feel the grain of it. It is cool but not cold.'

'Where are your shoes, then?' Laurence laid her arm down.

What Dangers Deep

Maria frowned again. 'I have no shoes, my feet are bare. And all around me is light: pink light.'

'What value of colour?' demanded Zamoyski. 'Pale? Brilliant? Dark?' Laurence stilled him with a raised palm.

'Not pale, but bright and soft,' replied Maria. 'A little like hyacinths, or pink tourmaline.'

'And do you see anything in this light?' Laurence folded his hands peacefully on his knee.

Maria closed her eyes. 'That is all I remember. Please, what is *burning*?'

'You'll find the smell grows fainter,' said Laurence. 'Well, Maria, we have little else to do, so we'll wait beside you here.'

And so began our watch. The hour passed, and the paroxysm did not come again.

At the Embassy, when I returned that evening, I found everyone safe. Dorotea had gone to bed at eight o'clock. Antony said, 'Philip, help me by concealing this business of Maria's until tomorrow. Dorotea has borne as much as she can today, and we must cherish the child. Perhaps by morning Father Laurence will judge Maria to be safe.' Of course I agreed.

In my room I found a letter from my brother Robert, one from my old teacher Hubert Languet, and two (I thanked God) from both my parents – my father writing from Ireland, my mother from Hampton Court Palace.

'My dear Philip,' began Father's letter:

What an amazing business. I have had a note, I am sorry to tell you, from Monsieur Languet, complaining of your unkindness, your want of frankness, your indifference to his letters, and your present dangerous escapade. Now there, do you know, I think the poor old gentleman is right. To get caught between an Imperial army and a

Polish one seems unthrifty, when I can offer you just such wretched foolishness here in Ireland if you care to come.

And my mother wrote:

My beloved son,
Forgive me for taking so long to answer. In addition to my distress for you I have had duties here. I have brought Mary to Court with me for the first time, and she plays a good deal with Penelope Devereux, whom you will not remember. Both are eleven, and I prefer Penelope to the men who already write verses to Mary – some of them (the verses, not the men) exquisitely bad. I enclose some samples for your amusement, and I assure you that these gentlemen write their poems to a very *distant* Muse. Still, I think she will prove a fashionable beauty, while Penelope is plain and pale, and looks the younger of the two. Odd, at that age, how some children begin to be women, while others lag behind. Still, they play happily together. Mary has outgrown her dolls (the favourite who shares *Penelope*'s pillow is still made of wood!) and retreats into dignity at any suggestion of such childishness.

I assume lord Zamoyski's searchers will have found the bodies of Maria and Yolanta, or else some news about the Turks. I gather raiders do take Polish women. One dares not judge, one dares not hope; but I think of you continually. Of course you cannot leave until your conscience absolves you. But Philip, you may find it necessary to let go of something that has no ending. Life, I have found, is miserly of fulfilments. I hope lord Zamoyski finds his nieces safe. If not, I hope he finds an explanation. But if no answer comes, judge the moment when you must loose your grip and let the matter go.

I could have cried with gratitude at the comfort of her love, her steadiness. Instead I ordered a bath, and a meal I did not eat.

Afterwards I lay, warmly wrapped, on the bed staring at the fire. Never before – I thought with a minor shock of annoyance – had I noticed the barley-twist marble pillars that flanked the fireplace. *I feel my feet standing on marble . . . It is cool but not cold. Please, what is burning?*

I frowned and shut out the light, arm across my eyes. Surely Maria's marble and her burnt smell both came of the brain's delusion: no memory set in such a context ought to be believed.

I remembered the voice of Stefan Báthory saying: 'Then shall two be in the field: one shall be taken, and the other left. Then shall two women be at the mill: one shall be taken, and the other left.'

Labrys by her nature strikes both ways: to destroy one and – to restore the other to freedom? Or to mock with freedom one who could never escape either ostracism or memory? For Labrys, being holy, is not kind.

I had been right, then, eight years ago, to re-bury in the Ring the ancient object that I might have chosen simply to cherish with my other treasures – the river-pearls, the blown ostrich-egg, the drops of amber and shards of iridescent Roman glass.

I drew my arm slowly down from my eyes. How had I come to link them – Labrys and the Grove? When I was three years old my mother had found me worshipping the moon, my head covered in an ancient posture of devotion. There had been holy things before we Christians came; and one should always treat a holy thing with reverence.

Freedom and safety for Maria, for Caspar Laurence, for me: I knew now what I must find, but not how I must find it. For an instant I wished my father were at Penshurst. To him I might have written, despite the weeks the exchange would take, 'Dig up Labrys from the place where I laid her, and send her to me. Send me Labrys and I will bury her in the Grove, which may accept the deepest sacrifice of which I know.'

You are a Christian man, I thought. *You dare not make idolatrous sacrifices: Christ's blood redeemed us, and after that, says Saint*

Ignatius, all magic was dissolved. Yet all my instinct moved me suddenly to *give* something to the Grove: not in expectation of reward, but in hope of penetrating its silence.

The Grove has dealt with you: there will be no more. And Labrys lay where she ought to lie – hundreds of miles from here. What else could I give that might implore help from a silence that had brought us nothing but destruction?

You think of Labrys, I reflected; *But you have a single, more valuable thing.*

Hope in exchange for hope: my longing for success, for favour – for time in which to achieve some worthy fame. I could go to the Grove and offer it myself.

'They won't let me get out of bed,' said Maria as I settled on a stool beside her. The waiting-women sat at a distance, sewing and glancing at us and chatting among themselves. 'It seems you see me only bedridden, or being made to do something by someone else.' I estimated she had lost three more pounds. Books lay scattered over the counterpane, her place marked by paper slips; she held a volume on her knees as if to form a barrier between us.

'I don't mind,' I said.

'Philip, may I speak to you honestly?'

I said with caution, 'Please.'

'And can you,' demanded Maria, 'speak honestly to me?'

Less and less, I thought; and, as I forced my gaze not to break from hers, I realized she intended this contest. *Honest about what? Do you know Jean Palmette is dead, and not alive in France? Do you know he existed, if it comes to that? Did you serve as pandar for your sister? Do you know I have met Prince Stefan, or that I have lain with Sabina? Has your uncle's conduct to you been impeccable? And why did you try to plunge into the fire?*

'I hear,' said Maria, 'that you went with *Pan* Nemet Josef to kneel beside a grave.'

'From whom did you learn this?' I demanded.

Maria shrugged. Her soft eyes with their flaxen lashes held mine, and their steadiness was not gentle. 'Let us say my waiting-women, who gossip.'

'And so?'

She glanced beyond me at our *dueñas* – a glance skilfully unobtrusive. 'I know who lies there. And I know an act of mine that helped drive him from this house. I pray for his soul, and for forgiveness on my sin. Uncle Jan says he fell from his horse and – and broke his neck against a stone.'

'And so he did,' I said.

We stared at each other. After an instant Maria replied, 'Thank you: I needed only your confirmation. Philip—' For I had turned my head away. She laid a hand on my arm.

I said, 'Maria, if anything I say to you brings on another paroxysm *Pan* Zamoyski will rightly be angry with me, and I will never see you again – certainly not in private. If you want to deal in honesty, consult your own safety. And think how selfish, how unwise you may be in asking me to risk that safety.'

'I am listening,' she said, and cast a glance of composure at a *dueña*, who sensed some tension and subsided. 'I repeat that I hear you have inquired into our affairs. I can answer some questions if you will ask them. Or will you force me (it would be the cleverest course) to cast answers at you at random, and so to reveal questions you have not even thought of? I should advise the second way: it would tell you more.' She found her place in the book by feel: I noted the steadiness of her fingers.

'In short,' I said, 'I must ask my questions or watch the consequences?'

She had finished the trial of wills: she glanced away from me into her own thoughts. 'Jean is dead,' she said. 'I accept that and do not question it. On one night, and one only, I let him and my sister use my bed: Yolanta entreated me on her knees. We meant to give out that she had been alone with me all night. *And as I listened to them . . .*'

'*Maria.*' My voice, soft as it was, did silence her.

For a moment she faltered. Then she eased her shoulders against the pillows and said, '*Ask.* Help me, for I have a question too. Ask me, I can help.'

'God forgive me, then.' I picked up a book – she moved her knees aside, assenting – and opened it. 'Is your uncle guilty of incest with you or with Yolanta? And, at this moment, are you his spy against me?'

'My uncle has dealt chastely with me and, so far as I know, with Yolanta. I am a virgin. I did not see my sister in the pink light, which, by the way, I remember: I never saw her after the Grove. And I am not my uncle's spy.'

'Do you know that Prince Stefan Báthory was here while you lay unconscious?'

This time, to my astonishment, she laughed. 'No! Did he come by the underground tunnels?'

'Yes, but he let a few people in the Palace catch a glimpse of him.'

She laughed again – a little bark of delight. 'And of course he left a rumour in the city. I hope he wins. The Emperor has taken two years to make up his mind, but they say he is mustering men, and buying up timber and grain and metals for the army. The Archduke Ernst has gone out privately from Vienna: our scouts say he has been seen on our borders.'

'I can believe it: he would hate his father's indecision,' I said, 'and he can at least help with the muster. I, also, hope Prince Stefan wins. Is *Pan* Nemet Josef his agent here, as well as being the Sultan's?'

Maria shrugged. 'Stefan and Nemet are friends, Philip. And remember, the next King of Poland will need Turkish, or Turkish-Hungarian, friends. I think the Turks want peace. Prince Stefan knows that, so does the Archduke Ernst. Whose promise then, I wonder, will Sultan Murad find more lucrative?'

'And why,' I said, 'did you try to plunge into the fire?'

Her eyes closed. After a moment she said, 'It was what they wanted. And to go where Yolanta is.'

'I am sorry,' I said softly.

Maria frowned, and the muscles wrung towards weeping. 'When I woke from the paroxysm I had so ravenous an appetite; and I felt *glad* I was alive. Glad and hungry.'

'That is natural,' I responded. 'Maria, why did Yolanta inflict hurt upon herself? And why did she seek to make others hurt her?'

'Ah,' she whispered. 'Barbara!' One of the younger women started up, and I straightened, certain Maria had ended our interview. But she said only: 'Will you bring me the drawing I made of our garden – the one taken from the gallery? I think you will find it in the second drawer.'

'I'll look, my lady.'

The woman moved away; the others, mollified by their interest, returned to their embroidery. Maria said, 'I think, somehow, that she felt the least, the smallest of us.'

Barbara handed me the drawing. 'Thank you,' I said. 'I haven't yet seen the garden in spring.'

'Our rose-stock came from Constantinople. Thank you, Barbara.' The woman curtseyed and left us. 'She had nightmares, my sister.'

'Forgive me for this,' I said.

'Help me in one matter, Philip.'

'If I can.'

She did not look away. 'I hear that, when you first found me, you and the Brother Infirmarer looked at me naked. I cannot remember.'

'Have your women told you,' I said, 'that the Abbot was there as well?'

'No. Three of you, then?' I nodded. 'For what purpose, Philip?'

'To stand witness for each other in case you had been raped or otherwise abused.'

She nodded. I felt desire rise, tired and cool. I said, 'Maria, no one of us was alone with you. I thought you – I think you – beautiful, but I no more lusted than if you had been a hurt child. We did nothing that should shame you; I did nothing it shames me to remember.'

'Then what of me have you seen?' she demanded, and, with a desperate stillness, began to weep. 'A creature at whom it is lawful to look, although any other woman could protect her nakedness?'

'Oh, my dear,' I said, and folded my arms around her. She came to me and lay against my shoulder and wept till she was empty; and the women obeyed my gesture to stay away, though all of them had risen. One went to the door; I knew she was calling Doctor Solniecki.

In my arms Maria's body felt warm – a finite composition of bones and processes, dear in its humanness but rousing no concupiscence. I wiped her cheeks with my handkerchief. 'Here comes Doctor Solniecki.'

Four mornings later, in the library, I began again on my letter to Hubert Languet. *My beloved master* . . .

'Sir, Father Laurence is here to see you,' said Marta.

'Good day, Father,' I greeted him, and held out my hand. 'How is Maria?'

'Well enough, I think,' he replied, sitting down. 'Philip, I feel I can take the risk of leaving her temporarily: a week has passed without the seizure's recurring. It was not, I feel cautiously hopeful, evidence of a pattern. Maria herself has consented that I go away for a few days. I have told *Pan* Zamoyski I intend to go to the Ancient Mass, and he has most reluctantly acceded.'

'Why?' I demanded. 'I admit I too have thought recently of going to the Grove, but why beg it to break its silence? Whatever took Yolanta – accident, human cruelty, or something we do not know – will not give her back again. The Grove tempts me, I think, simply to desperation.'

'What do you think of Maria's memory of falling into the pink light?'

'That it was a delusion, like the burnt smell.'

'I disagree. I think it – forgive me – offensively facile to dispute another human being's experience because she has had it and we have not. I hate the stupidity that takes another man's or woman's experience and says with brazen arrogance, *You are deceived*. I grant, in this case the context is troubling.'

'The context,' I said, 'makes it impossible for me to believe Maria; and I respect the experience of others, which I know I cannot share and in some ways cannot dare to judge, as much as you do.'

'And have you forgotten,' demanded Laurence, 'that when Maria first woke she made her only comment about Yolanta: *She fell down*?'

I had forgotten. My face showed it.

'When my patient remembers something – that is, when she tells me that an event appears in her mind *as memory* – I have two possible courses of action,' said Father Laurence. 'I can, in this case, dismiss Maria's memory because it lay in proximity to an admitted hallucination, or – though people never admit this motive – because I do not *want* it to be true. In fact, I must determine whether my motives for dismissing it are in themselves impure. This kind of dishonesty is a common, and commonly undetected, vice of the human mind. Or I can listen to Maria when she says *memory*, and can simply take her word. I think there is something in the Grove. I am going there to seek it out – perhaps to exorcize it, though I admit an exorcism will probably fail.'

My skin contracted as though to a delicate stimulus. 'I think we had better leave it alone. I don't fear a repetition of what happened in October. I don't know what I fear.'

'I have a letter for you from *Pan* Zamoyski,' said Father Laurence.

Philip,
Maria tells me she thinks that you may fear I am angry with you because of the sad way your visit with her ended. Of course I am not angry. Father Laurence intends to exorcize the Grove. I think this should be done, though I doubt its success. If he wants a co-celebrant, I am sure the Abbot of the Bernardines could supply one. You may go with him if your interest carries you there: I think it contemptible to be afraid of the place, and so, I suppose, will you. I make only this condition: that you accept the escort I send with you. Maria and I, and the Princess who is with me at this moment and who asks me to add her greeting, hope to see you back in Kraków within a week.

              Zamoyski.

I folded the letter. 'Father, have you your superiors' consent to an exorcism?'

'No.'

'Is that not necessary?'

'Yes.' Laurence spoke gently. 'I suspected you might decide to come with me. You may do so, though we'll be cumbered with sixty guards. The Bernardine monastery has space enough for so many pilgrims, and I hope to persuade their captain to let me approach the Grove itself with a smaller party. Do you want to come? You need not. Perhaps it is truly wiser to be afraid.'

I thought of the spot where I had knelt, where I had heard – voices? a choir? – and my mind had touched something I prayed never to feel again. 'We will come away disappointed,' I said.

'I know. But I have never seen the Grove and, though I expect to find it as bare as any ordinary place, examining it might help me to heal Maria, although I am not sure how.'

Labrys lay beneath the altar-stones of the Ring; and whatever I had dared imagine in the firelight, by day my impulse of sacrifice seemed dangerous and almost unintelligible. And yet I never doubted my answer. I said, 'I will come.'

'Then you had better tell the Ambassador,' said Father Laurence.

'The Ancient Mass again?' said Antony. 'Why? You'll find it plundered bare.'

'I'll be of age this autumn, Antony. I hope you won't oppose my going.'

'No, I will not stop you. But Philip, you are growing too close to Father Laurence.'

'I have fulfilled my commission,' I replied.

'I know. And I agree that Father Laurence is a good doctor, on whom we have all come to depend. But if friendship moves you to protect him—'

'—From becoming Her Grace's victim?'

'—From dealing with the Privy Council, then you will forfeit Her Grace's liking, perhaps for the rest of your life. Let him alone, Philip. As to the Ancient Mass, you may go. But heed me: do not make a friend of Father Laurence. See less of him for your own heart's peace; for he is a Catholic and an intriguer, and the Privy Council has not surrendered him; and you will lose him.'

Nineteen

We came to the Abbey at three o'clock of a cold, blue-violet day; we intended to go no further. 'Tomorrow,' said Father Laurence to Zamoyski's captain, 'I want to inspect the Grove by daylight. Will your men be afraid to go there with me?'

'Some will, Father,' replied the man. 'You have said you want the smallest party I can cull out without endangering you. I think I can find two dozen volunteers. I'll ask them when we've had supper in the refectory.'

'Two dozen would be excellent,' said Laurence. 'The monks will feed you well, I know. Master Sidney and I must call on the Abbot, so we will say good evening.'

The man knelt; Laurence's hand sketched a blessing. As he rose, the Captain said, 'And the Brothers will find warm pallets for us, I don't doubt. Sleep soundly, Father; and you, Master Sidney.'

The Abbot received us to supper. I felt glad to see him again. As we ate, the shadows grew grey with approaching dusk. Flames licked round the logs in yellow peaks melting up from their own white heat. Beyond the window I saw the bright coldness of a sky from which day was beginning to withdraw.

'I'll leave you to an early bed,' said the Abbot, 'since you seem tired. The news of the lady Maria is, at least, better than I had feared.' And he too wished us good night.

Laurence pulled his cloak from its peg. 'Come along.'

'What, now? To the Grove?'

'Of course.'

'You've less than an hour of daylight!'

'It will get us there. I saw no reason to mention to the Abbot or to the Captain that I paid a servant to saddle fresh horses, and to load mine with my bundles, which include torches.'

'Fire will catch the trees,' I protested. I had laced my cloak and was pulling on my gauntlets.

'Then let us hope the trees are iced solid. I *do* mean to go back tomorrow also, Philip – there I was not lying. Tonight let us hope we can get out the gate unnoticed.' He opened a door, and we ran, lolloping like a pair of schoolboys, down a stair that twisted round a stone column.

'*Why* must you do this?' I demanded, jolting behind him. 'I've no desire to get killed for my purse.'

'Then stay behind,' said Laurence, halting. 'But I will go, because whatever hallows the Grove may come out at night.'

I obeyed his gesture to speak softly. 'You'll find no holy power there, Father.'

He smiled. 'I have never, Philip, since the day I was received into the Order, found any holy power anywhere.'

In the clearing a thaw had left the mud-ruts bare. The chaos that succeeded our adventure in October had effaced all trace, all feel of the evening when Yolanta had sung '*Mignonne, allons voir si la rose*'; when I had described – to two sisters, not to the one survivor – the monk I had once seen confronting me in the August heat at the top of my parents' stairs. A line of verse, heard I could not remember where, came across my mind: *And to it I may well compare my love that is alone.*

Around us the forest, a tangle of grey and brown shadow, lay charged with awareness.

'Does it feel the same?' asked Laurence.

I hesitated. 'No. I think it is simply waiting for us to leave.'

'And so we shall soon: in peace, I hope.' He did not raise his voice, although he meant the words for some listener other than myself. 'Here are the torches.' I heard the scratch of flint and tinder. 'I risked this, in part, because the path sounded short and well known to you.'

'We'll still return along it after dark.'

'Can you pick out the entrance, Philip?'

'Yes. There.' I had drawn my sword, and pointed with it. Laurence too wore a sword, and a dagger as well.

Torches flared white: shadows deepened and sprang towards us. 'Then let us go,' said Laurence.

The mud had re-frozen. We stumbled over carved ruts and horses' dung towards a desolation of naked trees. As we entered the path – worn now as clear as a cart-track – we dodged, holding our torches low. This was the path where Yolanta had switched the bushes. Far above the twilight in which we walked there stretched a sky as gentle as spring lilac.

About our progress I remember the ground's texture, and the light. Search-parties and curious intruders had done their harm here too: the path rucked beneath our feet, and one had constantly to be watching one's next step. Our torches glittered off diamonds of ice, and off square crystals brittle as mica, all caught in the frozen mud. Around us lay a hush that increasingly baffled the eyes. I could feel the light ebbing from the wood.

We passed, in a grey that destroyed all beauty or scent from the moss, the apple-tree with the split arm. Here long ago Zamoyski's searchers had found the cap. *I do not care*, I thought, and drew my dagger. Perhaps Laurence felt my anger, for he had not spoken to me since I began to lead. As for me, I understood, with more kindness than I showed, the longing that had driven him here.

'Damn,' I said, and wished I had not cursed aloud. 'Feel the ground slope down. This is the lip of the dell. Can you see the water through the dark?'

'Yes.' It had not frozen over, being fresh and I do not know how deep: we could hear its lapping in a silence that I suddenly felt was too insulated, too profound. 'Yes, it shows black against the rock wall. Do you know where the bear-pit stood?'

'Not precisely. I think Maria said it lay near the water.'

'I want to go down,' said Laurence. 'Can you show me – only show me – where you knelt?'

'I'll do better than that,' I said; and (*One must not draw steel here*) sheathed both sword and dagger. Laurence, watching me with a sort of critical compassion, kept both his weapons in his hands.

I felt as drained as the trees, the ground, the light as, in a desolation that made me want to weep and run away, we descended the slope to the pool. Here, with the sky open above us, what light remained did fall. Shadow rose like smoke from the ground; everything swam in a twilight without colour.

'I found her over there.' Laurence nodded. 'And here is where I knelt.'

I knew the place: for a stone, pale in the dusk, had lain to my right on that October day. The searchers, I now saw, had not dislodged it. The pool sucked softly against its margin of ice: a shining crust where the leaf – long since, I supposed, rotted brown and sunk to join the caked matter at the bottom – had floated.

The question of Laurence's exorcism occurred to me and was dismissed. No rite had power here, either this day or tomorrow. I said softly, 'If I start to babble, or do anything that is in any way strange, defend yourself from me. Cut me down if you must: I do not know what may possess me. I must dare this place and speak to it aloud.'

'Do what you must, and God guide you,' said Father Laurence, and stood back from me.

In the place where the fear of madness had come upon me I sank, for the second and final time, to my knees. My mind remained composed as I gazed at the water, at the trees, at the shadowed rocks. A minute passed, then another. The wood slid into darkness; above us in a delicate glassblower's blue the first star shone.

Help me to pray, I thought. Drain me of anger, for anger is not kind or safe in a holy place, however inimical its darkness. Calm my heart. Help me to make a worthy act.

I spoke aloud, and felt Laurence start, then compose his body to stillness. 'If you are not an evil power–' (my voice shuddered in a compact echo from the rocks) – 'and from all such may God defend me – I entreat you. Long ago I made a sacrifice but did not know its meaning. Now I see why Labrys has a double blade.'

Double blade. Precisely echoed, it came back to me once. I said, 'I am ambitious: I long for praise, and for power to make my family happy. I entreat you, help me.'

I sensed a slight motion in the dark. I started violently, but only felt Laurence's hand on my shoulder: he had sunk to his knees beside me. He crossed himself and let me go. I said, 'Give me courage to choose loyalty, not praise; and help me to surrender Her Grace my Queen, for all my life if I must, rather than do a cruel thing that is against my soul.'

Beside me now, Laurence spoke to the listening dark. 'I add my voice to my friend's voice. Bring me to peace.'

Focused on us with live attention, the power that heard us made no sound – did not breathe. 'Shall we speak their names?' said Laurence.

I made the decision for us both, and raised my voice to the shadow that confronted us, enclosed us, and lapped in water and ice before us. 'Two women have suffered here. For Yolanta we beg release, and the relief she longed for. For Maria I entreat . . .' Here I paused, searching the stillness. It waited, full of patience. 'Maria must continue alive. Let her therefore remember goodness; for it also is real. Let human kindness find her out. Have pity, I beg you, on her desolation.'

I glanced at Laurence, who crossed himself once more. 'Amen,' he said. 'Now rise: let us not tempt it further.'

Cautiously we stood up, made obeisance, and retreated

up the slope. There we relit our torches, and amid shadow and prickling light we sought the path back to the clearing.

I was shaking with sickness of it, with rage to be done with it: gooseflesh chilled and thickened my muscles. In the sky above us lilac had faded into a grey intense enough to sustain starlight. Laurence slipped on ice and blundered into me: I cursed his soul aloud. I saw his startled and uncondemning eyes, and heard the authority he must often have used to calm a shaken child or student. 'Steady,' he said softly. Then, no less gently: 'Philip, look.'

She fled before us on the path, through that cold fantasy of twilight and bare trees and ice, of laced shadow and starshine: a woman whose gown flickered, crackling like some insubstantial taffeta, its hem an unstable border of mist twelve inches above the ground. Her hair flickered too, a sheaf of auroral light, as she ran, apparently fleeing from us. And when she glanced back at us – a proud brief declaration of a glance – her face, rendered in planes of light and sockets of shadow, was Yolanta's, but Yolanta's face transformed. Screaming in silent laughter, feral, evil, she bloomed and flared out.

Sobbing, I blundered out into the clearing. The men waiting for us must long since have located us by sound. Perhaps fifty men on foot, their cavalry (so I learned later) stationed out of earshot sealing off access to the clearing. In the dark we could scarcely see them; and in the fraction of time it took to wonder whether the Captain had come for us, the voice of Daniel Balinski said, 'Gentlemen, light your torches. Father, Master Sidney, I regret I must separate you.'

Laurence still held his sword poised. With calm he answered: '*Pan* Balinski, we had heard you were in the south.'

'And so I was. Put away your swords, or shall we take them from you?' Lights sprang up.

Laurence sheathed his blade. 'Give it up, Philip, we cannot win. Why separate us, *Pan* Balinski?'

'Because my men wish to return you, Father, to the Abbey,

and from there to Kraków. And *I* intend to show Master Sidney the Turkish border.'

'How long,' I demanded, 'do you mean to keep me away from Kraków? And who has paid you?'

'Oh, Robert, I should guess,' said Father Laurence. 'What did he give you, Lord Balinski?'

'A part of my mother's dowry that King Henri had stolen from us and presented to the Jesuits. Now I have what is my right: the deeds and the land.'

'And can therefore afford to betray your employer?'

Balinski grinned. 'But you were the man who spoke – did you not? – of Father Parsons. These men will conduct you to the Abbey, where I hope your own escort will not take the trouble to provoke them. Father Parsons is not a fool, but it was perhaps foolish of him to pay my price beforehand: for no priest rules me, and so he shall find. Master Sidney, in three or four weeks, if Turks or outlaws or slave-takers do not kill you, you also will return peacefully to Kraków: I have neither the commission nor the desire to harm you. This–' he gestured – 'is a simple service for a fee. I am sure Robert Parsons will succeed in explaining to you, Father Laurence, why he desires to interrupt your deepening friendship with the Privy Council's messenger. Please tell him he assumed my silence but neglected to ask its price: a pity, since there was one.'

'If he is lying and they kill me, there is nothing you can do,' said Laurence to me. 'God bless you, therefore, Philip, and absolve us both.'

'Then you think we did wrongly?' I gestured towards the forest. Men who did not seem unfriendly led up horses for us both.

Laurence mounted, and sat for a moment controlling his horse as his new escort gathered around him. 'Yes,' he said.

They were leading him away into the dark. I strained towards him, against the imprisoning arms, and called softly in the English our captors could not understand: 'And this thing, was it Yolanta?'

Perhaps they caught the name, for those who held him respected the next pause, glancing from his face to mine. At last: 'Would Yolanta have laughed?' demanded Caspar Laurence.

Twenty

I first saw service under Daniel Balinski. And although I know little about where in that wilderness of mountains, ravines and stony pastures our commander led us (his errands he explained to me himself, and they soon became clear enough), the memory of spruce-smoke and the icy fragrance of snow still brings back to me a memory of freedom, and – yes – of happiness.

The lowland cottages, with their roofs of moss-quilted thatch and their walls stained pink and turquoise, violet and yellow, yielded, as the hills rose, to houses of spruce logs; houses sometimes shingled from crown to base, sometimes made of interlocked trunks fifty feet long, bleached with winter. The people of these houses hid from us, as they would from any mounted company: Balinski had to coax them out, which he did with surprising gentleness; and only the men came, when they identified his red and silver.

I never saw inside these houses, but I noticed crosses stamped on many beams, and rosettes painted with a pigment made of milk and blood. On most dwellings I saw the great down-sweeping roofs that shed snow – sometimes with their lower edge fluted outwards, so the load would fall several feet away from the house-wall. And once, I remember, we passed a tree from which swung, in chains, the mummified corpse of a wolf. Balinski glanced at it and shrugged. 'When the villagers catch a wolf here, they try it at law and sentence it to hang,' he said.

Our errands, he told me, would take us through the mountains, and then perhaps back again if we found prey worth hunting. On the second day he rode beside me. 'Your father's son should know what we do here,' he said. 'Our enemy Islam, my lord Philip, always presses northwards, testing our defences. Neither we nor they know where next year's borders will be. Their scouts are watching us now, though I doubt even my scouts will see them. I intend to ride through a certain pass if avalanches have not blocked it, to the borders of their land. We may fight them, but I doubt it: I wish them to know how far we ride and what line we mean to hold. Slave-parties do use the passes in all seasons; these may not be Turks, but outlawed men looking for plunder and women they can sell. I will kill these if I find them; and to find them I will need the trust of the hill-people, who trust no one. I can get that trust, but they rightly fear all armed men, and I must control my own.'

'The Poles seem to boast,' I replied, 'that no officer can command them.'

'Nevertheless I can, and I will tell you how. If this does not prove a lucrative patrol, I must find one party – Turks, slave-takers, outlawed men, it does not matter – one party I can plunder. I give this to them, to amuse them and to pay them, and they know I will take no share for myself. My price is their obedience.'

But it is not the hill-men from whom we sought information that I remember – some of them slender, muscular and blond, others coarsened astonishingly by a life spent ploughing and picking stones from the shallow fields. Nor do I most remember the village streets we rode through, which seemed pure mud; nor the tales I heard of their pitiful meals, of boiled straw in starved seasons, tree-shoots, and a soup of thistles and nettles; nor the solid, rosy, pretty women who rarely showed themselves at the windows when their men, armed with crossbows, came out to talk with Balinski and his officers.

I do remember the men with whom I rode. They were Balinski's own – part of that private army he would, when the King called him, contribute to the *levée-en-masse* for the defence of the realm, for there was constant warfare but no royal army.

What Dangers Deep

'We can raise ten thousand,' he told me once. 'Ten thousand men to patrol all our borders, including the mountains and eastwards into Russia. We do not fight battles, my lord Philip – we raid. And because we need each man, each man is known, and becomes boastful and brave. I do not know how my lord your father fights his Irishmen; but if he finds them an elusive enemy, then our ruses and pursuits and ambushes may teach you something.'

They hated the Turks, these young men with their small swift horses; but I wonder if any soldier entirely hates his enemy. In any case they had taken some things from Islam: the turbans they affected, fine stolen weapons, drinking-flasks knobbled with turquoises, and more than one cuirass damascened with the names of God. They wore leopard-skin cloaks and the pelts of lynx or wolf for saddle-cloths; their harness was gilt leather with tassels of metal thread, and they docked their horses' tails and trimmed their manes down to the nape to give the enemy no handhold. Their coats were plain leather which covered them to the ankles, down to short boots with backslung heels. They carried all they needed. One man could bear his cooking-things, his longsword, bow and quiver, a lance, and a mace whose head resembled a steel segmented orange. Each man also wore a long dagger which they called a *misericordia*, since they used it to slit the throat of a fallen enemy.

I have never seen finer riders: proud, elegant and clean – for these men were fresh from the stockaded camp where Balinski hoarded his foodstuffs, and to which he sent his patrols for rest and his wounded to be nursed. And, during the weeks I rode with them, they cared for cleanliness when they could, and never laughed at me when I could not bear the combination of dirt and cold. One could, at the worst, wash with snow, and I thanked God for the occasional pot of water heated over the fire. This laborious and stoic cleanliness pleased me: one's body seemed suddenly to achieve its actual value, and hot water became what it is, a privilege and a delight. I admit I found it easier to grow a beard, which came out yellow. Some of the men did better, and actually shaved on mornings when the snowlight lay blue around us and steam rose from the cooking-pots.

I have never, even at twenty, been so hungry; and we never lacked game, stewed with dried roots and spices that came, so my friends said, from Hungary. Balinski allowed us calculatedly little wine: it surprised me his men accepted this, though we had brandy against the cold.

And so we rode up into the mountains, up through pastures where rivers chattered brown over the rocks. Here the shepherds grazed their sheep in summer. First undulating stony fields, cleared, I guessed, with much labour; then foothills whose pelt of spruce and fir grew thicker and rose in solid forest up the slopes. And then the peaks with their rivulets of avalanche.

Fog came on the milder days. I remember afternoons when mist steamed in the pine-trees fifty feet above our heads. I remember, on one track we took, a boulder nine feet tall that blocked our way, until we canted it down the slope. I remember trees twisted by their weight of creamy, sparkling snow. I remember fording rivers jade-coloured with cold. I remember learning to recognize the rough, crumbled quality of avalanche-snow. I remember camp-fires, each a haze of gold and orange sparks.

I disliked the peaks: they were dangerous, and we moved among them on narrow paths, trapped and diminished by the gigantic shapes above us. The snow took on all the colours of the changing light. At evening the slopes grew blue, then lilac-coloured, before yielding to the hard and brilliant stars; and at dawn, rose-coloured light almost garish in its brilliance flooded down the peaks.

After the villages we met no one, and if Balinski had heard news of raiders he did not tell me. Twice he examined, without comment, the ashes and frozen horse-dung of camp-sites his scouts had found. Born to this work, he loved it, and loved the power it gave him; I found him skilful, silent, patient. The

What Dangers Deep

dignity I had not understood, when he gazed down at Zamoyski out of a wantonness whose defeat he had also foreseen and accepted, now revealed to me its source. I never liked him, but he sought me out and taught me with courtesy and with a barely personal attention.

All one day we had moved through a pass in single file. It had thawed the night before, and that, I understood, rendered the snow more unstable and more dangerous. Balinski made us tie cloth around our horses' hooves, and said he would flog any man who raised his voice. On either side of the trail rose slopes whose first trees I could have brushed with my outstretched hand; and no more than forty feet higher, the mist fumed down among the trunks, hazing their rise into one solid blue-green shadow. One other party, I could see by the tracks, had gone through here since the last snow. Plunging dim out of the mist on the opposite side I saw the lane of an avalanche. The trees it had snapped lay strewn like a child's gamecounters on either side of it.

'My lord Philip,' said Balinski softly. We had come to the end of the canyon: before us and below us opened a white plain. 'The Turks occupy a village not twenty miles away, and patrol this far. Behold, therefore, your enemy Islam.'

I looked down and out over the grey-white snow. I could see neither house nor field nor road. Somewhere in that desolation lay the enemy for whom I had expected to feel hate. But the land went on unchanged, and I felt glad there were no women, in the emptiness below us, to look up to the hills with fear.

I said, 'Did you expect to meet them here?'

'Not necessarily, although they know we are here. I think the avalanches will secure us from pursuit. I want to draw back, but cautiously.'

'I cannot hate them,' I said.

'I can,' said Balinski. 'Have you ever seen how they ganch a man or woman? They tie the victim's hands behind his back, then force him over backwards into a bow-shape and press him down on a hook six feet long. This they drive between the ribs and through the trunk, till the man lies speared like a fish on a fish-hook. It takes them many days to die. And I have heard something even stranger: that if rescued within twenty-four hours, a few such men have been known to survive.'

I stared at him: at the fine handsome face, the mouth pinched in a smile that was not kind; at the blue eyes webbed with weather-lines. For a moment more Balinski's gaze invited me.

In that instant I understood what had seemed his coldness – the absence of any effort to attract, despite his beauty. The gaze I now sustained was both declaration and invitation. I met it as a lover of women must: with refusal.

Then, with a laugh, he kicked his horse's sides and gestured his men back.

Six nights later the coldness woke me before dawn. As an officer (by courtesy) I had a tent and a camp-bed; but even raised off the ground, dressed in my day-clothes and covered by a blanket and a wolf-pelt, I found the shuddering had interrupted my dreams. Then, since hunger had added itself to my other discomforts, I went out to relieve myself in the snow.

Balinski's tent, I saw, was lit. A quiet group of men and horses, apparently on the point of departure, stirred just beyond the light of the only fire left burning. All the other hearths had dwindled down to resinous, white-hot ash; therefore the warmth drew me, without thought of harm, over to Balinski's fire. I meant to warm my hands, thinking, at most, to wish good morning to his guests.

I reached the bonfire and stretched out my hands. One man turned and noticed me. At that instant I realized that a second man was holding the bridle of a chestnut already saddled; that a third was kneeling on the ground; and that his master had just swung from his servant's knee into the saddle.

The rider gathered the reins; his horse's head jerked, its breath pale in the growing light, for the sky above us had gone from indigo to a deep marine-blue.

Across the fire we stared at each other, as once on a feast-day in Vienna our eyes had met and held.

It was the Archduke Ernst.

Certainly he saw the recognition in my eyes. Around him his suite were mounting. He turned away, his manner abolishing from being the instant I could never prove. And then, in quiet, they rode away through the blue-rutted snow.

It was when we came back down into the high farmlands that we found what Balinski had expected: a farm where raiders had kicked in the door of the byre. Their fire had failed to catch the ice-glazed roofbeams, but the stolen stock had trodden the snow black. Inside the house we found every room ransacked – hacked, torn and overthrown, though they had taken little of the solid furniture, which some grandfather must have carved from the huge trees of the region, intending that his family need no better for two hundred years.

We found one man dead inside the house. Another lay, in blood only now starting to congeal, on his face beside the barn. We found no adult women but, crumpled beside the woodpile where she had sought to hide, a little girl with dark-blonde hair. One of Balinski's men, young and gentle, dismounted and lifted her: she came supple in his arms, not yet frozen by the cold or by the rigor of death. She had, I saw, vomited blood. The man signed a cross on her forehead and, looking up, spoke to his commander. 'She has not been dead half an hour.'

'Then take four men,' replied Balinski, 'and bury them with all decency, too deep for the wolves to find them. If they are driving the stock they cannot have gone far.'

They had not: we caught them with twenty minutes' pursuit. I had little time to judge before we killed them – I had never speared a man through before: I was to remember afterwards how the bulk of the human torso resists the blade – and we killed too quickly for it to matter; but I think they were mixed men, some Poles, some Tartars and Hungarians – even, I think, two Turks. They numbered about thirty, and defended well their two waggons (one proved to contain movable booty, the other women) and their driven flocks of sheep and cattle. I suppose they had meant to dispose soon of these latter: certainly the encumbrance had destroyed them.

Balinski's men kept none to torture: rage drove us to murder more quickly than I think the outlaws deserved. I had enjoyed the pursuit and, with an angry delight, the killing: the little girl had absolved me of pity – or so I thought. I did not realize that my rage had risen fragile as the truculence of a drunkard – had ripped upwards in a release compounded of fury and some more illicit, more suspect thing. As our own men, rendered restless and with nothing more to kill, opened up the waggons in the cold rosy dusk, I found my face greased with sweat and my hands shaking on the reins.

Balinski had detached the more stable men to light bonfires – we would soon need supper and warmth – to fence the sheep, and to slaughter several for our meal. Objects taken from the first waggon tumbled from hand to hand, and the women, who were dirty, climbed down. We needed food; the night air smelled good, and, whatever appetite made me shake, I had not, like the others, had enough.

I knew already that a small picked guard surrounded Balinski, visibly distinguished only by his trust in them. They sat round him as, still mounted, he questioned the women. He had drawn his sword, not in threat but in warning to his own party. Almost all the prisoners were blonde; all were young. From one after another he elicited, to their increasing confidence, their names and the names of the homes from which they had been taken. One after another he gestured aside, with courtesy, into a circle that I knew consisted of his own chosen, trustworthy guards. Three he requested gently to stay where they were, until only they of the original group remained standing before us.

I still remember them: a pretty one with braids tumbling out in wisps about her forehead; a child of about fifteen with white-blonde hair and a high-cheeked, innocent face; and a sturdy, decent girl of about twenty, with copper-brown hair and irregular features.

What Dangers Deep

Balinski pointed with his blade, and said in a voice loud enough for us all to hear, 'The others are all Poles. These women are Hungarian. Use them one by one.'

He withdrew. They held the first two while they stripped the third – the oldest, the girl with the brown hair. She made no sound as the men tore away her clothes. The snow was a foot deep, or would have been but for our trampling of it.

Abhorrence and lust held me still as I watched them strip her standing. I saw in her face the knowledge that existence ended here – in this place, in this hour. I do not know what home, what sustaining protection she was remembering as the sight of her breasts and haunches drew from us a laughter unlike any laugh I have ever heard: a roar, elemental and pitiless. Then four men bore her down into the snow, and two pulled apart her ankles, displaying what her pinioned hands could not close or conceal. I saw two or three open their smallclothes. As the first mounted her she did not make a sound.

I slid from my horse, the breathing of a complicated anguish tearing my lungs, and fought my way into the press – not to harm her, but to save her.

I could not get through: shoulders and bulk of bodies resisted me, and I could not hear my own shouting as another roar rose: the second man, I suppose, must have hurt her.

I could not see the other two girls, who were, I knew, being made to watch. I could not forget – have never forgotten – the image of a woman's nakedness in the snow, in the orange-yellow light of the cooking-fires. For I understood that we were punishing her: for what? For breasts that quivered with their weight; for haunches whose difference from our own roused a lust so genital it abolished pity; for the odorous cleft all women at some time deny us? For I could have raped her too, disgusted only, if at all, by the slime of other men's seed, and could have wept with laughter as I watched others rape her.

As I fought my way towards her I caught a glimpse of her among the onlookers. Blood had begun to pour from between her legs, why I am not certain: perhaps the second one had used

271

his blade. Now someone's sword transfixed her and she died, eyes open; and the second girl, the youngest, was flung down into the snow.

When my rescuers took hold of me I thought they were only Balinski's soldiers, and fought them blind and lost the fight, until the voice of Robert Sellier said, 'Sir, you cannot save them. They will only kill you too.'

Hazily I recognized faces from Antony's household. At least five men were mastering me, dragging me out of the crowd. And Nemet Josef said, 'Balinski's servants have set up your tent. We will sit there and wait till morning, and hope they forget to turn on you as well, Master Philip.'

Once in the tent I vomited. Rob Sellier held me with decent competence, and cleaned up the mess. The place was too small for seven men, and they stretched me out on the folding bed, which would have unbalanced had anyone sat beside me. When dark was several hours old, Nemet, stepping outside, brought back a platter of roast meat, from which no one ate much. All the time we listened. The second girl wept before they killed her; and the third, having watched too long, began to scream and gave them little pleasure. They beat her into silence and used her, I think, until she died.

By dawn I had a headache that started at the crown of the skull and that did not leave me for three days. I had not vomited again, nor had I wept. Nemet hunkered in front of me and said, '*Pan* Zamoyski sent us to find you. He has paid Balinski your ransom. Let us go, Philip.'

By now the Morning Star shone above the trees, and in the rich blue the camp lay silent, the embers orange with a core of gold, the waggons empty, the men stretched sleeping or sullenly wakeful. Someone had trowelled up the bloodstained snow. I could see no trace of the women's bodies; and I never saw Daniel Balinski again.

Twenty-one

At the first inn I shaved off my beard. March was coming in with swansdown flakes out of a brilliant silver sky. I had grown sick of snow: in England, I thought, the crocus-buds would perhaps be showing saffron or purple snouts through cracks in the earth.

'How is the city?' I said to Nemet.

He shrugged. 'Quieter, I think, and more resolute. They think now of an election, a king and a war. If Prince Stefan wins they say he means to conquer Russia.'

'Why?'

'To stop the Russians from conquering him.'

'Can he do it?'

'If he creates a standing army, and the Tsar continues to betray his people rather than to defend them, he can at least burn Moscow. I hear that is easily done, and as easily rebuilt in a day. They cut the logs to standard sizes, poor souls – it must make the burning and the raising so much easier.'

For a moment we rode on through a snow whose autumn I could not remember, as I could not imagine its spring. 'Has Kraków forgotten Yolanta, then?' I said.

'It seems so,' replied Nemet. 'And we will never know who among the crowds – what gentleman, what wife, what thoughtful artisan – is discovering he will never forget her.'

'Once,' I said, 'King Henry the Sixth – our mad King, who lived a hundred years ago – lost his way alone when he was out hunting. A little girl was picking mushrooms in the woods: the King stopped to ask his way of her. Her name was Mary

Littleton. Some years later King Henry died. Usurpers succeeded him, and civil war; lifetimes passed. But the little girl lived to be one hundred and ten years old; and six years ago she described King Henry to my father.'

'Then scan the crowds of Kraków,' said Nemet, 'and tell me which apprentice will live as long. What mark does he carry of the destiny no one covets: to outlive all those among whom he was born? And a century from now he may say: There was a woman named Yolanta Zamoyska.'

'And Maria?' I said.

He shrugged again. 'Endures, so I hear. She has her books, her priests and doctors, her cage. I think her a brave woman: such courtesy and patience come of the soul's grace. And I wonder how many of her attendants thank her, as they should, for the labour of waking to exist for another day.'

Twenty miles out of Kraków *Pan* Nemet said to me, 'Philip, I promised to bring you this far, but now I must leave you. I have another errand.'

'I'm sorry,' I exclaimed. 'I had looked to have your company all the rest of the way. When shall I see you again?'

'In some weeks, I promise.' As he turned away he halted, reined his horse in a close circle and came back. 'Philip, they will recover their purity, as you will recover your knowledge of your goodness.'

'I was not born,' I said, 'to kill for lust, or to take joy in raping.'

Pan Nemet frowned. 'It was not joy, Philip: it was despair and grief, and the mind's own self-salvation in extremity.'

Therefore it was without *Pan* Nemet that I brought my party to the Abbey where a timber hall raised its height above the graveyard, and where, having sent my people to the refectory, I sought out the stone Nemet had once shown me.

Beneath my feet clear beads of snow, melted and refrozen, still formed a crust on the ground. Clouds were blowing across

What Dangers Deep

a pale sky. It suddenly occurred to me that this cool, high cloud belonged to spring. Above the graves the branches still showed grey, not flushed with the red-brown that means the rising of the sap; but I saw each twig bent out of true, its line subtly rippled by the swelling of the buds.

In this chill of early spring the graveyard stretched serene. The dead who lay beneath its stones had left there nothing of themselves – nothing of the passions, duties, endurance that had moved them: only, delicately communicated with the wind, their surrender of our world – that gentle, implacable surrender which has made me doubt whether anyone who has ever left this world desires to come back. All passions resolved – not healed – into this silence; all fear of death enigmatically relieved, they and the trees communicated a peace that was not peace, but something more like a secret. I closed the gate: wind rustled the trees and the cold returned me to winter.

The Brother-gardener was there. I hesitated, then went up to him. 'Good afternoon, Brother. What are you looking for? I have seen you here before.'

He glanced round at me – a keen, sharp-witted man, and darker than any Pole I had ever seen. 'And I have observed you, sir. You came with *Pan* Nemet one day, I remember. As for me, I look for the spring. I almost hunger for it.'

'So do I. Will you accept this' (I held out a small purse of gold) 'for your alms-box?'

He took it. 'Gladly, sir. Can I serve you in return?'

'Perhaps. Some weeks ago *Pan* Nemet brought me here, as I see you noticed, to pray at the grave of one of his friends.'

The gardener nodded. 'The gentleman who lies over there under the stone with no name?'

'Yes. I found *Pan* Nemet much distressed, and dared not question him, but I gather this man died of wounds. I know the matter may be private; but have the Brothers heard any talk that might explain his death?'

The gardener stowed the purse into a pocket. 'The man came

to us apparently in coma. He was confirmed dead in our infirmary. His arm had been broken, in a fight as it seemed, and he was bruised, especially about the face: I remember because I assist Brother Scholasticus, our Infirmarer, when my other work does not require my attention.'

'Did he die of such curable wounds – bruises, a broken arm?' I demanded.

'No. His neck was broken too, and the back of his head cut open – not with a weapon, but as though, falling backwards, he had the ill luck to crack his head against a rock. I think the man he was fighting probably killed him by misadventure.'

And so, I reflected, chance had brought me with ludicrous simplicity where no search or bribery *inside* the monastery itself had succeeded in bringing the bewildered Nemet.

'Now compose yourself quickly,' said the gardener: 'Here comes someone we both know.'

I glanced towards the gate. His hat in his hand, the Grand Chancellor of Poland was approaching us among the gravestones. I think he had not yet come near enough to hear our talk. As he came up to us I bowed. '*Pan* Zamoyski, thank you.'

He smiled. 'Well, your latest catastrophe distressed Dorotea, so I had to send someone out to find you. Are you well, Philip?'

'Unwounded, my lord. I saw some action.'

'So I hear. Brother Gerontius, it will soon be spring.'

The gardener frowned. 'If we get a mild April, *Pan* Zamoyski. Will you excuse me?' Zamoyski bowed, and he left us alone.

'Come with me,' said Zamoyski. 'You know where he lies.'

As we walked I asked, 'What hope has Maria, sir, of rejoining the community of man?'

'As much hope as I can find for her. But I should think,' he said softly, 'very little.'

We knelt before the stone whose base would, I thought, in six weeks be hazed with grassblades. *Man comes forth like a flower, and is cut down.*

What Dangers Deep

The moment was so gentle that my question came naturally, without fear. 'Did you kill him, sir?'

'Yes, accidentally.' Zamoyski's averted face showed neither anger nor surprise. 'I meant to beat him, but I am – I was – the bigger man. I flung him backwards, and he fell.'

'What did he do to her?' I demanded.

This time his head did turn, and his eyes met mine with a hardness, still void of anger, that I found difficult to sustain. 'Under Islamic law I believe that when a woman wishes to divorce her husband because he has practised sodomy upon her, modesty prevents her from naming the crime to the judges. Instead she removes one of her shoes and lays it, inverted, on the ground.' I stared at him. Zamoyski sighed. 'Poor boy; poor children, both of them. I should have helped them.' The silence lasted perhaps thirty seconds. 'Prince Willem of Orange has chosen a husband for his daughter.'

Man comes forth like a flower. 'Then my moment is gone,' I said.

'One of them,' replied Zamoyski gently. 'One of them.'

I clenched my fist against my mouth, controlling a childish desire to weep. 'Well, I have spared her an unloving husband. I have always believed husband and wife should love each other.' Zamoyski nodded. 'In any case I am not fit to command. I wonder whether my father commands as Balinski does: by sacrificing those he must. He let three Hungarian girls be raped to death a week ago, to keep his men from the others.'

'I know. You cannot understand how we hate the Turks, as we can never understand, I suppose, the blood-hate between English and Irish.'

'These girls were not Turkish.'

'They were not our own.'

'Would you have done the same, my lord?'

'No. And for that decency I might have lost all the women.'

'If posterity remembers us–' I gestured to the gravestone – 'will it be, do you think, for anything we actually were?'

'No man is remembered, Philip: not for the truth that was in him. Posterity makes up fables around a hundred recorded names out of all the millions who have lived. You have gifts. There will be another moment. But I predict for you that you will not feel its falling, any more than one notices the first yellow leaf that falls in August.'

With the flat of his hand he signed a cross towards the stone, and stood up. 'Come with me. I must take you to the Wawel: the Princess Anna has asked to see you. You will find Antony there as well.'

'Master Sidney,' said the Princess, 'no apology I make can comfort them or save them. *Pan* Balinski is a competent commander and makes, I think, the best choices he can. I ask you to remember that there was one alternative, and to forgive us. In my nation's name I am sorry for what you have seen.'

Antony, his arms crossed, nodded at me in faint encouragement. I hesitated, then glanced from the Princess to Zamoyski. 'Madam, one dawn, while I was with *Pan* Balinski, I espied by accident something I think I should tell you about. It seems to me I owe lord Balinski no loyalty.'

'He captured you,' said Antony, 'he did not hire you, Philip. You owe him nothing.'

'What did you see?' demanded Zamoyski.

And so I told them about the Archduke Ernst.

As we rode home, surrounded by our guards in the torchlit dark, I said to Antony, 'Do you think it was a dishonourable choice?'

'No. Imagine how troubled you would feel if you had *not* told them . . . Philip, Her Grace has written to me. I will be succeeding Rafe Sadler in Paris at the end of April, or sooner if I can conclude my affairs here.'

I thought of Sabina, of Caspar Laurence, of Maria. 'We'll be going, then.'

'Not for some weeks. And then your road, I think, lies towards Italy, Philip; and after that, towards home.'

Twenty-two

I slept well that night; and next morning, after a bath and a meal, went at once to Collegium Maius to see whether Father Laurence was safe. I knocked on his door, and experienced a pulse of disappointment – I mean to say, of delighted relief – when his voice answered, 'Come in.'

It seemed I need not have feared: Balinski had kept his word. I opened the door. 'Father—'

Two men, both dressed in black, had been sitting in the window-seat, leaning towards each other in a conversation whose intimacy their posture still acknowledged as they straightened. One was Caspar Laurence; the other was Robert Parsons.

I threw down my hat and, ploughing across the room, carried Parsons up against the wall. He was older by twenty-five years, and also stockier and stronger; but he fought me with a released loathing that was a relief to us both. Laurence had now eluded my field of vision. As Parsons forced me, staggering, away from the wall, I heard Doctor Pasek's voice at the door, and Laurence's urgently answering.

Something – Parsons' nails, or perhaps some clasp or pin he had torn from his clothing – raked my face open (I will always carry the scar, though the portraits omit it; and Robert Parsons' broken nose is my work, thank God). His weight served him, but I am a good wrestler, and I had him on the floor and was striking him in the face, using my balled fist with the ring on it (astonishing what harm a ring can do) when Laurence closed the door and bolted it. 'Pasek is coming with the Rector's men:

you have, if he and I can get it for you, perhaps ten minutes. Have you finished?'

I found I had. Shifting with care, I moved away from Parsons and, steadying myself on one knee, held out a hand to my enemy. 'Thank you, Master Philip,' murmured Father Parsons, and let me help him up. 'Caspar, have you got a towel?'

'Yes, damn you. Are you hurt, Philip?' The supple doctor's hands were setting chairs, filling a basin with water, and stripping the towel-rack for us. One, flung with absolute accuracy, landed in my lap, one on Parsons' knees. Laurence scanned us and then, dismissing my hurts for the moment, he knelt beside his friend. 'Robert, someone ought to have broken your nose for you years ago.'

'I can't breathe,' observed Father Parsons, with the air of someone making a simple observation.

'Good,' replied Laurence. Blood was flowing down Parsons' chin into his mouth.

We sat opposite each other, cleaning ourselves and resting. Presently I saw Parsons assessing me. 'Master Philip, I am sorry only that I did it so badly. I hate your family, and I know you detest me. I regret nothing but that I neglected to purchase Balinski's silence, not having recognized it as a separate commodity. If it comforts you, Caspar hit me too, so I gained nothing, and made myself look a fool.'

'Now,' I replied, 'you have something else to hate my family for: I've marred your face for life.'

He grimaced – first in acknowledgement, then in pain. 'Can one *breathe* through a broken nose, Caspar?'

'Probably, when the bleeding stops,' replied Laurence testily.

I had at least wiped off the blood when we heard (by the sound) twenty men tramping down the corridor. 'Father Laurence,' called Doctor Pasek's voice, 'the Rector instructs me to ask you to unbolt the door. It is University property, and we will charge you the replacement if we have to break it in.'

'I'm coming,' called Laurence. Then he spoke to me. 'Philip, thank you for expressing so delicately your concern for my health.' I grinned, which hurt. 'Go with them; I'll send to Antony Marshall, and we'll have you out within twenty-four hours.'

And so began what *Pan* Zamoyski had hoped I would avoid: my acquaintance with the Small Dark Cell. Five men, looking frightened of me, brought me, most kindly, water to wash off the blood, and then (I gathered) the usual meal: brown bread and water. While resting on the pallet, to which the Rector refused to allow a pillow or mattress, I counted the names scratched on the wall. There were seven hundred and sixty-three; among them it pleased me to note Jan Zamoyski's signature repeated five times over, at dates which I averaged to have been one hundred and four days apart. It also pleased me to mention this to him next time I saw him.

Antony got me out; Dorotea, laughing rather more than I thought polite, tended my cuts; Antony threatened me with flogging if I did not go to bed for twenty-four hours; and Rob Sellier, laughing almost as much as Dorotea, carried a message for me to Sabina Korytowska.

On the day the Rector informed me in writing that I was banned for life from the University, I visited Sabina in the evening.

In the room where she had first received me – she had never, it occurred to me now, allowed me to see any other room of her house – Sabina offered me another supper. I ate enough for courtesy, then said, 'Sabina, I will not be visiting you again.'

Her eyelids fell; her posture showed undiminished dignity and her manner, after an instant's pause, undiminished gentle friendliness. 'May I ask why?'

'Two reasons. The Ambassador has been appointed to the Court at Paris. He has not yet told the Princess Anna.'

She nodded – an affirmation of discretion. 'They know, of course, the two of them. They read all his despatches.'

I shrugged. 'Then they re-seal them as expertly as thieves. Have you heard, Sabina, what *Pan* Balinski did just before I left him?'

'The rape of the Hungarian girls? Yes: the whole city knows

and does not care. I am sorry, of course, but I had a cousin taken in the raids. We never heard of her again. Each woman among us lives with the knowledge that, if the Turks take this city, she must pray at best to be sold in Constantinople. Did you know that among the Turks a slave has certain rights at law? I believe a man who wishes to buy a woman may not strip her naked, but he may handle her breasts.'

I felt heat on my skin, and bowed slightly, indicating that I was listening to her. Sabina said, 'Did you mount any of them?'

'No,' I said. 'But I watched.'

Her hand, used with a courtesan's trained grace, indicated the bed. Her tone was hard. 'Then bring it to bed with me. *I will understand.*'

'No.' The word came strangled out of me. 'Into some degradations I will not go.'

She watched me, her eyes brimming with pain for herself and with pity for me; and I went and took her in my arms. 'And so we take,' I whispered into her hair, 'and so we leave when it pleases us.'

'Yes. I am a servant.' With fingers that trembled she wiped her tears and stood away from me. 'I will miss you.'

'I will miss you also,' I said softly.

I held her chair and she sat down again. I said, 'I have left with your steward two bolts of cloth: the dark orange and morello colours you like.' It was an expensive gift; she acknowledged it with a nod. 'And I should like you to have these.' I pulled out a jeweller's case from my pocket and opened it. On a ground of white watered taffeta lay a pair of earrings, each consisting of three rubies, descending teardrops strung by delicate loops of chain.

Sabina smiled. 'I shall wear them and remember you. Thank you, Philip.'

As I walked away from her house I looked back. Sabina stood in the lighted window. As I gazed, she raised a hand to me, and then drew the curtain straight across.

Twenty-three

I did not tell Antony what Sabina had said about the despatches: I presumed he knew. Nor had he given me permission to speak of his departure to the Princess. I knew therefore, when Zamoyski invited me to a supper that would include only himself, Maria and the Princess Anna, that I could not tell them I was leaving them – could neither ask nor give comfort about all we had begun and now would never finish.

Yolanta is dead, I thought as my guard escorted me in the dusk across the town. Repetition had worn the words dull: the fact remained unsolved, unhealed. I glanced at the sky. Frost had arrested the buds; cloud steamed so low it hazed the church-towers. Wind had begun to rise. It smelt of ice and storm.

Life is miserly of fulfilments. The porters let me in at Zamoyski's gate; and as I rode up the corkscrew lane I thought: If we were now to find a bare answer – Yolanta's skeleton, or news of her slavery in Constantinople – yet the long questioning that had changed us could not be undone. Zamoyski's reputation had survived – had perhaps never actually risked any harm more serious than the flattery of the mob's fascination. Did Maria hate her people now? And if she did, to what refuge on Earth could she go?

I dismounted – greeted the servants, even as words formed themselves distinctly in my mind. *Marry her. Marry her and take her with you to England.*

I gave hat, cloak, gloves to a woman who smiled at me. My next birthday would free me from my family's authority if I brought home a Polish wife. Maria knew no English, but Dorotea might be near – might be in London if the Queen let Antony come home. Utter distance and the company of strangers were all I could give her, except myself.

I spoke pleasantly to the servant who led me upstairs. *Is this how my oath in the Grove will be required of me?*

Beyond the windows, the sky now showed plum-coloured with storm. Light shone beneath a closed door; my guide knocked, and as Zamoyski opened it I understood the coldness in which I had conceived what prudence warned me I still must weigh. I liked, desired, respected Maria; but I did not love her.

She was there, dressed in grey velvet, with her hair confined only by a braid interwoven with gold and silver thread. The Princess had brought no attendants. I bowed to Her Highness, and smiled quickly at Maria. 'My lord Zamoyski,' I said, 'it is March and winter again.'

'Is it bad?' Zamoyski bent to the window, squinting out at the dark.

'Coming on to sleet, I think,' I replied.

The chamber was a small dining-room, its walls panelled with the yellow grain of young oak. The ceiling showed gold-striped beams stamped with the words *In Hoc Signo*; the furniture was padded with purple velvet cushions, and beside the fireplace I saw trays of kindling – pine-cones and fresh logs. On a table in the corner lay a virginal with ebony and ivory keys, its lid painted with mottoes in Roman lettering.

'Do you play, Maria?' I said to her.

'No,' she replied. 'But I do play the *vièle*.'

'I thought we might have some music afterwards,' said Zamoyski. 'Her Highness, in fact, plays the virginal.' Anna smiled acknowledgement. 'Do you sing, Philip?'

'Yes, and I play the lute well enough.'

Zamoyski glanced from me to Maria. 'Of course.'

Wind rattled the panes in their cradles of lead solder. 'Good God,' said the Princess, glancing out. 'I hope this one proves the last this winter. I have always said, Jan, that our worst storm comes on April fourth or fifth.'

'Never mind: the buds survive their first check every year. Madam,' said Zamoyski, 'will you take supper?'

While we ate the wind continued, at last shaking the panes in a jarring, staggered rhythm that strained our conversation. Finally they gave us an apple-tart and a platter of marzipan fruits, each pear stained with reds and yellows, each little orange provided with a taffeta leaf. Also the servants set before me a goblet of the colourless hot wine. I think they made it from barley: perhaps one cannot hope for grapes in Poland. It smelt of mace and ginger, and the heat made it more potent.

We had talked all through the meal but, perhaps for reasons of decency, not of my adventures on the border. Maria had not seen me in five weeks: her acceptance of our silence indicated that she knew the stories current in the city; but she said nothing, though occasionally I saw her gazing at me.

I met her eyes, thinking: Keep your secrets, you and your uncle and Dorotea. I will never know the dead to whom all of you are loyal. I will never know whether, like me, you think of Yolanta every day. Are you *capable* of reaching us, or do you despair of your distance from us? Do you know the danger of being frozen as you are, and does it frighten you? For you have reachieved a life of ice, and I think it is false. Did you too perish in the Grove?

Maria was staring at me, though only a fraction of an instant had passed. She lowered her eyes, looking troubled. For a second her face, presented thus, was so womanly I felt a pang of astonished love for everything that made her different from myself: the thin soft lips, the eyes that in this light seemed ice-grey like her gown – for every secret proportion and animal grace that shone from her. The sounds in the room changed: she turned away, exposing to my eyes the line of her profile and the curve of young muscle along her throat.

'You're right, Philip, it is sleet,' said the Princess. I heard a hissing against the panes. The wind had stopped: instead a fine-grained, glassy snow was showering down on to the outside sill, which already lay several inches deep in it.

'This will freeze on the cobbles,' remarked Zamoyski. 'You had better stay, both of you.' Anna nodded. Zamoyski said to me, 'Philip, can you sleep here tonight? When the man can get across Market Square I'll send a message to Antony.'

'Perhaps it would be safer,' I agreed.

Afterwards we made up a consort (I found that Zamoyski could play the recorder, which balanced our *ensemble* of virginal, lute and viol) and made music for about an hour. The sleet still struck with a pattering hiss against panes now ringed an inch deep in ice. Zamoyski laid his instrument back in its case and sighed. 'No one will go out tonight. I hope the monasteries have opened their doors to the poor: two or three will freeze to death before morning. I will tell my steward to let them in and feed them. Enough, I think, madam?'

'As you wish,' replied the Princess.

'Then come back to the fire, Philip, and translate for me a title I cannot read. This–' he found it on a table where it had apparently been lying ready – 'is the only book in English that Collegium Maius possesses. I gather it was a present from Doctor Dee, and *Pan* Balinski's choir sang poetry from it, though where they got the settings I cannot guess.'

We had all now found seats in the firelight. I took the book and crowed with surprised pleasure: it was Tottel's *Miscellany*. I translated the title for them. 'This man Master Tottel first brought into public print the works of Thomas Wyatt and of the Earl of Surrey, the two best poets we have had since Chaucer.'

'Please,' said Maria in her calm, low-pitched voice, 'will you read us some, Philip, as it was written? Can you translate it and explain it to us? Dorotea is learning English, but finds it difficult.' I grimaced in sympathy. 'And no one here speaks it but Antony. I should like to hear your poetry.'

'I can render it into French, of course, but not into French verse,' I replied. 'The two languages lilt too differently. German would do better, but I know little German.'

'Then do as well as you can,' said Zamoyski.

I did not want to bore them with too many uncomprehended sounds, so I began with the short things – two of Surrey's sonnets: 'Alas, so all things now do hold their peace', and 'Set me whereas the sun doth parch the green'. I have loved these poems all my life; but I could not tell, from the gentle intelligent eyes that watched me with such courtesy, whether my language sounded beautiful to those who could not understand it. Zamoyski and Anna were following with close attention; Maria had turned towards the fire – the more intently, it seemed, to listen.

I came – it was the last piece I intended to read – to the great poem of regret in which Surrey, imprisoned for treason in Windsor Castle, remembers his playmate the Duke of Richmond (King Henry's bastard son, who died young) and the other vanished children, their companions. I know no better catalogue of the delights youth does hold; for though it is not a happy time, we still have then, I think, a sense of belonging to the world and to our friends, and also something that might be called unconscious hope.

Friends die, and we recognize both hope and health by losing them. So I already suspected at twenty; and so I have found it to be. Into a silence gone concentrated as rock-crystal, I recited Surrey's tale of the games that had once filled the now-empty courts:

> The stately seats; the ladies bright of hue;
> The dances short; long tales of great delight;
> With words and looks that tigers could but rue,
> Where each of us did plead the other's right.
>
> The palm-play where, despoilèd for the game,
> With dazèd eyes oft we by gleams of love
> Have missed the ball, and got sight of our dame,
> To bait her eyes who kept the leads above.

> With silver drops the mead yet spread for ruth
> In active games of nimbleness and strength,
> Where we did strain (trailèd by swarms of youth)
> Our tender limbs, that yet shot up in length.

Ice blew in a storm of sparks against the windows. Maria, her hands clasping her knees, sat gazing into the fire.

I blundered into it. In fact I closed the book, and simply went on reciting words I had known since I was ten:

> The void walls eke that harboured us each night –
> Wherewith, alas, reviveth in my breast
> The sweet accords; such sleeps as yet delight;
> The pleasant dreams; the quiet bed of rest;
>
> The secret thoughts imparted with such trust;
> The wanton talk; the diverse change of play;
> The friendship sworn, each promise kept so just –
> Wherewith we passed the winter night away.

Then the poet cries aloud to his prison – cries for the vanished children, using the word 'fere', which in an older English means *companion*:

> O place of bliss! renewer of my woes!
> Give me account where is my noble fere
> Whom in thy walls thou didst each night enclose –
> To others lief, but unto me most dear.

I simply stopped. After a moment I became aware that the Princess Anna's voice was saying, 'Philip. Philip, you must translate it.'

'I think not, madam, it is sad,' I said. 'Let us put the book away.'

'I shouldn't like to ask Antony Marshall.' Zamoyski's voice was gentle. 'But if necessary I will.'

And so I did translate it, into a silence already prepared by my distress. *To others lief, but unto me most dear.*

What Dangers Deep

And then Zamoyski held me while I wept, and said at last, 'That settles it, of course: you must sleep here tonight.'

The aftermath of violent weeping resembles a drug, or so I have found, and leaves an enjoyably empty weariness – a pleasure unlike any other kind of fatigue. Zamoyski's people had given me a room; I had washed away tears and sweat. My dayclothes hung airing on a rack by the fire. The storm had stopped at about one in the morning.

I felt too well in body to rebel against my wakefulness. I had rid myself of Zamoyski's huge borrowed robe, and lay naked in sheets long since grown warm with my body. The bed-curtains were white, embroidered with serpents and griffins in black thread. The solid pillow smelt of rosemary.

I woke from a conviction that I had been staring quite comfortably at the fire. The clock showed two. Had I slept with my eyes open, or had I dreamed I was awake?

I got up, pulled on my robe, and rinsed both face and mouth with water from the basin. I was towelling myself dry when a knock, almost too soft to hear, came at the door.

I had bolted it. I went to the peg from which my sword-belt hung, and quietly drawing the weapon, stood to the door. 'Who is it?' I made my tone soft and neutral.

'Let me in.' The whisper was Maria's.

I unbolted, pulled her in and closed the door again, securing bolt and lock behind her. She was wearing a night-robe of dark blue taffeta; from the way the folds fell I guessed that it, like my bedrobe, was lined with fur. She wore ermine slippers, she was not barefoot – another sign she had not come on impulse. The robe's collar rose to her chin, as concealing as a ruff. The garment's sleeve showed the *voile* of a white nightgown.

'*Maria!*' My whisper was as furious as if I had shouted. 'What prank is this? If your uncle catches us he will kill us both.'

'You should know that is the last of all things he would do.' Her eyes were frightened, assessing my opposition.

'Well,' I said, 'do not force on me the semblance of your seducer: or is it to be *attacker*, Maria? Are you seeking your own—'

She turned from me; my arm denied her the door. 'My own Jean Palmette?' She crossed herself, and said in a furious whisper, 'My poor sister: how good she was, how courageous, how humble. All this you will never know of her. I will think of her every hour until death relieves me.'

'So will I.' She lunged for the key: I stopped her. 'You can cry out and make me guilty: no one will believe me.'

Maria stared at me with composure. 'You know you are safe from that. This is your room, Philip: it is obvious I came here. And now I will go. I am sorry about the poem, but I could have shown it best by silence. It was selfish of me to interrupt your sleep. I apologize.'

I blocked the door with my shoulder. Her own actions – her own decency, I admitted to myself – had denied her any help. If she had come for mine, I could not have begun more badly. I said, 'Maria, I am sorry – for my anger; above all for what I implied about Yolanta. You could not be like her, and I know she deserved your love.'

Maria knelt down to stir the fire. With a gesture identical to one I had seen her uncle make, she began to rebuild it. When I spoke her sister's name she did not glance at me.

I put my sword away and came to her cautiously, my arms crossed – but still blocking the line between her and the door. 'If you came to talk with a friend, you have found only a cruel vulgar insult, and for that I am sorry. I must ask you to tell me why you came here.'

She placed a third log, building the rough cone that would steeple the heat upwards. 'I was lonely, and I had a chance to be with you – a chance I will never have again. Also I had a favour to ask; I cannot ask it now.'

She set down the poker; I watched her, reflecting that it was a weapon. 'Are you afraid of me, Philip, or do you dislike me? I saw your look at supper. I know about Antony's departure. So we must settle it now, you see.'

'Whatever we have begun,' I said: the lilt made it an affirmation.

Maria nodded. 'May I sit down, Philip?'

'Good God, yes. Here, come to the window-seat.' I led her there and sat beside her, our backs to the desolate garden. The curtains were drawn as close as they would go: they fell about three inches short of meeting. I hoped no watcher across the quadrangle could identify us by the strip of light that fell on the rimed snowbanks two storeys below. I glanced out. The sky was clear; stars glittered like cold bonfires.

As two people will who have come close to quarrelling, we had both settled into an anxious, over-warm courtesy. I gazed at Maria where she sat, compact and elegant, beside me. She freed her hair from its concealment, looping it out of her robe with a practised twist; the velvet fell around her with exquisite precision. Had Zamoyski thought of using her marriage – of giving her to one of his friends to make an alliance? If so, the Grove had ruined her for him; but still, I thought, with love and perseverance she made herself elegant for him; for he needed the women to do him honour.

What had I learned about her, now I could expect to learn no more? Of Tomaśz my mind had gradually formed a picture of a man mature, shrewd and good, and (so my imagination insisted) brown-haired, unlike most Poles. Helena also had been brown and slender – decidedly Yolanta's mother. But time had broken open years ago a family I could not imagine in its unwounded wholeness. Maria had once been a youngest child, secure in the activities, in the love of her vanished family.

I said, 'Maria, what did you think of them all?'

She had clasped her hands around her knees; I saw her fingers lock, but otherwise she did not stir. 'Has anyone told you,' she answered, 'that you are cold, Philip?'

It shocked me: for a second I did not reply. Then I said, 'Never.'

'You are cold,' replied Maria.

I stared into her eyes, and discovered that one can smile with anger. 'I do not believe you.' I could have touched her, for anger had begun to rouse lust.

'A liar too, then,' composedly replied Maria. 'A cold huntsman, to follow with such perseverance my family's suffering, to which you have no right. What will age make of you, I wonder, Philip? What,' she said softly, 'will your Queen make of you?'

'Whatever she pleases,' I said.

Maria laughed. I did not strike her. When I did not move she said, 'What is it you want to know?'

'Did you love Helena?'

She thought. 'My mother? No, because I could not respect her. She was a fool, Philip: all she did I could have done better. I loved my father, who chose me out above my sisters. I will always be grateful to him.'

'And your mother's death?' I said. It was inexcusable, and I therefore dared it gently, despite my anger at her.

'My mother's death,' said Maria, 'was a damnation of us all.'

'Do you hate her for it?'

'Yes, I hate her.' Maria's eyes, beautiful as grey crystal beneath the finely cut precision of her lids, gazed at the fire. 'For like all suicides she ensured that we should love her, in despair and without help: for her act also damned any atonement we can make.'

She straightened, unclenching her hands. 'You know, we had a nurse when I was small. This woman used to tell a story about her own mother's childhood – tell it to Yolanta, Dorotea and me.'

Her voice now held the slight, formal lilt of the storyteller, which dictated a response trained into me by my own nurses. 'Let me hear this tale,' I said, for after my unkindness I owed her this courtesy.

Maria nodded. 'One night this child lay in bed awake, gazing at the moonlight on the panes. And as she watched, there

What Dangers Deep

appeared a white shadow looking in at her from outside the glass. It grew in colour, gained resolution, and became a woman – a woman in white cere-cloths, with a shock-head of hair uncombed, and the face of a skull.'

I stirred uneasily. 'Well, Maria, I can swear that *my* mother lay in bed when she was eight years old. And I can swear she looked at the window-pane: God himself could not reprove me for it. And I could guess she drifted into dream, and that her fears took shape and gazed at her.'

'Perhaps. But how sad–' said Maria softly – 'how sad for the skull-woman, and how sad for those who fear her. I have always thought she was human, and yearned, perhaps, to be transformed – yearned to come in out of the cold dark. I have always pitied her.'

'You must not choose such objects for your pity,' I said. 'To pity the unnatural is dangerous, Maria: we should only abhor it.'

She said, 'Philip, *I* have been thrust outside the window. All my life people will stare at me as I imagine that child's eyes staring at the skull in the dark.' I gave her no response but my attention. 'That I can endure,' she said. 'I have had five months in which to think what I can do: leave this city for the rest of my life; use this as a trial of our solitude with God. I have decided to survive Yolanta's legacy *in* the world, among my fellows, not by escaping to some convent. I will appear, if I succeed, to be like other people.'

'Can you endure such a pretence without breaking?' I spoke with all the gentleness I could.

'I do not know. But there are two things I *cannot* endure.' She gestured away my comfort. 'The first is this. I remember falling into the pink light. *It did not happen here, Philip.* Time has no space for it. The world embraces no place, no instant in which it happened. I have been where I was not.'

'There are names for such states, Maria.'

'And for those who remember them. "Liar" is one, "madwoman" another.'

'Dismiss those words if they are not true! Leave any room in which they are spoken; leave any friend who speaks them, or who allows them to be uttered in your presence.'

Maria laid her hand over mine. Warm, gentle, supple, her fingers raised gooseflesh on my skin. 'Is that bone, Philip? Because *I am Yolanta: look at me.*'

Thus seduced: helpless in its own goodwill: all the mind's defences voluntarily discarded – thus in silence, in shadow, in the modelling of normal forms – thus monsters are made from daylight, having hidden within the light. I saw Maria's chin lengthen, her face flow into a longer, more oval, yet still kindred shape; saw her mouth compress into the sour-sweet witty smile my mind suddenly remembered whole; saw thicker brows beneath which brown, not grey eyes stared at me.

I think that, my mouth covered with both hands, I stifled a scream. The moment flared, incandesced, stabilized and faded. 'No,' said Maria's voice. 'You create your own witches, Philip. I am only Maria and, may God have pity on me, I am sane.'

Her face with its too-pretty planes – its small muscular chin and the feminine proportions of nose and eyes – was her own: had never changed, never flowed into another form. Alone Maria gazed at me, having forced me to enact her utter solitude.

I straightened and said softly, 'Maria, you had no right.'

She was trembling. I grasped her wrists and pulled her bodily from the window-seat, flinging her on to her knees on the floor. She gave an exclamation of pain.

I lifted her by the shoulders, and flung her back without grace on to the cushions. She sprawled here, staring up at me. I unknotted my robe and came down on her naked, crushing her: committed to the act now by lust, by anger, and by an anguish close to tears.

She did not receive me, but fought me gropingly, in silence. I knew she would not cry out. This clumsy battle – of mouths, of fingers, of closed fists – reduced me to the unskilled play of boyhood, and lasted for some minutes.

What Dangers Deep

Suddenly I lifted my head. 'Maria, is it your time?'

She gasped. 'It is not my time. I have had no courses since you found me in October. Father Laurence says they may come back if I am patient.'

She had gone tense beneath me. I held her, gentling her. 'No, you smell only of lavender. I wondered by the taste of your mouth – a clean copper taste that sometimes means blood.' If shock had stopped her courses, I could perhaps take her without giving her a child.

Her tension had changed; for now I did intend to have her, and my weight and strength were greater. I unlaced velvet and gauze and found her breasts – applied my tongue to a nipple, and felt her wince with surprise. She squirmed away from me: I blocked her with my thigh and bore her down.

It was the cramped size of the window-seat that brought us, ultimately, into a half-sitting posture. By then Maria's shoulders and breasts were bare. She glanced behind her, in a natural caution, at the curtains that did not quite meet – and she froze, an arrested motion so full of authority that I stopped with her. '*Philip*,' she said.

He stood where the roses bloomed in summer; only now, shrouded in straw and burlap, their stocks rose up through four feet of snow. The storm had stopped hours ago: ice rimed the drifts, glazing their undulations, glistening on the single spike of snow that the wind had lashed into the angle of a wall. Our window cast only dim firelight: against it I hoped the two of us were just black shapes to any watcher. The light fell on the snow in embers of blue and yellow crystal.

If, on the night I buried Labrys, I had been able to imagine him, I would have pictured him in a warrior's stance: feet planted broad, arms open in a posture of declaration. But he had not chosen to come so to us. Naked – muscled like an archaic bronze – he stood with his arms folded and his head bowed. I could not see his face.

He consisted of blue light, which flowed through him, pulsing with the delicate naturalness of blood. I suppose it was pale blue, at times almost white. Blue fire rimmed his body. He cast no shadow. And he had lowered – not in threat but in contemplation – his head crowned with its ancient ornament: the horns of Minotauros, Lord of the Labyrinth.

I do not know how long we watched him. I was kneeling, my arm around Maria's shoulders, all our lustful game forgotten.

The figure turned without motion, shedding, I now saw, a narrow base of reflection on the snow. He had not eased his pose of meditation. Naked – weightless above the drift – he bent the great sickle-curved horns away from us. And then, without vanishing, he was gone.

Maria slumped against me. I cradled her, fearing she had fainted; but she was conscious. As I laid her down on the pillows she whispered, 'Yes, I saw it.'

We embraced and rested, and did not make love. An hour later she left me.

Next morning no one I met in Zamoyski's household showed any awareness of scandal between Maria and me; nor did my host betray whether anyone had seen us. No one talked of an apparition in the garden. The house seemed serene. The weather gave me no excuse to go into the quadrangle, but I did contrive to rest for a moment leaning on a window-sill.

This window faced, at ground level, the same view as my last night's bedroom. A stick tipped with sacking poked above the snow, and the rime had congealed into a crust slick as grey glass.

But no human being had waded through the snow. The drift with its sparkling crust flowed over the rosebushes as though no one had stood there.

Twenty-four

Spring, increasingly urgent in its changes, dealt quickly with the blizzard. Those among the poor who had frozen to death were coffined and forgotten; water sluiced in torrents down the streets. Above us the sky showed a remote, gentle blue; and in Market Square I saw, and bought for too much money, the first twined braid of lily-of-the-valley. The season was still too young for it; I did not know what lord's glasshouse had fostered these early flowers (for the lords did not disdain to earn money for their goods in Market Square).

In any case I carried it home, the little perfumed bells twined with pink ribbon, and dropped it gently over Dorotea's head. 'Here is spring's first necklace,' I said.

'Oh, *muguet*! I love them. They are the first to come except the crocuses and snowdrops. Mmmmm.' She inhaled, while I watched her in some anxiety: I had heard perfumes could cause nausea in a pregnant woman.

And Dorotea now looked pregnant. I could not help remarking how her hair had acquired a new sheen of healthy oil; how colour and solidity now rendered her body beautiful; and how white breasts, enlarged, now crushed her bodice above the front-laces she had taken to wearing. A dowdy fashion from our grandmothers' day, but useful if we are busy making their great-grandchildren. Every week the cross-ribbons came a little looser, a little more comfortably adjusted over Dorotea's bulge. It seemed a solid, hard little bulge. I longed to cup my hands over it, but shyness prevented me, and I feared to hurt her: one never knows, with women, what may break inside them if one is not careful.

'Are you happy?' I said.

'To my surprise, yes,' she replied. 'Happy as a cat dozing on a wall. I want only to sleep and eat and dream. I sleep so much I forget—' her head bowed – 'forget the sister I will never see again. I wake and remember that I love Antony. I wish Maria had such a friend, and such a consolation.'

'The child gives you pleasure, then? More than you had hoped?'

'Far more. With my stillroom, suckling and bearing, and mounting poor Antony only to get more – what a complacent creature I shall sound.'

'Do you fear the birth?' I asked.

Dorotea shrugged. 'One fears pain, especially an unknown pain. And I am not young, Philip: Doctor Solniecki admits this first one may not be easy. He knows a woman of thirty-two who gave birth in half an hour – and that with her first child. And I know another who had to be cut open. Well, Antony will be with me there. Surely it knows we long for it to be born, and will call it forth in all the love and safety we can, into a world we will teach it not to fear.'

'Lucky baby, then, and God be with you.'

'Call me lucky when—' she rose: I helped her – 'when it is safely and blessedly born. I had not believed I could forget Yolanta. I never will, I know. I had not expected any respite so innocent as this pregnancy. It *is* a respite, but it may become a truth: may become a family I can serve.'

'Be careful,' I said: I had never before seen Dorotea apparently lightheaded.

Her sad, brilliant eyes, which had not changed, assessed me suddenly without pretence, without euphoria. 'I am in my middle years, Philip, but my doctors say I am healthy. My courses come as they should; my husband will sow each child in love. Never mind—' she gathered up her sewing-silks – 'it is an *endeavour*, to build three or four healthy children against such obstacles. And Antony will love them so. I must go to bed: Doctor Solniecki sends me there by eight o'clock.' She kissed my forehead. 'Good night, my dear.'

Therefore her room was quiet and dark had fallen when Antony summoned me to his study. There I also found Father Laurence, who rose to greet me.

'Please, Father, sit down,' I said. 'Antony, if this conference involves us three alone, I can think of only one matter that concerns us all. You have called us here about the Privy Council's message.'

Antony pursed his mouth; concern quirked his eyebrows upwards. 'Marta, bring us wine, please. Father Laurence, will you believe me – we do have some acquaintance, you and I – when I say that no man-at-arms in this house has orders to overpower you, and that any wine I give you will be offered in goodwill? If you fear drugs, I will drink first from your cup.'

'I believe you will not harm me here, Sir Antony,' replied Laurence. 'At the same time you are Her Grace's servant. I will drink your wine in trust, as a friend should. And I will ask myself when your secret orders from Sir Francis Walsingham will force you to give me to the Privy Council.'

'Where, six months ago, you ardently desired to go,' said Antony.

I watched Laurence sip his wine. 'Ah,' he said, 'I have just confessed to fear. Nevertheless, my lord Ambassador, I am at your mercy in your house.'

'And I,' said Antony softly, 'have an order to fulfil. Father Laurence, would you be willing to take an oath of silence?'

'That depends upon the matter to be concealed. Offhand I should say no.'

'Then I am risking my career; but nevertheless I have decided to tell you. You are a good man, Father Laurence; and sundered though our nation has become – Protestant against Catholic – we are still one community.' Laurence nodded. 'I have observed you over many months,' said Antony. 'It seems to me that your life has value to your countrymen – to all of us: more value than would your death. It seems to me also that perhaps you should not be allowed to seek that death.'

'I cannot permit the word *allow*, Sir Antony.'

'Then consider this. I cannot tell you the name of my informant: you must take the statement bare, unsupported and unproven. Her Grace has granted Ulmerstead to her favourite, Christopher Hatton.'

After a moment Laurence whispered, 'She has given my home to—?'

'To Christopher Hatton, with all its lands and rents.'

Laurence rose, seemed to seek an objective, then walked, almost stumbled, to the window. Antony's gesture forbade me to help him.

Antony gave him (I estimated) sixty seconds. Then he rose and with gentle caution approached the other man, whom he did not touch. 'Father Laurence, Philip and I are here. If you are in distress, will you not return to your chair?'

Without a word Laurence accepted the arm he offered and, seating himself, bowed his head into his hands. Antony held out his cup; Laurence shook his head.

Antony said, 'Father Laurence, as one Christian man to another, I ask you to listen to me.'

Laurence straightened. 'I will hear you.'

'Her Grace never meant to keep faith with you.'

Through two closed doors we heard sounds of an arrival in the hall. 'It seems she did not,' said Laurence. 'She meant simply to torture me for what I know.'

'After which you could at best, like Queen Mary's Chaplain Doctor Feckenham, rot for twenty years ministering to your gaolers in the Tower. Or be quartered as a Jesuit and a preacher of sedition.' Laurence's eyes closed. Antony said, 'Stripped of all normal inducement, Father, do you still seek that death? You need not answer. I do not know what drives you. But I tell

What Dangers Deep

you this: *it need not stop* before you can help yourself. I beg you to do two things. Refuse whatever impels you: act as a Christian should – in charity to preserve yourself.' Laurence nodded. My godfather continued, 'The second thing is harder still. Accept your exile. Home and death are easy. You will never go home, Father Laurence. *It is lost to you.* Die an exile, in what time or way God wills. You are as old as I: you know, as I do, that Time exacts from us the humility of surrender. What greater sacrifice can we consecrate to God than the admission: *It is lost?*'

Robert Parsons had come quietly into the room. He nodded to Antony, and gestured greeting to me with as much friendly familiarity as though he had been my uncle. He moved with that silence which is the gift of certain heavy, muscular men; and lingering as he did in the shadows near the door, Laurence did not at once see him.

Caspar Laurence said, 'What an ignoble pretence. I have not, indeed, the courage of our martyrs – Thomas More and Bishop Fisher and the rest whom King Henry slaughtered. I suppose I never had it.'

'Neither have I,' remarked Antony. 'Some virtues, I think, can only fill us with awe and pity, not with the duty to emulate them. What did Thomas More say: *It is God's part to bring us to such a pass*? You have the skill of healing, Father Laurence. You have honesty and kindness and wit and love of truth. Can you not love, a little, the man your friends love?'

Laurence's mouth pinched in a calm, haggard smile. 'If I look within, I find, yes, love for that good man.'

'Then do not murder him,' said Antony.

Laurence glanced at me, but spoke still to Antony. 'I had thought, you know, to go back, as this young man will go back: somehow to reclaim the choices and undo the past. There comes a year, my lord Ambassador, when we know all our choices are done.'

'And the past gone beyond reach of our longing,' replied

Antony. 'I know. But no man who hungers for it has ever been given the past again.'

'And you have no hope, Caspar,' said Robert Parsons, coming gently forward, 'that a Redemption that shall renovate all things can somehow render to us all we have sacrificed – even the beloved past?'

Laurence shrugged, apparently unsurprised by a presence so delicately introduced to his notice. 'Robert, in all my life God has never visited me with the mercy of hope. In my young manhood I chose to follow my own soul. Perhaps I secretly hate that choice now because it has brought me no reward. I have lost my country, my home, my family, my youth, and the time God gave me in which to exist as a living man.'

'My dear old friend,' said Parsons, 'you did the best you could. So have we all. I, I suppose, fight also in my way, to take back the home to which I have as much right as Philip Sidney or Antony Marshall, or you. Come back with me. Let yourself rest. I believe the love you have served will some day visit you with peace.'

'Not before I break with longing for it.'

'Yet it is our duty, William's and mine, to tell you that agony must some day stop, because it was not infinite.' Laurence bowed his head. Parsons spoke to Antony. 'My lord Ambassador, this secures the safety of the English Jesuits on the Continent, and of those who harbour them at home. I am grateful for your decency. I will not afflict you, also, with the thanks of Cardinal William Allen and of the English College.'

Antony smiled. 'We may need Cardinal Allen's gratitude, Philip and I. We will not get Her Grace's.'

'So I fear. Caspar, come,' he said softly. 'If doctors ever take their own medicines, I hope I can persuade you to swallow a spoonful of your own poppy-syrup.'

'I will. I think,' said Laurence with sudden wounding clarity – 'I think that I have not been well in mind.'

Parsons' voice, dissembling all distress, was gently practical.

'Yet you will mend. And William as your superior orders you back to Rome for a course of rest.'

'Yes,' whispered Laurence, 'perhaps that is indeed the best.'

Parsons slipped an arm about his friend and raised him. 'Sir Antony has given us a coach. I'll take you home.'

'I cannot leave Kraków – not yet.'

'I know: the lady Maria. Of course she is your patient.'

At the door Laurence glanced back. 'Philip, I haven't spoken a word to you since I came in – forgive me. Will you come share a cup of wine with me – say, the day after tomorrow?'

'Most gladly, Father,' I said, and held the door for them.

Servants lit candles before we spoke again. At last Antony glanced up at me, and was in the motion of addressing me when the steward announced the Princess Anna.

We started to our feet. 'Madam, what is the matter?' exclaimed Antony.

The Princess drew off her glove and held out her hand to him. 'Good evening, Antony – Philip. Excuse me for coming in so rudely. I have a message for both of you, and also for Dorotea. It comes from Prince Stefan Bathóry. He asks that you meet him at a place to which my Captain will take you safely, Dorotea only excepted if she is not well. You are to start immediately.'

'Why, madam?' I demanded.

'Because,' replied the Princess, 'he says he has learned something about Yolanta.'

'Let him find what he may,' I said: 'unless it is Yolanta living or her body dead, I am beginning to believe a power has been at work here that we cannot force to answer us, and that we cannot call to justice.'

Twenty-five

I did not see Father Laurence next in his own chambers. After she left us, the Princess Anna visited him. Next day at ten in the morning he joined the cavalcade Antony had hurriedly assembled; and he served as doctor to Dorotea as her litter, slung between two horses, set a slow pace for us southwards through the rain.

Polish roads are better than English ones, and frost still came every other morning to congeal the last day's waggon-ruts. Dorotea lay on her back, bored or stoically reading; rain drummed on her canopy, and flowed off the cloaks of oiled cloth with which we sought to keep dry. Her Highness's Captain left us no fear of robbers; so we took it in turns to entertain Dorotea, riding beside her and talking.

Antony had allowed me Ambrose as my body-servant, and also Rob Sellier. On that first day I had just glanced back at Dorotea: Father Laurence, his face alight with kindness, had just said something that had made her laugh. Then Sellier drew level with me. 'It's filthy riding, sir.' I nodded. Sellier said, 'You asked me once for any rumours in the city. I can tell you that today before dawn – six hours earlier than our own setting-out – *Pan* Zamoyski left Kraków with the lady Maria and an ample guard. If they are going to the same destination as we then they will maintain their lead, as they have no pregnant lady to keep safe.'

On a day when snowdrops blossomed through the last rotten drifts, we halted by a river. Its spate had drowned the reeds.

The rain had drawn itself upwards, forming clouds upon the mountains. It was still falling, I guessed, in the mist several hundred feet above us: falling on spruce-trees that carpeted, with a thick blue-green nap, the swell of the mountain.

Beneath that slope Prince Stefan's hunting-lodge looked small. The belt of its outer wall rose up the hillside. I could see gardens, and a second, inner circle of wall which protected buildings with steep turrets of red tile. It seemed the Lodge consisted of a patchwork loop of houses built from the brown or orange-red stone of the region. I could see a small Hall, its roof tiled in red and patterned with a dicing of black stone.

We crossed the river safely, riding a ferry made of logs; it had a railing, and the keepers winched it from one shore to the other. We paid them well for the drenching they had taken to rescue us, and entered the first gate.

Beyond it lay gardens washed in a desolation of spring rain. The outer circle sheltered a considerable household – we saw a squadron of cavalry drilling, and barnyard beasts, and children playing in the mud. The second gate was guarded by two turrets capped with red roofs. This admitted us, I found, to the main house: a circle of lodgings apparently built as they had been needed, all joining to enclose what had, with centuries of addition, emerged as the central court. On one side of the circle stood the little Hall I had seen, with its tower and parapet.

This courtyard was less crowded, and indeed had no room for stables: they led our horses out again, and lodged me in a charmingly odd building only one room deep, though it had pointed windows and a ceiling whose beams smelt of pine. The fire, like the bath and meal that followed when I had warmed myself, was pleasantly adequate. No door opened from my little building to the adjoining one where the servants had taken Father Laurence: to talk with him I must either tap a code on the wall or go from my door to his, through the courtyard.

After supper a man brought me a letter from my host.

What Dangers Deep

My dear Master Sidney,

Excuse this summons, and the inconvenience of your room. I am delighted Father Laurence can be here, as the danger to Dorotea distresses me; but Antony tells me she insisted, and she has the right, as my business concerns her family. Jan is with me now; I have not seen Maria, though she is also here, and well. I truly had expected, when we met in Kraków, to encounter you only once. As it is, I hope you will consent, with our friends, to meet with me tomorrow afternoon at two. Sleep if you can, and ask my people for anything you may want. I must talk with Jan, and then rest for a few hours – excuse, therefore, all this discourtesy. You will be sleeping on Polish soil, by the way: this manor was King Zygmunt's gift to me, and I come here only as its master.

Chilled and ravenous, I enjoyed my meal. I went to bed at ten, and fell into sleep like a stone.

Rain shone on the cobbles when, after a solitary midday meal, I climbed the rise to Prince Stefan's hall. In the courtyard I could see no one, except one figure robed to the feet in brown leather. I called out. '*Pan* Nemet!'

'Master Philip!' He raised his hat, which he had tilted against the rain, revealing the sardonic Tartar face of my friend. He held out his hand to me. 'Good afternoon.'

'Good afternoon. What does His Highness want of us, do you think?'

'I think perhaps he wants to help.' We had halted, the rain sluicing off our hat-brims. 'It is time this business ended, Philip.'

I glanced around. We stood near the place where the low buttressed wall joined the main hall; I saw that the last buttress jutted out, protecting a nook in the right-angle of the two structures. Two human beings might stand upright in it, hidden from sight if not from hearing. I wondered with amusement how many maid- and menservants the nook had hidden for five minutes' work on summer nights over the centuries. I said quietly, 'May I speak with you?'

'Of course.'

We stepped into the little sheltered place. 'I made you a promise once.' Nemet nodded. 'It would violate confidence,' I continued, 'to tell you the little I have learned.'

I saw his eyes assess the possibilities, and wondered for an instant whether – among the elders with whom in any case I felt I could barely deal – he were not the cleverest of all. 'I see,' he said with caution.

I glanced out. The courtyard was still empty. 'He was killed by a friend – in anger but, as I believe, by accident.'

'For what crime?' demanded *Pan* Nemet softly.

'For no crime. For an act any man might commit if lust made him, for a few moments, neither wise nor kind.'

An alternative possibility existed, as I had long been aware; but for it I had no proof beyond the fresh-printed placard from the illicit press, the placard Caspar Laurence had destroyed; and in it I did not believe. Therefore I did not speak it: that Zamoyski had killed Jean Palmette not for what the secretary had done, but for what he knew.

Nemet stared at me. After a long second he said, 'Would Yolanta forgive Jean?'

So in this deserted place she rose before us – the girl I had scarcely known: the woman who had vanished with the silent elegance of a sickle reaping grain – without our noticing, without farewell. The girl whose history I had traced as best I could – through her mother's ostracism from the University to her sickness and her suicide; through the father's scholarship, his favouritism for the other child, and his violent death abroad. The girl who had destroyed Jean Palmette. Elements of a shattering within the soul whose agony I could, with pity, surmise, but whose truth I would never know. What moment of her youth had destroyed Yolanta, in the fragility she had so truculently shielded? And what choice, what power had doomed Maria to return? For 'with the dead all is very well'; but Scripture gives us no equal assurance for the living.

All this I thought while the rain rustled around us, sweeping the cobbles in wind-driven veils. I heard *Pan* Nemet say again, 'Would Yolanta forgive him?'

I replied, 'I believe – I hope – she would. He was young. His friends should love him and commend his soul to God, who surely has received him.'

'Thank you, Philip, for remembering your promise.' He was silent for an instant. 'I will miss him. I will miss them both.'

'I know.'

Nemet shook his cloak, glanced at the sky and sighed. 'Well,' he said. 'Let us go and hear why the Prince has called us all together.'

Twenty-six

More recent owners had paved over the hearth from whose fire, once, had risen all the hall's warmth. Now a fireplace with a carved Italian lintel warmed our backs as we found our places at Prince Stefan's table; but the smoke of the old hearth still charred the interlacing beams above us and lent its redolence to the air, mixed with the smells of cedar and whitewashed stone. Ranged down the long room I could see tables; plate made of gold and silver and maiolica, displayed on buffets between the tapestries; and a trace of the old rusticity that it seemed Prince Stefan had not cared to change – the dry spiked horns of deer slaughtered a hundred years ago.

'No, I have changed little.' Prince Stefan smiled at me. Around our table, which lay at the warm end of the hall, I saw Maria, to whom I bowed; Dorotea, her face serene in answer to the Prince's glance of concern; *Pan* Nemet, Antony, Caspar Laurence, Robert Parsons and Jan Zamoyski. Servants had lit candles, for the silver sky beyond the windows already showed a depth that promised twilight.

'Forgive me for this summons,' said the Prince. 'Especially I apologize to Dorotea. Only the King should, I think, at this point enter Kraków openly: I cannot. I have found something all of you should judge, and I will show it to you almost immediately.'

Dorotea frowned; Maria bowed her head. Prince Stefan glanced around at us; his big-featured, comely face was kind. 'My own searchers have continued at intervals to examine the

Ancient Mass. Ten days ago I thought to make one final search. Other parties, and public interest also, have almost destroyed the Grove, but we have all had a season in which to lose hope, and few visitors go there now. Therefore I sent my people once again. They examined the Grove in daylight, twenty-four hours after a light fall of snow.'

Zamoyski had steepled his hands to hide his mouth. His eyes were half-closed. Dorotea stirred: Laurence bent quickly towards her, then straightened again. Prince Stefan continued: 'My men found nothing in the pool, which they dragged; nor in the wood for a square half-mile; nor around the margin of the pool; nor at the place where Yolanta vanished. They did discover the trove of bear-skulls, which they searched to the bottom, replaced, and covered over: for it was holy to the ancient people, and it is not well to meddle with a holy thing.' *Pan* Nemet frowned and nodded. 'Among the pines at the top of the cliff, however,' the Prince continued – 'to be precise, among the exposed roots of one tree, they found this.'

His steward had come up carrying a tray. The man bowed and presented to Prince Stefan a small bundle tied in brown cloth. Not – the shock appalled me and branched, searing, through my veins to my fingers' ends – not brown cloth: brown velvet.

'I have retied the bundle, as I could not avoid examining its contents. Originally I found it tied in a loose, simple knot. Jan?' Prince Stefan's gesture offered the parcel to Zamoyski, who declined with a single motion of the hand. The Prince touched the bundle. 'It is velvet, probably from Yolanta's habit. And it contains her jewels.'

His fingers worked gently and nimbly with the folds. Against the fabric, shining untarnished as on the day I had last seen them, lay a ring of white jade and a brooch enamelled with the arms of Coligny.

'She is dead, then,' said Maria.

Caspar Laurence cleared his throat. 'My lord Prince, you

said, "twenty-four hours after a light fall of snow". Did these things lie on top of the snow, then?'

'They were found under it,' replied the Prince. 'My men judged they had lain on the ground since the day before: no longer. There were no footprints.'

'The fabric is not rotted, then?' inquired *Pan* Nemet.

'Not rotted, only damp.'

Nemet nodded.

'And the jewels,' said Antony. 'Is there any blood, any earth on them?'

'None.'

I spoke. 'Has the fabric been ripped, or cut?'

'A clean rip,' said Prince Stefan.

Maria held out her hand. 'Give them to me, sir. They are the last of her I shall touch.'

He gave them into her palm. She bent and kissed them, and tipped them in turn into Dorotea's cupped hands. Dorotea was weeping without a sound. Maria's face was harsh: she suddenly looked, I thought, forty years old.

And as we all sat absorbed in watching her, Caspar Laurence leaned to me and uttered one soft sentence. *We should be tender of her good name.*' The laughing apparition in the Grove, whatever it had been, must not destroy the calm of these survivors – must never threaten the sanctity, the fragile peace in which those who loved her must lay Yolanta at last.

'May God curse them,' said Jan Zamoyski. 'May God curse them.'

'Have you any enemies who would torment you so, my lord Zamoyski?' demanded Robert Parsons.

'I have enemies, Father Parsons: none I had thought capable of this.'

'Only an enemy would have preserved them in this state,' observed Parsons. 'I mean undamaged. To judge by their condition they have not been recovered from a grave. There is no blood. Thieves would never have returned them. Unless you have an enemy capable of such intricate malice—' He shrugged.

'But *intricacy* is precisely the point,' I exclaimed. '*Pan* Zamoyski, I will not be so impudent as to say you may have many enemies.' Zamoyski raised his brows, but nodded. 'I am a stranger here,' I continued: 'You all know much that I do not. But only two enemies of yours seem to me to be implicated here: *Pan* Balinski and the Archduke Ernst.'

'As far as I know, Philip,' replied Zamoyski, 'that is correct.'

'Then Father Parsons is right: the method is too intricate. The Archduke Ernst has only a pragmatic enmity towards you. I cannot believe he would interest himself in anything so cumbersome and irrelevant as this torturing of you through Yolanta.'

Zamoyski nodded again, his attention focused on me with intensity.

'And this placing of the jewels just beneath new untrodden snow,' I said, 'as well as many other things that have happened here, exceeds the physically possible in a way that would be almost bizarre to authorize or successfully to achieve from Vienna, through intermediaries, only for the aims the Archduke has. None of us knows him for a cruel man, only for an ambitious one. I think he is not guilty of this crime.'

'Very well,' said Zamoyski.

'Then,' I continued, 'I must ask you, *Pan* Zamoyski: forgive me. You and *Pan* Balinski are about the same age; you have, I suppose, known each other for many years. You were perhaps boys together. Do you hate each other? Might Balinski have *hated* Yolanta?'

Zamoyski considered, visibly reckoning up memories he did not intend to confide. 'Yes, we were boys together. Balinski and I endure each other, Philip: we do not hate. Each of us does his work too well. As for Yolanta, I know of no passion he might have had for her, no refusal on her part that might have justified revenge. I cannot conceive that he hated her.'

'I have heard that *Pan* Balinski slit the bellies of captured

Turks, and then left them to crawl home alive. Might he,' I said gently, 'torture you?'

'For pleasure? You have ridden with Balinski, Philip. He is capable of cruelty, but no madman – no man who *delights* in cruelty – can command sane, decent men as successfully as he has done. That kind of madness would be a fatal luxury in a soldier, and his own comrades would, for their own safety, destroy him. Balinski is capable of having *seized* Yolanta. No,' said Zamoyski, 'he might wish to force me; but to torture me as this affair has done would be to him irrelevant.'

I glanced again at Maria: saw again in her eyes the memory of the presence we had seen glowing blue in the barren garden, where nothing could have been. 'Then,' I said, 'Yolanta was rapt from earth by a power we do not understand.'

Maria kissed the jewels again, her hair falling around them. As she surrendered them to Prince Stefan she stared at me, and I nodded. There was no refuge here from the blue light we had both seen above the snow.

Prince Stefan sighed and pushed back his chair. 'My heart tells me there will be no more. If this is the last, my friends, perhaps we must now be gentle with the living. Can I help, or can we help each other?'

'My sister is dead,' said Maria. 'And, God forgive me, I am *glad*.'

No one broke the silence soon enough. And the voice that did so was my own – offering, to my astonishment, the only hope I possessed. 'Maria, will you marry me?'

Zamoyski looked up abruptly. I was the son-in-law Prince Willem of Orange had not despised, and, though I felt my skin go hot, it was not with shame. Prince Stefan made a soft sound of enjoyment that was not quite a laugh.

It did distress me to see that the idea had thunderstruck Maria. Her face – soft, astonished, gentle – revealed how little she had connected me with any such intimate decency. I said, 'I would take you far away, but we could visit. My family would love you, and would respect your religion. Forgive me for speaking of it, but I admit we are a Protestant nation. Do not be afraid of us for that. Marry me, Maria, and let us make a home together. Will you come with me?'

She held out her hand: I took it, there in the sight of everyone. Very softly she replied, 'I do not know, Philip.'

A long moment afterwards Prince Stefan said, 'Jan, we will find nothing more. I recommend that all legal inquiry into the matter be closed. Let us grieve and heal over the long years if we can. I will keep the two children here with me for a day, as it seems they have private business to discuss. The jewels, of course, are yours.'

'I will bury them in our vault,' said Zamoyski. 'They are all of her we have left to bury. Father Laurence, will you pray with us for her peace, and for the absolution of the living?'

'Very gladly,' replied Father Laurence.

After thinking a moment, he bowed his head and said aloud – and I sought above, below our strained attention for some presence that heard him, and found no tremor of its listening: 'We have done all we could. Comfort us in our helplessness and in our ignorance. We entreat you, comfort the dead. Help us to accept this parting: in Christ's name, Amen.'

They left the next day. As he shook my hand, *Pan* Nemet said, 'Master Philip, I have enjoyed you. Let me hear of you – and from you, if I may. Prince Stefan will know where a letter might find me.'

And Antony smiled at me. 'The baby may take us by surprise, so I do not know where I shall see you next – Kraków or Paris. His Highness has promised to send a messenger to the Embassy for your baggage if you decide on Italy.'

Dorotea embraced me and said gravely, 'Will you be the child's godfather, my dear? We can find some friend to stand proxy for you if you cannot reach us in time.'

'With all my heart,' I said, and kissed her. And some time

later I became godfather to their first daughter, whom they named Philippa.

Father Laurence kissed me, held me at arm's length, and said, with a hesitation whose simplicity charmed me, 'Will you accept a blessing?'

'Most gladly, Father,' I replied.

I knelt before him to receive it. As I rose he glanced towards Maria, who stood out of earshot, and said, 'So powers exist. That is, after all, the truth I formally affirmed when first I took my vows. All my life I have sought for confirmation of that hope, and now—' he gestured, and his hand suggested something, fragments or ashes, falling through the fingers, scattering on the wind. 'Now power has shown itself, and it is enigmatic: it is barren.'

'They say that God is love,' I replied.

Laurence stared at me. 'I wonder in God's name,' he said, 'what *reason* they found to say it. A bad place, the Grove: will its obliteration last, do you think? The bear-skulls still lie hidden, the stream still flows, and the apple-trees, I suppose, will nourish their birds and small creatures through years we shall not see.'

'Does it matter?' replied Jan Zamoyski, joining us. 'This foul mystery is unworthy of you, Father, as it is of me: I long to be washed clean of it. Philip, you have surprised me – and pleasantly. If Maria accepts you, come back to us at Kraków. If not, and if I do not see you again, I wish you every good. Farewell.'

I hugged him, weeping and smiling. Then, to my surprise, even Robert Parsons had a word of kindness for me. 'Master Philip, we will take good care of Caspar – William and I. And if you ever hear the ghost-monks chanting, write to me.'

'Then you will never hear from me, Father Parsons,' I said; and we shook hands.

'Pray for me, Philip,' said Laurence as he turned away. And indeed he has not lacked my prayers, every night of my life since then.

And Rob Sellier said, 'May I claim your promise, sir? The Ambassador is leaving Poland. I should like to go with you to Italy, or wherever you go.' I shook his hand and we agreed on it. He is with me still.

They rode away into the rain.

For a moment Prince Stefan and Maria and I listened to the silence. Then, 'Damn this gloom,' remarked the Prince. 'I have something to cheer you both. Come along.'

Dodging the rain, we climbed with him up to the battlements. Here the masonry widened to make a terrace as broad as a small house; and someone had built a glasshouse, a bell of glittering little panes, freckled with rain and steamed from within with a heat that promised summer. Inside I saw puffs of colour: dim pastels. 'I made this,' said the Prince. 'Come in.'

Above us rose a roof of panes leaded together – a roof frosted with vapour. Here, in winter, it must be bright if glass could gather any light from the snowclouds; but today, down an aisle perhaps as long as two houses set end to end, we saw in the rain-light the vaporous colour of spring shrubs, their sprays creased and pleated with new green. From the humidity rose the smell of earth. Perfumes of flowers separated themselves delicately on currents of air: lilac, *muguet*, violet. Bushes trembled with young leaves; and around their roots lay powderings of the scentless flowers – bluebells, snowdrops, saffron and purple crocus.

Prince Stefan led us forward, talking gently of grafts and cuttings and of bulbs purchased, even smuggled from the Turks. He hoped, he said, to bring new blooms from the Americas: he had heard of sunflowers ten feet tall, each with a blossom the size of a gold plate – of a vine covered with exquisite blue flowers that opened only in the cool of the day, and of another vine that turned wine-purple in the autumn. In China, he said, there were fields of wild roses blooming unregarded, for the Chinese do not esteem the rose. And from

What Dangers Deep

Japan came brown chrysanthemums for which he would pay the mariners any money.

For an hour we wandered in this magic cell of spring, while half-dissolved snow spattered against the panes. Maria had taken off her coat. Ever since our conference yesterday she had not troubled to cover her hair with a coif: humid with sweat, it fell with a sheen like parcel-gilt over her gown of green broadcloth. She spoke little; her manner to me was open, shy and grave.

As for me, I had used my man's privilege of asking – a form of mastery that shamed me slightly by its unfairness, but it had transformed her – and we both knew it – into a girl I could have. I hoped she had not noticed (do women look, I wondered?) how this affected me. I eased myself unobtrusively, and cursed.

Prince Stefan had, for the only moment in that hour, left us alone. Otherwise he had escorted us, I thought, with delicacy and gentleness, never seeming to observe us – though I felt his interest – nor forcing us, by his desertion, into an intimacy we might not want. Now, however, he had found a gardener to whom it seemed he must talk about a shipment of tulips; and with an apology he left us.

I looked down at my companion. 'May I come to you tonight?'

'Yes, of course.' She bent to sniff a spray of white lilac. 'We mustn't pick them, must we? Ah well: it's stupid to kill a flower, or so I've always thought.'

'Can you stay awake till one?'

'Yes.'

'At one o'clock, then,' I said, and smiled at her.

Our host, his eyes bright with an interest I did not acquit of common curiosity (I suspected that Prince Stefan, for all his solidity, was a gossip among his friends), had turned back to us. We stepped apart – Maria lifting the burden of her hair away from her neck with a natural gesture. I saw our host's smile congratulate us, though gently.

* * *

I should say now that Prince Stefan, to judge by his subsequent history, was probably one of the most intelligent human beings I have ever met. The silence between Maria and me was perhaps a little heavy: in any case, that night after supper, our host set out to relieve it, and did so with brutal daring. I have never seen a handsomer man, and few, even including my uncle Robert, who were taller; and I remember clearly his characteristic gestures, including a sudden widening in interest of eyes that were ice-blue, keen and kind. Now, over the nuts and marzipan fruits, he hitched back his chair, crossed one leg over the other and said, 'So, Master Sidney, is Queen Elizabeth a virgin?'

I had leisure later to reflect that this man was a gossip, if with zest, then also with calculation. At the time I heard Maria's smothered laugh of surprise, and felt myself blush. 'My lord, I have parried this question all the way from Paris to Rome. Surely your own spies have informed you?'

'Indeed. May God forgive the French and Spanish Ambassadors, who pay well to know the state of Her Grace's monthly linen.'

'That, surely, is another question.'

'But it seems Queen Elizabeth *can* bear,' remarked my host. 'How interesting, then, if she were to do so.'

'To a Spanish prince or a French one? She never will.'

'A Danish prince would at least be Protestant.' He cracked a walnut and offered the meat, extracted whole, to Maria. She took it, glancing at me with a smile of interest that reminded me of Zamoyski. 'And I hear,' resumed Prince Stefan, 'I hear she once said to your uncle's face—'

'She once said to my uncle's face, "I will have but one mistress here – and no master."'

'Precisely,' replied the Prince. 'Yet when she lay near to death of smallpox—' Here he did have the decency to stop. Very gently he resumed. 'I do beg your pardon. Did she not, believing herself to be dying, will fifty ducats to the groom who slept in your uncle's bedchamber?'

'Yes, she did. This gossip seems to me unworthy of you, my

What Dangers Deep

lord.' Stefan nodded, as friendly to this assertion as to any other I might make. I could not hit him, he was my host; and in any case the conversation was moving too quickly. I found that, without knowing how, I had forgotten my dread of one o'clock. I said, 'Perhaps the groom had reason for silence; but Her Grace and my uncle love each other, and ought to have the rights of any lovers – among them the right to a decent secrecy. And even so my parents, who have known her from her childhood, judge, sir, that she cannot.'

'And yet,' said Prince Stefan, 'when she was fifteen – perhaps you are too young to have heard the story? – her stepmother Queen Katherine Parr and the Princess Elizabeth's own governess conspired to remove her most suddenly from Queen Katherine's household, where she had been a ward. In fact Queen Katherine's husband had found his way into the Princess Elizabeth's bedroom, had he not? And after they sent her away, she fell ill in her retirement, and was confined to bed for six months. A miscarriage, one wonders?' *An abortion?* The question hung unsaid.

'Misery and exhaustion merely, sir. She was only a child.'

'So she was,' assented Prince Stefan.

Thereafter, as if judging he had gone as far as I would endure, he led me with adroitness away from intimate or intrusive questions. He asked me about Queen Elizabeth's imprisonment of her cousin Mary Stuart Queen of Scots, whom we have had in jail in England ever since her own subjects expelled her for murder and vicious incompetence. This subject led us to another: the conspiracy against Her Grace of the Catholic North. Prince Stefan asked, 'Will the North of England rise again, do you think?'

'It is too soon to be sure,' I replied. 'The Council hanged many poor men at the crossroads of their own villages. I think they broke the North.'

'Which is the ancient Catholic constituency.'

'Insofar as one remains in England, yes.'

'Both the New Religion and the authority of London are now secure, then.'

'Not secure, my lord; not so long as Mary Stuart can conspire to bring in the Spanish,' I said.

'And yet Queen Elizabeth protects her cousin's life. Is it true the Council want Mary Stuart dead?'

'Not only the Council, the people too.'

'Why, then, does the Queen spare her execution? She has evidence enough – for instance that Mary Stuart was party to her own husband's murder.'

'Yes,' I said, 'a court found her guilty on the evidence, and guilty she is.'

'Then why not kill her?'

'Perhaps because Her Grace remembers the beheading of her own mother, Anne Boleyn. But *I* think . . .' I hesitated. 'I think she believes that, if once one touches the life of an anointed Prince, the precedent will not stop in Scotland: it may descend in the future on England as well.'

'How lucky you are,' Prince Stefan observed, 'that the lesser of two sisters, poor Queen Mary Tudor, died, and that the greater sister both survived and chose, Master Sidney, to be a light to the Protestant cause.'

But this time I would not take it. I said merely, '*We* think ourselves lucky, sir.'

He glanced at Maria, who had bowed her head – as I then thought, because the conversation had up to now excluded her. When he drew her in she had to follow him, which she did with a troubled smile.

And from this hall hundreds of miles distant – from the humidity of the glasshouse, and from the day's sorrows – as if it had been Prince Stefan's gift to me, I felt suddenly a hunger for my home: primitive as these people would think it, with its gentle landscapes, its savageries, its foreignness to the human beings among whom I had lived the past years.

Prince Stefan led the conversation towards subjects in which he cajoled Maria to join. It was perhaps nine-thirty when she rose, shaking out her skirts. There were prints of exhaustion beneath her eyes. She did not look at me. 'My lord – Philip –

What Dangers Deep

please excuse me. I should like to call for a bath and, I think, wash my hair.'

'It's cold for that, my dear, but my people will make your room as warm for it as they can.' The Prince pushed back his chair and rose to a height that rendered her childlike in comparison. He kissed Maria's cheek, with a sudden sweet gentleness that I ever after remembered and liked him for. She fell from his hands into the full obeisance of a Court curtsey. Then she straightened, saluted me, and left us.

'Stay with me, Master Sidney, if you please,' said Prince Stefan, making no comment on the salute that had named him King, not only for my eyes, but in an act of love privately declared.

'Gladly, sir,' I answered. Maria had shown me the way the vote would go on Warsaw Plain. My head ached with the wine, and I would rather have gone away. Why can one not *want* such an opportunity when at last life offers it?

'I know,' said the Prince. 'Shall I send for coffee, or will that make it worse?'

'That would make it better,' I admitted.

It took some time to come; the Prince's silence did not press me. When at last His Highness poured coffee into the thimble-shaped cup, I saluted him. 'Excuse me, sir, for being too tired to value as I should the only time I will, probably, ever again have alone with you. And thank you for keeping us here, Maria and me. It was kind of you.'

'I met her when she was little,' he replied. 'I liked Dorotea for her courage, and Maria for her decency. But Yolanta I pitied: not that her gifts were any less, but that she seemed unhappy. I hope she has found peace . . . Master Sidney, your father wrote to me two months ago, enclosing a letter which he asked me to keep for you.'

'Wrote to *you*, sir?' I exclaimed. 'Two months ago I expected never to see you again.'

The Prince shrugged. 'I gather Doctor Dee instructed him. You will surely wish to read it.'

No one had visibly tampered with the seal. I glanced up at

Prince Stefan, wondering how many people – certainly Zamoyski, perhaps also the man before me – had read my letters since I came to Poland. His answering smile was peaceful and amused. I unfolded the sheet. From it dropped into my palm a small object wrapped in tissue, whose weight I recognized.

My dear son,
I think Prince Stefan will find you, even if I have been wrongly advised. For myself I should have asked lord Zamoyski to forward this letter, but never mind.

Your mother saw you go that night, though she took many years to tell me; and she guessed your errand at the Standing Stones.

I said to you once that gold should not slumber in the dark. I return to you, therefore, what is yours.

With hands that shook, I undid the tissue-paper. Between my fingers there shone in the Polish winter-cold an object alien in its purity and heaviness and in the dark colour of its gold: Labrys, the Double-Headed Axe.

The quality of Prince Stefan's attention reminded me of my own grip upon the ancient, precious thing. At last he said, 'I can see it is very old. Will you not tell me what it means?'

'I *buried* it–' I brought my voice under control – 'and it would not *stay* buried. I fear and hate the spoil of graves.'

'May I touch it?' he said.

I gave it to him.

For a long time he weighed it in his hand. At last, as if reaching a conclusion, he clipped it in his palm and gave it back to me. 'Philip, I am no diviner; but there is a truth here that someone must say to you. I know some things about you, for Jan has spoken of you. Watching you has told me more; and Labrys also has spoken in her fashion. Wear the Axe next to your skin. Why bury what you cannot escape? And do not judge yourself a failure: not,' said the next King of Poland, 'until you know for certain all that you have given.'

Twenty-seven

The departure of his other guests had left some chambers empty. Accordingly, our host had moved us to rooms in the main building. By his kindness too, I suspect, my door now lay only five yards across the corridor from Maria's.

In a house gone still I drowsed in a bath, then towelled myself and dressed in clean day-clothes, and yawned over a book while the clock ticked out the hours till one. Now that Maria's answer, and perhaps another culmination too, had come upon me, I found myself as one often does at such moments: cool, reluctant, almost irritated.

No servant observed, no one opposed me as I stepped towards the line of light beneath Maria's door. I knocked twice, softly, and heard her voice call, 'Who is there?'

'May I come in?'

She unbolted the door and opened it, to reveal a room that seemed calculated to soothe me: a concavity of warm firelight and the colder shadows of candles. She had dragged a settle before the fire, and it touched me to see that a bowl of warm milk-punch (had Dorotea told her I liked it?) lay ready on the table, with its ladle and red glass cups.

She had not, I saw, washed her hair, which hung shining like spool-silk over her shoulders to her waist. The robe, brown velvet and warm for winter, was not the one she had worn on a night we both remembered. She turned from me and said, 'I ordered some punch. I *think* it has not curdled.'

I had come to her tired, and her coolness was that of a

hostess, not a lover. With a smile I obeyed her invitation to sit down, and let her serve me. As she leant down over me her hair, masking her shoulders like a shawl, fell across my knee. My flesh crept at its unsubstantial softness. She had not perfumed it: it was redolent only of her warmth.

She had not meant, I think, to convey so primitive an invitation, and drew away; but I grasped at the soft curtain, twining my fingers in it gently, and said, 'Sit here by me.' When she had obeyed, her face sober, I let her go. And so we sat for a few moments: as chaste, as motionless as strangers.

'It goes away, doesn't it?' she said at last.

'Sometimes,' I replied. 'And sometimes it seems to go away.' The punch was a mixture of milk, spices and fine brandy, and it had not curdled; I drank it without touching her.

I could feel her dread of any coarse approach. In the end it seemed kindest simply to slip my arm around her shoulders and embrace her. After a long moment I heard her sigh.

'Maria,' I said, 'will you let me touch you? You need do nothing.'

'Of course, Philip.' Her face was grave. I laid her against the back of the settle.

She watched me as I went to work with lips and palms, smoothing her, savouring her – enjoying the gentler senses. I kissed her hair, her cheeks, her throat. Finally my fingers found her breasts. She had begun to breathe more quickly. After that I used her hard with mouth and hands; and in our kissing I did not spare her my tongue.

Finally, since it is ludicrous to go there in haste, I took her hand and led her to the bed. Under the robe she was wearing a voile nightgown, which, not wanting to frighten her, I did not hurry to remove. She watched me as I laid her on the pillow and freed myself from clothing down to the waist.

The gauze gave me access to her breasts; and their feel abruptly transformed the rhythm I had intended. 'Maria, forgive me, but I think I must come to you now.'

What Dangers Deep

'Then help me, and yes,' she replied.

I had thought she must be afraid: but her face in its calm exaltation had a quality of competence, and also of that compassion that has astonished me once or twice on the breast of a woman I loved – the compassion they show us at the moment of our supreme joy. I rucked up her gown above her breasts and guided her.

I had meant to take care against the tearing of the membrane, but I forgot it and so, I hope, did she; for she received me as Nature had formed her to do – with a grip and inward textures that cost me the last of my self-command. I gasped an apology, I think, before I clasped her waist and mounted her, and thrust upon her the primitive surrender that is animal at its root, and that, in its dissolution, touches an ecstasy so holy our senses can barely sustain it.

One such encounter exhausted me; but I had not finished with her. Her heat gone soft around me needed the barest friction, and I used her again without leaving her body.

It left me shuddering, still tranced inwards; and I think I slept. She did not wake me. I did not see the blood on her legs, but when I woke she was gone from the bed, and I heard her dealing with water and a sponge behind the screen. She came out, her gown pulled down, and lay beside me in the firelight. I shook out a blanket – our work had made me cold – and said, 'Did I hurt you?'

'No.' Her eyes, dilated, were soft and brilliantly calm. 'This was the favour, that first night.'

I gazed at her with my head propped on my arm. 'Give me my answer,' I said.

Maria sat up. She swathed her hair around her shoulder, twisting it into a braid. 'You do not love me, Philip.'

It was not an accusation; and in the silence that opened between us I could not counter it. At last I said, 'I desire, respect, enjoy you, Maria. I know half a dozen marriages built on less than that, and they flourish well.'

'I am Catholic, Philip, and I love my faith. I dread to go with you to a Protestant country.' I nodded. 'I am a Pole: I love my home as deeply as you can yours. I cannot go with you so far away. I cannot become your client, your pensioner–' I started: she laid her hand on my arm – 'and begin again. I am too exhausted: I do not contain a new beginning. Yesterday afternoon the Prince spoke to me in private. Madame Marguerite has written him that she will gladly take me, departing from here, until it is safe for me to return to Kraków. My work is to exist: not to found anew. My answer is no. Rescue yourself from the Grove and all its legacy. Let me go, Philip: I am beyond your saving.'

I remembered the sisters my father had spoken of long ago: the Trojan Princesses Cassandra and Polyxena. Cassandra, whom a god loved – a love that drove her to witness his presence unbelieved, and to die in isolation from all humankind. And Polyxena, annihilated on the grave of Achilles, to be his slave in the Underworld.

Both women had been the elect of god or hero – elected to endure, with open eyes, a power to which they must go alone. Men are not grateful for such witnesses; and to behold such powers is a labour that goes unthanked.

I thought of the stone beast that writhed, forever frozen, on a panel in the torchlight; thought too of a wild horse rolling in the snow; of living hair, perfumed with the delicacy of its innocence – hair brown and blonde together. I thought of flames that burned before the Madonna; of Adam Kózmian, his head pillowed in his blood; of running through the dark. I remembered the kind face of the Princess Anna, and Dorotea's face when, with fear and tenderness, I had longed to touch the place where the child lay. I remembered a wolf, its body set to swing from chains in the wind; and Sancta Maria with its golden saints; and the sustaining patience of Antony Marshall; and the eyes of Caspar Laurence as I had seen them, wakeful in the firelight. I remembered a girl's voice singing *'Mignonne,*

What Dangers Deep

allons voir si la rose'; and the commands of my Queen; and the sacrifice I had cried aloud to the dark at the Ancient Mass before Balinski took us. I remembered Antony saying *It is lost*; and my own voice – *Then my moment is gone*; and the words of the Grand Chancellor of Poland – *If you matter again, it will be for some other achievement.*

Every man longs to matter in his time.

I should, probably, have left it all there, respecting the instinct that warned me. But the sleep of exhaustion had begun to overtake me, numbing kindness, prudence, foreknowledge. I said therefore, 'Maria, what do *you* think happened that day to Yolanta and you? What do you know that you have not told?'

She shrugged, arms laced around her knees. 'Something no one wants to hear. I admit, since everyone demands admission from me, that my memory goes a little way into the dark: to cool marble and gentle light – things not unkind, except that they do not exist. Then there seems to me to be a soft *crackle*, and all memory ceases. There is no secret, Philip. Something bereaved me of being. When I opened my eyes in my bedroom I was not a new creature: I was Maria, allowed to *be* again.'

'There *is* a secret,' I protested, my voice slurred, made cruelly persistent by fatigue. 'I held you living in my arms. I saw your eyelids move, your lips move, as if some presence held you.'

'If one did,' she replied, 'its gift to me was the knowledge that we exist at a whim of power: exist, then cease, and then perhaps exist again.'

'I cannot believe that. You slept, you forgot.'

She flung herself back on her elbow on the pillow: rigid, combative, confronting me. 'For Yolanta, annihilation; for me, the memory of annihilation. Endure it, Philip, for it makes nothing of your Faith: *nothing*.'

A miracle of destruction, Jan Zamoyski had said. 'Then,' I whispered, 'I refuse it.'

Frantic-eyed we stared at each other. Then she folded into my arms, and I held her while she wept. And as I crushed her into an embrace that sought desperately to convey all warmth, all humankindness, I thought, This certainty I have, Maria: that men and women love. Let the dark contain no other warmth: let memory be annihilate, and with it, those we have loved; let love encounter Power and lose, or seem to lose. Let Power reveal itself, and reveal itself as void. But if something were to reave me of my name, my history, my life, yet love has been born in me and cannot be destroyed.

I thought once to restore my family's honour: to be a statesman, or perhaps a general. I see now that my true work is primitive – is simple. My task is to cry love into the void, for love is greater than the void. Let me take up my work of courage, then, for death and Time are both revealed, and my labour at its core is simply this: that neither shall destroy me.

Twenty-eight

Hampton Court Palace,
October

The Court would soon leave Hampton for Whitehall: after their summer stay, the place smelt of human habitation. Servants had opened the windows. Through them came the scent of the last roses, and the occasional damp October leaf. The trees of the park blew yellow in the wind.

They let me in to Cardinal Wolsey's retiring-room, with its walls of warm linenfold-carved wood and its ceiling of worked plaster, where Tudor roses bulged red and blue from a net of gold strapwork. Around the ceiling ran a band of mural painted by an Italian master whom Wolsey had patronized before King Henry broke his heart and killed him: a Via Dolorosa worked in bright pastels.

She was there, sitting on a cushion on the floor, and she had only two companions: my uncle Robert of Leicester, who knelt beside her, and a little girl who was playing for her on a lute. In these past years her face had aged – the skin delicately creased at forehead and eyes, and lines triple-indented at the corners of her mouth. She held up her hand to me. She wore black and white; opals trembled at her ears. My uncle smiled at me. I sank down on both knees.

'Master Philip.' She gestured to the desk that stood in a corner. 'I have a letter over there. The King and Queen of Poland ask me to greet you for them. The Poles have elected

Stefan Bathóry, and he has married the Princess Anna. And King Stefan has reappointed Jan Zamoyski Grand Chancellor of Poland.'

I smiled. 'Madam, I am glad.'

'So you lost us Caspar Laurence,' she said.

I held my eyes on hers. 'He chose, Your Grace, to go with Father Parsons to Rome. I believe he was ill, and that the nursing they offered him was the best choice. I conveyed to him Your Grace's offer.' She nodded; for no one here had spoken to me of the gift of Ulmerstead, and my eyes must not say: *betrayer, liar*. 'Madam, I broke Parsons' nose, at least.'

She exchanged a glance with my uncle, and pursed her mouth expressively. I felt myself go red. 'Forgive me, madam. I lost him, I admit, but I tried fairly.'

'I believe you.' Her gaze did not release me. This trick alone convinces one she can see anything, and panics the unwary, which amuses her. 'And the disappearance in the Grove? I hear they talked of it in Paris for weeks, until other entertainments diverted them. Will Mistress Maria be safe from them there, do you think?'

'If Madame Marguerite can keep her so. I should have thought that England–' I swallowed, cursing myself, and went on – 'I should have thought England safer.'

I felt my uncle's sudden attention. The Queen's eyes dropped; her face went gentle. 'Ah. And what was the truth of it?'

'Of the disappearance, madam?'

My uncle cut across her answer, as only an intimate may do. 'It was a slave-party, surely, or some trick of the ground. There is an answer, whether or not the searchers have found one. It was some natural event strangely concealed – or perhaps investigated with a strange incompetence.'

'The searchers, sir, were adequate,' I said, 'and if not, then their successors were. Lord Zamoyski does not preside over incompetence.'

What Dangers Deep

My uncle grunted. 'Well, I agree we cannot judge from so far away; but one is tempted to common sense, Philip, and to all the natural objections.'

'I think that would be wrong,' remarked the Queen. 'It *is* usually wrong to dismiss someone else's experience simply because we did not share it. You were there, I was not: therefore you are lying.' She shrugged. 'This pink light, for example, of which we have all heard. You knew Maria, Master Philip. Did she ever admit to hallucination? May she have lied? Of course no woman so shattered would lie deliberately; but did she ever recant that memory in any way?'

'Never, madam. She saw the light, whatever it may have been. I think she may, at least in her mind, have gone where it was.' My uncle stirred impatiently.

'In her mind,' said the Queen. 'And perhaps in her body too?'

'Your Grace, I do not know.'

'She dreamt a dream,' said my uncle. 'I have heard that exposure, even death from cold, can beyond a certain point seem like a pleasant dream. Nature's mercy, perhaps.'

'In short, it is our unadmitted purpose to dismiss Maria's memory on *any* grounds,' objected the Queen. 'Master Philip, what is your opinion?'

'About the Grove, madam?'

'About the annihilation of Yolanta. Was there nothing, for you yourself, beyond the sickness, the forgetting, the distortion of Time? Was there never anything else – no other experience?'

There had been a pale veined light that flowed through all degrees of blue from white to turquoise, casting a glow on the snow-crystals beneath. There had been a girl-shape, its face contorted. There had been the naked figure of a man, his arms folded, his face bowed into shadow – a figure weightless and yet substantial, crowned with a helm that roused primordial memories. There had been a turning without motion. So much my memory informed me. But somehow I could not directly contemplate the recollection: though it existed in my consciousness, the emotion it had caused – the sensation of its presence – had vanished like a conjuror's handkerchief.

'You never *saw* anything, then?' The Queen's voice shocked me into attention.

'No, madam.'

I am an indifferent liar. Now, staring into her face, I knew for certain that she knew I was lying, as though the admission had passed from mind to mind.

The interview had gone badly from first to last; but still, she deserved my honesty. 'I do not know what took Yolanta. But it seems to me like a wave into which one drops a stone. For a few moments there is turbulence; but at last there is only the wave, as if no stone had fallen there. And then what does it matter which stone you flung, or what hand threw it?'

To that she did not answer. The silence between us was almost one of friendship. At last she said, 'Have you seen your mother?'

'Not since I landed, madam. She is with Ambrosia, who lies dangerously ill.'

'I know, and I am very sorry. Ride down to Penshurst and comfort her. You may go.'

I rose, bowed to her and slightly, also, to my uncle, and backed towards the door. As I reached it the Queen's voice said, 'Master Philip.'

I stopped. 'Madam?'

She sat in profile to me: I could see the superbly straight back, the high flat planes of her face, and the nose that is pointed and not straight, though the portraits make it so. Then she turned to me, although I knew her short-sighted eyes could no longer see me so many paces away. Perhaps it was this strain that gave them, with their big pupils and the uncertain colour of the iris, a serious gentleness. 'Master Philip, what do you believe happened in Kraków last year?'

'A story, madam, that came to no conclusion before life wrenched it from us. I had hoped for answers: had longed – by willing it, by praying, by earning – to deserve them. But Kraków has taught me a new thing: that life has the power absolutely to deny.'

'Then let go,' she replied. 'For only if we loosen our grip – without any secret condition, without any remnant of our original hope – may something drift back into our hands.'

'Your Grace,' I said, '*Pan* Zamoyski once quoted to me the words of a Muslim sage: Shall I serve like a labourer, in expectation of my wages?'

She smiled. 'And yet I see,' she said, 'a priest who has chosen self-preservation, and who has surrendered the impulse, if not the substance of despair. I see a girl who surrendered all hope of resembling other people, to choose instead the lonely courage that survives. Master Philip, what did *you* surrender at the Ancient Mass?'

My voice replying held – I think she heard it – the first steadiness of my maturity. 'The hope of your favour, madam.'

My uncle froze – then glanced, uncertain, at Her Grace. But she sat still. At last she said, 'What did you choose instead?'

'Your Grace, I chose to serve the truth in honesty – and if I can, with love.'

For an instant more the silence lasted, precise as a quartz-crystal. 'Then,' replied the Queen, 'go and comfort your mother.'

Conclusion

Her Grace did not advance me. Oh, she appointed me Royal Cupbearer, and once sent me on a minor embassy. She knighted me only when I had to greet a visiting king, lest my rank insult him. She stopped me from going with Francis Drake to America. Now, twelve years after Poland, she has at last appointed me Lord Governor of Flushing.

To beguile my idleness during those years I began to write poetry. I made an *Arcadia* to amuse my sister Mary; also a *Defence of Poesie*, and some love-sonnets – for I succeeded her dolls on little Penelope's pillow when she grew up and became most beautiful. At thirty I married Frances Walsingham, daughter of Sir Francis. I love her, and we hope for children, which are the greatest comfort in the world.

As for my years of study in Europe, I once wrote:

> For since mad March great promise made of me,
> If now the May of my years much decline,
> What can be hoped my harvest-time will be?

The poetry amused me, and I did it well; but I do not want the name 'poet' graven on my tomb. I had hoped to be a statesman and a soldier. Two things about those years I do not regret: my devotion to the Protestant cause, and the letter I wrote Her Grace when it seemed she meant to marry a French prince twenty years her junior. I told her why our people would hate a foreign-born King. I have heard Her Grace wept as she read the letter. I can only suppose they were tears of rage.

And yet I believe she liked me, and hoped to employ me. Perhaps, in the end, she found me too intractable.

'Mad March great promise made of me', but little came of it, Maria. And now I find a strange thing. I have begun to notice shadows: the patterns of shade that trees cast in the rich light of afternoon. *How beautiful are the shadows*, I think: *the day will soon be over*.

The man at the desk glanced up at his servant, who sat on a joint-stool, quietly working with oil and leather and metal. 'Ambrose, leave those. I'll do without my thigh-pieces tomorrow.'

Ambrose Hyde frowned. 'Are you sure, Sir Philip?'

'*You* would be, if you'd ever tried to grip a horse with them. Our footsoldiers go into battle armed far worse than the officers: one at least of us ought to feel some shame about that. Leave them, man, and go to bed.'

'Very well, sir, but you are wrong.'

'That may be. Good night.'

'Good night, Sir Philip.'

When Hyde had gone, his master rose, stretched, sighed, and wandered to the tent-door. There for a moment he gazed up at the stars, humid-ringed with yellow mist. Then he returned to the letter on the desk.

> Of all the actions of my youth [she had written] I most regret my reply to you, and that I turned from you with so little real explanation. Real explanations are not within the command of the young; but I have known ever since that in thrusting you off, even on a true excuse, I had been unkind to you. I have never been unkind to any other creature. I thought then, Philip, to spare you my affairs, with which an unnatural self-sufficiency had taught me to deal alone from my childhood onwards. My mind and tongue had forgotten the habit of communion, or that happy expectation that confides in others.

I should, that night, have risked much more and told you everything I felt. And yet I cheat myself: for if, in memory now, I go back to the bed and the firelit room, it is to tell you all that twelve more years have won for me of charity, of openness, of knowledge. Only a decade more – a decade we did not have together – could have enabled me to talk as I wish I could talk to you now. Only ten years' more experience could have given us the friendship for which I now long with so vehement a regret that it takes my breath sometimes.

I have hesitated to say this to you, since it seems to me that one's suffering should be private. But more: perhaps one's love must be acknowledged when at last one recognizes it. On the night we lay beside each other I did not love you, Philip, or did not know I loved you. I know it now.

I cannot tell to what mystery we go: to annihilation or to manifest love. For annihilation, betrayal and loss we have evidence enough; for love, only that fellowship which, I find these days, outwears both hate and wrong. And I would not want my life back again. But a certain human excellence withstands Time; and one finds it rarely, and recognizes it only when one has grown to meet it.

Well, I rejected you and lost you, and have made a life with a husband and with friends I love.

Philip, forgive me that I turned from you – cold as an inexperienced mistress can be, and too young to be a friend. Time gives nothing back, and it will not give me back my youth and the friendship you offered me. There is no re-beginning. If I could have that night again, I wish I could fill it with the vehemence of my present knowledge: *I love you*. When we slight another person – his goodness and beauty being unique and ephemeral and precious to us – then we impoverish his life and ours; and that is a wrong Time punishes.

And so that October day unites us doubly: we were there together – and we must remember *for* each other what few other living minds can now treasure, and none explain. I still recall that distant jewel of a day, and for many years I asked its meaning. Then I found that friends had become indifferent, and that they ordered me to forget – as they believed, for my own good; and that for arrogant young minds Time did not contain the morning on which my life was shattered into stillness. And at last I found in my own intellect, not peace, but a conviction that there would be no answer; and that I must loosen my grip without hating what has repaid my devotion with so adamant a silence. Not only we, but the beauty, the mystery, the goodness we have loved must go into the past; and our adventure and our story must vanish into silence.

Have you ever admitted to yourself that you should have married Prince Willem's daughter? That was your chance, Philip: did life ever give another?

You know that, on the death of Monsieur Hubert Languet, the portrait of yourself you gave him was recently returned to you through acquaintances in Paris. And because your friends in France remember you, many of us went to view it before the English Ambassador despatched it on the final stage to London. I saw it at his house.

The portrait had an oval frame and showed you, I suspect, at about the age of thirty – for I recalled abruptly, looking at it, that in my memory you are younger. The artist had chosen to depict you in part-armour, wearing a slashed doublet of dark yellow velvet and a gorget of black steel. You stood turned three-quarter-face, your hand on the hilt of your poniard – your hair brushed into a style that, also, I did not remember. A pleasant, competent, half-smiling face: a static Court portrait – an oval of gold and dark that glowed smaller as I walked away from it down the gallery. Suddenly I remembered your smile, and – retrieved whole from some abyss of memory – the scent of your skin.

Well, they exist, the ambushes of Time, though they are rare. Nothing changed around me as I acknowledged the shift by which a truth we have always known attains the accuracy of admission. Humbled – most deservedly rebuked – I turned back to the oval of gold and dark, remembering the doubts about you that had been, I know, also true and accurate within my young measure.

I think I would like you better now. That I loved you I never knew. Forgive me.

Philip Sidney sat a long time reading that. Then he softly turned a page. She had written it (perhaps without realizing) in bold ink.

I told you I had dreamt about Yolanta. But more, Philip: I have seen her. I had always feared to confront the dead, for I dreaded the skull at the window; but this moment fell as wholesomely as the crumbling of a late-summer rose.

We have a garden set down four steps and surrounded by a low wall. Here I grow my white and yellow roses. Few remained last week before the first frost, so I meant to gather the very last of them for the house. I took my shears and basket, and went out on one of our last fine evenings. I remember a streak of coral cloud fading to dun, and a few first gentle stars.

I came down the steps. Beside a rose-bush I saw a woman standing with her back to me; she was dressed in grey, and held a white rose in her hand. She wore no headdress; her dark brown hair flowed unbound down to her waist. As I came near her, she turned, looking over her shoulder at me. It was Yolanta.

Quizzical, intimate, severe she gazed at me, but she was not angry; nor did she smile. And then, with no transition, I was alone in the garden.

Her reader sat for an instant biting his lower lip, in a gesture she would not have recognized. Then he touched his breast, where Labrys hung from her golden chain, and wrote: *Dear fellow-pilgrim, I think, at least, it was no mockery*.

He lifted his head. From some ruined farmstead half a mile away a cock was crowing dawn. He smiled, an acknowledgement of finishing, of sleep – and, already half-turned from the desk, picked up the pen for the last time, and wrote in English and in French below his signature:

> For Rachel have I servèd
> (For Leah cared I never),
> And her I have reservèd
> Within my heart forever.

Historical Note

Philip Sidney did visit Poland in 1574; events of the Second Interregnum then stood roughly as I have given them. A girl did study at Collegium Maius, disguised as a boy, for two years during the Middle Ages. A Catholic mob did burn the Protestant Chapel in Jana Street: a poster celebrating the event still exists, like Hubert Languet's recorded (but here reproduced only in spirit) complaints about Philip's letter-writing. The Richard Saltonstall who brought Antony news from Turkey was an ancestor of my own. Father Robert Parsons was still an active pamphleteer against the English government at least fifteen years after this story occurs. The marker beside the road outside the gates of Hamelin is rumoured to have existed until the eighteenth century, but has since disappeared. The Small Dark Cell can still be seen at Collegium Maius.

Philip Sidney died on October seventeenth, 1586, as the result of a wound in the thigh which he received during an action near Zutphen. Witnesses believed his death could have been averted had he consented to wear his leg-armour on that day.

A selection of bestsellers from Headline

LONDON'S CHILD	Philip Boast	£5.99 ☐
THE GIRL FROM COTTON LANE	Harry Bowling	£5.99 ☐
THE HERRON HERITAGE	Janice Young Brooks	£4.99 ☐
DANGEROUS LADY	Martina Cole	£4.99 ☐
VAGABONDS	Josephine Cox	£4.99 ☐
STAR QUALITY	Pamela Evans	£4.99 ☐
MARY MADDISON	Sheila Jansen	£4.99 ☐
CANNONBERRY CHASE	Roberta Latow	£5.99 ☐
THERE IS A SEASON	Elizabeth Murphy	£4.99 ☐
THE PALACE AFFAIR	Una-Mary Parker	£4.99 ☐
BLESSINGS AND SORROWS	Christine Thomas	£4.99 ☐
WYCHWOOD	E V Thompson	£4.99 ☐
HALLMARK	Elizabeth Walker	£5.99 ☐
AN IMPOSSIBLE DREAM	Elizabeth Warne	£5.99 ☐
POLLY OF PENN'S PLACE	Dee Williams	£4.99 ☐

All Headline books are available at your local bookshop or newsagent, or can be ordered direct from the publisher. Just tick the titles you want and fill in the form below. Prices and availability subject to change without notice.

Headline Book Publishing PLC, Cash Sales Department, Bookpoint, 39 Milton Park, Abingdon, OXON, OX14 4TD, UK. If you have a credit card you may order by telephone — 0235 831700.

Please enclose a cheque or postal order made payable to Bookpoint Ltd to the value of the cover price and allow the following for postage and packing:
UK & BFPO: £1.00 for the first book, 50p for the second book and 30p for each additional book ordered up to a maximum charge of £3.00.
OVERSEAS & EIRE: £2.00 for the first book, £1.00 for the second book and 50p for each additional book.

Name ....

Address ....

....

....

If you would prefer to pay by credit card, please complete:
Please debit my Visa/Access/Diner's Card/American Express (delete as applicable) card no:

Signature ....Expiry Date ....